Cindi Myers is the ~~a~~ novels. When she's not ~~~~ she enjoys skiing, gardening, cooking, ~~~~ daydreaming. A lover of small-town life, she lives with her husband and two spoiled dogs in the Colorado mountains.

Juno Rushdan is a veteran US Air Force intelligence officer and award-winning author. Her books are action-packed and fast-paced. Critics from Kirkus Reviews and Library Journal have called her work 'heart-pounding James Bond-ian adventure' that 'will captivate lovers of romantic thrillers.' For a free book, visit her website: junorushdan.com

PURSUIT AT PANTHER POINT

CINDI MYERS

WYOMING MOUNTAIN COLD CASE

JUNO RUSHDAN

MILLS & BOON

First Published in Great Britain 2023
by Mills & Boon, an imprint of HarperCollins*Publishers* Ltd
1 London Bridge Street, London, SE1 9GF

www.harpercollins.co.uk

HarperCollins*Publishers*
Macken House, 39/40 Mayor Street Upper,
Dublin 1, D01 C9W8, Ireland

Pursuit at Panther Point © 2023 Cynthia Myers
Wyoming Mountain Cold Case © 2023 Juno Rushdan

ISBN: 978-0-263-30741-2

0923

MIX
Paper | Supporting
responsible forestry
FSC™ C007454

This book is produced from independently certified FSC™ paper to ensure responsible forest management.

For more information visit: www.harpercollins.co.uk/green

Printed and Bound in the UK using 100% Renewable Electricity at CPI Group (UK) Ltd, Croydon, CR0 4YY

PURSUIT AT
PANTHER POINT

CINDI MYERS

For Lucy

Chapter One

Anna Trent had been drawn to search and rescue work because she wanted to help people. But sometimes, like today, helping hurt more than she had bargained for.

"I'm sorry to have to ask you to do this, but he's been missing more than twenty-four hours now and Sandy is worried sick. We all are, really." Eagle Mountain Search and Rescue Captain Sheri Stevens rested one hand on Anna's shoulder. The women stood on the side of a snow-packed road in a remote section of the county, a brisk wind sending devils of snow swirling around their feet. "I know Dave is your friend, too."

"He is. I want to find him as much as everyone else." Anna looked down and met the gaze of her search dog, Jacquie. Maybe it was fanciful to think so, but the poodle's brown eyes seemed to reflect Anna's own concern. When word had spread that Dave Weiss, a popular volunteer fireman and owner of a local bakery, hadn't come home the night before last, Anna's first thought was that he had had an accident while out ice fishing or back-country skiing. Eagle Mountain Search and Rescue was on standby to look for him, but in a county comprised mostly of wilderness area full of ski trails and fishing holes, there was no logical place to begin.

Anna was a newer member of the SAR team and, ordinarily, would be grouped with the other rookies to sweep a designated area. But Jacquie, a three-year-old standard poodle who had recently been certified by Search and Rescue Dogs of Colorado, had already proved valuable in finding other missing persons. As tense as searches could be, she was glad to be able to do more to help find her friend.

A few hours earlier, someone had spotted Dave's pickup truck parked in this out-of-the-way location designated on some maps as Panther Point. An inch of snow from last night's storm covered the truck's windshield and hood, and obscured any footprints he may have made after he'd parked the vehicle. Had he met someone here and driven away with them? Anna looked down at Jacquie. The dog's black curly coat was flecked with snow, like a sprinkling of powdered sugar. She stared up at Anna with solemn brown eyes, as if she sensed that today wasn't merely a training exercise. "If anyone can find Dave, Jacquie can," Anna said.

Sheri moved in a little closer, her voice low. "I have to warn you. When Sandy called about Dave not coming home, she told the dispatcher she was worried he might have gone somewhere to kill himself."

Anna rocked back on her heels. "Dave? Why?" She pictured the man who had become one of her first friends after she had moved to Eagle Mountain five years before. Dave was a cheerful, burly blond, who still had a distinct Austrian accent despite two decades in Colorado. She had been a newlywed who'd known no one other than her new husband, Jonas Trent. Dave had been one of Jonas's best friends and he had welcomed Anna with open arms—literally enveloping her in a warm hug the first time they'd met. After Jonas's death, Dave had always been there, to shovel snow or repair a leaky faucet, or buy her a cup of coffee when they ran into each other downtown. In the past six months, they hadn't seen as much of each other. Anna felt more comfortable standing on her own feet and she suspected Dave's wife, Sandy, had been a little jealous of the attention her husband had paid his friend's widow.

"Sandy said he's been worried about money," Sheri said. "Apparently, they've been stretched pretty thin."

That didn't sound like Dave, either. Jonas had always said his friend was one of the smartest men he knew. He had a solid business and the couple didn't live extravagantly. "I guess we never really know what is going on inside people," Anna said. Maybe in the past six months something about Dave's situation had changed.

Sheri patted her shoulder. "It's terrible, but I wanted to warn you that this search might not have the happy outcome we're all hoping for."

Anna took a firmer hold of the long lead clipped to Jacquie's collar. "We'll do our best to find him. Even if the news is the worst, his family and friends deserve to know what happened." She always reminded herself of this when she and Jacquie set out on a search. Not every hunt, or even most of them, ended with good news, but the work they did was still important.

"Thanks." Sheri stepped back and looked toward the Rayford County Sheriff's Department SUV parked at the edge of the Forest Service road. She raised her hand and the door opened; a man with ink-black hair in sheriff's department khakis and a black leather jacket stepped out.

"Who is that?" Anna asked as the deputy started toward them. She thought she knew all the local officers, but this one didn't look familiar. She guessed he was about her age—early thirties—fit and good-looking, at least from what she could see as he walked over, head down.

"He's with the Mesa County Sheriff's Department," Sheri said. "He's filling in while Jamie Douglas is on maternity leave."

"Jamie had her baby?" Anna smiled. The force's only female deputy was a familiar figure around town.

"Two nights ago," Sheri said. "A little girl."

"Hello."

Anna turned her head to the deputy but realized he wasn't addressing her. Instead, he had stopped to pet Jacquie, who vibrated the stub of her tail and leaned into the ear scratch he offered. Smiling, he looked at the women, his eyes meeting Anna's. "Hello," he said again. "Thanks for agreeing to help us."

"Of course." Anna tried to look away, but she couldn't. She didn't know this man's name, but they had definitely met before. A hot flush of embarrassment rose to her cheeks as she remembered their last—and only—encounter. Over two years ago, at the Junction hospital. She had been screaming at a nurse in the corridor, furious that Jonas had been waiting more than an hour for something to relieve the agonizing pain of his end-stage pancreatic cancer. Not her finest moment, made even more embarrassing by the arrival of this officer, who had led her away and persuaded her to calm down.

Was it possible he wouldn't recognize her? After all, she was two years older now, quite a bit calmer and better rested.

"You're looking much better than the last time we met," he said, proving that he hadn't forgotten.

"You didn't see me at my best," she said.

Sheri looked from one to the other. "Do you two know each other?" she asked.

"Not really," Anna said quickly.

"I'm Lucas Malone."

He held out his hand and she took it, his grip firm. "Anna Trent." Had she told him her name that long-ago evening? She couldn't remember.

Sheri looked from one to the other, obviously curious. "We'd better get started," Anna said before her friend could ask any more questions.

"I've never worked with a search dog before," Deputy Malone said. "What do you need from me?"

"Since we're looking for a specific person, it would be good to have something of Dave's for Jacquie to scent," Anna said.

They looked toward the white pickup angled into the brush on the side of the road. "I can probably pop the lock on the truck for you," Malone said.

He returned to his SUV and came back with the tool for jimmying the lock open. While his back was to her as he worked, she studied him. That night at the hospital, she had been too upset for more than his general features to register. Now she noticed the way his leather jacket clung to his broad shoulders, and how the sun glinted on his thick, dark hair. The flutter this awareness sent through her startled her.

He pulled open the door of the truck and turned to her. "Try not to touch anything except the scent item," he said as he stepped back to allow Anna access.

Mind once more on the solemn task ahead, she shoved her right hand into a wrong-side-out plastic bag and leaned into the truck. She scanned the interior, searching for something that might hold Dave's scent. She spotted a can of snuff in the tray on the console. He probably handled that multiple times a day, but she worried the strong mint aroma of the tobacco might dilute his own smells. Jacquie was capable of distinguishing the different scents. Why make things difficult for her?

Instead, she chose a bandana tucked in the tray next to the snuff tin. She picked it up and withdrew her hand from the bag, turning the plastic inside-out as she did so, capturing the bandana neatly in the bag. Jacquie sat, eyes focused on the bag, every muscle tense with anticipation. She knew what came next.

Anna bent and offered the open bag to the dog. Jacquie stuck her nose inside, inhaled deeply, then sampled the ground around the open truck door. Snuffling excitedly, she walked around the truck to the passenger side, sniffed the snowy ground around the truck then turned and dove through a narrow gap in the underbrush alongside the road, tugging hard on the lead.

"Wait here," Sheri called over her shoulder to Malone as she took off after Anna and Jacquie. "I'll radio when we find anything."

Anna's pack slapped against her back as she jogged to keep up with the excited dog. Thirty yards from the road, Jacquie swung right, up an incline, weaving around the white trunks of a thick growth of aspen, bare of leaves this time of year. Anna's boots slipped in the snow and the legs of her pants were already wet from plunging through stands of post oak, dead leaves coated with snow.

"She's heading to the river." Sheri caught up with Anna. She carried the bag with the bandana, which Anna must have dropped in her haste to follow the dog. "I brought this in case we needed it," Sheri said.

"Good idea," Anna said. If Jacquie lost the scent, they could use the bandana to refresh her memory. But for now, the dog was definitely keen. They reached the river and Jacquie waded right in, crashing through the ice on the shore into the rushing water. Anna moaned. If Jacquie decided to wade or swim across, she would need to follow, but she didn't relish doing so.

"That water isn't deep enough to drown in," Sheri said. "Did Dave decide to go fishing after all?"

But only a few steps into the water, Jacquie whirled around and headed south along the riverbank. Anna took a firmer grip on the long lead and stumbled after her, Sheri close behind. Jacquie veered around a large beaver dam and sniffed along the edge of the pond that had formed as a result of the beaver's efforts. She slowed, her nose pressed to the icy mud, snuffling loudly. The trainer Anna had worked with had explained that this snuffling was a way of pulling in more scent particles. Dogs had the ability to store up these particles. There was more ice here at this stiller water, and Anna studied it, searching for any sign that someone had fallen through. Dave liked to ice fish, but surely he would recognize this ice wasn't safe.

Jacquie tugged left, headed down a narrow path leading away from the pond. The neat imprints of deer hooves showed in the otherwise pristine snow of the trail. "She's not following the deer, is she?" Sheri asked.

Anna shook her head. Jacquie didn't do that. In the months since she had completed her training, she had proved to be an adept tracker, finding everything from lost hunters to—once—a discarded knife used in an assault along a jogging trail in Delta County.

Jacquie had slowed her pace, no longer eager, though her attention remained focused on the ground. Suddenly, she veered again, this time down another animal trail lined with wild roses, last year's hips crimson against clumps of snow. Jacquie barked and Anna looked up then pulled back on the leash. A wave of grief washed over her as she stared at the figure swaying from the tree branch in the midst of a grove of cottonwoods. She looked at the face only long enough to make sure it was Dave—contorted in death but recognizable by his neat goatee and hatchet nose.

Sheri pressed her palm to Anna's back. "I'm sorry," she whispered. "I was really, really hoping he had just gone fishing."

Anna turned her back to the body in the tree and called Jacquie. The dog came, tail down, head hanging. Though Anna told her she had done a good job and gave her treats and water, Jacquie knew finding a dead person was never as good as finding a live one. The dog had known Dave, too, and that probably made this even more upsetting for her.

"One of us needs to go back and get Deputy Malone and lead him back here," Sheri said. "I can stay here with the body while you do that."

"I'll wait here," Anna said.

Sheri frowned. "Are you sure?"

"It's all right." She looked up at the spreading branches of a cottonwood, the thick gray bark patterned with orange and white lichen. "It's peaceful here."

"Okay, then. It's liable to take a while. Will you be okay?"

"I'll be okay." She offered a small smile. "I'm not the hysterical type, and this isn't my first suicide recovery."

The first had been a teenage boy who had shot himself near the family's summer cabin. That had been far worse, seeing those parents' grief. Staying here with Dave's body would be a last service she could perform for him. And she would rather do that than have to spend the long walk back in with Lucas Malone, knowing what he must think of her after that day in the hospital.

"All right," Sheri said. "I'll be back as soon as I can." She turned and trotted away.

Anna led Jacquie back up the trail until she spotted a fallen log where she could sit. *Why had Dave chosen to end his life here?* she wondered as she contemplated the snow-covered scrub oaks and bare trunks of cottonwoods. The county was full of more scenic spots and places that were easier to get to. Had he come here because he hadn't wanted to be found? But parking his truck along the road guaranteed someone would eventually spot the vehicle and make inquiries. People who didn't want to be found at all tended to disappear in mountain wilderness, miles from anyone, not within a quarter mile, as the crow flies, from a road.

Jacquie leaned against Anna's thigh and rested her head in Anna's lap. Anna combed her fingers through the dog's curly hair and thought about Dave. When was the last time she had seen him? Last Friday. She had gone into his shop to buy cookies to bring to a SAR meeting. He had smiled a big smile and clasped her hand warmly. "How are you doing?" he had asked, and looked into her eyes. "Tell me the truth."

"I'm good," she had said. "Things are starting to feel more…settled." She felt more in control of her life now, still missing Jonas, but the pain wasn't as intense. She could go whole days without thinking of her husband. She wasn't exactly happy, but she was content.

"I'm glad to hear it," he had said, and turned to box up her order, as usual throwing in a few extra cookies. The heady aromas of cinnamon, vanilla and chocolate perfumed the air of the shop, and she'd resisted the urge to tell him to add in one of the pink-frosted chocolate cupcakes in the display case. Surprise Cakes, the label read. That was one of Dave's specialties. The center of the cupcake was hollowed out and contained a surprise—a dollop of fruit filling or ganache, a marshmallow, nuts or a chocolate truffle. For Anna and Jonas's wedding, Dave had made a cupcake tower, each cupcake containing a silver charm.

I should have asked him how he was doing, she thought now. If she had, would he have told her the truth?

Jacquie's whimper interrupted her thoughts. The dog was staring toward the clearing where Dave's body hung. "You don't want to go back there," Anna told her.

Jacquie stood and headed toward the clearing. "Jacquie, come back here," Anna called.

But the dog pretended not to hear. Anna caught up the end of the long lead before it slipped away and stood to follow.

At the clearing, Jacquie avoided the body but circled the area, sniffing among the trees. Anna shivered as a chill wind swept through, but she was grateful for the cold, which would keep down the smell. She told herself she shouldn't, but something in her compelled her to look again at the body.

Her first thought was that it was so high in the tree. Standing ten feet away, Dave's feet, in Merrell hiking boots with red laces and red trim, hung at about eye level. How in the world had he gotten up that high? More curious than horrified now—or maybe just numb—she walked to the base of the tree. It was an old cottonwood, with a trunk five feet thick or more, towering a hundred feet overhead. The trunk rose straight up ten feet before it divided. She didn't think she could have climbed it. But Dave had, and with a rope in his hand.

Jacquie had moved over to join her, then put her nose to the ground once more and headed toward the ground directly beneath the body. "Jacquie, come back," Anna called. She didn't think either one of them should be there. Maybe they were disturbing a crime scene. Well, not exactly a crime, but would the sheriff's department want to investigate?

Again, Jacquie played deaf. That wasn't really like her but, like people, dogs had moods, too, Anna had discovered. Maybe because she had been asked to find a dead person instead of a live one, today Jacquie was being contrary. The dog stopped now and alerted on something in the ground. With a growing sense of dread, Anna moved forward to see what had caught the dog's attention.

She stared at four square indentations in the ground beneath the body. They were deep enough to still be discernable in spite of the snow. The first two were about two feet apart. The second set was parallel to the first, three feet away. Anna stared. Where had she seen indentations like that before?

She thought to this summer when she had decided to repaint her bedroom. When she'd finished the job and cleaned up, she had found indentations just like those in the carpet, where the ladder she had used to reach the top of the wall had stood.

She looked around her, confused. If Dave had used a ladder to get into that tree, where was the ladder now?

Chapter Two

Lucas had been startled to run into Anna Trent in this remote setting. When the search and rescue captain had explained they were waiting for a canine search team, the name hadn't clicked for him. After all, it had been two years since he had last seen Anna, and a great deal had happened since then. But when he'd looked into her distressed blue eyes, he had been thrust back to that hospital corridor, in the glare of fluorescent lighting that made even healthy people look ill, listening to her rage against the inability—or as she'd seen it, unwillingness—of anyone to relieve her dying husband's pain.

The nurse Anna had been screaming at had welcomed Lucas's intervention. "Deputy, please take this woman away until she learns to control herself," she had said before stalking off.

Lucas hadn't responded out of any duty as a law enforcement officer. He had stopped by to see his girlfriend Jenny after a long shift, still in uniform, and had stepped into the corridor to allow a nurse to check a dressing and had heard the shouting and gone to see what was wrong. After the nurse left, Anna—he had only learned her name later, after checking at the nurses' station—turned on him.

"If you're going to arrest anyone, it ought to be the people here for letting a man suffer so," she said and then burst into harsh, painful tears.

Lucas had held her until the front of his uniform shirt was soaked with her tears, and wanted to join right in with her. "I'm not going to arrest anyone," he said, though he doubted she heard him. If only dealing with life was as easy as locking up whoever was responsible for problems. Too often there was no one to blame and nothing to do but try to endure the pain.

They hadn't said anything else. When her tears had subsided a little, she jerked out of his arms, stared into his face with a horrified expression, and turned and ran down the corridor. He took a few steps after her, then decided maybe it was better if he left her. Sometimes suffering was easier done in private. At least, it was for him.

Now here they were, in another terrible situation. Anna looked better now. He had been aware of her beauty before, but in an abstract way. Today, her attractiveness was more concrete. He'd noticed the soft curve of her cheek and the deep blue of her eyes framed by dark lashes, and the lush pink of her lips. And he'd noticed that he'd noticed—something that hadn't happened to him in a long time.

Sheri jogged out of the underbrush and Lucas stepped from the SUV and went to meet her. "We found him," she said. "Hanging in a tree."

He grimaced. So the wife had been right to suspect suicide. "Anna is with him?" he asked.

"Someone had to stay and she insisted she could do it."

"Let me radio for the coroner and some more officers to help," he said. "Then you can show me."

The dispatcher promised to notify Dr. Butch Collins

and to send two more officers to help retrieve the body. Then Lucas followed Sheri back into the underbrush. She set a brisk pace, moving more quickly than he would have thought for someone making the slog for the third time in the last hour. "I didn't like leaving Anna there alone," she said, as if to explain her haste. "I didn't want to leave her at all, but she insisted."

"You're sure it's suicide?" he asked.

Sheri stopped and looked back at him. "Are you saying someone else could have put him in that tree?"

"We can't assume anything," he said. "Every suspicious death has to be investigated."

She nodded. "But his wife said he was upset. She thought he might try to kill himself."

"I didn't see a note in the truck," Lucas said. "But we'll do a thorough search. And not everyone leaves a note." They set out walking again, not as fast now that the trail had narrowed and the going was more difficult. "Did you know him?"

"He ran the local bakery and he was a volunteer fireman," Sheri said. "I knew him to speak to, but not well." She paused. "You should ask Anna about him. Her late husband and Dave were good friends. Dave spoke at Jonas's funeral."

Hadn't the poor woman suffered enough? First, she'd lost her husband to cancer and now she had to find his friend's body? Lucas put his head down and trudged forward. A lot of things about his job were unpleasant, but today was moving to the top of his list of worst days on the force.

Anna met them on the trail before the clearing. She had a look about her Lucas had seen before. "What's wrong?" he asked.

"Maybe nothing." She pressed her lips together, as if uncertain whether she could continue. "I found something. Something that doesn't make sense."

"Show me." He started to follow her then turned to Sheri. "Stay here and wait for the others, please." No sense having anyone else in what could turn out to be a crime scene.

"I painted my bedroom recently," Anna said as she led the way up the trail. Most people would have wondered at the direction the conversation was taking, but Lucas had learned that many witnesses, especially witnesses under stress, preferred to approach explanations indirectly, sneaking up on a horrible truth. "When I was done, I noticed the ladder I'd used left impressions in the carpet." She glanced back at him. "There are impressions like that under Dave's body. But I can't find a ladder anywhere."

He put a hand out to stop her. "You saw these impressions in the snow?"

She nodded. "They're deep enough that the snow has settled into them. There was probably mud there before it snowed. We had a string of warm days before this latest storm."

"Did you see any footprints?" he asked. "Any disturbed ground?"

She shook her head. "No."

"Stay here," he said. "I'll go on and look for myself. How far is it to the body?"

"Not very far. You'll see a grove of cottonwoods. The body—Dave—is there."

He hurried past her and soon reached the cluster of cottonwoods. The man's body was near the center of the grove—a shocking, terrible sight. Lucas forced himself to study the image, to note the type of rope and position of the knot. Then he moved slowly toward the body, approach-

ing at an oblique angle, studying the ground for any sign
of footprints. He spotted fresh tracks in the heavier snow
along the outer edge of the clearing from the woman and
the dog, and partial shoe impressions moving toward the
body. He thought these belonged to Anna.

He located the marks she had told him about and crouched
down to study them. They definitely looked like indentations made by the legs of a ladder sunk deep into the mud,
perhaps under the weight of a man. He glanced overhead
again, trying to judge the height and weight of the body
overhead. Not a small man, maybe as much as one-eighty to
two hundred pounds. He stood and it struck him how high
up the body was. If the ladder was, say, eight feet, and a
six-foot-tall man stood on the step just below the top of the
ladder, he could have just reached the branch the rope was
tied to. So he fastened the rope and...then what? Jumped?
Kicked over the ladder?

But where was the ladder?

He walked back to where Anna and the dog waited. "I
see what you mean," he said. "We'll have to look into it."

"Does this mean Dave didn't kill himself?" she asked.

"We can't know at this point," Lucas said. "Sheri said
you knew him?"

She nodded. "He and my husband were good friends."

"Sheri told me he died—your husband," he said. "I'm
sorry for your loss."

She looked away. "Thank you."

He took a step backward. "You should go back to the
parking area. I'll need to get a statement from you, but you
can come into the sheriff's department this afternoon. I'll
wait here for the coroner and the other deputies."

She nodded and gathered up Jacquie's leash.

"It was good seeing you again," he said. "Despite the circumstances."

She didn't say anything, merely looked at him a long moment then turned and walked down the trail. He waited until she was out of sight before he turned to walk back to the clearing and the ugly business of death.

ANNA AND JACQUIE emerged from the search area onto the road as two sheriff's department vehicles and a black SUV arrived. The vehicles parked behind Deputy Malone's SUV and half a dozen men emerged, including an older, portly man in a heavy overcoat, carrying a doctor's bag.

Sheriff Travis Walker, sporting a deep tan despite the winter weather, a souvenir of his recent tropical vacation, approached Anna and Jacquie. "Hello, Anna," he greeted her. "Lucas said you found the body pretty quickly."

"Jacquie took me right to him." She looked down at the dog, who raised her ears at the sound of her name.

"Not a fun job, I know, but you spared the family a longer wait."

"Deputy Malone said I need to give a statement," she said.

Travis seemed to consider this. "Let me talk to Lucas and someone will be in touch."

Then he left and she was alone, everyone else disappearing down the now-beaten trail through the snow. She walked over to Dave's truck. Careful not to touch anything, she looked into the cab. Funny, Dave had left the can of snuff behind—he usually kept it in his back pocket. All of his jeans had circles worn into the back pockets where the tins always nestled. But maybe he had emptied all his pockets before walking into the woods. Someone distressed enough to kill himself might have all kinds of ideas that didn't seem logical to her.

She turned away, back to her car, and drove the six miles to Eagle Mountain's main street. Traffic was light this time of year. The bulk of tourists would arrive with warmer weather, though several cars with out-of-state plates parked in front of the Cake Walk Café attested to ice climbers or skiers who appreciated the beauty of the mountains in winter. She turned into an alley and parked in a small lot behind the buildings that fronted Main.

Jacquie leaped out as soon as Anna opened the door and trotted to a green door at the rear of one of those buildings. Anna used her key to open the door and stepped into a narrow hallway flanked by a restroom on one side and a storage closet on the other. A buzzer announced her entrance and a round-faced woman with a tumble of shoulder-length gray curls looked down the hallway. "I wasn't expecting you in this morning," the woman said. "Are you okay?"

Gemma Taylor, Anna's sole employee and best friend, bent to pet Jacquie, who had scurried up to meet her, then straightened and regarded Anna. "From the look on your face, I'm guessing not well," she said.

"Not well." Anna hung her coat and Jacquie's leash on hooks beside the storeroom, then followed Gemma into the large front room of Yarn and More, the store she had opened last year.

Gemma moved a box of yarn from a chair at the long table at the back of the room. "Have a seat and I'll make some tea and you can tell me about it. Or not, if you'd rather not talk about it."

"I think I need to talk." Out in the field, she had been able to distance herself from what was happening, even after the shock of seeing Dave's body. Now the protective shell of adrenaline was dissolving, leaving her shaken. She needed to put things into words to process them. She sat and picked up a partially knitted scarf from a basket at the center of the table. She was working on a piece to use in a display of the New Mexico wool she had just begun to stock in the store.

Gemma slid a full mug toward Anna and sat across from her. "Your message said you were called on a search. Was it Dave?"

"It was Dave." She sipped the tea. It wasn't brewed enough yet, but the hot water soothed her anyway. "He's dead. Hanged."

Gemma gasped and put a hand to her mouth, then leaned across the table and gripped Anna's wrist. "I'm so sorry."

Anna nodded. "It's awful. And how horrible for Sandy. I'll have to call her later. After the sheriff's department has had time to notify her."

"Dave always seemed like such a happy guy," Gemma said. "But I guess you never know what's really going on with people."

Anna began to knit the scarf. The feel of the needles in her hand and the rhythm of the motion soothed her. Dave *was* a happy guy. In his early twenties, he had survived cancer and said he was grateful for every day he'd had since. Had his cancer returned? Or had something else happened to so drastically change his outlook?

But then there were those marks, as if from a ladder. What did they mean? "I don't think I can talk about it anymore," she said. She wanted to tell Gemma about the ladder but maybe she should wait to see what the sheriff's department had to say about that. She nodded toward the box of yarn. That was a much safer topic of conversation right now. "I see that shipment of Malabrigo silky merino came in."

"Yes, and two cartons of hand-dyed sock yarn. The Sock Sisters will be pleased." The Sock Sisters were one of several knitting groups who met at the shop. Organizing such groups had been Gemma's idea, and a great strategy for recruiting regular customers.

"We've got four sign-ups for the spring break Knockout Knits class for teens," Gemma said. "I'm going to drop more flyers at the library and the Teen Explorers group. I'd love to have young people meeting here regularly. I want kids to know fiber arts aren't just for grandmas."

Anna smiled at her friend, who wore a deep red tunic sweater of her own design over patterned red leggings. "You don't look like anyone's grandma," she said.

Gemma grinned. "But speaking of grandmas—Jamie Douglas's neighbor came in first thing this morning with Jamie's sister, Donna. Turns out Donna has taken up knitting and they were looking for simple patterns she could make for the baby. I hooked her up with a couple of receiving blanket patterns, a soft knit cap to try, and some adorable but really simple diaper shirts and that baby yarn that's washable. I guess Jamie is on maternity leave for the next six weeks. The neighbor said the sheriff's department has an officer on loan from Mesa County while she's out."

"His name is Lucas Malone," Anna said.

"You've met him?" Gemma began removing hanks of yarn in a rainbow of colors from a box.

"He was the responding officer this morning. He opened Dave's truck so I could retrieve something for Jacquie to get Dave's scent."

Gemma leaned forward. "So, what's he like? How old is he? Is he single? Good-looking?"

"He's about thirty, I guess. Good-looking. Black hair, brown eyes. I have no idea whether he's married or not."

"Too young for me." Gemma went back to unboxing yarn. "But he's about your age."

"Don't get any ideas," Anna said, and cursed the blush that heated her cheeks.

"I was just making an observation." She picked up the empty box. "There are three more boxes of yarn to unpack, and we still have all the kits to put together for the Knockout Knits class."

The two women spent the rest of the morning into early afternoon unpacking new arrivals, adjusting displays and waiting on customers. Word of Dave Weiss's fate had apparently already spread and a couple of the women who'd stopped in had clearly hoped to glean more information. A terse "I really don't want to talk about it" from Anna had sent them on their way.

A little after four, the chime on the door signaled a new arrival. Anna emerged from the back room to find Deputy Malone standing before a large display of variegated sock yarn. "Are you a knitter, Deputy?" she asked.

He took a step away from the yarn. "No, um, I came to see you."

Jacquie trotted over to greet him and he bent to scratch her head. "Is something wrong?" Anna asked. Her heart pounded.

"I need to get your statement and thought it might be easier for me to come to you." He straightened and looked around the shop, his gaze pausing briefly at the table, where two women had stopped knitting to stare at him. "If there's somewhere we can talk?"

"I'll watch things up here while you and the deputy use the back office," Gemma said.

Anna widened her eyes at Gemma. The back office was what Gemma insisted on calling the storeroom whenever there was someone around she wanted to impress. But it wasn't a real office, and it was scarcely large enough for two people.

"That would be great," Malone said. He and Gemma both turned to her and the awkward moment stretched.

"Fine," she said at last. "Come this way, Deputy." She swiveled on her heel and led the way to the storeroom. At least if she embarrassed herself any more in front of the deputy, she could do it surrounded by yarn she loved.

Chapter Three

The room—more of a large closet—Anna led Lucas to held one of those high-top tables he had seen in bars, the surface all of two feet square, with two spindly-looking metal chairs. The rest of the room was filled with yarn—yarn of every color spilling from shelves, some in boxes or baskets or bags, other balls of it loose in pyramids and piles. A wooden crate on the floor held still more yarn and a box next to it was filled with packages of knitting needles.

"This isn't really an office," Anna said, as if reading his puzzlement. "It's our store room. But it's the only private place in the shop unless you want to try to squeeze into the bathroom."

"This will do." He pulled out one of the chairs. "Let's sit down."

She perched on the edge of her seat and he settled into the chair across from her, which squeaked under his weight. Their knees brushed before she angled hers away. He pretended not to notice, though the zing of awareness lingered. "How long have you had this place?" he asked, making conversation, trying to put her at ease as he pulled out his digital recorder and a statement form.

"A little over a year." She looked around at the rainbow

of yarns. "I had some insurance money from Jonas, and this building came open. There isn't a good fiber store within a hundred miles of Eagle Mountain, so I thought I'd take a chance."

He nodded. "I'm going to be recording this," he said. "Could you go ahead and state your name for the recording."

"Oh. Sure. Anna Simmons Trent."

"And you were at the scene this morning in what capacity?"

"I was there with my search dog, Jacquie. I'm a volunteer with Eagle Mountain Search and Rescue and we had been asked to help look for a missing person, Dave Weiss."

"Tell me about your search and what you found. Start at the beginning."

She took a deep breath and paused, as if gathering her thoughts. "I met Sheri Stevens at Search and Rescue headquarters at seven thirty and followed her to the location where Dave's truck had been found." Then she took him through the rest of the morning, up to the moment she had located Dave Weiss's body hanging in a cottonwood tree.

"Describe the scene for me, please," he said.

"It was—remote," she said. "But not really. As the crow flies, it's only about a quarter mile from the Forest Service road. The map we consulted labeled the area Panther Point, but there aren't any named hiking trails around there. And the trail we followed in wasn't made by hikers or hunters or anything like that. It was an animal trail. I don't think it's a place anyone would go to fish or even to take pictures."

"Do you think that's significant?" he asked.

"How did Dave even know about it? Why would he have been there at all? He went to a lot of trouble to get back there, but why there?"

"Do you have any idea?"

"None."

"What else did you notice while you were waiting for Sheri to return with law enforcement?"

"Jacquie was restless. She insisted on sniffing around under the body. I thought she was upset because it was Dave and she knows him. Sometimes when I stop by his bakery, he gives her a treat. He *gave* her a treat." She looked down for a moment, gathering herself.

"Would you like me to get you some water?" he asked.

"No. I'm okay." She took a deep breath. "I followed her, trying to get her to come away from the area, but she stopped right beneath the body, sniffing at something on the ground. That's when I saw the impressions of what looked like a ladder."

"The impressions were on top of the snow?"

"No, it had snowed on top of them, filling them in partially, but not all the way."

"What made you think a ladder made those marks?"

"I remembered when I painted my bedroom, the ladder left impressions just like that in the carpet."

"Did you notice anything else?"

She hesitated.

"Anything at all could be useful," he said.

"The body was up really high. Like—ten feet in the air. That seemed really high up for someone to be hanging if they did it themselves. And the tree he was in was really big, and it was a long way up before there were any good branches to climb. Dave was a volunteer fireman and he was in good shape, but I wondered how he got up that tree."

"Did you notice how the rope was tied?"

She shook her head. "No. Why?"

"I'm just wanting your impressions." The rope had been secured fairly low around the trunk of the tree. Accessible to someone standing on the ground but, to his mind, awkward for that same person to then drape the other end over that high branch. Not impossible, though.

"Has anyone told Sandy?" Anna asked. "Dave's wife?"

"Yes. The sheriff and I notified her that her husband's body had been found."

"Poor woman. I'll have to go see her. She must be devastated."

"She was obviously very upset." She had stared at Lucas and the sheriff for a long moment then burst into noisy sobs. Lucas had summoned a neighbor to sit with her, but Sandy had been too grief-stricken to answer any of their questions. He would need to talk to her soon, though.

"Do you really think Dave killed himself?" Anna asked. "I know Sandy told the dispatcher he was worried about financial problems, but was he really that upset? Was there anything else?"

"Mrs. Weiss wasn't able to speak with us," he said. "But, apparently, when she reported her husband as missing, she'd said he had taken out loans to expand his business and was having trouble meeting the payments."

"I didn't know he was expanding his business."

"I understand he was friends with your late husband."

"Yes. And my friend, too, after Jonas and I married. He was a big help after Jonas died. But I hadn't seen much of him in the last six months."

"Why is that?"

She shrugged. "I think maybe Sandy might have been jealous of the attention he was giving me. There was never a hint of anything untoward between us, but I got the impression, from little things he said, that she was the jealous type. But I was doing better on my own, and Dave had plenty to do between looking after his business and his volunteer work. I still saw him when I shopped at the bakery and he never acted any differently toward me."

"Had you seen him recently?"

"I saw him Friday. He seemed fine."

"What about Mrs. Weiss? How well do you know her?"

"Not as well. Jonas and I spent a lot of time with her and Dave—barbecues at their house, dinners at ours, things like that. The guys were best friends and they wanted us to be friends, too. Sandy and I get along fine, but we're so different. She never said anything, but I got the impression she didn't approve of me. Or she thought I wasn't good enough for Jonas."

"What about her marriage? Did she and her husband get along?"

Anna stared at him. "You can't think Sandy had anything to do with Dave's death. The two of them adored each other. And they did everything together. They ran the bakery together and they were both firefighters. When they were younger, they competed in body-building competitions. That's how they met. They were really a team."

"It's just a routine question."

"Does this mean you don't think Dave took his own life? Someone with a ladder? Someone who could have put the rope that high?"

"It's much too early to draw any conclusions," he said. "Is there anything else you noticed that might be significant or that seemed unusual to you?"

"Dave left his tin of snuff in his truck," she said. "That was odd because he always carried it in his back pocket."

She frowned. "I don't see how that could be significant, it just struck me as odd."

"Anything else?"

"No. I just…is it okay if I contact Sandy? We weren't close, but I want to offer my condolences and any help she might need."

"Of course. I told her you were the one to find the body."

"She would have figured that out soon enough. Anyway, I want to talk to her. I probably come closer than most to know how she's feeling right now, widowed so young."

"Is there anything else that struck you as unusual or significant about the place where you and your search dog located the body?" he asked.

She shook her head. "No."

He leaned over and switched off the recorder. "When did your husband die?" he asked. "If you don't mind my asking."

"I don't mind. It happened not long after that day in the hospital." She didn't say what day—she didn't have to. "He slipped into a coma and never woke up."

"I'm sorry," he said again. She was younger than Sandy Weiss. Under thirty. She couldn't have been married that long.

"I shouldn't have yelled at that nurse the way I did," she said. "It wasn't her fault. It wasn't anyone's fault. But I couldn't let him suffer that way and do nothing."

"It's okay," he said. "No one is blaming you. Least of all me."

"I apologized to her after Jonas died. It was…awkward." She covered her face with one hand. "I had this idea when Jonas was first diagnosed that I was going to be so patient and loving and gracious. I wasn't anything like that. It was…so ugly."

"Yeah. It's like that."

She lowered her hand and her eyes met his, clear and laser-focused. "You know?"

He concentrated on putting away the recorder and his notepad. "I wasn't at the hospital that night because someone had called me about you," he said. "I was there because my girlfriend was there. She died, too. Three months after your husband."

Her face crumpled a little, eyes crinkled, mouth compressed, expression turned more inward. "I'm sorry."

"I used to get pretty frustrated with things at the hospital, too," he said. "The person in that bed is your whole focus and to the staff they're just one more needy person they are trying to care for. Not that they were callous, but everyone can't be their priority the way your loved one is for you."

"I wish I had been more understanding, that's all," she said. "But I do feel better knowing the hospital didn't call you in to arrest me." She stood and he rose, also. He looked at her across that tiny table and became aware once more of how intimate this space was. There was scarcely room for one of them to move without touching the other.

"I think someone who gives up her time to go out and search for other people, in rough terrain and all kinds of weather, has a lot of compassion," he said. "That's more important than one outburst at a weak moment."

"Thank you for saying that. I hope you find out what really happened to Dave. And why."

"The whys are a lot harder to figure out sometimes."

"I guess so."

She started to move past him to open the door and jostled against him. They both jumped away, as if shocked, and she laughed nervously. "Maybe we should have met at the sheriff's department."

"No, this was better," he said. He liked being close to her. He hadn't felt that way about a woman since Jenny had died. He took it as a good sign.

ANNA PHONED SANDY that evening after she got home, but no one answered her call. She hung up without leaving a message. She couldn't say anything to make the situation better, but at least she could offer her sympathy in person, where she was sure it would mean more than a recorded message.

She moved into the kitchen to feed Jacquie and her gaze came to rest on a framed photo on the refrigerator—she and Jonas, Dave and Sandy, all standing atop Dakota Ridge the summer before Jonas became ill. The men stood together in the middle—both tall, fit and handsome, flanked by the women. Sandy was only a few inches taller than Anna's five feet, three inches, but stockier and more muscular. She had very short blond hair and light blue eyes, and looked directly at the camera, grinning widely to show the slight gap between her upper front teeth. Anna was looking at Jonas, leaning into his side. Pain pinched at her heart, remembering that day. She had thought their whole long future together stretched out ahead of them.

Jacquie whined, reminding her what she was supposed to be doing. She measured out the dog's food and set it on the floor, and wondered what Sandy was doing right now. The evening after Jonas had died, Anna had wandered through this house feeling detached from reality. Jacquie had been only a year old, just starting her search and rescue training, and looking after her had been Anna's only tether to routine. Jacquie had had to be fed and walked and petted and played with. She'd had to practice her search techniques several times a week and attend classes and training. Having her to focus on had helped Anna so much.

Sandy and Dave hadn't had a dog or any children, so what was Sandy focusing on?

Anna regretted telling Deputy Malone that Sandy hadn't liked her. They had never been close, but Sandy had never been rude or said anything negative to Anna. They were just very different people. Anna liked reading, knitting, and growing flowers. Sandy raced dirt bikes, fished, and hunted. She was competent and competitive, and Anna had felt awkward around her. Anna had even worried that she was the kind of woman Jonas admired and secretly preferred, though those fears had gradually left her.

When Jonas had died, Sandy and Dave had brought a tray of pastries and offered to drive Anna to the funeral. Sandy had wept alongside Anna and kept people away when the condolence calls became too much for Anna. Anna wanted to do the same for her.

Tomorrow, she told herself as she shut off the light for the night. Tomorrow she would go to Sandy and do what she could to help.

SHORTLY BEFORE TEN the next morning, Anna headed to Yarn and More to open the store. Gemma had Wednesday mornings off and, if the store was quiet during that time, Anna would catch up on some bookwork. But she was surprised to find Sandy waiting at the back entrance to the store. She had the hood of her blue parka pulled up, shielding her face from view, but there was no mistaking her sturdy frame.

"Could I talk to you for a minute?" Sandy asked as Anna exited her car, before Anna could even say hello.

"Of course. Come in." She hurried to unlock the back door and ushered Sandy inside. Jacquie followed, her attention focused on their visitor.

"Sit down and let me take your coat," Anna said, gesturing to the wooden worktable. "I'll make us some coffee. Or would you rather have tea?"

"Nothing." Sandy sat but didn't remove her parka. "I just want to ask you a few questions then get out of here before anyone sees me."

"Of course." Anna pulled a chair out to face Sandy. She would leave the Closed sign in place a little longer. A large shelf of yarn would hide them from the view of anyone peering in the front windows. "I'm so sorry about Dave," she said. "This must have come as a huge shock."

"Everyone's sorry," Sandy said. "I'm sick of hearing about it. All the sorry in the world isn't going to bring him back."

Anna started to say how sorry she was about that, but stopped herself in time. "What do you need from me?" she asked. "I'll do anything I can to help."

"The sheriff and that other cop who came to see me yesterday said you were the one who found Dave's body."

"Yes. Jacquie and I were called in to search." Jacquie moved to rest her head in Anna's lap and Anna fondled her soft ears.

"They said his truck was parked on a forest road, down near the river. That kind of marshy spot past Panther Point."

"Yes."

"Where exactly? The cops didn't give me a lot of details."

"The truck was parked on the side of the road, nosed up in some oak brush," Anna said. "Jacquie and I followed a game trail to the river, then down to where a beaver dam had formed a pond, then past that to a grove of cottonwoods. Dave was in the cottonwoods."

"Hanging. They said he hanged himself."

Even though she had been there and seen it for herself, the words sounded so harsh and ugly to Anna. But then, the situation was harsh and ugly. "Yes," she said.

Sandy nodded and said nothing else. She had dark circles under her eyes and looked drained but still strong. She wasn't the type of woman to ever look fragile, Anna supposed. She had often envied Sandy's physical prowess, but she saw now that her strength went deeper.

"Why would Dave go there?" Anna asked. "Do you know?"

"No idea." Sandy shook her head. "There aren't any good ski trails back in there, and it's too close to the road for legal hunting. And it's too marshy for fishing."

"So you know the area?" Anna asked.

Sandy's eyes met hers and there was no mistaking the disdain in her expression. "I've lived in this county all my life. There isn't any place I don't know."

"Of course." She stared down at her lap, once again feeling awkward. It annoyed her. No one else she knew made her feel this way.

"You said something about this being a shock," Sandy said. "Well, it was and it wasn't. I knew Dave was stressed out, but I never thought he'd take the coward's way out like this."

Anna felt the anger behind the words. That was part of grief, she remembered—being so angry at the person who had left. "Why was he stressed out?" she asked.

She half expected Sandy to tell her that was none of her

business, but instead she said, "About six months ago, we were approached by this restaurant supplier who offered us a way to expand the business. This guy agreed to buy desserts from us. He'd distribute them to restaurants in the area. Locally sourced food is a big selling point these days, and Dave had built up a reputation for his pies and especially those Surprise Cakes. It was too good a deal to pass up— too good to be true, really." Sandy pressed her lips together and the fine lines around her eyes tightened.

"If it was such a good deal, why was Dave stressed?" Anna asked.

"We had to take out a loan to add another walk-in cooler, to hire another baker, and purchase more cookie sheets and muffin tins and another commercial-grade mixer. It was a big investment, but we were sure it would pay off. But the money coming in wasn't as much as this guy had promised, and the commissions we owed him for every sale took a big chunk of our profits, so we were really squeezed."

"What's going to happen now?" Anna asked.

"I'm trying to get out of having to pay off the loans," Sandy said. She seemed calm enough. "That may mean losing the business. We never should have agreed to the deal in the first place, but Dave was really excited about it, at least at first."

"But would he really have killed himself over something like this?" Anna asked.

"He did, didn't he?" Sandy glared at her.

"What if he didn't?" Anna asked.

In the silence that followed, Anna could hear Sandy breathing. Jacquie whimpered then lay down, her chin resting on Anna's shoe.

"What do you mean?" Sandy finally asked. "Dave hung himself. The sheriff said so."

"Did he say it like that, exactly?" Anna asked.

Sandy frowned. "He said they found Dave's body hanging in a cottonwood tree near the river. His truck was parked nearby. There wasn't anybody else there." She leaned toward Anna. "That's right, isn't it? You didn't see anyone else there, did you?"

"No. But it was just such a strange place for him to go to die. His body was so high up in that tree. How did he ever climb it?"

"Dave was a good climber. He would scramble up any trail. He did rock climbing, and he could shimmy right up a tree. I've seen him do it."

"Maybe so." She hesitated. Should she say anything about the marks she had seen on the ground? She couldn't be sure if they were made by a ladder. But if she were in Sandy's place, she would want to know. "There were some marks on the ground underneath the body," she began.

"What kind of marks?" Sandy demanded, her voice sharp.

"Some indentations, like from the legs of a ladder."

Sandy let out a bark of not-quite laughter. "Are you saying somebody hauled a ladder out there and strung up Dave's body? You do know the man weighed over a hundred and eighty pounds? And you probably haven't carried around too many ladders in your life, but let me tell you, they're heavy and they're awkward. It's not something you want to lug around in a bunch of underbrush, through frozen swamp. If someone did want to kill Dave, there were a lot easier ways to do it."

Anna could see how absurd the situation was when Sandy described it like that. But was it any more absurd than a man taking his own life? "I'm just telling you what I saw. The sheriff's department is investigating and I'm sure they'll come to the right conclusion."

"The only conclusion is that Dave killed himself." Sandy knotted her hands in her lap. "I know he looked happy and upbeat to everyone, but take it from me, he had his dark moods. And he grew up without a lot of money. He had a real fear of being poor. He thought we'd default on our loan and lose the business and be out in the street. I tried to tell him he was being foolish, talking like that, but he wouldn't listen to me."

"You certainly know him better than anyone," Anna said.

"I wondered why the sheriff asked me if Dave had any enemies. I guess I know now. But everybody liked Dave. The customers liked him. The other firefighters liked him. They liked him more than they like me."

"You have a lot of friends in this town, Sandy," Anna said. "I know it can be hard to accept help from others, but if you need it, don't hesitate to ask. You're going to have a lot to deal with now that Dave is gone."

"I'll handle it." She stood. "Most people don't know this, but I'm the one who's kept the business going for years. Dave was good at baking, but he was really lousy with money. He worried about making those loan payments, but I knew we'd be all right. Part of being successful in business is knowing when to cut your losses and move on. That's what I'm going to do now."

Anna rose, also. "If there's anything I can do to help, please let me know," she said. "You and Dave were such a help to me after Jonas died."

"Like you said, I've got plenty of friends who will help me if I need it." She nodded. "I can let myself out. You'd better open up before some woman with a yarn emergency gets upset."

Anna watched until Sandy had let herself out the back door then went to the front door, unlocked it and turned the sign to Open. Was that "yarn emergency" remark Sandy's attempt at humor or a way to belittle her and her customers? And what should she make of that comment about Sandy having friends who could help her? It was only as much as Anna herself had said.

Still, the words stung. Sandy had always had a way of getting under her skin.

One of the Sock Sisters came in to look at the new shipment of sock yarn, and another regular wanted help figuring out the directions in a pattern for a sweater she was knitting. Anna made a few other sales, paid some invoices, filed others, and finished up a new display of crochet thread. At twelve thirty, she had just finished eating the sandwich she had brought from home when Kyle Saddler came in.

"Hey, Anna," he said, offering a shy smile.

A tall man who hunched his shoulders as if to appear smaller, Kyle was another friend of Jonas's who had, by default, become Anna's friend, too. As the county building inspector, he'd frequently gone to Jonas's job sites to approve the work Jonas had completed. Lately, he had also made a habit of stopping by Yarn and More.

"What can I help you with today, Kyle?" Anna asked.

He looked around, as if suddenly remembering where he was. "Um, my niece is turning ten next week," he said. "She likes crafty stuff, so I thought maybe…some yarn?" The shy smile again. "Could you help me pick out something she would like?"

"Sure." She led the way to the display of needles and no-tions on the side wall. "We have some Learn to Knit kits geared toward teens and tweens that I bet she would enjoy." She pulled one of the kits from the hook. "This comes with yarn, instructions, needles and a link to a video she can watch to help with the basics."

Kyle took the kit. "Great. I'll take it."

She was walking toward the cash register when Gemma rushed in from the back. She stopped short when she saw Kyle. "I forgot something in my car," she stammered, whirled around, and exited again.

"Is there anything else?" Anna asked as she rang up Kyle's purchase.

"Yeah," he said.

She looked up at his emphatic tone and met his steady gaze. "Would you have dinner with me this weekend?" he asked.

Her stomach dropped to her toes. Kyle looked so hopeful. And he was so nice. "That's so sweet of you to ask," she said. "But I'm not really interested in dating again. Not yet."

"I understand." He handed her his credit card. "I was just thinking, though. It's been two years. You're still a young woman. Maybe you should try going out. With a friend."

She processed the card then handed it back to him. "I'm just not ready," she said.

His smile was gone, replaced by a woeful look. He tucked his wallet into his back pocket. "Let me know if you change your mind."

The door hadn't fully closed behind him before Gemma hurried in from the back room. "Didn't I tell you?" she said, equal parts censure and triumph in her voice. "Kyle Saddler didn't take a sudden interest in yarn because he wanted a new hobby. He wanted you!"

Anna tucked the credit card slip into the cash register drawer and pushed it shut. "Kyle is a very nice man, but I'm not interested in dating anyone."

"Why not?" Gemma asked. Her expression softened. "I'm not saying you have to get involved with anyone, but dinner wouldn't hurt."

"Kyle wants a lot more than dinner." At thirty-four, Kyle had said more than once that he was ready to settle down. When she looked in his eyes, she saw "serious romance" not "casual friendship."

"You're too young to spend the rest of your life alone," Gemma said. She patted Anna's hand. "I'm only saying that because I love you."

"I know," Anna said. "I'm just...not ready." Though, lately, something inside her had shifted. If the right man—someone she was attracted to, who wouldn't expect too much—came along, she might at least agree to go out. Maybe. The thought made her stomach twist in knots, but life was all about taking risks, right?

"I stopped by Sandy Weiss's house on the way over here," Gemma said as she moved to the worktable. She had shed her coat to reveal a colorwork sweater in shades of purple and green. "She wasn't there, but did you know there's a For Sale sign in the yard?"

"No. I spoke to Sandy this morning and she never said anything about that."

"You went by the house and the sign wasn't there?"

"No. She was waiting for me at the back door when I got to work this morning."

"Then she probably didn't tell you the bakery is for sale, too. There's no sign there, but I called the real estate agent who has the listing for the house and pretended to be interested and she said the business is for sale, too."

"Gemma, you didn't!"

"I'm sure I'm not the only one." Gemma set a large pink travel mug on the end of the worktable. "Barely twenty-four hours since Dave's body was found and Sandy has already contacted a broker?"

"That does seem really sudden," Anna said. "But Sandy mentioned something about money problems. Maybe she feels like she needs to sell out to pay debts Dave left."

"You would think she would at least wait a week or two," Gemma said. "Don't they tell people dealing with grief not to make any drastic, life-changing decisions too quickly?"

"Yes." But when your life had already been changed so completely by the death of a person you loved, everything else seemed secondary. In the days following Jonas's death, Anna had considered selling the house and moving away, even though she and Jonas had talked about her staying. At least she had had time to discuss those things with him before he died. Sandy hadn't had that luxury. "I'm sure she's doing what she thinks she needs to do," she said. "This has got to be really hard for her."

"I'm sure it is, but selling out? Where is she going to go? She's lived here all her life."

"Her parents died several years ago," Anna said. "And her siblings moved away. Maybe she thinks now that Dave is gone, there's nothing here for her. Maybe she wants to make a fresh start. She said she was ready to cut her losses and move on."

"She's certainly not wasting any time," Gemma said. "People are going to talk. They're going to wonder what she's running away from."

Maybe she was running from grief, Anna thought. Plenty of people had tried, though they all learned, as she had, that unlike justice or retribution, grief always caught up with you.

Chapter Four

"He died from a broken neck." Rayford County Medical Examiner Dr. Butch Collins looked down on the body of Dave Weiss, arranged on a metal table in the basement room that served as his lab and the county morgue. A stocky man with the weathered face of someone who spent a lot of time outdoors, he had the calm, matter-of-fact delivery of someone who had seen it all and was surprised by nothing. "Nothing unexpected about that. From what I saw at the scene, that tree branch he was tied to was high enough off the ground to ensure a big drop."

"So that's how he did it—climbed up there, put the noose around his neck and jumped?" Lucas asked.

"That would have done it," Collins said.

"We didn't see any marks on the tree trunk or limb to show he had climbed up there," Travis said. The sheriff and Lucas had driven to the medical examiner's office shortly after 11:00 a.m. on Wednesday, after two hours going over the scene at Panther Point again. "I don't think I could have made that climb."

"Dave was pretty athletic," Collins said. "Maybe he had practiced and knew he could get up there."

"Anything else?" Travis asked.

"He had a hefty dose of barbiturates in his system. Looks like he washed them down with a strawberry-banana smoothie. Phenobarbital."

"Where would he get his hands on phenobarbital?" Lucas asked.

"We don't prescribe it much for people these days," Collins said. "But it's fairly common in veterinary medicine. They use it to treat seizures in dogs."

"Dave didn't have a dog," Travis said.

"Then maybe he knew someone who did? Or he got a doctor to prescribe it for him?" Collins shrugged. "I can't help you there. In any case, the pills didn't kill him—the fall did."

"So why take them?" Lucas asked.

"He took enough to calm him down some. Maybe to give him the courage to go through with it."

"So he climbed that tree while he was doped up?" Travis asked.

"Adrenaline can negate the effect of sedatives to a certain extent," Collins said.

"Could someone have doped him up, hauled him out to that tree and strung him up?" Lucas asked.

"If you're skeptical Dave climbed that tree by himself, what makes you think someone else could climb up there with him?" Collins asked.

"What if they had a ladder?" Travis asked. "Force him to climb up the ladder, maybe at gunpoint, put the noose around his neck, then shove him off, or kick the ladder away."

"They'd have to have a lot of physical strength. Dave wasn't a little guy, and even drugged, he would probably fight back."

"But would the injuries you saw be consistent with that scenario?" Travis asked.

"They would." Collins regarded Dave's still features. "He's got some bruising on his arms and legs, but he was an active guy and they're the kind of marks anyone who's into rock climbing, skiing, hauling around big bags of flour and fire hoses and whatever else might have on them. Nothing unusual under his fingernails, no signs that he fought anyone." He looked back up at them. "That's it. I didn't find anything that isn't consistent with suicide."

"Thanks, Butch." Travis nodded and they turned to go.

Back in the sheriff's SUV, Travis started the engine but didn't move out of the parking spot. "What do you think?" he asked.

"I think suicides are usually suicides," Lucas said.

"And why would anyone kill Dave Weiss?" Travis said. "His wife says he was distressed. He's athletic enough to have climbed that tree himself."

"What about the ladder marks? That's the only sticking point for me."

"We don't know they were from a ladder," Travis said. "Maybe they were from rocks someone dug up? Or impressions made weeks ago." He shook his head. "The easiest explanation is usually the right one."

"So Dave Weiss killed himself?"

"Unless we find other evidence to the contrary, yes. Did Anna Trent's statement turn up anything of interest?"

Other than the fact that I'm attracted to her? "No, sir," Lucas said. "She noted the same things we did, about the height of the rope and the indentations in the mud and snow. Oh, and she thought it was odd that Dave left his snuff in the vehicle."

"People who are distraught can vary from their usual routines," Travis said. "I can't see any significance in snuff in the truck and not in his pocket."

Lucas shifted. "I'd still like to interview the widow," he said. "I want to hear what she thinks now that she's hopefully not as distraught as she was yesterday."

"Talk to her. Then give me a final report and we'll close this out."

"Yes, sir." The sheriff was right, yet those indentations in the mud and snow still bothered him. He didn't like unanswered questions and loose ends, but only on television did a case end with all of those tied in neat bows.

ALL DAY WEDNESDAY, Anna kept returning to her conversation with Sandy. Why had this mysterious businessman approached Dave—owner of a small bakery in a small town—to make a deal to supply desserts for restaurants? Yes, Dave was an excellent baker, but was his reputation that widespread? Was the man buying from many small bakeries or only from Dave? And why would Dave, who had always said he was content with the life he had, suddenly decide to take on the stress of expanding his business? He and Sandy didn't have children to provide for, and Dave had sometimes joked about how he was "the opposite of ambitious."

After she returned home that evening, she called the one person she thought might help her understand the situation better. Justin Trent, Jonas's older brother, answered her call on the second ring. "Anna! What are you doing calling me?" he said, raising his voice to be heard over the clink of glasses and hum of conversation. She pictured him, a stouter, grayer version of Jonas, with swept-back salt-and-pepper hair and a runner's lean frame, standing in the bar of Red Mesa, the restaurant he owned in downtown Junction.

"I was talking with a friend today and heard something that piqued my interest," she said. "I thought you might be able to give me some more information."

"Information about what?" The background noise ended abruptly. He must have moved to his office, behind the bar.

"Do you remember Dave Weiss?" she asked. "Jonas's good friend?"

"The baker, right? I think I met him a time or two."

"He was found dead yesterday. It may have been suicide."

"That's terrible. I'm sorry, Anna. And his wife is a friend of yours?"

"Yes." No point explaining all the background or that she was the one who'd found the body. "She said Dave was really stressed because he had taken out loans to expand his bakery business and was having trouble repaying them."

"It happens," Justin said. "People get in over their heads. What does this have to do with me? No offense, but I've got a full house tonight and I really need to get back out there."

"I won't keep you long," she said. "Dave's wife said a man approached him six months ago and offered to buy all the desserts he could provide, at a very good price, to supply area restaurants who want to advertise that they use local products. Do you know anything about that?"

"She's probably talking about George Anton," he said. "We use his company for some of the items we serve at Red Mesa. He's negotiated some really competitive prices for local meat, vegetables and baked goods. The suppliers get a good profit, restaurant owners like me get to offer a quality, local product to customers at a price point where I can still make money."

"So it's legitimate?"

"Why would you think it wouldn't be?" Momentary static as he moved around. "What's really going on, Anna? What do you care about this other guy's business dealings?"

"Jacquie and I found his body," she said. "We were called to help after Dave was reported missing and his truck was found, abandoned. I was there at the scene and I'm just not sure it was suicide. Dave had no reason to kill himself."

"Whoa, there. What do the local police say? What does the man's widow say?"

"His wife—his widow—thinks he killed himself. I don't know that the sheriff's department has decided."

"You need to stay out of this and let them do their job. It isn't any business of yours. I'm sorry about your friend but, seriously, don't think you can play amateur detective. Real life isn't like TV."

"I'm aware of that, Justin." She clenched her jaw. How could she have forgotten Justin's insufferable superior attitude? He had always—but especially since Jonas had died—treated Anna as if she didn't have the brains to find her way across town. When he'd learned she'd planned to open Yarn and More, he had accused her of throwing away Jonas's life insurance money. He told her to sell the house, move to the city, and go back to school to get a degree in something that would allow her to support herself.

"Maybe you need to find some volunteer activities to devote yourself to," he said. "That little yarn store you opened obviously isn't keeping you busy enough. Or I can always use help at the restaurant. We could probably set you up in a little apartment here in Junction, where I'd be close enough to help you when you need a hand. Jonas would have liked that, I think."

Jonas would have hated that, she was sure. And if she ever needed a job, Justin would be the last person she would ask to hire her. "Thank you for answering my question," she said. "How is Gloria?"

His pause was too long—he was probably framing how to word his answer. "Gloria is good," he said finally. "She and I are good together. I made a mistake and she's forgiven me."

"That's good to hear," Anna said, though she wasn't so sure. She liked her sister-in-law, and she had seen how hurt Gloria had been when she'd discovered Justin's affair with a coworker. Jonas had been furious with his brother, but Justin had dismissed his concern. "I know how to handle myself," he had said. But, apparently, he had done the right thing and gotten back together with his wife. "I'm happy for you," she said.

"Whether you are or you aren't doesn't really matter to me. I have to go now."

Silence, indicating he had ended the call. She stared at the screen, then stowed her phone once more. Talking with Justin always left her irritated, but at least he had satisfied her curiosity about Dave's new business venture. Apparently, it was legit, and she had a name, too. George Anton. Nothing she had learned contradicted what Sandy had told her. Dave had made a business deal that hadn't worked out the way he'd hoped, he had gotten in a financial bind and been so upset at the results he couldn't live with himself. It was upsetting and, in many ways, unfathomable, but that didn't make it any less true. Maybe this was the case in all suicides—they never made sense to the grieving people left behind.

A text pulled her from her reverie and she read the summons from Search and Rescue.

Lost hiker. Sunshine Ridge trail.

Before she could respond that she was on her way, a second text arrived. This one from Sheri.

I think we need you and Jacquie on this.

We're on our way, Anna typed then went to retrieve Jacquie's harness and her pack.

DIANE SEYMORE, described as a fit, fifty-seven-year-old woman who hiked every week year-round, had failed to return to her condo after telling her neighbor she was going to hike Sunshine Ridge if the trail was clear enough of ice. Lucas had driven to the trailhead and found Diane's vehicle, but no sign of the missing hiker, and summoned Search and Rescue.

"I walked about half a mile down the trail before a snowslide blocked the path," he told the Search and Rescue volunteers who met him at the trail, including, he couldn't help but notice, Anna Trent and her dog, Jacquie. "I could see what looked like fairly fresh prints from a smaller-sized hiking boot until that point. I called out for Diane Seymore, but didn't get an answer."

"It's possible she was caught in the snowslide," one of the volunteers, a tall, thin man the others addressed as Tony, said.

"Or she might have tried to go around the slide," Carrie Andrews said.

"We could waste valuable time trying to figure out the best place to look," Captain Sheri Stevens said. She studied the sky. "The sun is going to set behind that ridge in less

than an hour. We need to get Anna and Jacquie on this before the trail goes any colder."

"I'll open Diane's car so you can retrieve a scent article,"
Lucas said. He'd been thinking a lot about Anna since they
had last talked. Being near her made him feel more alive
and awake than he had in the two years since Jenny had
died from cancer. Those were feelings he wanted to hold
on to after being numb for so long.

She followed him from his department SUV to Diane's
Jeep. Jacquie pranced on the end of her leash ahead of them.
She had the traditional poodle cut, with pom-poms of curly
hair around her wrists and ankles, another pom-pom on the
end of her stubby tail. But her orange Search Dog vest and
intense focus marked her as a working animal, ready to get
down to business.

Anna trotted along behind the eager dog, a trim figure
in gray snow pants, blue Search and Rescue parka and blue
daypack, a bright knit cap over her dark hair. She looked
very different from the distraught woman he had met in
that hospital corridor two years before; competent and in
control, a healthy flush in her cheeks and a brightness to
her eyes that grief and frustration had drained away during
her husband's illness.

She retrieved a half-empty paper coffee cup from the
front of Diane's car, emptied the coffee and offered the
cup to Jacquie to sniff. Then she and the dog disappeared
down the trail, one of the other Search and Rescue volunteers jogging after them. Lucas returned to lean against his
sheriff's department SUV to wait. The tall, thin volunteer
walked over to join him. "Tony Meisner," the man introduced himself.

"Lucas Malone. I've only been here a week, on loan from

Junction, and this is the second missing person's search I've been involved in. I'm beginning to wonder about this place."

Meisner, a lean man in his late thirties, leaned back next to Lucas against the patrol vehicle. "Maybe you're jinxing us. Though I can tell you from working search and rescue for fifteen years that calls tend to come in clusters. We'll get a trio of vehicle accidents or several falls in a row. This time it's missing persons, though let's hope this call has a happier ending than the last one."

"Did you know Dave Weiss?" Lucas asked.

"I did. We climbed together a few times, and we talked fishing whenever I went into his bakery."

"I didn't know him, but from what I've been told, he sounds like a great guy."

"He was."

"Did it surprise you that he'd take his own life?"

"They're sure it's suicide?" Tony asked.

"That seems to be the case. His wife said he was stressed lately."

"I wouldn't have said Dave would do something like that, but I guess you never know."

"Apparently, he was under a lot of financial stress."

"I didn't know that."

"When was the last time you saw him?" Lucas asked.

Tony rubbed his chin. "Saturday. I stopped in the bakery to get a loaf of sprouted grain bread and a bear claw."

"How did he seem?"

"I didn't actually talk to him. A teenager who works there part time waited on me. But Dave was there. I could see into the office he has behind the front counter. The door was open and he was arguing with someone. I didn't see who, and I only heard Dave's side of the conversation, but he was upset about something."

"You think he was arguing with someone?" Lucas asked. "What about?"

Tony shook his head. "I have no idea. I heard Dave say, 'No, that's not going to happen,' but then the clerk handed me my change and I left. Dave isn't the type to get angry easily, but he was really upset at whoever was in there."

A cheer rose up near the trailhead, and both men straightened as Anna and another woman emerged from the trail.

"Oh, I hate that you all had to come out here for me." Diane put her hands to her cheeks as she took in all the Search and Rescue volunteers gathered around her. "But I'm so glad you did." She turned to Anna. "And I'm so grateful to Anna and Jacquie for finding me."

"Are you all right?" Sheri asked.

"Oh, I'm fine," Diane said. She laughed. "Well, I'm looking forward to a nice hot shower, a glass of wine and dinner, but really, I'm fine. I was just foolish and got off the trail. I thought I could go around that snowslide and get back on the trail on the other side, but obviously I was wrong."

"She wasn't even that far from the trail when we found her," Anna said.

"Yes, but I didn't know that," Diane said. "I've hiked this trail half a dozen times, but everything looks different with all the snow."

"We're glad you're all right," Sheri said.

"Thank you all again, so much." Diane went around the group, shaking hands. She paused when she reached Lucas. "Oh, and the sheriff's department, too. I really have caused a lot of trouble."

"I'm glad you're okay." Lucas echoed the others. "Don't worry about the trouble. It's what we're here for."

"And I'm so grateful, really."

She moved on toward her Jeep and Lucas turned to Anna. "Good job," he said. "It didn't take you long to find her."

"Jacquie does all the work," she said. "I just follow her lead."

"I imagine it's nice to have a good outcome like this after what happened earlier in the week," he said.

"Oh, it is." She glanced around them then leaned in closer. "Have you learned any more about Dave's death?"

"The evidence points to a suicide," he said. "I'm sorry."

"What about the imprints from the ladder?" she asked.

"We don't know they were from a ladder, or when they were made," he said. "There's no indication that he had any enemies. His wife says he was upset enough about his financial situation to have killed himself."

"Yes, she told me the same thing." She hung her head.

"I'm sorry," he said. He wanted to put a hand on her shoulder to try to offer some comfort. But that wouldn't be appropriate.

"It's not your fault," she said.

"Still, I hate to see you so sad."

She raised her head and her eyes met his. "That's a very nice thing to say."

"Can I say something else?"

The pause was only as long as an inhale, but it felt much longer. "What do you want to say?" she asked at last.

"Will you have dinner with me?"

He had meant to say "coffee" or "a drink." Nothing as formal as dinner. He waited for her to say no, maybe even tell him he was way out of line. Instead, her cheeks flushed a little pinker and a dimple formed at the left side of her mouth. "Yes," she said. "Yes, I'd like that."

Chapter Five

Was this a date? Dinner was a date, right? But she didn't date. She wasn't ready to date. She felt too married to date. She wasn't married, of course. But she still felt that way, inside. She should call Lucas and say no. She could say something had come up. Or she could tell him she wasn't ready.

Anna paced back and forth across the bedroom, mind in turmoil. She couldn't remember the last time she had been so flustered. She forced herself to stop and take a deep breath. She had nothing to be nervous about. Nothing to feel guilty about. She could have dinner with a good-looking man who made her feel more like a woman than she had in over two years. There was nothing wrong with that, and maybe everything right.

Jacquie lay on the end of the bed, front paws neatly crossed at the wrists, intelligent brown eyes fixed on Anna. She sometimes wished the dog could talk, to render her opinion on the subject. She thought about calling Gemma, but Gemma would whoop and tell her it was about time she went out with someone, especially someone as good-looking as Lucas Malone.

Yes, he was handsome, but Anna didn't care about that. Or at least, it wasn't the most important thing. She wanted someone who had a good sense of humor. A man who was smart and kind. Lucas seemed like all of those things. And he had pointed out if they were going to have dinner together, she should stop addressing him as Deputy Malone. His first name, Lucas, felt a little awkward, but she was growing to like it.

"It's just one dinner," she said out loud. "It will be fine." But her stomach wobbled in a way that wasn't fine at all.

In the end, she managed to dress and do her hair and makeup in time to answer the doorbell when Lucas arrived. He wore the same black leather jacket she had seen him in before, but with black slacks, shined shoes and a blue button-down that made his eyes look even darker. "Hello," he said, and she felt the impact of his soft, deep voice, and the smile that went with it, just below her belly button.

They made small talk on the way to the restaurant, until after they had given their orders to the waiter. She began to relax. Lucas was easy to talk to. Why had she been so nervous?

"Do you know a man named Justin Trent?" he asked.

The water she had just sipped went down the wrong way and she started coughing. Several awkward moments passed before she could speak. "Justin is Jonas's brother," she said. "How do you know him?"

"He called me this morning."

"Why would Justin call you? He lives in Junction." And he definitely didn't know the two of them had agreed to go out.

"He wanted to know the cause of death for Dave Weiss. He said Dave was a friend and he had just learned he had died."

"Dave was Jonas's friend," she said. "Justin hardly knew

him." She searched his face for some clue as to where this was leading. "What did you tell him?"

"I told him it looked like Dave had taken his own life."

"I told him that when I talked to him Wednesday," she said. "I don't know why he would call you. Maybe he didn't believe me." She took another sip of water, more cautious this time. "He always treats me as if I'm dim-witted. He thinks he knows what's best for everyone, including me."

"He said you had asked him a bunch of questions about some business deal Dave was involved in. He thought it might be a good idea for me to warn you not to interfere with a police investigation."

This time she was glad she wasn't trying to drink, or even holding a glass. "What did you say to that?"

"I told him you weren't interfering with anything."

The server arrived with their salads and she used the break in the conversation to try to think of what to say.

"I wasn't interfering," she said. "But Sandy told me Dave had signed a contract with someone who distributes food to area restaurants. He agreed to buy desserts from Dave at a good price, and Dave invested in a new walk-in cooler and more help and equipment in anticipation of a big pay-off. And I guess he owed this middleman commissions, too. But he didn't earn as much as he'd thought he would and the loans were at risk of being in default. Justin owns a restaurant in Junction and I thought he would know how an arrangement like that might work and could help me understand why Dave—who never showed any sign of wanting to expand the business or have more money—would have signed a contract with this guy."

He poured dressing onto his salad. "What did you find out?"

"Justin says there's a man named George Anton who acts

as a middleman between small suppliers and restaurants. He pays good prices to the suppliers and offers competitive prices to the restaurants. Justin said Anton supplies some items for Red Mesa, Justin's restaurant. Then he made some snide remark about how I shouldn't be playing amateur detective. Which was bad enough, but to have him call you is infuriating."

"I'm impressed," Lucas said. "You found out a lot more than I knew about. Sandy didn't give me any particulars about Dave's business dealings. She just said they owed a lot of money he realized he couldn't pay back."

"If I was her, I'd be frantic right now about that debt," Anna said. "But Sandy was perfectly calm. She said she'd let that loan default and move on."

"Do you think she'll continue to operate the bakery?"

"I would have thought so. I knew Dave was the original baker, but my impression was that she helped a lot. And he told me when he catered our wedding that Sandy did most of the decorating. He said she was the more artistic of the two of them. Still, maybe the work was too much for her on her own, and she didn't want to hire someone to take Dave's place. I can see how that would be awkward." She stabbed at her salad. "Apparently, both the bakery and her home are up for sale."

"Maybe she's not as blasé about the debt as you think," Lucas said. "Maybe she needs to sell the house and the bakery right away to pay off the loans her husband took out."

"I'm really surprised Dave ended up in such a fix in the first place," she said. "He was never one of these people who is always out for more, looking for new ways to bring in more money. He and Jonas were alike that way—not exactly unambitious, but content to keep their businesses smaller. 'Manageable,' Jonas used to say."

"What kind of business did your husband have?" Lucas asked.

"He owned a small construction company. He built custom homes mostly, and did some remodeling." She pushed lettuce around the plate. "He had people who worked for him, but really, the business was all about him and his leadership and skills. Without him, there really was no business."

"So you decided to open your own business?"

She shook her head. "No. At first I thought I'd get a job working for someone else. I had done all the bookkeeping, payroll, etcetera, for Jonas for the past few years, so I started applying to offices around town. I got one job offer from a man I didn't particularly like, another builder in town. The pay he offered wasn't really enough to live on. I could have supplemented my paycheck with Jonas's life insurance money, but the whole idea of the job depressed me. I was walking back to my car after the job interview and I saw the For Lease sign in the window of the building that houses my shop. I'd thought about doing something like this for years and I figured, why not now?"

"And it's worked out for you?"

"It has." She smiled, happy to talk about something that had become so precious to her. "I look forward to going into the store every day and I've made some wonderful friends."

"It's good to hear you're doing so well. I bet your husband would be pleased."

She tried to hide her disappointment in his remark. So far they had talked about her husband's brother, her husband's friend and now her husband himself. Lucas didn't sound like someone who was interested in any kind of romantic relationship. "I have no idea what Jonas would think," she said. "He liked having me working for him. I liked it, too, but the few times I talked about doing something with my knitting—opening an Etsy shop, for example—he wasn't exactly encouraging. I think he saw knitting as a quirky little hobby, not a real business."

Opening Yarn and More and making it a success was the first thing she had done solely for herself since her marriage. Along with pride in her accomplishment came so many other emotions—sadness, guilt, regret. She shook her head and pushed aside her half-eaten salad. She didn't want to go there. Not tonight. This was supposed to be a time for her and Lucas to get to know each other better. At least, that was how she had viewed the evening.

"Are you enjoying your stay in Eagle Mountain?" she asked.

"It's a beautiful place," he said. "I've been here a number of times before. Junction is only a little over an hour away, after all."

"Have you lived in Junction long?"

"Seven years. I moved there from Fort Collins after I graduated from the state's police academy. Jenny, my girlfriend, moved over about a year later."

Their entrées arrived and Anna wrestled with what to say next. Were they going to talk about his girlfriend now? She was curious about the woman who had apparently been dying about the same time as Jonas. Such an odd thing for the two of them to have in common and yet there was comfort in knowing he probably understood a lot of what she had gone through. Why not let him know that she could empathize with him? "You had been together quite a while, then," she said. As long as she was married to Jonas.

"We were." He looked even sadder.

"There are so many emotions to process," she said. "Grief, of course, but also guilt."

He leaned toward her. "You feel guilty?"

She nodded. "I think everyone who is left behind feels that way. Sandy is probably feeling it now. I always wondered if I had urged Jonas to go to the doctor sooner, or if we had eaten healthier, could I have saved him? The answer is probably no, but still, we torture ourselves with questions like that."

He sat back. "I guess so." He seemed to gather himself and his expression took on a new warmth. "I'm sure Jonas knew how much you loved him. How devoted you were. You should take comfort from that."

She nodded and neither of them spoke for a long moment, but in the silence there was closeness—she had seldom talked to someone who knew so intimately what she had gone through.

After a moment, he touched her hand and smiled. She felt the heat of that look all the way to her toes. "I'm feeling better about life in general these days," he said. "What about you?"

She returned the smile. "'Life goes on' sounds so trite," she said. "But it's true. I remember the first day I woke up and felt excited about the day ahead. I felt lighter. Not exactly happy, but not depressed, either, as if a cloud had lifted. Of course, the next day I cried half the day, but it was one baby step forward and then there were others. Now, most days, I feel pretty good. I can see possibilities again, and that's such a relief."

He nodded and cut into his chicken. "You're in a good place—your own house, friends, a business you love. And, hey, if the yarn store doesn't work out, you could always be an amateur detective. You seem pretty good at it." He winked and she burst out laughing. Their eyes met and she felt lit from within.

From that moment on, the evening changed, as if, having acknowledged the ghosts of their pasts, they were ready to focus on this moment. She told him about training Jacquie to be a search dog, volunteering with Search and Rescue, and about some of their adventures. He shared amusing encounters he had had as a law enforcement officer, including retrieving a marmot that had hitched a ride in a tourist's SUV from a high-mountain parking area to downtown Junction.

"I decided right then I'd never make it as a wildlife officer," he said. "The ungrateful little rodent bit me and I worried I'd have to get rabies shots, but the doctor finally decided that wasn't necessary."

"The poor thing was probably frightened," she said.

"He wasn't the only one. You think they're cute when you see them on the side of the road, but up close, in a confined space, they look twice as big and fierce."

She laughed more than she could remember laughing in two years. When the server asked for the third time if they needed anything else, she looked across at him and felt grateful and happy—and definitely attracted. "We'd probably better go," he said.

She nodded and they stood and collected their coats. He slid hers onto her shoulder, his fingertips lightly brushing her collarbone as he did so, sending a hot tremor through her.

He drove back to her house in comfortable silence, music

playing softly on the radio. At one point, he reached across and took her hand and she didn't pull away. She felt closer to him than she could have imagined she would to someone she had known such a short time.

Then again, she could say she had known him for two years. They hadn't been together during that time but, for a while, they had led parallel lives, each dealing with one of the worst things a person could go through. That made for a kind of kinship most people would never have.

He parked in her driveway and they got out. She debated whether or not to invite him in, and what kind of message that sent. In front of her door, the light she had left on bathed them both in a golden glow. He leaned closer. "Is it okay if I kiss you good night?" he asked.

She nodded, suddenly tongue-tied. She was about to tell him it was more than okay, but his lips covered hers, sending a thrilling heat all the way through her. She gripped his shoulders and arched up toward him, and he wrapped his arm around her and drew her close. She opened her mouth and his tongue teased across her lips. It had been a long time since she had been kissed this way, and she realized how much she had missed. Missed this physical surge of pleasure and the sensation of being someone's complete focus. Missed the tingle of desire that made her feel giddy and daring. Missed the anticipation of what might come next. Something good.

She would ask him inside, she decided. Reckless. But she wasn't an unsure girl. She didn't have to wonder what he'd think of her or care what the neighbors would say. Life was short and they both knew that better than most. Why not enjoy whatever they could, right now?

They parted, both breathing hard, and she smiled and

started to turn toward the door, but a movement over his right shoulder made her gasp. She pulled back and he whirled around, pushing her behind him, shielding her with his body. "Who's there?" he demanded.

Sandy Weiss moved out of the shadows into the path of the porch light. "It's just me." She smirked. "Sorry to interrupt."

Anna pressed a hand to her chest, trying to slow the racing of her heart. "Sandy, what are you doing here?"

"I wanted to talk to you."

"You have my phone number, don't you?"

"This wasn't something I wanted to talk about on the phone." She looked at Lucas.

"I'll go," he said, but made no move to leave.

"You can stay," Sandy said. "Maybe you need to hear this, too."

"What are you talking about?" Anna asked. "You're scaring me."

"Could we go inside? It's cold out here. Besides, I don't like being out here where anyone can see us together."

"Of course." Anna pulled her key from her purse. "But give me some idea of what has you so frightened."

"I'm not frightened!" She sounded angry. "I'm just being smart."

"What are you being smart about?" Lucas asked.

Sandy ignored him, her focus still on Anna. "I'm beginning to wonder if you were right the first time," she said.

"Right about what?" Anna fit the key in the lock and turned it.

"Maybe Dave didn't kill himself. Because now I think someone is trying to kill me."

Chapter Six

Lucas followed the two women into the house. While Anna greeted the dog and switched on lights, Sandy shrugged out of her parka and settled onto the sofa. The room's furnishings were simple and homey, with a braided rug on the hardwood floor and furniture upholstered in brown or soft blue. A knitted throw in those same colors draped across the back of one of two armchairs. "Can I get you anything?" Anna asked. "A glass of water, or I could make coffee or tea."

"Always the perfect hostess." Sandy shook her head. "Don't you want to hear what happened?"

Anna sat at the opposite end of the sofa. "Of course."

Lucas took the chair across from the women, the one with the blanket. "What makes you think someone is trying to kill you?" he asked.

Sandy crossed and uncrossed her legs. She was dressed in jeans, a gray sweatshirt with Downtown Gym in black letters across the chest, hiking boots and a black fleece beanie pulled over her short blond hair. Dark shadows beneath her eyes testified to sleepless nights. "It started with phone calls," she said. "The first one came the afternoon after Dave's body was found. Someone called the bakery and, when I answered, a man said, 'Keep your mouth shut or you're next' and hung up."

"Did you recognize the voice?" Lucas asked.

"No. It was very deep. Really, it sounded like someone trying to make his voice deeper."

"Did you contact the sheriff's office?" Lucas asked.

"No, why would I? It was just some creep."

"You said 'phone calls,'" Lucas said. "There was more than one?"

"Yes. I got another call the next morning with the same message." She shifted on the sofa, as if trying to get more comfortable. "And one that afternoon. That third time, I told the caller to get lost, though I didn't use such polite language. No calls today, so I figure that solved the problem."

"Now you don't think so?" Anna asked.

"No. Because this evening I got this." She leaned onto one hip, pulled something out of the back pocket of her jeans and handed it to Anna. Anna unfolded a piece of paper, read it, then passed it to Lucas.

He studied a sheet of lined notebook paper, the ragged left edge indicating it had been torn from a spiral notebook, with pasted-on letters that appeared to be cut from a magazine that read "Keep your mouth shut or you'll end up like your husband." He looked up at Sandy. "Keep your mouth shut about what?"

"I have no idea," she said. "It's silly, really." She glanced at Anna. "But then I started thinking about what you said about Dave's body being so high up in that tree, and how you had seen what looked like marks from a ladder. I wanted to talk to you and see if you really thought that meant that Dave didn't kill himself."

"Mrs. Weiss, do you believe your husband was involved in something that could have gotten him killed?" Lucas asked.

She turned to him, fine lines on her high forehead. "I don't," she said. "I thought Dave was on edge because of the money we owed, but what if that wasn't it? What if he was so stressed because someone was threatening him?"

"Have you found anything to indicate that was the case—any notes your husband received similar to this one?" He tapped the paper in his hand.

"No. And Dave never said anything. But he wouldn't have wanted to worry me."

She wouldn't be the first spouse who was in the dark about her partner's business affairs—legal or illegal. "I spoke with someone who said they came into the bakery last Saturday and heard your husband arguing with someone in his office," Lucas told her. "The customer couldn't see who the person was, but they said Dave was very upset. Do you know who that was?"

She pressed her lips together. "Last Saturday morning or afternoon?" she asked after a pause.

"Afternoon."

She shook her head. "I have no idea. I wasn't at the bakery then."

"You have someone who works for you?"

Sandy nodded. "Ashley Dietrich. She's a high school student. But I don't think Dave would argue with her. She's such a timid kid. She would crumple if you raised your voice at her."

"When does she work her next shift?" Lucas asked.

"I had to let her go. I can't afford to keep an employee with Dave gone. I'll handle things myself for now."

Lucas made a note in his book. "This person said they

heard your husband tell the other person 'No, that's not going to happen.'"

Sandy relaxed a little. "Dave was probably on the phone. And I'm pretty sure he was talking with George Anton. That's the restaurant supplier we agreed to sell desserts to. But they weren't arguing. They were just discussing the next delivery. This customer—whoever it was—must have misunderstood." She turned to Anna again. "You know Dave. He never got angry with anyone. That wasn't like him."

Tony Meisner had said he could see Dave and he was sure he was talking to another person, not on the phone. Tony hadn't struck Lucas as the type to exaggerate or misinterpret. "If your husband didn't kill himself, do you have any idea who was responsible for his death?" he asked.

Sandy held out both hands, palms up. "No idea at all." She leaned toward him. "Do you think he was murdered?"

"If this was a random crime, the killer went to a lot of trouble, going to that remote location, hauling out a ladder and rope, and your husband," he said. "Suicide seems more likely."

"If someone murdered Dave, you need to find out who," she said.

"You said you believed your husband was upset enough about his financial problems to kill himself," Lucas reminded her.

"I don't think that anymore. Not after these threats."

"We can see about getting you into a safe house," Lucas said. "Someplace whoever is threatening you won't be able to reach you."

"Oh, no, I'm not going anywhere." Sandy crossed her arms over her chest. "I have a business to run. I need to plan

Dave's funeral. I'm not going to hide. You just do your job and find whoever is doing this."

"We'll certainly look into the matter," Lucas said. "We can start by examining your phone records. Maybe we can track the caller."

The lines on her forehead deepened. "You can really do that? Our bakery gets dozens of calls a day and we don't have caller ID or anything."

"It will help if you can remember what time the calls came in."

"The closest I can get is morning or afternoon." She leaned toward him. "My husband died. I'm going to have to sell my home and my business. I'm not sleeping. I don't know whether I'm coming or going. Grief does that to you, you know?"

He knew. "We'll do the best we can," he said. "Is there anything else you can think of that might help? Anything your husband said to you? Anyone who was angry with him about anything? A former employee who left unhappy? A customer?"

She shook her head. "Nothing like that. Dave was a really nice guy. If anything, he was too nice. I always worried about people taking advantage of him."

"What do you mean?"

"Nothing important," she said. "You know, if someone complained they didn't like the pie they bought, Dave just automatically refunded their money. He didn't argue or ask questions or anything. He'd stay late to fill an order for someone who waited until the last minute to call. He let people take advantage of him like that."

"Everybody liked Dave." Anna hadn't spoken for so long,

the sound of her voice seemed to startle Sandy. "I never heard anyone say a word against him."

Right. The man was a saint. But if Sandy was right, someone had disliked him enough to kill him.

"Sandy, you're welcome to spend the night here," Anna said. "You can stay as long as you need to, while the sheriff's department checks out these threats."

"I'll be fine in my own home." Sandy stood. "I'm not the skittish type."

Lucas stood and followed Sandy to the door. "I'll follow you home, just to make sure you arrive safely," he said.

"Aren't you the gentleman?" Sandy looked him up and down then glanced at Anna. "I'll wait in my car while you say good night," she said.

ANNA TOLD HERSELF she should be grateful for this offer of privacy, but the smirk that accompanied the words spoiled the mood. Lucas waited until the door had closed behind Sandy before he turned to her. "I'm sorry to leave you like this," he said. "But I really should make sure everything is all right at Sandy's house."

"Of course you should." She forced a smile. "It's getting late anyway."

"Dinner was nice," he said.

"Yes." She couldn't meet his gaze. She had been feeling a lot bolder until Sandy showed up. Now she felt awkward and unsure.

Lucas touched her shoulder. "Good night."

She lifted her gaze to his. "Good night," she said then, impulsively, she leaned forward and hastily kissed his cheek. She pulled away. "You'd better go. Sandy will be getting impatient."

He let himself out and she waited until she heard both vehicles drive away before she sat on the sofa again. Jacquie jumped up beside her and laid her head in Anna's lap. "I don't know if I'm ready for this, girl," she said as she massaged the dog's ears. Being on her own was easier, and she had thought she was happy that way. But now she had a good-looking, interesting, intelligent man who seemed interested in her as well. Being alone didn't seem so happy, after all, but opening herself up to someone else felt pretty scary. "Unlike Sandy, I guess I am the skittish sort," she said.

Jacquie whined and Anna went to the back door and let her out then, instead of following the dog, she opened the door into the garage. She flipped on the light and studied the tarp-covered shape that filled half the space next to her Outback. Jacquie came to sit beside her, and let out a low whine.

Anna walked around her car and lifted the tarp. Beneath it, the 1974 Dodge Dart was a patchwork of Bondo, primer and remnants of the original red paint, now oxidized and nicked. A dusty collection of parts salvaged from junkyards around the state filled the front and back seats of the vehicle, which Jonas always referred to as "The Dart" as if it were the only one ever made. It was the only one for him anyway. He'd also called it "my baby" and she'd known he wasn't even joking.

After he'd died, Anna had donated his clothing and sold his tools, but she hadn't been able to part with the Dart. He had spent so much time with it, invested so much of himself into it, how could she let it go?

Minutes ticked by as she stared at the car, trying to picture Jonas bent over the engine, singing off-key to country radio as he worked. In the early days after he'd died, it was as if his ghost haunted this space. She had been able to see him here. To hear him. But not in a while.

She lowered the tarp and smoothed it over the fender, then turned to go back inside. Time for bed. Alone. No new lover and no ghosts to keep her company.

ASHLEY DIETRICH WAS a slight, pale, sixteen-year-old who told Lucas she had worked for the bakery for three months. She sat on the sofa next to her mother, who had somewhat reluctantly agreed to the deputy's request to interview her daughter before Ashley left for her new part-time job Saturday morning. Ashley tucked her long, strawberry-blond hair behind one ear and stared down at the chipped red polish on her nails. "Mrs. W. told me a couple of days ago that she's planning on closing down the place since Mr. W. died, so I had to find another job."

She looked up at Lucas, light green eyes wide. "That sounded terrible, didn't it? I didn't mean that. I'm really sorry Mr. W. died. He was a super nice guy. He was always thanking me and telling me I was doing a good job." She bit her lower lip. "This was my first job and I was really nervous, but he made it easy."

"I want to ask you about the Saturday before Dave Weiss died," Lucas said. "That would be Saturday, March 12. You worked that morning, is that correct?"

Ashley nodded. "I worked every Saturday. Seven a.m. to three p.m."

"That afternoon, you waited on Tony Meisner," Lucas said. "Do you remember him?"

Ashley's brow furrowed. "He's a regular customer. He

bought a bear claw. And maybe a loaf of bread?" Her voice rose in question.

"That's right. Tony said while he was in the store, he heard Mr. Weiss in his office, arguing with someone. Who came to the bakery to see him that afternoon?"

"No one came to see Mr. W. that afternoon," Ashley said. "It was just me and him and Mrs. W. there all day. And she was only there for a couple of hours. She had fire department stuff to do, or something like that."

"Could someone have come in a back door to the office?" Lucas asked.

"There isn't a back door to the office," Ashley said. "There's a door on the loading dock, but that goes right into the freezer, from when the building was a meat market, so it doesn't get used much, though they keep flour and stuff in the freezer. The only way into the office is through the front door and behind the counter."

"Could someone have come in while you were away, maybe using the restroom or something?"

"I guess. But I would have heard them in there with Mr. W. He never closed the door or anything."

Tony had told Lucas the door was open and he could see Dave. Maybe he had the day wrong. "Did you ever hear Mr. Weiss argue with someone when you were at the bakery?" he asked.

"You mean besides his wife?" She blushed. "I mean, it's not like they fought all the time, but they did have some, um, loud conversations when I was working."

Everyone had painted a picture of Sandy and Dave as devoted to each other, but Lucas wasn't really surprised to hear they hadn't always gotten along. Every couple rubbed each other the wrong way from time to time, and he would imagine it could be even worse if you not only lived but worked together. "What did they argue about?" he asked.

Ashley shrugged. "The foolish stuff people fight about," she said. "She thought he was careless about picking up his clothes off the floor or paying bills. He thought she was too uptight about money."

"Do you remember any specific argument?" Lucas asked.

"No. I really didn't pay attention. I mean, why would I?"

Why would a teenager care about an older married couple's squabbles? "Thanks, Ashley. Just one more question. Do you think Mr. Weiss was worried about anything before he died?"

"You mean, like, was he upset enough about something to kill himself?" She shook her head, the large gold hoops in her ears swaying with the movement. "I was really surprised when I heard what happened. He was a really upbeat kind of guy. Not the type to stress over stuff. I dropped a whole box of cupcakes one time and I was sure he'd fire me, or at least yell at me for being clumsy. Instead, he helped me pick up everything and made a joke about how he was glad he wasn't the only person in the shop who was a klutz." She dabbed at a tear in the corner of her eye. "I can't imagine how much he must have been hurting inside to go and hang himself. It's terrible."

Mrs. Dietrich handed her daughter a tissue from a box on the coffee table between them. "It's almost time for Ashley to leave for work," she said.

Lucas stood. "Thank you for talking to me, Ashley," he said.

Mrs. Dietrich walked Lucas to the door. "What is this

about?" she whispered. "Is there something going on besides Dave Weiss killing himself?"

"I'm just getting a better picture of his last days," Lucas said.

She frowned but didn't say anything more.

Lucas checked his watch. He had a few minutes before he had to be at a meeting at the sheriff's department. His conversation with Ashley hadn't provided any new information, though it had added another name to the list of people who were surprised to learn Dave Weiss had taken his own life. He had thought finding the person Dave had argued with that Saturday might lead to a reason for Dave's suicide, or a suspect in his murder, but maybe Sandy was right and Dave had been having a phone conversation with George Anders.

He made a note to call Anders and set up an interview. His name kept popping up in this investigation, one more piece of the puzzle Lucas needed to complete the picture of Dave Weiss's final days.

Chapter Seven

Saturday morning, Anna had scarcely set her mug of coffee on the worktable when Gemma pounced, "I ordered take-out from Mad Thai last night. When Terry went to pick it up, he said he saw you and some really good-looking guy having dinner. He said the two of you looked really cozy."

"Did Terry really say he was good-looking?"

Gemma's husband could have posed for photos as a "mountain man" with big biceps and a bigger beard. Anna had never seen him in anything but jeans and a plaid flannel shirt and work boots. He drove a pickup truck with over-sized tires, owned a hunting dog named Minnie and had visibly paled and then refused when Gemma had asked him to hold her purse while she went into the ladies' room at a local music festival.

"No, but he said the guy was about your age, had really dark hair and looked fit—that sounds like good-looking to me." She slid into the chair across from Anna. "Was it that new sheriff's deputy who was in here the other day? He had really dark hair and I thought he was really into you."

"You saw the man for all of five minutes." Anna shifted, pinned by Gemma's avid interest. "You couldn't possibly tell something like that."

"It was him, wasn't it?" Gemma said. "I can tell because you're blushing."

"I am not." Anna put one hand to her hot cheek. Good thing she had never aspired to the stage—she was a terrible actor.

"Liar." Gemma laughed. "And I guess all those excuses you made about not being ready to date were lies, too."

"I wasn't lying," Anna protested. "Not intentionally anyway. This just...happened."

Gemma leaned closer. "Tell me all about the deputy. What is his name again?"

"Lucas. Lucas Malone."

"He even has a sexy name. So, you had dinner, then what?"

"Then we went back to my house to talk."

Gemma raised both eyebrows. "Did you really just talk or is that a euphemism for something else?"

"When we got to my house, Sandy Weiss was there, waiting for us."

Gemma sat back, eyebrows in their normal position now. "What was Sandy doing there?"

"Apparently, she got some threatening phone calls and a note. She's wondering if the same person was threatening Dave. And maybe he didn't really kill himself."

"You mean he was murdered?" Gemma popped out of the chair then sat again, as if she couldn't quite contain her excitement. "But Sandy said it was suicide, right? Because Dave was having money problems?"

"She said that, but now she's not sure." Anna sipped the coffee, trying to organize her thoughts. "You knew Dave. He wasn't the brooding type. As far as I know, he had no history of depression. And so many things about that scene by the river seemed so odd."

"It did seem like a lot of trouble to go to," Gemma said. "Dave never struck me as one for making a production of anything. Sandy was the drama queen in that relationship."

"Do you think so?" Anna asked. Sandy had always struck her as blunt, quick to anger maybe and even cynical, but not one for hysterics or exaggeration.

"Trust me, I've known Sandy since she was a teenager. She was one of the popular girls, and she used to go on and on about how she was going to marry a rich guy and live in a mansion in California and have a great tan while the rest of us shoveled snow all winter. I was pretty surprised when she ended up marrying one of her fellow firefighters. Dave was a great guy, but he never had that kind of ambition."

"They were wild about each other," Anna said. "I know losing him has been so hard on her."

"And now someone's threatening her," Gemma said. "What kind of threats?"

"Nothing specific. Just 'keep your mouth shut or else.'"

"Shut about what?"

"She doesn't know, and I believe her."

"Yeah, I doubt the wife of a bakery owner in a small town knows anything most people would care about," Gemma said.

They turned as the bells on the front door announced a customer.

Lucas stopped just inside the door. He wore his khaki sheriff's department uniform, starched creases and very official-looking. Very handsome. Her stomach fluttered as his eyes met hers.

"Good morning, Deputy," Gemma called, breaking the

spell. She grinned and gave Anna a thumbs-up. Anna shooed the gesture away.

"Hello, Lucas. What can we do for you this morning?" She stood and went to meet him.

"I need to ask a couple more questions," he said.

"Sure." She looked around. There were no customers in the store but one could arrive any minute. "We can go back to the store room."

"Don't bother," Gemma said. "I have a sudden urge to walk down the street and get another cup of coffee." She stood and hurried out the front door before Anna could protest.

Anna turned back to Lucas. "What is it you need to ask me?"

"Did Dave and Sandy ever have a dog?"

She frowned. "I don't think so. Maybe before I met them, and for a few years they had a cat. Sparky. They haven't had a pet at all for a while now."

"Any friends or neighbors with dogs who have seizures?"

She stared at him. "I don't know. What is this about?"

He winced. "It's confidential."

"Does this have something to do with Dave's death? Are you thinking now it isn't suicide?"

He moved closer and lowered his voice. "You can't tell anyone."

"Of course not. I wouldn't."

"The autopsy found a sedative in Dave's blood. A drug that is used to control seizures in dogs."

"Somebody killed him with dog meds?"

"No. He died because of the hanging. He may have even taken the drug himself, to calm down and make what he was going to do easier."

"Maybe you should talk to the local vet," she said. "There probably aren't that many dogs around here on that drug."

"I have an appointment with the vet's office this afternoon," he said.

"How is Sandy doing?" Anna asked. "I mean, how did she seem when you left her last night?"

"Tense, exhausted. About like you would expect. But she's determined to stay in her own home. She seemed more annoyed by the threats than frightened."

"Have you found out any more about those threats?"

He hesitated.

"Tell me," she said. "I already know one big secret. I promise I can keep the rest. I found him, remember? And Dave was my friend. I'm not just asking because I'm nosy."

"We were able to identify three calls about the times Sandy reported receiving the threats," he said. "They were all from an untraceable cell phone. One of those pay-as-you-go things you can buy at gas stations and other stores."

"A burner phone!" She flushed. "Sorry. I like detective fiction."

"We're not going to have any luck tracking down that phone," he said. "I stopped by the bakery just now and told her we need to look at her husband's computer. She said he didn't have a laptop. There's just the computer at work."

"What about his phone?" Anna asked.

"Dave's phone?"

"I don't remember him having a laptop, but he did everything on his phone. Have you found it?"

"No. Sandy said she didn't know where it was. I thought he might have pitched it into the pond before he killed himself."

"Or his killer has it."

"We can try to trace it." He made a note. "Thanks." He looked up.

"Anything else you want to tell me?" she asked.

"Just that I'd like to see you again. Though I'm not sure when. This investigation is probably going to require over-time."

"I'd like to go out with you again," she said. "But find-ing out what really happened to Dave is more important."

"We still can't rule out suicide," Lucas said.

"I know. But you can't let a killer go unpunished, either."

"No," he agreed. "And I want to stop whoever it is be-fore they hurt Sandy. It would help if we could figure out who would benefit from his death. Not Sandy—she still has to deal with the debts Dave left behind. He had a small life insurance policy, but it's not a big payout." He scanned his notebook again. "I know Dave owned a bakery. Were there any competing businesses, someone who would gain by killing off the competition?"

"I think one bakery is about all Eagle Mountain can sup-port," she said. "It helped that Dave had such a good reputa-tion in the area. He catered weddings and things like that."

He nodded. "I know these questions might seem random, but with so little to go on, I'm trying to look at every angle."

"I understand. If I think of anything useful, I'll let you know." She glanced over in time to see Gemma peering in the front window. When Gemma realized she had been caught, she straightened and hurried away.

"I'd better go." Lucas touched her arm. "I'm glad I got a chance to see you again."

"Me, too." She couldn't hold back a smile, though she felt a little foolish, so giddy over a man she scarcely knew.

She walked with him to the door, but as they reached it,

her phone alerted her to a text message and his shoulder-mounted radio crackled. She stepped away to read her message while he responded to the dispatcher.

"I've got to report to a traffic accident near Dakota Ridge," he said.

"So do I. Search and Rescue says there are two people trapped in the car."

"Do they need a search dog for that?" he asked.

"No, but I volunteer with Search and Rescue as more than a search dog handler. They were recruiting volunteers last fall and I already knew everyone and I thought, *Why not? I'm learning a lot.*"

"You're pretty amazing," he said.

"I don't know about that." She pocketed the phone. "We'd better go."

"Can I give you a ride?" he asked.

She shook her head. "I need to get to Search and Rescue headquarters, but I'll see you there."

IN HIS TIME in the mountains, Lucas had seen many similar motor vehicle accidents. Drivers going too fast, not paying attention, or simply unlucky enough to meet with bad road conditions, went off the side of a steep pass. Sometimes the cars rolled. Sometimes they crashed on rocks or hung up on trees. Sometimes drivers or their passengers died, but he had seen many survivors, too.

He didn't yet know the fate of the occupants of the black Escalade on its side in the river below Dakota Ridge. He met up with the driver who had called in the accident and they stood on the side of the road, looking down on the wreck. "I think he must have hit a patch of ice," the caller, a slight man in his fifties, wispy blond-white hair combed over a pink scalp, said. He twisted his hands together and made a clicking noise with his tongue against his teeth. "I sure hope they're not dead."

They both turned at the sound of an approaching vehicle to see the orange Search and Rescue Jeep pull in behind Lucas's cruiser. The SAR volunteers, including Anna, piled out. She had changed into technical pants and boots, and a blue Eagle Mountain Search and Rescue parka. SAR captain Sherri Stevens and volunteer Tony Meisner joined Lucas and the caller, who introduced himself as Alex. "Have you heard any cries for help or anything like that?" Sheri asked.

They both shook their heads. "All right," Sheri said. "We'll take it from here."

Lucas collected Alex's contact information and told him he could leave. "Is it okay if I stick around?" he asked. "I want to know what happened to the people in the car."

"All right, but you'll need to stay back, out of the way."

"No problem." Alex retreated to his car, where he stood and peered down at the scene below.

Rescuers were already running rope lines and making their way down toward the Escalade. Two men secured the vehicle with chains and blocks, then two other volunteers with full packs followed. Sheri directed the others to ready a litter and handle more ropes. Anna moved with assurance among the tangle of people and equipment, kneeling to help with one task then moving to the next.

Down at the Escalade, the two first responders with the packs leaned into the vehicle. They managed to wrench the passenger's-side door open and the smaller of the two climbed in. Then both swarmed into the cab.

"Two people, a man and a woman, both alive and responsive," Sheri announced. The radio in her hand beeped again and she listened intently. Lucas moved closer and heard the crunch of Alex's footsteps behind him.

"The female passenger has multiple cuts and a possible broken forearm," came the message over the radio. "The driver is dazed, after apparently hitting his head. No other obvious injuries. We'll need litters to bring both of them up."

The team went into action once more. Some volunteers rigged more lines, while others climbed down with two metal litters and a variety of medical gear. Anna worked with Tony, rigging one set of lines. In the canyon, volunteers fitted the driver and passenger with neck and back braces, then gently moved them from the vehicle onto the ground, where they conducted more examinations. They eased the woman onto a large orange air mattress then lifted the mattress into one of the litters. She was strapped in and fitted with a helmet like the ones the volunteers wore. The litter was attached to a line and the slow climb toward the top began.

The man, whom Lucas judged to be in his forties, had dark hair and a middleweight boxer's build. He loudly protested that he could walk, but he was coaxed into the litter and he, too, was carried to the top with a volunteer walking on either side of the litter.

"The ambulance is on its way to transport these two." Sheri joined Lucas beside his cruiser, where he had retreated to be out of the way. After hearing that the two people in the car were alive, Alex had driven away. "The man's name is George Anton. The woman with him is Shaylin Brown. He says he wasn't driving too fast. He hit a patch of ice and the Escalade went flying."

"George Anton?" Lucas confirmed.

"Yeah. Do you know him? He said he was from Junction."

"Not exactly."

A cheer rose up as the stretcher with Ms. Brown reached the top. Anna hurried to unfasten the litter from the ropes and then helped carry the injured woman to a level patch of ground. A second group of volunteers worked to do the same with George, though he insisted on being allowed to sit up on the litter once it was on a level patch of mud and snow.

Lucas approached the man. "Mr. Anton?" he asked.

The man looked up at Lucas with sad brown eyes. "Don't tell me you're going to give me a ticket," he said. "I didn't do anything wrong. It was the ice. Why do they even keep this road open in winter if it's so dangerous?"

"No ticket." Lucas squatted down until he was eye-level with Anton. "Where were you headed when you hit the ice?" he asked.

"I was coming from a meeting with a client in Eagle Mountain, on my way to meet a different client in Paradise."

"Who did you meet with in Eagle Mountain?"

"Why are you asking?"

Lucas shrugged. "It's a small town. I'm just curious."

"Her name is Sandy Weiss. You know her?"

Lucas thought he did a good job of hiding his surprise. "She and her husband have the bakery."

"That's right. I'm a restaurant supplier and I get some of my desserts from the Weisses. Here." He dug in his pocket and pulled out a business card. "Anton's Finest—restaurant provisions. Local products are our specialty."

"You know Dave Weiss died last Sunday," Lucas said. "His body was found Monday."

"I heard. It's a terrible shame, but Sandy called and asked me to meet her. She wants to make sure we're on the same page."

"I understood you dealt mainly with Dave Weiss before."

Anton gave him a long, considering look. "It doesn't matter now because he's dead, so she's the one I deal with."

"Who is the woman with you?" Lucas asked.

"Shaylin. She works with me. I thought it would be good to have a woman along when I spoke to Sandy. In case things got emotional, you know?" He pulled out his phone. "I need to call my client in Paradise and let him know we're not going to make it." He swore. "There's no signal." He shook his phone. "What's wrong with this thing?"

"There's no signal right here," Lucas said. One of many dead spots in this remote mountainous area.

"Mr. Anton?" Sheri approached them, a paramedic beside her. "This is Emmett. He's going to check you out then take you to the hospital." Nearby, another volunteer and a paramedic examined Ms. Brown.

Several minutes later, as the ambulance pulled away, Anna came to stand beside Lucas. "I think they're both going to be all right," she said.

"Did you know that was George Anton?"

She stared. "The man Sandy talked about? The one who contracted with Dave to supply restaurants with baked goods?"

"Yes. He said he was on his way from a meeting with Sandy when his car went off the road."

"Who was the woman with him?"

"Her name is Shaylin Brown. He said she works with him."

Anna sucked in her breath. The sound made him look at her more closely. "Do you know her?" he asked.

She shook her head. "It's probably someone else with

the same name. You did say Shaylin, right? Not Sheila or Sharon?"

"Shaylin. It's not a very common name. Who is the woman you know?"

She blew out a breath and gave him a rueful look. "She's Justin's mistress."

Chapter Eight

Lucas stared at Anna. "Justin Trent, your brother-in-law, the restaurant owner?"

She nodded. "Not long before Jonas died, Gloria, Justin's wife, got a call from a woman named Shaylin Brown. The woman said she and Justin had been lovers for two years and Gloria needed to do the right thing and give Justin the divorce he wanted. Gloria said she was completely blindsided. She had no idea anything was wrong and Justin had never mentioned divorce. She was devastated, and when Jonas found out, he was furious."

"What happened after that?" Lucas asked.

"Justin groveled and begged Gloria to take him back. He quit seeing Shaylin—or at least he says he did—and he and Gloria went to counseling. But none of that happened until after Jonas died. Maybe I'm being petty, but I'm still angry about that. Jonas was really upset about the affair, and knowing Justin was doing the right thing would have made him so happy." Her eyes met his. "He didn't have much to be happy about in those last weeks."

He nodded and looked away, giving her time to pull herself together.

"Justin said he and Shaylin worked together," she said

after a moment. "I always thought it meant she worked at the restaurant, but maybe they met because she worked for George Anton."

"You said it's been two years. Maybe Justin fired her, or she quit when he ended the affair, and she went to work for Anton then."

"Do you think he was in Eagle Mountain to put pressure on Sandy about the contract Dave signed with him?" Anna asked. "Is he the one threatening her?"

"He said Sandy asked him to meet her."

"He could be lying," she said.

"I'll do some checking." He would start by finding out where George Anton had been when Dave Weiss died.

Someone whistled and Anna put a hand on Lucas's arm. "I have to go," she said. "It was good to see you."

"It was good to see—" But she was already gone, back to the group of volunteers who were loading up equipment and preparing to leave. Lucas strung tape to close off the pullout where the emergency vehicles had parked, to keep the curious from stopping to look. He had worked one wreck where, though the driver of the vehicle escaped with only minor injuries, a would-be good Samaritan who'd decided to check out the wreck had fallen and died.

Then he headed back to the sheriff's office, intent on finding out as much as he could about George Anton.

ANNA CHANGED CLOTHES at Search and Rescue headquarters, back into the wool skirt, hand-knit sweater, tights and boots that were her winter work uniform. She had intended to drive straight to the shop, but instead turned onto the side street that led to Weiss Bakery.

A single car was parked in the gravel lot in front of the

white-brick structure. A former meat processing plant, the building sat by itself at the end of a street on the edge of town, surrounded by empty pasture. A sign at the end of the street and another on the building itself directed customers to the bakery. Dave's talent for producing delicious and beautiful desserts had attracted customers who were willing to go a little out of their way to shop there, though today the place looked almost empty.

Anna pushed open the door and inhaled the familiar aromas of sugar and vanilla. The front room was empty, the glass bakery case about half full of various pastries, cookies and cupcakes. Anna looked around. "Hello?" she called.

A moment later, Sandy emerged from a back room, a twenty-five-pound bag of flour under each arm. The frown lines on her forehead deepened when she recognized Anna. "What are you doing here?" she asked. She deposited the bags of flour on a wooden table at the far end of the counter and brushed a white smudge from the side of her blue sweatshirt.

"I wanted to see how you were doing." Anna moved to the bakery case.

"I'm fine." Sandy picked up a white bar towel and began wiping down the glass case at the end of the counter.

"I just came from a search and rescue call," Anna said. "An Escalade went off the road on Dakota Ridge. The driver was George Anton."

Sandy went still. "Is he dead?" she asked.

"No. Just a bump on the head. He's on his way now to the hospital to be checked out. The woman with him, Shaylin Brown, wasn't so lucky. She had a lot of cuts from glass, and maybe a broken arm. She was in a lot of pain." She watched Sandy carefully, trying to read her reaction, but she only blinked a couple of times then went back to wiping down the glass.

"Mr. Anton said he had just come from a meeting with you," Anna said.

"So what if he was?" Sandy stopped wiping and glared at Anna. "Maybe you think I should be collapsed in a heap, mourning my husband, but I don't have that luxury. I have a business to take care of."

Anna drew back, stung. "I don't think that at all," she said. "I'm not judging you, Sandy. Not at all. I've always admired how strong and practical you are. And I know there is no one right way to mourn."

Sandy tossed the rag into a white plastic bucket behind her. "Sorry. I've just had my fill of people telling me how 'shocked' they are that I'm selling the house, or they can't believe I didn't close the bakery for a week 'out of respect for Dave.' Until they're paying my bills, they need to shut up." She bit her lip and looked away, blinking rapidly.

Any other person, Anna might have reached out to offer a literal shoulder to cry on, but she doubted Sandy would appreciate the gesture. "Maybe you could negotiate with your creditors," she said. "I'm sure the local bank would understand you need more time..."

"George Anton is our creditor," Sandy said. "He's the one who loaned us the money to expand. Low interest, good terms. He promised to send enough business our way, we would be more than able to pay, but that didn't happen."

"Is that even legal?" Anna asked.

"Don't look at me like I'm a fool," Sandy snapped. "I never should have told you."

Anna took a step back. "I'm sure you'll deal with things the way that's best for you," she said.

"I'll deal with them all right."

Silence stretched between them. Anna searched for something to say that wouldn't make Sandy even angrier. "Have you had any more threatening calls or letters?" she asked.

Sandy shook her head. "Maybe it was just a prankster," she said. "Apparently, death can bring out sickos who like to prey on the families left behind. Or so I've read."

"If there's anything I can do to help, please tell me," Anna said.

"Why do you want to help me?" Sandy challenged, defensive once more.

"I know what's it's like to be in your shoes," Anna said. Widowed young, with no family close. Alone in the worst way.

"I doubt that," Sandy said.

The door opened and a couple entered, talking loudly about their dinner party plans. Anna debated waiting until they'd made their purchases and left and trying to resume her conversation with Sandy, but decided against it. She wasn't doing anything but upsetting the poor woman, who either couldn't—or didn't want to—tell her any more about the threats or George Anton or anything relating to Dave's death.

Anna knew she had no "right" to such information. But finding Dave's body had shaken her more than her other body recoveries. Dave had been Jonas's friend, and her friend, too. How could she—or Sandy—lay him to rest without knowing what had really happened to him?

"Goodbye," she said. Though Sandy, who had already turned to wait on her customers, didn't acknowledge her words. She returned to her car and drove to Yarn and More, still unsettled by Sandy's prickly attitude. She needed to lose herself for a while in the soothing colors and textures of yarn.

"How did it go?" Gemma asked when Anna settled beside her at the worktable.

It took a moment before Anna realized her friend was referring to the rescue. "It went well. Some injuries, but both driver and passenger should recover."

"That's great," Gemma said. She leaned closer, studying Anna's face. "But you look upset. Did something else happen?"

Anna picked up the half-finished scarf from the workbag beside her chair and began to knit. "I stopped by the bakery to see Sandy."

Gemma sat back. "Did she say something to upset you?"

"What makes you think that?"

"Because I know Sandy. She's always gone out of her way to be rude to you."

Anna almost dropped a stitch, she was so startled. She pushed the knitting away. "Sandy isn't rude, she's just… brusque."

"She was rude to you," Gemma said. "Frankly, I think she's always been jealous."

"Why would she be jealous?" Anna asked. "There wasn't anything in my life she wanted."

"Except that people like you. People put up with Sandy because of Dave. And she pulls her own weight at the fire department, I'll give you that. Her fellow volunteers respect her, but I don't think many of them really like her. She doesn't have the easy way with people you have."

"I'm sure you're wrong about that," Anna said. "Sandy has lots of friends, not just with the fire department. There are the people she bikes with, and climbers."

"They were Dave's friends first," Gemma noted. She began straightening items on the table, stacking pattern books and corralling yarn into a basket. "What did she say to upset you?"

"I told her to tell me if there was anything I could do to help her and she all but accused me of having an ulterior motive. I tried to tell her I understood what she was going through and she took it all wrong."

"I don't know why you bother," Gemma said. "If she doesn't want your help, why keep offering?"

"Because I know what it's like to lose the man you loved so young," Anna said. "I remember how much I appreciated everyone who came to help me, and I want to pass that on to Sandy. It doesn't take away the loss, but it does help." She picked up the scarf again but didn't resume working on it. She held the project in her lap, stroking the soft yarn and admiring the interplay of colors. "I'm sure I was upset and said things to people I shouldn't have. Grief exposes every nerve. People were willing to overlook that for me, so I'm trying to do the same for Sandy."

Gemma reached over and squeezed Anna's wrist. "I can't imagine you ever said anything terrible to anyone, but if you did, it's easier to forgive a nice, likeable person."

"I always thought the challenge of forgiveness was supposed to be that it's hard." She slipped the tip of the needle beneath the first stitch and wrapped the yarn. "Anyway, I'm trying to give Sandy the space she seems to want, but also be there if she needs anything. Dave wouldn't want her to have to handle everything by herself, and he was dear to me, and to Jonas."

"That just proves you're a better person than I am." Gemma checked her watch then bounced to her feet. "I have to go. I promised Terry I'd meet him for lunch." She grabbed up her purse and coat, and hurried out the door.

Anna continued knitting, her mind still racing as she completed each stitch. She wanted to call Justin, but he would tell her she was interfering with things that didn't concern her. He would probably be angry. He might even accuse her of trying to upset him on purpose.

He wouldn't be entirely wrong. But she had long since stopped caring what he thought of her. She set the scarf aside and pulled out her phone. Justin answered with his usual brusqueness. "Two calls in one week, Anna. What is going on?"

"Shaylin Brown was injured in a car accident this afternoon," she said. "I thought you'd want to know."

Silence, though she thought she heard him get up and close the door. He was probably in his office at the restaurant. "How do you know anything about Shaylin?" he asked.

"Eagle Mountain Search and Rescue responded to the call," she said. "Shaylin was with George Anton. Apparently, she works for him now."

"I know that. What happened?"

"His car hit a patch of ice and went off the road at Dakota Ridge. They were lucky they weren't killed."

"Why did you call to tell me this?"

"I thought you might want to know."

"Shaylin and I aren't involved anymore. That was a mistake I will pay for for the rest of my life, and I don't appreciate you bringing it up."

"I just thought you might want to know she was hurt. She's in the hospital in Junction."

"I'm sorry to hear that, but it's not my concern."

"What do you know about George Anton?" she asked.

"I already told you. He supplies food to restaurants. He supplies my restaurant."

"But what else do you know about him?" Was he the type who would threaten a customer like Sandy? Could he have killed Dave?

"I don't have to know the life story of everyone I do business with," Justin said. "We came to an agreement that benefits both of us and that's all we have to know. Why are you even asking these questions?"

"Because someone has been threatening Sandy Weiss, Dave's widow," she said. "I wondered if it might be George."

"Why would George threaten Sandy?" Justin asked.

"She owes him money."

He laughed. "A lot of people owe me money and I don't threaten them. It's not how most businesses operate."

She decided to shift the conversation. Maybe she could throw him off guard. "Why did you call the sheriff's department about me?"

"I don't think it's safe or smart to meddle in a police investigation," he said, seemingly unmoved.

"I don't need you to look after me, Justin."

"Apparently, you do, if you're going to go around playing amateur detective. You're Jonas's widow and I feel an obligation to him."

"He's been gone two years and this is the first time you've showed any concern for me," she said.

"This is the first time I've become aware that you're behaving so foolishly."

She took a deep breath and forced herself to count to ten. Justin was saying this to make her angry and to deflect attention from him and his motives. She had seen him do it before, or attempt to do it. Jonas had seldom fallen for his brother's manipulation.

"I don't think I'm being foolish, but I am trying to help a friend," she said. "And I thought you might want to know about Shaylin. Even if you aren't seeing her now, you were close once."

"Do me a favor and don't make any assumptions about me and my feelings." He ended the call before she could say anything.

She pocketed her phone. That went about as well as she had expected. Justin wasn't her favorite person, but his restaurant had a good reputation and Jonas had always said his brother was one of the savviest business people he knew. Justin stayed out of debt and made money.

He wouldn't have signed a contract with George Anton unless he thought it was a way to make more money, so how had Dave ended up in debt to Anton? And not just a little debt. Sandy made the situation sound dire, if she was having to sell her house and the bakery building to make the payments.

The list of questions she wished she could learn the answers to grew longer every day. The bell over the door rang and she looked up, a smile on her face, determined to focus on the things she did know, including how to help her customers find just the items they needed. If only she had someone to help her do the same.

ON MONDAY MORNING, one week after Dave Weiss's body had been found, the sheriff convened a meeting to review the case. "The medical examiner has ruled the cause of death was a broken neck, but he's unable to determine whether this was due to suicide or murder," Travis said. "I want us to review what we know and see if we can draw any conclusions."

"Those dog tranquilizers in his system seem suspicious," Sergeant Gage Walker, the sheriff's brother, said.

"And why that location?" Wes Landry asked. "If Dave was intent on hanging himself, there are a lot of places it would be easier to do it."

"Maybe the location had some significance to him we don't know about yet," Shane Ellis interjected.

"Or maybe he didn't want his body found easily," Dwight Prentice said. "Even with his truck there, we might not have found him for days or weeks if not for Anna Trent and her search dog."

"Anna knew Dave and she seemed surprised he would take his own life," Lucas said. He wondered how much her doubts had influenced him. If he hadn't been so focused on her and her emotions, would he have automatically taken the scene at face value—a man in despair who had decided to end his life?

"The branch the rope was tied off on was pretty high up in that tree," Travis noted. "Not an impossible climb, but a difficult one."

"He wanted to make sure the drop was far enough for a quick end," Gage said.

"Or his killer wanted that," Lucas said. "And there are those impressions in the ground beneath his body. They sure look like a ladder to me."

"So his killer not only gets Dave back to that remote location, he hauls a ladder back there?" Shane shook his head.

"Dave wasn't a little man," Gage said. "Even doped up, he would probably try to fight. I don't see how anyone could get him up that ladder."

"Order him up at gunpoint," Dwight suggested.

"Or threaten his family," Wes said. "Promise to kill his wife if he didn't cooperate."

"Sandy doesn't think it's suicide," Lucas said.

"Families often are in denial," Wes observed. "That's understandable."

"She thought at first that he had killed himself," Lucas said. "But those threatening phone calls and the note made her think differently."

"We weren't able to trace the calls or find anything significant about the note," Gage said. "It was on common notebook paper and the letters were cut from a magazine, but we can't get more specific than that. The message was vague and threatening, but nonspecific."

"So maybe just a prank," Dwight proposed. "Someone with a sick sense of humor."

"We need to take a closer look at George Anton," Travis said. "Sandy says the contract Dave signed with him was the source of their financial trouble."

"She confirmed she met with Anton yesterday afternoon," Lucas said. He had spoken briefly with Sandy after the accident. Apparently, Anna had already broken the news of the rescue, shortly before Lucas called. "Anton was coming from that meeting when he was injured in that accident up on Dakota Ridge."

"What about the woman who was with Anton?" Gage asked. "What was her role in this?"

"Anton said she worked for him and was along to put Sandy at ease," Lucas told him. He didn't bother mentioning Shaylin Brown's former relationship with Anna's brother-in-law. It was interesting, but he didn't see that it had any bearing on the case.

"That doesn't sound threatening," Dwight said.

"I ran Anton's name and didn't come up with anything," Lucas said. "No criminal record, and his only online profiles are in relation to his business, Anton's Finest. I didn't find a motive for him to threaten Sandy or want to harm Dave. With Dave gone, his chances of getting money he's owed from commissions, or the desserts Dave contracted to supply, go down."

"Any other ideas where the threats came from?" Gage asked.

Lucas shook his head. "Sandy says no. And she doesn't know of any similar threats Dave might have received before he died."

"We need to go through Dave's belongings and his business records," Travis said. "Maybe we'll find something there."

"I'm headed to the bakery to do that this morning," Lucas advised. "It would help if we could find Dave's phone. It's missing, and Anna says he might have used it instead of a laptop or tablet. I've requested his phone records but I'm not having any luck tracing the phone's location."

"For now, the case stays open," Travis said.

When the meeting was over, Lucas drove to the bakery. The business sat at the end of a dead-end street on the very edge of town, surrounded by empty fields. A small corral behind the white-brick structure was empty, and a large roll-down door on one side of the building had a sturdy padlock on it.

Sandy was on the phone when Lucas stepped inside. "What do you want it to say on the top of the cake?" she asked her caller, and made a note on the clipboard in front of her. "What color would you like the lettering?"

While he waited for her to finish the call, Lucas looked around the bakery. There were posters advertising wedding cakes and holiday pies, and a row of photographs in black plastic frames: Dave and Sandy in bunker gear. Sandy on a mountain bike on a trail. Dave with a massive lake trout. An active life spent outdoors.

"Have you found out anything, Deputy?"

He turned back to Sandy. She stood behind the front counter, her hands in the pockets of a blue apron. "Not yet," he said. "I need to look through Dave's office and the bakery's computer."

"I've already looked," she said. "You're not going to find anything."

He had dealt with this kind of reluctance before. No one wanted a stranger, much less a police officer, going through their personal records. "I might see something you didn't," he said. "And anything I find is held in confidence, unless it's evidence we need to use at a trial."

She pursed her lips. "It just seems so…intrusive."

It was intrusive. In the course of investigations, he had read personal love letters, people's attempts at bad fiction, and accessed secret porn accounts. He hadn't lingered over any of those, as they hadn't pertained to the cases he'd been involved in at the time. But just knowing he was going to see such highly personal things made most people uncomfortable. "It's important to gather as much information as possible to find out what happened to your husband," he said. "And to track down who threatened you."

"I haven't heard anything else," she said. "I think it was just a sick joke."

"I still need to look through Dave's things."

"Aren't you supposed to have a warrant or something?"

Now he wondered just what she thought he would find. "I could get one, but it will be faster if you agree to let me search. The sooner we gather information, the better."

She chewed her lower lip. "All right. But I don't think you're going to find anything. Dave kept everything personal on his phone."

She led the way through the door behind the bakery counter, into a surprisingly spartan office. The desktop was clear of everything except a page-a-day calendar stuck on the day before Dave had died. The cinder block walls were bare and the single window high in the wall looked out onto an alley. "This seems like a remote location for a bakery," he said. "There aren't any other businesses around."

"This building used to be a meat processor," Sandy said. "They kept cows in the corral out there until slaughter. You don't really want that kind of thing right downtown. We bought it because it was cheap. We figured the baked goods we made were good enough people would drive out here, and we were right."

"I heard your specialty is something called a Surprise Cake," he said.

"That's right. You can choose one of our surprise fillings or we'll include your own. We've put engagement rings, birthday gifts, party favors—all kinds of things inside. The hollow to hold the surprise is made after the cake is baked, so you can put anything in there. We once put a positive pregnancy test in a cupcake." She shrugged. "If the customer wants it, we'll put it in there."

"I'd better get started," he said.

"Suit yourself."

She left him alone. He started with the desk. Deep drawers on either side of the desk held files full of the forms people filled out to order cakes or pastries. There were receipts for supplies, licensing paperwork, health department paperwork, and records of donations the bakery had made to local softball teams and other charities.

After less than thirty minutes, Lucas had seen everything there was to see in the space. He moved to the doorway and spoke to Sandy, who was marking down the price on a tray of bear claws. "Where are the financial records?" he asked. "The day-to-day accounts, I mean."

"Our CPA keeps track of all that," she said, not looking up from her work.

"Don't you have computer records here?"

"Dave didn't like computers."

How did anyone operate a business in this day and age without computerized records? "What about an old-fashioned ledger?"

She shook her head. "Our CPA takes care of everything."

"Then I'll need to talk to your CPA."

"I'll have to talk to him about that. He's probably going to want to see something more official."

If he was any good at his job, he would, Lucas thought. "Where is the contract Dave signed with George Anton?" he asked.

She glanced over her shoulder at him. "You didn't find it?"

"No."

She slid the tray of pastries into the glass case, stripped off her gloves, dropped them in the trash can, then followed him into the office. She opened one of the desk drawers. "It should be in here," she said, and riffled through the files. She closed that drawer and turned to the others. At last, she looked up at him. "It should be right here, but it's not."

"Was it there when you searched the office?"

"I didn't notice. I was just looking for anything out of place."

He frowned. He hadn't found any threatening notes, and he hadn't found the contract with Anton. Nothing that pertained to the case. Nothing to indicate Dave was thinking about suicide, either.

"I'd like to see the house. Maybe he kept some things there you didn't know about."

She thrust her hands back into the pockets of her apron. "You'll have to wait until I close at five-thirty."

"You can give me a house key."

She took a step back. "I don't want you nosing around when I'm not there."

He could have pressed, but didn't. "Did you and Dave ever have a dog?" he asked.

"No."

"What about before you married? Did you have a dog? Did Dave?"

"No. I mean, I think he might have had a dog or two when he was a little kid, but not as an adult. We had a cat for a few years, but after he ran off, we decided pets tied us down too much. Why are you asking about a dog?"

"The medical examiner found that Dave had a sedative in his system when he died. It's a drug commonly used to control seizures in dogs."

She stared. "That's the strangest thing anyone's ever told me. You're saying Dave took dog tranquilizers?"

"It's a human medication that is used in dogs, too. But the vet here doesn't prescribe it." The Eagle Mountain vet had explained he preferred different medications that didn't have the side effects of phenobarbital.

"Maybe your lab got something wrong," Sandy said.

He doubted it, but wasn't going to debate her.

"What's going on with you and Anna?" Sandy asked.

Her question caught him off guard, which may have been why she'd asked it.

"We had dinner together," he said. It wasn't any of her business, but it wasn't a secret, either.

"You know she's a widow. Practically a newlywed still when her husband died."

"I know." Did she think the fact that Anna had been married before would put him off?

"I'm a practical person. Sad as I am about losing Dave, I know life goes on. I have to move forward and make the best of things. Anna isn't like that. She idolized Jonas. No other man is ever going to measure up."

He stiffened. "I'm not looking to 'measure up' to anyone. We just had dinner."

She shrugged. "Suit yourself." The phone rang. "I have to go." She pushed past him into the office again, and shut the door behind her.

He stared after her, half a dozen different retorts stalled in his head. But ahead of all the snappy comebacks he might have made was the question Sandy's words had raised in his mind. Was Anna still in love with her dead husband? Should he walk away before he made a mistake and started thinking past dinner?

Death changed so much. It was awful in the moment, and awful for months or years afterward, as those left behind lived with the reality of unrealized hopes and regrets for all they would never say or do. People learned to live with that, and to be hopeful and happy again, but they couldn't live as if death hadn't changed them. Those who knew them best could see the scars. He saw them in himself, and he recognized them in Anna. That shared suffering made him feel close to her, but he wasn't so sure it was a good basis for a relationship.

Not that he wanted a relationship. It was just…good to be with someone who knew his story. Anna wouldn't expect too much from him.

Jenny had expected too much from him. His greatest regret was that he hadn't been able to give her what she'd expected, much less what she'd deserved.

At five-twenty, Lucas left the sheriff's department and drove to the Weisses' house. The red For Sale sign stood out against the accumulated snow on the front lawn. The house already looked empty, with no furniture on the porch, no car in the drive. He parked at the curb and five minutes later Sandy pulled into the drive. She got out of her car and headed to the front door without acknowledging him. "You're wasting your time," she said as he came up behind her while she was unlocking the door. "There's nothing here that will help you figure out what happened to Dave."

"You never know," he said and followed her inside.

The first thing he noticed was how empty the house felt. The living room and the dining room next to it were almost devoid of furniture, only a single upholstered chair and a lamp sitting in the middle of an expanse of dull beige carpet. "There's no point in keeping things if I'm going to be moving," Sandy said.

He followed her farther into the house, past the door to the kitchen, down a hallway to a room with a queen-sized bed, a small table with a lamp and a row of cardboard boxes along one wall. She pointed to a closet. "That was Dave's, but I've already given away most of his things."

He opened his mouth to ask why she had done that, but she cut him off. "I thought he killed himself. Seeing his things was too painful, so I bagged everything up and took it to the humane society thrift store in Junction."

He nodded. He had been tempted to do the same with everything that had belonged to Jenny after she'd died. Instead, he had asked her sister to take everything.

He opened the closet door and looked at the empty shelves and hangers. A single shirt button rested on the edge of one shelf, and a worn belt hung from a nail at the very back. He shook his head and closed the door behind him.

Sandy had left the room, so he moved to her closet. In contrast to Dave's, her space was crammed with clothing—shirts, pants, a few skirts and dresses and winter coats, as well as at least twenty pairs of boots and shoes, various cycling and workout gear, a hamper of dirty laundry. He sighed and began going through everything.

He found several shirts that might have belonged to Dave, but there was nothing in the pockets. He moved on to the dresser, which also yielded nothing of Dave's and also nothing that revealed any insights into Sandy. She wore little jewelry, preferred casual clothing and practical footwear, and if she had displayed any personal photos in the bedroom, she must have packed them away.

He found her in the kitchen, standing at the counter, drinking coffee from a mug that advertised a local bank. "Did you ask your CPA about those financial records?" he asked.

"Not yet." She sipped the coffee and fixed him with a cold stare. Not exactly hostile. Annoyed, maybe.

"Did Dave keep any financial or business records here?"

"No," she said.

"Did he have a home office?"

"He had a desk. But I already gave that away, too."

"What did you do with the contents of the desk?" he asked.

"I burned it all." She smiled, as if pleased to frustrate him with this news. "I looked through it all before I lit the match," she added. "There was nothing there. No personal diary, no suicide note, no plans for his demise."

"What about threats? Did you find anything like that?"

"Nothing."

He looked around the kitchen. Two cabinet doors stood open, showing the insides were empty. Three more cardboard boxes sat on the counter, one open to reveal packed dishes. He was wasting his time here. "Where's your bathroom?" he asked.

"Down the hall, next to the bedroom," she said. "There's only the one."

In the bathroom, he did a quick check of the medicine cabinet and the shelves beneath the sink. He found an assortment of over-the-counter remedies and some expired prescription allergy medication for Sandy. No phenobarbital. No sleeping pills or antianxiety medications or anything that might indicate Dave or Sandy had been dealing with extra stress.

Sandy appeared in the doorway. "Are you done yet?" she asked.

He looked up from examining the spare towels under the sink. "I want to see the garage," he said.

She led him out the back door to a detached, single-car garage behind the house. It, too, had been stripped bare. Not a single old paint can rested on the shelves between the studs of the walls, and only an oil stain on the concrete floor gave evidence that the building had ever been used at all. "A guy from Delta made me a good offer on everything that was in there," Sandy said. "He hauled it all off yesterday."

Lucas shook his head. Maybe he would have found something significant if he had gotten here before Sandy had donated or burned all of Dave's things. But he was too late now.

He left and sat in his cruiser for a moment, debating whether he should return to the office and go through the case files one more time. His phone rang and his spirits lifted when he saw Anna's name on the screen.

"Hello," he answered. "How are you?"

"Not so good right now."

The shake in her voice made him sit up straighter. "What's wrong?"

"I just got home from work. There's a note on my front door. It says…" Her voice faltered and he heard her inhale shakily. "It says if I'm not careful, I'll be the next person to die!"

Chapter Nine

Anna sat in her porch swing, coat pulled tightly around her against the cold, and waited for Lucas to arrive. Jacquie curled against her, her head in Anna's lap. She threaded her fingers through Jacquie's curls and watched the street, resolutely averting her eyes from the single sheet of lined paper tacked to her front door. But she didn't have to see it to remember what it looked like or what it said: Mind your own business or you will be the next to die.

The words were melodramatic, bad B-movie dialogue. But they were also terrifying.

A black-and-white sheriff's department SUV turned onto her street and she stood and walked to the edge of the porch. Jacquie jumped up and came to sit beside her. They waited while Lucas parked and strode up the walk toward them. "Are you all right?" he asked, searching her face.

"I'm fine." She turned toward the door. "It's just a piece of paper, but who would do something like this?"

She followed him to the door. He studied the note a moment then took out his phone and photographed it from several angles. Then he took a large, clear, plastic envelope from his jacket, along with a pair of nitrile gloves. He put on the gloves, then carefully pried loose the thumbtack holding the note in place and slid both tack and note into the envelope. He completed a label on the front and tucked the whole thing back into his jacket, along with the gloves. "What time did you find it?" he asked.

"I close the shop at six and I drove straight home, so about ten after six," she said.

"Did you touch it?"

She shook her head. "No. I read the words. Then I read them again. I looked around—I don't know why. It's not as if whoever did this would stand around waiting for my reaction. And Jacquie didn't act upset, as if she sensed a stranger nearby. Then I sat in the swing and called you." She had sat because her legs wouldn't support her, and she had called him because she knew she would feel stronger and safer if he were with her, instead of whatever deputy might be on duty.

"What time did you leave the house this morning?"

"A quarter to ten. I usually try to be at the shop by nine, so I have an hour to work before we open, but I didn't sleep well last night, so got a late start." She had tossed and turned much of the night, her emotions in turmoil.

"I want to talk to your neighbors and see if any of them noticed anyone near your house today." He touched her shoulder. "Will you be all right here while I do that?"

"Of course." She glanced down at Jacquie, who sat beside her, leaning heavily against her leg. "And I have Jacquie." The poodle didn't have an ounce of meanness in her, but she could bark loudly, and her large size intimidated some people.

He left and crossed the street. Anna shivered and decided it was ridiculous for her to stay out here in the cold. She unlocked the front door and went in, letting the dog go first. If a stranger did lurk inside, Jacquie would find him or her.

But the house was empty. Jacquie trotted to her water bowl and drank loudly while Anna hung up her coat and then followed her into the kitchen. She put on the kettle and looked out the kitchen window, hoping to glimpse Lucas on his way to or from a neighbor's house, but the street was empty.

A knock on the door announced his return just as the teakettle began to whistle. She shut off the stove then hurried to open the door. "A woman across the street saw a delivery person here just after noon," he said. "Someone in a brown shirt and pants, a ball cap, with short hair. She said 'he' but admitted it could have been a woman. The person went up to all the houses on this side of the street. I double-checked, and none of them received any deliveries today."

"Come into the kitchen," she said.

He followed her, shedding his coat once there and draping it over the back of one of the chairs around the table. "I'm making tea," she said. "Do you want some? Or cocoa?"

"No thanks." He pulled out a chair and sat. "Can you think of anything that might have set someone off?" he asked. "Something that would have triggered that person to post this note? Something that made them feel threatened?"

She sat across from him. "No! It's just bizarre. I'm not a threat to anyone."

"Tell me everything you did the last three days," he said. "Everyone you talked to."

"There was the search and rescue call Saturday—you know about that. When that was done, I stopped by the bakery."

"Why did you do that?"

"I wanted to see how Sandy was doing. And I wanted to find out more about George Anton and Sandy's meeting with him." She flushed. "I know it's none of my business, but I want to know."

"What did she tell you?"

"Not much," she admitted. "She ranted a little about how she was angry at people for judging her for running the bakery and putting it and the house up for sale instead of collapsing in a grief-stricken heap. I told her about Anton's accident, but once I assured her he wasn't dead, she lost interest. She really didn't tell me much about the meeting, only that they had had one." She stirred her tea. "I would make a terrible detective. I don't know how to be subtle when questioning people."

"Did Sandy seem angry with you?"

"No. She was how she always is with me—not hostile, but not terribly friendly. The two of us rub each other the wrong way. She makes me feel inadequate and awkward, and she seems to think I'm silently judging her. I actually admire her a great deal, but she never believes me when I say so."

"All right. Anybody else?"

"There was Gemma and customers at the shop, of course, but none of them are going to threaten to kill me." She sipped her tea, choosing her words. "I talked to one more person Saturday. And he's not my biggest fan, either." She forced herself to meet Lucas's steady gaze. "I called Justin. I wanted to gauge his reaction when I told him about Shaylin Brown. That's probably petty of me, and he called me on it, which I deserved."

"What else did he have to say?"

"Just that George Anton offered a good deal to suppliers and restaurants." She gripped her teacup more tightly as a new thought swept over her. "Do you think Justin could have told George I was asking about him? If he's the one who made those threats to Sandy, maybe he decided to do the same to me."

"We haven't found any evidence linking George Anton to those threats," he said. "We haven't found evidence linking anyone to them." He pulled out his phone. "Let me check something right quick."

He waited for a moment then identified himself to the person on the other end of the line. "Can you tell me when George Anton was released from treatment? He was transported to the hospital from Rayford County yesterday morning."

Another pause then he said, "What about the woman who was with him? Shaylin Brown?"

He made some notes, said thank-you, and ended the call. "George Anton was treated and released yesterday afternoon," he said. "Shaylin Brown was discharged at two this afternoon. So she couldn't have been the person who left this note, but Anton could have been."

"If he is the one sending these threats, that must mean he has something to hide," she said. "Something to protect." She shuddered. How far would he go to hide or protect whatever that was?

"I'll talk to him, see if he has an alibi," Lucas said. "And we'll compare this note to the one Sandy gave us."

"It looked the same," she said. "They both might have been torn from the same notebook."

"We'll double-check to be sure, but they look the same to me, too. What about the rest of the weekend and today?" he asked. "Who did you see or talk to those days?"

"Sunday, I cleaned house and watched TV and knitted. I

didn't see or talk to anyone. Today, I worked at the shop. I talked to Gemma and customers, but nothing upsetting or unusual. Mostly, we talked about yarn and knitting."

He nodded and made notes on a small pad he'd pulled from his pocket. She sat up straighter. Now that the first shock of that note had worn off, she was growing angrier. "Have you found out anything else about Dave's death?" she asked.

"I searched his office today, but there was nothing," Lucas said. "No sign that he was either being threatened or that he was contemplating suicide. But not everyone writes that sort of thing down."

She took another sip of tea, which had grown cold and bitter. She pushed the mug aside. "Something struck me when I was talking to Justin," she said. "He was talking about how the arrangement with George Anton was a good deal for both of them. Justin has run a successful restaurant for almost fifteen years. He's a good businessman. He wouldn't make a deal that didn't benefit him and make him money. So how did Dave, who was also in a contract with Anton, end up with so much debt? He wasn't as wily as Justin, but he had never had financial trouble as long as I've known him."

"Maybe things weren't as advantageous on the supplier's side," Lucas said. "Or maybe the debt isn't due to the contract with Anton, but with how far he extended himself with loans for the new cooler and more help and supplies."

"But all those loans were with Anton, too."

"They were? How did I miss that?"

"Sandy let it slip then acted like she wished she hadn't told me. Apparently, Anton agreed to loan them the money to expand in order to supply more desserts for the restaurants that were also his clients. Sandy said he offered a low interest rate and promised to give them sufficient business to enable them to pay on the loan and take a small profit, but it didn't work that way."

"I wonder how many other people Anton has with similar agreements," Lucas said.

"Is what he's doing illegal?"

"I don't think so, but that's not my area of expertise. I'll ask my colleagues in Junction if they know anything." He slid back his chair. "How are you feeling now?"

"Steadier." She smiled. "That note is so ridiculous, it's hard to be afraid now that I've had time to think about it. It's unsettling, yes, but also too over-the-top. If you really intended to kill someone, would you give them so much warning?"

"Maybe the aim isn't murder, but silence," Lucas said.

"Then it would help if they told me what I'm supposed to be silent about."

"Will you be okay here alone?" he asked. "I'll ask the deputy on duty tonight to drive by a few times to check on things. Or you could come to my house. I have a decent guest room."

Her heart beat a little faster at the thought of spending the night at his house—though not necessarily in the guest room. She stood, also. "I'll be fine alone," she said. "Though, why don't you stay for dinner? Do you really want to go home and eat alone? I know I don't."

He smiled. "I'd like that."

She pulled out chicken and vegetables to make a pasta dish. "You can chop the peppers while I peel carrots," she said and handed him several bags of produce from the refrigerator.

When she closed the refrigerator, he paused to study the

pictures there. He nodded to the photo of her and Jonas, with Sandy and Dave, atop Dakota Ridge. "Is that your husband?"

"Yes."

"You look happy together. I imagine you loved him very much."

"Yes. I always will. I'm sure it's the same with you and your girlfriend."

He met her gaze briefly, something troubled there, then looked away. "Yes." He turned and set the produce on the counter then pulled a knife from the block. "How do you want these peppers sliced?"

She was determined to overcome this sudden awkwardness. They ought to be able to talk about their exes without feeling like this. "How did you and Jenny meet?" she asked.

He didn't look up from his chopping. "She worked at the tax office, just down the hall from the police department where I did a stint as a civilian volunteer, while I was waiting to get into the academy."

"A cousin introduced me to Jonas," she said. "We hit it off right away."

"Jenny refused to go out with me for three weeks," he said. "She said she never wanted to be involved with a cop."

"What changed her mind?"

He finally looked up, his wicked grin making her laugh. "My devastating charm, of course." He held up the cutting board. "Do these look okay?"

"They're great. Now, would you start a pot of water boiling for the pasta?" She paused before returning to their conversation. "What drew you to police work?" she asked as he filled a pot with water.

"It sounds corny to say I wanted to make a difference, but

it's true. And I thought I had a good temperament for it. I don't mind working alone, and I don't have trouble talking to people. Every day is different. A lot of the job is boring, but some of it is intensely interesting. It's not for everyone, but I like it."

As the topic shifted to their backgrounds and interests, the mood grew more relaxed. This was more like a first date than the dinner they had had the other night, she thought. Then, they had talked mostly about Dave's death. Now, they were getting to know each other, and she liked what she was finding out.

"This looks delicious," he said later when they sat down to dinner. "Thanks for inviting me to stay."

"You're good company," she said.

"So are you." Their eyes met and she felt a tingle down to her toes. The sensation surprised her. It made her a little nervous. But it also made her hopeful. Not all of her had died with Jonas.

He insisted on helping clean the dishes and she considered asking him to stay a little longer, for coffee or a glass of wine. Would she ask him to stay the night? *Too soon*, she thought, but she enjoyed contemplating the idea. It didn't make her nearly as nervous as she would have thought such a big step would. Maybe that was because at least part of her was ready to move on into a future without Jonas. Yes, he had been gone two years, but he was still such a huge, important part of her life. Maybe she was working toward letting him go, so they could both rest in peace.

"I'd better go," Lucas said, wiping his hand on a dish towel. "If you're sure you'll be okay on your own?"

Here was her chance to ask him to stay but, clearly, he needed to leave. "I'll be fine," she said.

She waited while he shrugged into his coat and followed him to the door. Jacquie watched from her place on the end of the sofa. "Thanks for dinner," he said.

"I had a nice time," she said. She put a hand on his arm. "We'll have to do it again sometime." Her eyes met his, trying to tell him how attracted she was to him. She shifted her gaze to his lips and leaned a little closer, sure he would take the hint and kiss her good night, and maybe continue what they had started the other night before Sandy had interrupted them.

"I'll look around outside before I leave," he said then opened the door and was gone.

She waited by the window, watching as he switched on a flashlight and circled the house. When he reached the front once more, he gave her a thumbs-up gesture and strode to his SUV. She hugged her arms across her stomach and stalked back to the sofa. So much for her own "devastating charm." Lucas Malone was apparently immune.

Chapter Ten

Tuesday morning, Anna was marking down yarn for the sale bin when Sandy called her. "Can we get together for drinks after work?" Sandy asked.

"Uh, sure." Sandy had never asked Anna to any activity that didn't include Dave and Jonas, too. Now that they were both widowed, were Anna's efforts to be Sandy's friend paying off? "I'd love to."

"Meet me at Mo's at six fifteen." Not waiting for confirmation, she ended the call.

"Is something wrong?" Gemma dumped an armload of yarn onto the worktable. "You look upset."

"No, nothing's wrong." She picked up the pricing gun again. "Sandy Weiss invited me for drinks at Mo's tonight."

"You don't look too happy about it," Gemma said.

"No, I'm happy. It was just…unexpected." She picked up a skein of cashmere. This orange shade had been a slow seller and she needed to clear it out to make room for new stock. "I'm thinking of doing a display of one-skein projects. What do you think?"

"It's a good way of encouraging people to buy some of the pricier yarn," Gemma said. "One skein doesn't make such a dent in the budget. Does Sandy knit or crochet?"

"I don't think so." Sandy had never showed interest in Anna's own hand-knit items, and she had once declared she didn't see the point of crafts of any kind.

"Maybe you can convert her. It's a great stress reliever."

Sandy probably relieved her stress by trail running or lifting heavy weights. Nothing wrong with that, of course, though Anna preferred yoga and knitting. She smiled at the thought that she and Sandy were truly opposites when it came to almost everything. But that didn't mean they couldn't be better friends.

A trio of customers entered—two women who were clearly together, and Kyle Saddler, who caught the door as it started to close behind them.

"Hello, Anna," he said, zeroing in on her.

"Hello, Kyle," she said. "How did your niece like her birthday gift?"

His expression clouded for a moment then cleared. "Oh, my niece. She liked it a lot. You made a great choice."

He moved closer and Anna wondered if he didn't feel Gemma's gaze burning into him. "What can I do for you today?" she asked as she turned to neaten the display of yarn to her left.

"I heard you had dinner with the new sheriff's deputy the other night."

Her hand stilled and she cringed inwardly. Of course, people had seen her and Lucas at the restaurant. And some of them had talked. It was what people did. It wasn't a small-town-only pastime, but living in a place where you knew everybody made it easier to notice what they were up to. She turned to Kyle. "I hope you haven't been gossiping about me." She tempered the words with a warm smile.

His ears turned pink. "Not gossiping," he said. "But I

figured maybe it meant you'd changed your mind about dating. So I thought I'd ask again if you wanted to have dinner with me."

She pressed her lips together, buying time to think of kinder words than the ones that first came to mind; that who she went out with was none of his business and he should be gracious and accept no for an answer. Now she was probably going to end up hurting his feelings. "Thank you for the invitation, Kyle, but I'm not interested in having dinner with you." She forced herself to meet and hold his gaze as she spoke.

"How did you even meet that deputy?" he asked.

We met when I had a meltdown while my husband was dying, she might have said. Or, *We met when my late husband's best friend died*. Neither was an auspicious circumstance to begin a closer acquaintance. "It doesn't matter," she said.

He frowned. "I hope you know if you're ever afraid of anything or need protecting, you don't need to call a cop. You can call me."

What an odd thing to say. "Who do you think I need protecting from?" she asked.

He shrugged. "Somebody told me they saw that cop at your house last night. In uniform and everything. I thought that meant you called him about something, but maybe you invited him there for something else."

She drew herself up straight and made her voice frosty. "What I do in my own time is none of your business." Then, to avoid continuing the increasingly awkward conversation, she grabbed a ball of yarn from the display. "Mary Louise, you have to see this new mohair and silk blend we just got in."

A frequent customer, Mary Louise obligingly examined the ball of yarn Anna thrust at her, and they discussed the projects that might work well with the weight and fiber content of it. Anna smiled and nodded, and pretended to be fully engaged in the conversation, but she was too aware of the sound of the door slamming as Kyle exited the store.

Mary Louise ended up buying ten balls of the silk and mohair blend to knit a sweater, while her friend purchased the makings for a baby blanket. When they were gone, Gemma came to stand beside Anna at the cash register. "Kyle didn't look too happy when he left," she said.

"No, he wasn't." Anna turned toward her, arms folded. "He heard I had dinner with Lucas and decided that meant I was ready to date again."

"You mean he thought you were ready to date him," Gemma said.

"Yes. And now he's angry because I turned him down." She sighed. "Nothing I can do about that, but now things are going to be awkward between us, and I hate that."

"I bet you turned down a lot of men before you met Jonas," Gemma said.

"What makes you say that?"

"Because you're very pretty, but you're also particular," Gemma said. "And I mean that as a compliment. Unless I'm wrong, you weren't the type of social butterfly who accepts all invitations."

"You're right," Anna said. "I did pick and choose. I guess I'm out of practice letting men down easily."

"I hope Lucas Malone knows how lucky he is," Gemma said. She picked up a box of pattern books and carried them to the display at the front of the store.

Anna tidied the counter and thought about what Gemma

had said. She hadn't hesitated to accept Lucas's invitation to dinner. Why was that? Why did she find him so attractive when other men left her cold?

Anna turned the sign on the front door of the shop to Closed shortly before six and swung by her house to drop off Jacquie before heading to Mo's pub. No sinister note greeted her today and, while Jacquie wasn't happy about being left behind, she didn't sense anything unusual about the house.

At Mo's, Anna made her way through the happy hour crowd to the table where Sandy waited. "Thanks for suggesting this," she said as she shed her coat.

"I wanted to talk to you," Sandy said. A server delivered a glass of beer and asked Anna what she would like.

"A glass of pinot noir," Anna said. When they were alone again, she asked, "What did you want to talk to me about?"

Sandy didn't answer right away. She took a drink of beer and studied Anna for so long that Anna began to feel uncomfortable. She wore an oversized fisherman's sweater Anna thought might have belonged to Dave, and her short-cropped hair looked freshly cut. Pearly earrings and a sweep of dark mascara added a feminine touch. "I heard Lucas Malone was at your house last night," Sandy finally said.

Anna flinched. "Who told you that?"

"Don't be so jumpy. Alma Bettinger, who lives down the street from you, was in the bakery today and she said a sheriff's department SUV was parked in your driveway and a very good-looking cop—her words, not mine—was asking questions of all the neighbors. He wanted to know if they had seen anyone around your house that day while you were at work."

Anna hugged her arms over her stomach. "Someone left

a note on my door. A note like the one you received, with the words cut from magazines."

"What did it say?"

"It said, 'Mind your own business or you'll be the next to die.'"

"Huh." Sandy sat back. "Why would anyone threaten you?"

"I don't know."

"Do they think you're connected to me or something?" Sandy asked.

"I don't know." She waited while the server set a coaster and a glass of red wine in front of her, thanked her then took a sip.

"You worked that rescue last Saturday with George Anton," Sandy said.

"Yes."

"Did you say anything to him about me or Dave?"

"No. I didn't even talk to him." She hesitated then added, "I asked my brother-in-law about Anton. Justin has a restaurant in Junction. Red Mesa. He knows Anton. He told me he's signed a contract with him to supply his restaurant."

"What did your brother-in-law have to say about him?"

"That he made a good deal and has a good reputation."

She nodded. "That's true. I mean, Dave said he checked the guy out before he signed that contract. It just didn't work out for us the way it does most people."

"Why didn't it?" Anna asked. "I mean, if Anton loaned you the money to expand, it was in his best interest to make sure you got enough business to pay him back."

"If I knew the answer to that, I wouldn't be in this fix." She set aside her empty beer glass and signaled the server for another one. "Did Lucas say what the cops have found out so far? No one at the sheriff's department will tell me anything."

"He said he looked through Dave's office and didn't find anything."

"Yeah, he was there half the day. At least he was neat about it. We talked about you."

"You did?" Anna tried not to sound alarmed.

"I told him not to fall for you, that you're still married to Jonas."

"Jonas is dead," Anna said.

"Yeah, but you still feel married to him, don't you? No sense in a guy like Malone wasting time with you when there's so many women in this town who are desperate to hook up with a man."

Were those the only two categories of women Sandy saw—desperate and unavailable? "I will always love Jonas," she said. "But that doesn't mean I couldn't love someone else, too."

"Still, I can't really see you with a cop. Maybe a professor or a librarian or something."

"Jonas wasn't a professor or a librarian."

Sandy shrugged. "You were younger when you met him. Less set in your ways."

I am not set in my ways. Anna took a large swallow of wine to keep from saying this out loud. She hadn't come here to argue with Sandy, and she didn't like being put on the defensive.

Instead, she forced her shoulders to relax and smiled in a way she hoped was enigmatic. "I guess we'll just have to see," she said. "How are you doing? I know you've got a lot of arrangements to make. I found all the paperwork involved when a spouse dies a little daunting."

"I'm still waiting for the county to release the body."

"Are you using Hawkins and White for the arrangements?" Anna asked. "They were very helpful with planning Jonas's service."

"I'm not going to have a service," Sandy said.

"You're not?"

Sandy accepted a second beer from the server. "I'm not into that sort of thing and neither was Dave. I'm going to have him cremated and I'll scatter the ashes in the mountains somewhere this spring."

Anna started to argue that Dave's friends would welcome the opportunity to acknowledge his passing, but she kept back those words, too. This wasn't her decision to make. Maybe Sandy, as strong as she was outwardly, didn't want the pain of a formal ceremony and all those condolences. "That sounds very meaningful," she said instead.

"I got an offer on the house today. I still have to wait on the death certificate and some other paperwork, but the buyer isn't in a hurry."

"That was fast."

"It's a hot market. I still have to sell the business, but I'm hopeful I'll clear enough to pay what we owe."

Apparently, Sandy had decided against skipping out on her bills. She sounded so calm. Anna would have been devastated to have to leave her home and give up her livelihood. "What will you do then?" she asked.

"I might travel for a while, or go down to Mexico and hang out. I've got money of my own tucked away, so I'll be all right."

Anna tried to hide her shock. "Oh. That's nice." If Sandy had money, why was she selling everything? Maybe it was family money, or tied up in a trust or something.

Sandy smirked. "You didn't think I was going to let George Anton and the bank have everything did you?"

So much for thinking she was hiding her feelings from this woman. "A fresh start will be good," she said.

"It will, but I can't go anywhere until the sheriff's department finishes their investigation."

"Knowing who killed Dave won't bring him back, but it has to be terrible, not knowing," Anna said.

"At this point I don't really care if they rule his death murder or suicide, I just want everything settled." She drained the beer then took out her wallet. "Tell your boyfriend to hurry it up so I can get on with my life," she said, setting a twenty-dollar bill on the table.

"He's not my—"

Sandy laughed. "Gotcha!" she said and walked away.

Anna stared at her half-full glass of wine, cheeks hot. Sandy had always made her uncomfortable, but it was worse now without Dave and Jonas to serve as buffers. "She just has a different sense of humor," Jonas had told Anna once. "Don't take anything she says personally."

Except it was hard not to feel like a target when Sandy took it upon herself to warn off the first man Anna had been interested in since Jonas had died.

She remembered Lucas's remark when he'd seen Jonas's picture on the refrigerator. Anna had said she would always love him. She had thought he was acknowledging that bond with a loved one who is gone—the same bond he shared with his girlfriend who had died. But, really, he must have been alluding to Sandy's statement that Anna was still too tied to Jonas to be open to another relationship.

Six months ago, that might have been true, but not now. She ought to call Lucas and tell him so.

Before she could gather the nerve, another thought occurred to her. Maybe Lucas had brought up her love for Jonas as a way of letting her know he wasn't ready to move on from his relationship with Jenny. The idea settled in her stomach like a lead weight. Maybe he wasn't the one who needed to be warned off—she was.

Anna drained the glass of wine and thought about ordering another. Instead, she took out her wallet to pay. Better to go home to her dog and her knitting and keep things the way they had been. Quiet. Comfortable.

Lonely.

ON WEDNESDAY, Lucas drove to Junction to see George Anton. The office for Anton's Finest was a single-story, red-brick building in an industrial park next door to a cemetery. Lucas was surprised when Shaylin Brown came to the reception desk to greet him. "I didn't expect to see you, Ms. Brown," he said. "I thought you'd still be recovering from your accident."

She looked down at the navy blue sling on her left arm, a cast visible inside the sling. "I'm still dealing with this thing, but that doesn't mean I can't work. George is so busy, he needs all the help he can get."

She led the way down a hallway. A trim brunette in a tailored gray pantsuit, she moved briskly, heels making muffled taps on the low-pile carpet. She opened a door near the end of the hallway and George Anton rose from the head of a conference table. "Hello, Deputy," he said. "Have a seat and we'll take care of this as quickly as possible."

The three of them sat at the table and Lucas took out his recorder and notepad. "I just have a few questions," he said.

"Of course." Anton folded his hands in front of him, relaxed. "Though I'm surprised Rayford County would send someone all the way to Junction to answer questions about a traffic accident. We could have done this on the phone."

"This isn't about the accident," Lucas said. "I need to ask you some questions about your relationship to Dave and Sandy Weiss."

Anton and Shaylin exchanged looks. "What about them?" Anton asked.

"Where were you on March 13?" Lucas asked.

Anton frowned. "I was a lot of places that day. Calling on clients. Here at the office some, I imagine. Why is that important?"

"I'll need a list of all the places you were on that day," Lucas said.

"Why?"

Lucas met the older man's confused gaze. "Dave Weiss died that day."

"He killed himself," Anton said. "I heard. I'm sorry, but I don't see what that has to do with me."

"Dave owed you a lot of money. He wasn't going to be able to pay you back."

"Are you saying that's why he killed himself? Did he leave a note that said that?"

"I just need the list of your whereabouts."

Anton looked to Shaylin. "Get my datebook, would you?" he asked.

She left the room and Anton turned back to Lucas. "I'm old-fashioned. I still like to keep things on paper." He ran a hand over his almost-bald head. "This is the first I've heard that Dave wasn't going to be able to pay me back," he said. "He was making the payments. He was bringing in plenty of money."

Shaylin returned and handed Anton a slim black note-book. Anton flipped through the pages, then ran his hand along one to flatten it, and passed it to Lucas. "It's all right there."

Lucas made note of the list of appointments. Anton had spent the morning at the office in a meeting with at least three other people, including Shaylin, and the rest of the day calling on clients, including Justin Trent.

He returned the notebook to Anton. "Mrs. Weiss said you financed the expansion of their business. Was that usual?"

"Sure. I like dealing with small businessmen like myself. I try to give them a break. It's a good investment. I can offer my restaurant clients a really quality product that is truly local. They get to advertise that they're supporting local growers and producers, and I'm supporting the little guy instead of some faceless corporation. It's a win all around. And all legal. I keep the two businesses separate, you see? I don't want any trouble with the IRS. It's all on the level, I promise. I have a team of lawyers and tax people who look over every contract to make sure it's so."

"How did that work for the Weisses?" he asked.

"The same way it works for any other supplier I deal with. I give them a good interest rate and scale the loan to the amount of business I project I can throw their way."

"What happens if your projections are off?" Lucas asked.

"They aren't." Anton tucked the notebook into his suit pocket. "I've been doing this a while now. I know what the market will bear."

"Sandy Weiss says they weren't getting enough income from you to make their sales."

"Maybe you misunderstood her. I can show you the fig-ures. Here." He swiveled his chair and took a laptop computer from the credenza behind them. "It will just take me a minute to boot this up."

"I can ask Lisa to bring in some coffee or water, if you'd like," Shaylin said.

"No, thank you," Lucas said. He watched as Anton typed rapidly then began swiping at the screen.

Anton turned the computer toward Lucas. "That's the last six months' figures for Weiss Bakery," he said.

Lucas studied the spreadsheet on the screen, which showed amounts in the thousands to ten thousands for each month. It was a lot of money. "But what do they owe?" he asked.

Anton swung the laptop toward himself once more and scrolled again. "There." He angled the computer to Lucas again. "That's their note. See—they owed under half of their net take from me. Plenty left over for a little profit. And they still had all the income from their regular bakery and catering business."

Lucas made note of the figures. "This doesn't match with what Sandy Weiss told me," he said.

"Maybe her husband told her he wasn't making enough money because he was skimming money for something else," Shaylin said. "Drugs or gambling or an affair. A lot of women are completely ignorant of their husband's businesses."

"Not Sandy," Anton said. "If anything, she was more involved in this stuff than he was."

"Are you saying Sandy Weiss was involved in this contract?" Lucas asked.

"He signed it, because the business was all in his name, but she handled all the bookkeeping over there. I transferred the money I owed them into their account by electronic transfer every month and she paid me what they owed on their loan in a handwritten check. Her signature was on the checks."

"Sandy said Dave didn't like to use computers."

"That's right." Anton nodded. "I hesitated to do business with him because of that. It's too easy for things to get lost in the shuffle without computer records. But clients had been asking about his baked goods—his reputation was that good, so I took a chance. And they never missed a payment or screwed up an order. If anything, they were too generous. They were always throwing in extra things for the clients to try or sending goodies for the staff. People loved it, though."

"What about your contract with Justin Trent?"

Anton's gaze sharpened. "What about it? He doesn't have anything to do with the Weisses, does he?"

"I'm just wondering how an agreement with a supplier differs from your agreements with restaurants."

"I don't loan money to any restaurants," Anton said. "And the profit margins might be different. That's confidential information."

"I understand. I'm just trying to get a feel for how you operate."

"How do you know Justin?" Shaylin asked.

"I'm friends with his sister-in-law. She mentioned he works with your company."

"Yeah, I've known Justin a long time," Anton said. "Shaylin used to work for him. That's how we met."

"Back to the Weisses," Lucas said. "Someone sent Sandy Weiss a threatening letter, and she received some phone calls threatening her, too. Do you know anyone who would do something like that?"

"No. You think it was me? Why would I threaten her?"

"What about Anna Trent?" he asked. "She received a threatening letter, too."

"Is she related to Justin Trent? I've never met her. Never heard of. I sure didn't send her any letter."

"What kind of threat?" Shaylin asked.

"The letter writer threatened to kill these women," Lucas said.

Shaylin looked horrified. "That's terrible."

"I don't know anything about any letters," Anton said. He closed the laptop. "I don't know what else I can tell you."

"Thank you," Lucas said. "I appreciate your cooperation."

He stood and Shaylin rose, also. "I'll show you out."

Chapter Eleven

Shaylin Brown led the way back down the hall, through the reception area and out the front door. Then she turned and said, "Anna Trent is Justin's sister-in-law, isn't she?"

"Yes."

"I remember when she used to come into the restaurant, though we were never introduced." She rubbed one hand down the lapel of her suit. "She probably told you already that Justin and I had an affair. He ended it when his wife found out."

"She mentioned it when she saw you at the accident."

"She was there?"

"She's a volunteer with Search and Rescue."

"Those people are amazing." She shook her head. "Anyway, I just wanted you to know that George is telling you the truth when he says he doesn't know her. He knew Justin because Red Mesa has been in town for years, but I'm the one who talked Justin into signing with us. We're not together anymore, but we're still friends. And Justin knows a good deal when he sees it."

"Do you know anything about Dave Weiss's death?" Lucas asked. "Maybe something you didn't want to say in front of George?"

"No. I never met him. I never met Sandy, either, until the day of the accident. George wanted me to go along on the visit because Sandy's husband had just died and he thought it would be easier with another woman along. I think he was afraid she'd start crying or something." She rolled her eyes. "You know how some men are about tears."

"How did the meeting go?" Lucas asked.

"It went fine. Sandy was very composed, all business." Her eyes met his. "I'm not going to give you any details, but I will say she seemed happy with the business arrangement her husband had made and gave no indication she wanted to end the deal."

"She told you she wanted to continue the deal."

"Yes. On the same terms. She seemed happy about that."

That didn't match with what Sandy had told Anna about wanting to get out from under the debt. He made a mental note to check with Sandy about this.

"Is George in trouble?" Shaylin asked.

"If his alibi checks out, Mr. Anton has nothing to worry about," Lucas said.

"We heard that Dave Weiss killed himself—Sandy even sent a message to George saying that. But now you think it was murder?"

"We don't know. It's important to follow up on everything."

"I thought Eagle Mountain was such a pretty town," she said. "Very peaceful. Now I hear there are people being threatened and possibly murdered. I guess looks really are deceptive." She rubbed her shoulders, as if chilled.

"When will you see Mrs. Weiss again?"

"George is going to see her tomorrow. I'm sure he'll ask her why she told you he wasn't paying them enough money to manage the loan. That isn't true. George is a very smart businessman, but he really does care about people."

And you care about him, Lucas thought. "Thank you for your help," he said. "I won't keep you any longer."

She took a step back. "Right. I hope you find whatever you're looking for."

So did he. Though it would help if he had a clearer idea of who or what that was.

After talking to Anton and Shaylin, Lucas stopped by the sheriff's department in Junction to say hello. "How's life in the mountains?" his good friend, Del Alvarez greeted him. "Are you tired of ticketing jaywalkers and putting cows back in pastures, and ready to deal with real crime again?"

"Actually, I'm working a really interesting case," Lucas said. "A possible murder."

"Possible?" Del raised an eyebrow in question.

Lucas outlined the particulars of the case. "Do you know anything about George Anton?" he asked.

"Never heard of him," Del said. "Does he have a rap sheet?"

"Nothing. Nobody in this case has anything worse than a parking violation."

"So maybe your guy really did commit suicide," Del said.

"Maybe." Lucas crossed his arms. "It just feels off. The more questions I ask, the more things don't add up."

"Don't let it get to you," Del said. "Sometimes we just don't have enough information to solve every case."

"I know."

"And I know you," Del said. "You don't let go of things. That can be good and bad." He slapped Lucas on the back. "Walk out with me. I have to get going."

They said goodbye in the parking lot.

Lucas checked the time and decided to have lunch before he headed back to Eagle Mountain. He drove to a mom-and-pop café downtown that had become a favorite over the years. He was walking up to the door when it opened and a woman with long dark hair emerged. She stopped abruptly when she saw him.

"Lucas!"

"Hello, Tanya." Jenny's sister looked enough like Lucas's former girlfriend to cause a tightness in his chest, but her expression was anything but friendly. "How are you?" he asked. She and Jenny had been close, and the last time he had seen her, a few days after Jenny's funeral, she had been devastated by grief.

"I'm better," she said. "I've been seeing someone. A therapist, I mean. She's helping me come to terms with everything that happened."

"That's good."

"It is." She started to move past him then stopped. She was close enough to touch him now and her gaze burned into him. "She told me I needed to forgive you for what you did to Jenny."

He opened his mouth to speak but she held up her hand. "I don't want to hear your self-justification," she said. "Just know I'm working on this. If Jenny could forgive you, I ought to be able to."

He hadn't intended to defend himself. He probably would have said something like, *I'm sorry every day about how things turned out*. Now, he could only say, "Thank you."

"Don't thank me. I'm doing this for my own mental health, not yours."

She moved on, hurrying to her car. Lucas pulled open the door to the café and went inside, shaken by the encounter.

He ordered at the counter and carried his food to a booth, then stared out the window, not eating. He and Jenny used to come here, in the early days, when they were happy.

They came here the day they'd moved in together, after spending hours carrying furniture and unpacking boxes. He had been happy about the move, looking forward to seeing more of her.

He hadn't realized she had seen this as the first step toward marriage. Two years later, she had finally confronted him. "Are we going to get married?" she had asked.

The question hadn't surprised him. Jenny had been hinting for months that she wanted to make their relationship more permanent. He had gone so far as to visit a jewelry store to look at rings, but in the end, he couldn't buy one. "I love you," he'd told her. "But I'm not ready for marriage." Marriage was forever, and he wasn't sure his feelings for Jenny were that strong. Part of him was ashamed to admit it, but he'd known that he'd needed to be honest with her.

That had been a horrible night. Almost as horrible as two months later, when they learned she had cancer. She had been preparing to move out of their apartment and start dating other people, but her diagnosis had stopped everything. Lucas had committed to sticking by her through her treatment and, they hoped, her recovery. But the treatments didn't stop the disease.

Tanya had come to him near the end and suggested he marry Jenny anyway. "It's all she ever wanted," Tanya had said. "I think it's the least you could do to make her last days happier."

So he had bought a ring and gotten down on his knees in front of Jenny's wheelchair and proposed. She had looked at him, tears streaming down her face. "If it wasn't right nine months ago, it isn't right now," she'd said. She had put her hand on his shoulder. "I appreciate the gesture, but I think we both know we're better friends than we ever were lovers. You've showed that all these months, standing by me, and that means more to me than a ring or a wedding."

Jenny had forgiven Lucas for not loving her enough to marry her. But he was still a long way from forgiving himself. And now there was Anna. He was so attracted to her, and she seemed to respond the same way. But he could feel the ghosts of her late husband and Jenny standing between them. He didn't know how to get past that, or if Anna even wanted to.

He was contemplating all this, his food growing cold, when his phone rang. He checked the screen and answered quickly. "Hello, Sheriff."

"Are you on your way back from Junction?" Travis asked.

"I'm finishing lunch and headed that way," Lucas said. He gathered up the uneaten food as he talked.

"Get here as soon as you can. Someone shot out the windows in the bakery."

WEDNESDAY MORNING, just before noon, a tall young man with a long blond ponytail came into Yarn and More. Three women were shopping at the time and they all stopped to stare as he moved through the shop.

"Hey, Anna!" He grinned when he saw her. "Is now a good time to talk about those shelves you want?"

"Now is perfect." Anna set aside the patterns she had been collating for an upcoming Knit Your First Sweater class and stood. "Thanks for stopping by, Bobby. I know a small job like this isn't usually worth your time."

"Anything for you." Bobby Fitch had worked for Jonas for

two years before Jonas died, and he and his wife had ended up buying most of the business tools and equipment from Anna. "Do you have a sketch of what you want?"

"I do." She turned back to the worktable and shuffled through a pile of papers until she found the one she wanted. "I want a whole wall of shelves, on the diagonal, like this." She indicated the X-shaped pattern of boards she had drawn on a sheet of notepaper. "I want to end up with all these cubbies where I can stash yarn."

Bobby studied the paper then looked at the wall she indicated. "Oh, sure, we can do that," he said. "Do you want the wood painted or stained?"

"Stained, to match the other wood in here." She indicated the mahogany trim around the windows and doors. "And then over here." She turned to indicate a narrower space next to the checkout counter. "Here, I want vertical shelves for books. They need to be spaced fairly far apart—eighteen inches. A lot of needlework books are tall, and I can display other things there, too."

Bobby nodded. "Oh, sure. I can do that, too." He folded the sketch and tucked it into the front pocket of his denim work shirt. "I'll get you an estimate in a day or two. Or Melody will. That's her forte."

"No rush," Anna said. "I know you're busy."

"We are. It's been great." His expression sobered. "I owe you and Jonas everything, giving me this chance. Not many guys my age have their own business."

"You deserve it," she said. "Jonas would be so proud." She blinked rapidly, eyes stinging and her throat tight.

"Thanks. Hey, I've been meaning to ask you. What happened to that old Dodge Dart Jonas had in his garage?"

The reference to the Dart surprised her. "It's still in the

garage," she said. "Jonas never finished it." He had never had time.

"If you ever want to sell it, I'd make you a good offer," Bobby said.

"I didn't know you were interested in old cars."

"Kind of." He shrugged. "That one was special anyway. Because it belonged to Jonas."

She nodded. "I'll let you know if I ever decide to sell it," she said.

"It was good to see you again." He patted his pocket. "Melody or I will call you with that estimate."

He strode out of the business and Anna exhaled. The shoppers went back to examining skeins of yarn and Gemma finished adding up a customer's purchase.

Anna's phone rang and she was surprised to see the call was from Sandy. "Anna, I'm sorry to bother you," Sandy said. "I know you're at work."

Sandy didn't sound like herself. Her voice vibrated with tension. "You're not bothering me," Anna said. "What's wrong?"

"I was here at the bakery, working in the office. There weren't any customers, and I heard this...this explosion. I ran into the front room and glass was everywhere, and tires squealed as someone drove away."

"Sandy, what happened?" Anna fought back alarm.

"Someone shot out the front window. The one with the Weiss Bakery sign." Sandy choked back a sob. "I could have been killed."

"Did you call the sheriff?" Anna asked.

"Yes. They're on their way."

"I'm coming, too," Anna said.

"Thanks," Sandy said. "I didn't know who else to call."

"I'll be there in a few minutes. Just hang on."

She looked up to find two of the shoppers and Gemma staring at her, open-mouthed. "Someone shot out the window of the bakery?" Gemma asked.

Anna stared at her. "How did you know?"

Gemma shrugged. "Sandy talks pretty loud. And I have good hearing."

Anna pocketed the phone. "I need to go over there. She's frantic and the sheriff's deputies are on their way."

"Go," Gemma said. "We can handle it here. That poor woman has certainly had more than her share of bad luck."

She had, Anna agreed. But was it really bad luck that plagued the Weisses or something much more sinister and dangerous?

Chapter Twelve

Lucas recognized Anna's car ahead of him as he turned onto the dead-end street leading to Weiss Bakery. A trio of sheriff's department SUVs were already pulled up in front of the building, and the parking lot was strung with yellow crime-scene tape. Anna parked on the side of the road and skirted the tape as she made her way toward the front door.

Lucas jogged to catch up with her. "Anna, what are you doing here?" he asked.

She stopped and waited. She wore some kind of knitted wrap that gathered in folds around her neck, framing her face and drawing attention to her full lips and wide-spaced eyes. "Sandy called me," she said. "She sounded terrified."

She looked past him, toward the front of the bakery, and he turned to take in the large front window, several big shards of glass still hanging from the wooden frame, more glass glittering in the gravel of the parking lot. Sandy stood in front of the door with the sheriff and Deputy Dwight Prentice. She wore a stained blue apron over jeans and a green sweatshirt.

Sandy looked up as Anna and Lucas approached, her face blotchy, as if she'd been crying. "I got here as soon as I could," Anna said.

"I shouldn't have called you," Sandy said. "I don't know what I was thinking. It was just…"

"You were upset and you didn't want to be alone," Anna said. "That's perfectly natural."

"Hello, Anna," Travis said. "Would you take Sandy inside while we finish processing the scene?"

"Of course." Anna stepped forward and took Sandy's arm. "Let's go into your office."

Lucas waited until the women were inside with the door shut before he spoke. "What happened?" he asked.

"Sandy says she was in her office, getting ready to eat the sandwich she had brought from home for her lunch, when she heard tires on the gravel in the parking lot," Dwight said. "She started toward the front, thinking she had a customer, but before she had taken three steps, the front window exploded. She screamed and hit the floor and whoever fired the shot drove away. By the time she got to her feet and looked out the door, whoever had done this was gone."

"Just one shot?" Lucas asked.

"Just one." Travis held up an evidence bag with a spent shotgun shell. "Number 9 birdshot. This was lying in the parking lot."

Dwight looked around them. "There aren't any other businesses on this street and the closest house is two blocks away," he said. "We'll ask around, but the person who did this probably knew they wouldn't be seen."

"Did Sandy get a description of the vehicle?" Lucas asked.

"No. I asked if she had had any new threats, and she said no," Travis said. "She didn't have any customers here at the time, and no one had come in either the half hour before or the few minutes after the shot was fired."

"We don't have much to go on," Dwight said. "The ammo is pretty common. There aren't any tracks in the gravel lot. No cameras. No neighbors or customers to hear anything."

"Did you talk to George Anton?" Travis asked.

"I did. He says he never threatened the Weisses. And he said their proceeds from the bakery sales to him were more than enough to cover their loan payments. He showed me figures on his computer that backed up this claim. He gave me his schedule for the day Dave Weiss died. I still need to check that out, but if it holds, I don't see how he could have been involved in Dave's death."

"He could have hired someone to do it," Dwight said.

"But why would he?" Travis asked. He glanced at the broken window again. "What time did you talk to him?" he asked.

"I was with him from eleven to about eleven twenty," Lucas said.

"It's just possible he could get here from Junction in forty minutes," Travis said. "Call him right now and see what he says."

Lucas tried George Anton's number but the call went to voice mail. Then he dialed Shaylin Brown. She answered on the second ring. "Hello?"

"This is Deputy Lucas Malone. I'm trying to reach George and he's not answering his phone."

"He turns off his phone when he's in a meeting," she said.

"Can you tell me who he's meeting with?" Lucas asked.

"Sure. Hang on a sec." A long beat of silence then she was back on the line. "He's meeting with Justin Trent."

"Thank you."

"Is there anything I can help you with?" she asked.

"No. Just routine follow-up." He ended the call and looked

up the number for Red Mesa. A woman answered. Lucas identified himself and asked to speak to Justin Trent. Moments later, a man came on the line.

"Hello?"

"Mr. Trent, is George Anton there?" Lucas asked.

"He just left. Why?"

"How long was he with you?"

"We had lunch together. Why is a Rayford County Sheriff's deputy interested in George Anton?"

"It's just routine. How long was Mr. Anton with you?"

"Almost two hours," Trent said. "Does this have anything to do with Anna?"

"No, sir, it does not. Thank you for your time." Lucas ended the call. "Justin Trent says George Anton was with him for the last two hours."

"Let's have another word with Sandy," Travis said.

Anna and Sandy sat across from each other in the office. Both women looked up when the three men entered. "You can go now, Anna," Travis said.

"No," Sandy said. "I want her to stay." She glanced at Anna. "You'll stay, won't you?"

"Of course." Anna adjusted the knitwear around her neck.

Travis pulled a folding chair over in front of the women and sat. "What haven't you told us?" he asked.

Sandy stared. "I don't know what you're talking about."

"I'm looking at this picture…" Travis said. "Your husband dead under mysterious circumstances. Debts that don't fit Dave's historic behavior. Anonymous phone calls and a couple of threatening notes that look like something out of a kids' book. A drive-by shooting that on the surface appears unprovoked. We're missing too much information. Things you haven't told us."

"I've told you everything I know," she said.

"Tell us more about this debt," Travis said. "George Anton says you were earning more than enough from the meat contract to make the payments on the loan he extended you for improvements to your business."

"He's lying." The muscles along her jaw tightened.

"Had Dave borrowed any other money?" Travis asked. "Was he involved with loan sharks? Was he into drugs?"

Her face paled, freckles standing out across her nose. "Drugs?"

"Maybe he was siphoning off money to feed his habit?" Travis asked. Lucas wondered what Travis was getting at. The autopsy on Dave Weiss hadn't showed any sign of drug use, other than the dog tranquilizers, and they certainly weren't a commonly abused substance.

"No. How can you say such a thing?" Sandy buried her face in her hands and began to sob, loud, shaking sobs. Sandy Weiss had been stoic to this point, almost emotionless at times. This sudden weeping shocked them all into silence.

Anna leaned over and put a hand on Sandy's shoulder. "I think you've upset her enough," she said and frowned at them.

Travis stood. "We'll leave for now," he said. "But we may want to talk to you again."

The men filed out. Lucas paused in the doorway to look back, hoping to catch Anna's eye, but she was focused on Sandy, murmuring something to her, so softly he couldn't make out the words.

He followed the sheriff and Dwight back into the parking lot. "You didn't come up with anything suspicious when you searched the office here?" Travis asked.

"No, sir." He rubbed the back of his neck. "Maybe if we could find Dave's phone…"

"His provider says they haven't been able to track it," Travis said. "Which probably means it's been destroyed. I'm going to try to get a warrant to search the Weisses' home. I don't know if I'll succeed, but we need to find out more about what Dave was up to right before he died. Sandy isn't helping."

"She may not know," Lucas said.

"I have a feeling she does," Travis said. "But maybe she's trying to protect her husband's reputation." He shifted his gaze to Lucas. "You might suggest Anna be careful. If Dave was involved in something dangerous, she wants to watch her back. Maybe that threat someone left at her house was more serious than we thought."

ANNA AND SANDY sat in silence as the sheriff and his deputies got into their vehicles and drove away. Sandy let out a long breath as the noise of their tires on gravel faded. "Nothing like having the cops accuse you of lying to really cap off a horrible day," she said.

"They're frustrated because they aren't finding any more evidence," Anna said. "I don't think they really believe you're lying."

"The sheriff does." The desk chair creaked as Sandy shifted. "And he's not exactly wrong."

Anna stared. "What do you mean?"

"There is one thing I didn't tell them." Her eyes met Anna's, her gaze unblinking. "It's not anything that important. It may not even mean anything. But I think it's probably safer for me not to tell."

Anna sat again and leaned toward Sandy. "What is it?"

"When I saw George Anton on Saturday, I told him I was thinking of closing the business," Sandy said. "He got so upset when I mentioned it that I backed off. I pretended that I intended to keep things going, and to keep repaying the money he had loaned Dave, and keep supplying desserts to his restaurants. But I think he was suspicious."

"You should tell the sheriff this," Anna said. "It could be important. If George was upset about losing your business…"

"No." Sandy shook her head. "I can't say anything to the sheriff because of the other thing I didn't tell him."

Anna waited, holding her breath.

"George had a gun with him," Sandy said. "He wore it in a holster under his jacket, and he made a point of pulling back the jacket so I could see."

"What did he say?" Anna asked. "Did he threaten you?"

"He didn't say anything. I think he was letting that gun do the talking. And that's why I can't go to the sheriff. Shooting out my window is one thing, but the next time, the bullet might be meant for me."

"That's horrible." Anna gripped Sandy's hand. "You really need to tell the sheriff. You shouldn't be trying to deal with this on your own."

Sandy pulled her hand away and stood. "I am dealing with it. I'm going to sell everything and move to where George Anton can't find me. Until then, I'm going to make him think I'm going along with his plans. It's the only way."

Anna didn't agree, but this wasn't her decision to make. "Is there anything I can do to help?" she asked.

"Thanks for coming today," Sandy said. "The cops were probably easier on me because you were here." She laughed. "Your boyfriend's face when you gave them all the stink eye when they tried to question me was priceless. Like a hurt little boy."

"He's not my boyfriend," Anna said.

"You may not think so, but he does, and that's what counts." She picked up a stack of papers from the desk. "Before you go, let me give you something from the case up front. A treat to repay you for your trouble."

"You don't have to do that," Anna called after Sandy, who was already on her way to the front. Anna hurried to collect her coat and purse then followed Sandy to the front of the store.

"It's just a couple of cupcakes." Sandy turned to the counter behind the front case and arranged something in a small bakery box. "I know the chocolate ones with pink frosting are your favorite. Could you hand me that tape there on the top of the case?"

Anna searched and found the tape dispenser sitting on top of the glass case. "Here you go." She handed it to Sandy, who tore off a strip and sealed the box shut.

Sandy handed the box to Anna. "I need to get back to work and you probably do, too," she said. "Thanks, again."

"What about the window?" Anna asked. "You can't leave everything like it is."

"I've got some plywood in the back I can nail over it," Sandy said. "I'll have to close for a few days, but that will give me time to take care of some other things." She shrugged. "Don't worry about me. I can take care of myself."

Anna left, suddenly anxious to be away. She didn't understand Sandy, who was terrified one moment and completely calm and in charge the next. She didn't act like any friend Anna had ever had. Their only real connection was through their dead husbands. But Anna's loyalty to Dave and to Jonas kept her reaching out to Sandy. She didn't seem to have any other friends to rally round her, and she shouldn't have to go through all this alone.

Gemma was leading a sock-making class when Anna returned to the shop, so Anna didn't have to face immediate questions about what had happened. She fetched her lunch from the refrigerator in the storeroom and sat at the little café table to eat. The sandwich was chicken left over from some she had grilled a couple of days ago. She had taken the first bite when Gemma swept in. "The estimate for the shelves is on the table in the workroom," Gemma said.

"Thanks," Anna said. "Is the class over already?"

"The students are focused on turning the heels." Gemma slid into the chair across from Anna. "I've got a couple of minutes before they get frustrated and start calling for help. How is Sandy?"

"She's fine. Determined to be strong and not let anything get her down."

"That's Sandy," Gemma said. "She's not the kind of person I would ever feel I could confide in, but if I was ever stranded in the wilderness, she'd be a good person to have along. She'd know how to fix the car, find dinner, and navigate out of there. She's scary competent that way."

"She is," Anna agreed. Sandy had won awards with the fire department, and bragged that she was a better businessperson than Dave. She probably would know how to survive in the wilderness. But Anna wouldn't want to be stuck there with her. It was an ugly thought, but she wasn't so sure Sandy wouldn't go her own way and leave someone like Anna behind.

She looked down at her sandwich, her appetite gone. "I'll save the rest of this for tomorrow," she said and wrapped up the remains of her lunch before Gemma could comment on how little she had eaten. "Why don't we see how the students are doing on turning those heels?"

"It always confuses everyone at first," Gemma said.

"It does. Then when you figure it out, you feel like a genius," Anna said. She would ask Lucas if he ever felt that way when he solved a case.

That is, if they ever had that kind of conversation again. When he had left her house Monday night, he had seemed intent on putting some distance between them, as if he sensed her growing feelings for him and didn't want to encourage her. At the bakery this morning, he had been all business. What else could she expect, though, considering he was on duty and dealing with a serious matter? If only she could read him better.

For that matter, if only she could understand her own feelings. Apparently, romance didn't get any easier with age. She still felt like a teenager playing the will-he-won't-he guessing game. And she wasn't even sure what she wanted his answer to be.

Chapter Thirteen

Travis asked Lucas to come into his office when they got back to the sheriff's department after leaving the bakery. "What's your take on this?" Travis asked. His desk chair creaked as he leaned back.

Lucas sat in the visitor's chair across from the sheriff and tried not to squirm like a kid in the principal's office. He wanted to come up with some brilliant observation that proved he had insight into the whole case. But everything was a muddled mess in his mind. "Why would someone go after a small-town baker and his wife?" he asked.

Travis nodded. "Whatever is going on there, I don't think it started with those notes to Sandy. This goes back to before Dave died. Whether he took his own life or was murdered, I think it's connected to these threats."

"Shooting out the bakery window is escalating things," Lucas said.

"Sandy has the house for sale," Travis said. "She says it's because she needs to money to pay her debts. George Anton says different, and he showed you figures to prove it."

"Maybe she owes money to someone else," Lucas said. "Someone she doesn't want to tell us about."

"Did you find anything in the bakery office about how much they owed and to whom?"

"No. She said the financial records are with their CPA and she wasn't in a hurry to provide them to me. Without a warrant, I couldn't press."

Travis sat up, elbows on the desk. "What if we're wasting all this time investigating what turns out to be a suicide?" he asked. "Was there a ladder at the bakery?"

"I looked around and didn't see one. And none at the house, either. In fact, she had already gotten rid of everything of Dave's—clothes, tools, everything in the garage and most of the furniture, too."

"Why is she in such a hurry?" Travis asked. "I keep coming back to that."

"Because she's grieving and can't stand to be in the house and business she shared with her husband," Lucas said.

"Maybe. Or because she's guilty of something and wants to leave before she's caught."

"Guilty of what?" Lucas asked. "I can't see her hauling a man Dave's size up a ladder in the middle of nowhere. And she hasn't gained anything from his death. If anything, she's going to lose everything."

"Then that takes us back to these threats," Travis said.

"She wants to leave Eagle Mountain before the person who threatened her does to her what they did to her husband," Lucas said.

"Who's making the threats?" Travis asked. "George Anton?"

"Or someone he hired."

Travis drummed his fingers on the desktop. "What's his motive?"

"If we could find that out, we might have the answer to the whole case," Lucas said.

"Stay on Anton," Travis said. "Find out as much as you can. And we'll keep a close eye on Sandy, too. Maybe the person making threats has made other contact with her and she's too frightened to tell us."

Sandy had never appeared very frightened to Lucas, but he knew people could be hard to read. Behind her stoicism, she might be panicked. If Dave had been murdered, killing him had to have been difficult. His widow would make a much easier target.

ANNA NEEDED TO move to sort out her thoughts, so after work she took Jacquie for a long walk. While the dog sniffed at the bare branches of shrubs and rolled in the snow, Anna pondered what to do with the information Sandy had given her. The sheriff needed to know about this, and if something happened to Sandy because Anna had kept quiet, she would carry the guilt for the rest of her life. Sandy hadn't sworn her to secrecy. Reviewing the conversation, Anna even wondered if Sandy had told her the story about George Anton so that she would pass it on to Lucas.

She got home after seven. She had no idea what Lucas would be doing right now, but she called him anyway. If he didn't answer, she would leave a message asking him to call. But he answered quickly.

"Hello, Anna," he said. "How are you doing?"

"I'm fine," she said.

"I'm glad to hear it. I know our questions upset you," he said. "But it's our job to ask the hard questions. People lie, and those lies make it harder for us to help them."

"I know that," Anna said. She traced a finger through the

dust on a side table. Past time she did a little housework. "Listen, about Sandy. You were right. There was something she wasn't telling you."

"What is that?" She sensed a new tension in his voice.

"I've been debating all evening whether or not to tell you. But Sandy didn't say I shouldn't, and she's wrong for not telling you herself. I told her so."

"What is it she didn't tell us?"

"She says at her meeting with George Anton last Saturday, he had a gun."

"What kind of gun?"

"A handgun," Anna said. "He was wearing it in a shoulder holster under his coat. He didn't exactly threaten her with it, but she said he made sure she saw it, and she felt it was a threat. She said he was upset because she told him she was going to sell the business and wouldn't be able to fulfill the contract Dave had signed."

"He didn't say anything about this when I talked to him yesterday."

"Later on, she said that she decided to pretend to go along with George, even though she plans to sell the business and leave town. Maybe he believes her."

"Anton couldn't have been the one who shot out her window," Lucas said. "He was meeting with Justin at the time."

Justin again. Why did one of her least favorite people keep popping up? Anna didn't know whether to laugh or shake her head in exasperation. "I can't get over all the ways everyone is connected. Does that happen in all your cases?"

"Sometimes. I'll talk to George again and see what he has to say. Thanks for telling me. You're helping Sandy, whether she appreciates it or not."

"I'm sure she doesn't appreciate it, but that doesn't matter," Anna said.

"I won't let Anton know how I got this information," he said. "But promise me you'll be careful. Call me if anything happens that seems unusual or unsettling."

"Now you're scaring me," she said.

"I don't mean to. I'm going to drive by later to check on your house. I won't stop, but I want you to know I'm out there."

His words warmed her. She started to tell him to stop by, but held back. Her feelings for Lucas—and his for her— weren't clear, and she didn't want to expect anything from either of them that they weren't ready to give. "Thank you," she said. "That makes me feel very safe."

Safe was good, but was it what she really wanted? Maybe it was time to think in terms of less safety and more adventure. Lucas might be the man she wanted as her guide.

GEORGE ANTON SAT behind his desk and didn't conceal his frustration with yet another round of questions from the deputy. "Yes, I own a handgun," he said. "No, I don't carry it around with me. And I've never threatened anyone with it."

Anton was dressed in a suit identical to the one Lucas had seen him in before. But today, Shaylin Brown wasn't with him. "So you weren't upset with Mrs. Weiss when she told you she was closing her bakery and wouldn't be able to fulfill the contract Dave Weiss made with you?" Logan asked.

Anton's scowl deepened. "Sandy Weiss told me she wanted to continue the contract. I'm supposed to pick up a new shipment of pastries from her next week. She never said anything about canceling the contract."

He planted both hands palms down on the desk, as if

about to shove up out of his chair. "I don't know why she's telling you these lies. First, she told you I wasn't paying her and her husband enough for the baked goods they provided and that's why they were in debt. That's not true. I've showed you the numbers to prove it. And she told you she was closing the bakery and canceling her contract with me, but she told me she wanted to continue the contract and wanted it to be even bigger. She told you I was carrying a gun and I wasn't."

"What would she have to gain by lying about you?" Lucas asked.

"Nothing," Anton said. "But whether she wants to end our contract or not, I have the option of canceling it myself, and I'll do so if she keeps spreading these lies about me."

"Someone shot out the front window of Weiss Bakery yesterday afternoon," Lucas said.

"Is that why you're asking all these questions about a gun?" Anton shook his head. "I wasn't anywhere near Eagle Mountain yesterday."

"I'm aware of that," Lucas said. "Do you know anyone who might do such a thing?"

"No." He leaned forward. "Look, I'm sorry the woman lost her husband. I liked Dave Weiss. He was a good man, I think. But he was just one of my clients. If I lose one, I find someone else to take his place. I'm not going to waste time trying to bully someone into continuing to do business with me. It doesn't make any sense."

Lucas stood. "Thank you for your time, Mr. Anton."

Lucas left the office, but he didn't return to Eagle Mountain. He turned toward the center of town and Red Mesa. At just after eleven in the morning, the restaurant was already busy. A hostess in a sleeveless black blouse and slim trousers greeted him just inside the door. "One for lunch?" she asked with a welcoming smile.

"I need to see Justin Trent," he said.

The smile faltered and her gaze swept over his khaki uniform once more. "Wait just a moment, please."

While he waited, he studied the award commendations that filled the wall behind the hostess's stand. Best local eatery year after year from the local newspaper. An environmental award, and one from a regional food and wine publication. More diners entered and gave him curious looks before being led to tables by a second young woman.

Justin Trent was a slender man several inches shorter than Lucas, dressed in an expensive-looking suit and highly polished shoes, his dark hair gelled and slicked straight back. "What can I help you with, Deputy?" he asked.

"I have a few questions for you, Mr. Trent," Lucas said. "Can we talk somewhere private?"

A trace of a frown creased Trent's forehead before it was banished. "Come this way," he said and turned to lead him away from the dining room.

They passed through an empty bar area and through a door into a dark-paneled office with a polished wood desk and shelves filled with more awards. Trent leaned back against the desk and crossed his arms over his chest. "What's this about?"

"George Anton came to see you yesterday afternoon."

"Yes, I told you when you called that he had just left. What is this all about?"

"Does George Anton carry a gun?"

"A gun!" The word exploded in a bark. "I don't know. I've never seen him with a gun. Why would he?" He gripped the edge of the desk with both hands. "Has George shot someone?"

"Not that I'm aware of," Lucas said. "Do you know a woman named Sandy Weiss?"

"She's Dave Weiss's wife, isn't she? Widow now, I guess."

"How well do you know her?"

"Not at all. I may have met her once, but I don't recall. Dave was my brother Jonas's friend, not mine."

"The Weisses supplied desserts to George Anton," Lucas said. "I believe you contract with Anton, also."

"Yes. He supplies lots of restaurants. Meats, vegetables, baked goods, all from different local sources." He straightened. "Is George involved in something illegal? Because I want no part of it."

"There's nothing illegal going on that I'm aware of," Lucas said. "I'm just trying to understand the arrangement Anton had with the Weisses."

"I don't know anything about it," Trent said.

"Thank you for your time." Lucas turned to leave.

"Wait," Trent said.

Lucas faced him once more.

"Let me ask you a question," Trent said. "What do you know about drug trafficking in Junction?"

Lucas hid his surprise. "There's a drug problem here," he said. "Mostly opioids. That's no secret. It's a problem in a lot of places."

"One of my workers, a sous-chef who's been with me for five years, was arrested yesterday for dealing," Trent said. "He was caught red-handed, apparently. I had no clue." He shook his head. "He's been one of my best employees. Never a hint he was involved in drugs. His lawyer tells me he doesn't take them, but he says he came across a deal that was too good to pass up. An easy way to make a lot of money. When I first saw your uniform, I figured you were here to talk about him."

"What kind of deal?" Lucas asked.

"I don't know. He's not saying, apparently hoping to bargain his way to a lesser sentence. But now I'm worried he wasn't the only one involved. He was supposedly dealing out of this restaurant and I can't have that. I won't have it."

"Do you think this has some connection to George Anton?" Lucas asked.

"No! I just... I'm trying to find out everything I can and I thought you might know something."

"I'm sorry, I can't help you."

Trent nodded. He looked older, truly worried.

Lucas left the restaurant and took out his phone.

"You miss me so much you can't stay away, is that it?" Del said when he answered Lucas's call.

"That's it," Lucas said. "What can you tell me about a sous-chef from Red Mesa who was arrested yesterday for dealing drugs out of the restaurant?"

"I heard something about that," Del said. "But you need to talk to Detective Jacobs in Vice. That was her collar."

"Is she around today?"

"I just saw her."

"I'm on my way."

Ten minutes later, Del met him in the hallway outside the bullpen. "What's this about?" he asked.

"I'm looking into a connection with a case I have in Eagle Mountain," he said.

"I told Jacobs you were on your way over to see her," Del said. "You rated a big smile. Word is, she and the dude from the city that she was dating split up. You ought to ask her out."

Lucas shook his head. Detective Michaela Jacobs was a striking brunette with a wicked sense of humor. A few weeks ago, he would have been flattered to learn that he'd merited a smile from her. But a few weeks ago, he hadn't been interested in dating anyone. And he hadn't met Anna Trent.

"Lucas, when are you coming back to Junction?" Michaela looked up from her desk, smile set to dazzle. Yes, there was definite interest there. He was flattered but felt nothing in return.

"I should be back in a month or so," he said. "I won't keep you long. What can you tell me about this sous-chef from Red Mesa you arrested for dealing?"

"He's not the first restaurant employee we've pulled in." She sat back, all business now. "There's apparently a whole network of people working out of restaurants. But we haven't found their supplier, or even how they're getting the drugs."

"Any connection to a man called George Anton?"

Her eyebrows rose. "How do you know George?"

"I'm investigating a suspicious death in Eagle Mountain and his name has come up."

"We've been keeping an eye on George," she said. "He supplies every restaurant where we've made an arrest, but we can't find anything tying him to the drug smuggling. Do you think he killed this guy?"

"I don't have any evidence of that. The man who died was one of his suppliers."

"If you come up with any connection to drugs—fentanyl, mostly—let me know. The supply has really expanded in the past year and we think it's coming from this group of restaurants, but we can't pin anything down."

"I will."

She relaxed again and leaned forward. "Maybe we could get together next time you're in the area. I'll buy you a drink."

"Thanks," he said. "But I've sort of met someone. In Eagle Mountain."

She laughed. "'Sort of met'?"

"I've met her. We went out once, but it's a little complicated. She's a widow and maybe not ready to get involved yet."

"Then *maybe* you should ask her if she wants to get involved. With you." Michaela laughed again. "Good luck, Deputy. And if things don't work out with the widow, I'll still buy you that drink."

"HOW ARE THINGS with you and Lucas?" Gemma asked as she and Anna sat down to eat lunch at the worktable Friday afternoon. The whine of a power drill and banging of hammers disturbed the normally peaceful vibe of the store, but Anna was thrilled to have her new shelves. Bobby had offered to come in after the store closed, but she hated to ask him to work late. In the meantime, she had hung a Construction in Progress, Watch Your Step sign on the door and retreated with Gemma to the table at the back of the front room.

"There is no 'thing' with me and Lucas," she said. They had eaten a couple of meals together. She liked talking to him. She liked kissing him. But a second kiss had never happened and, in any case, it was far too early for there to be any "thing" between them. She unwrapped her sandwich and frowned at it.

"How long has that been in the refrigerator here?" Gemma asked.

"Only a couple of days." She took a bite and chewed. The sandwich was a little dry, but she couldn't let it go to waste.

Gemma drizzled dressing on her salad. "Have they found whoever shot the window out of the bakery?" she asked.

"How would I know?"

"I thought Lucas might have said."

"Do you think all we talk about is his job?" They did talk about that a lot, but Gemma didn't have to know that.

"I hope not. When do you see him again?"

"You're really nosy, did you know that?" Anna said.

Gemma grinned. "I like to think of it as caring about my friends."

Gemma was a good friend, the kind you could call on to listen to your problems, or help you bury a body. "I don't know when we'll see each other again," she said. "We're both very busy."

"If he doesn't call you, you should call him," Gemma said.

"Gemma."

She held up both hands, surrendering. "Okay, okay. I'll back off."

Bobby stuck his head around the shelf that divided the workspace from the rest of the store. "Want to come take a look?" he asked.

Anna abandoned the half-eaten sandwich and followed him up front, Gemma right behind her. The smell of sawdust and fresh wood stain almost overwhelmed the more famil-iar odor of wool, but the results were worth a little disruption to the store's usual atmosphere. "They're perfect," she said. She ran her hand along the smooth wood, picturing the diamond-shaped cubbies filled with colorful yarn skeins.

"I'm glad you like them," Bobby said. "We'll get out of your hair now."

"You're going to be able to display a lot of yarn with this design," Gemma said. "Do you know how you want to lay things out?"

"I have a plan." Anna started toward the front counter and the drawer where she had stashed her notebook. But she only took a couple of steps before the door opened and Lucas entered.

He was in his khaki uniform, sans leather coat as today was sunny and warmer. He removed his sunglasses and his brown eyes fixed on her. "Hi, Anna," he said.

"Hi, Lucas." They stood there, smiling at each other, but neither speaking. Anna felt a little like a girl with a crush—something she would have sworn she was far too old for, but apparently not.

"That's everything, then." Bobby picked up a plastic bin full of tools.

"Thank you so much," Anna said. "Everything looks perfect."

"No problem," he said. "Call me anytime you need anything. And let me know if you decide to sell the Dart."

Lucas watched him leave then turned back to Anna. "The Dart?" he asked.

"It's a car Jonas was fixing up. I probably should pass it on to someone who will care about it as much as he did." She moved closer to him and lowered her voice, though she knew Gemma was listening and would probably overhear every word. "What brings you here?"

"Turns out I have the night free. I know it's last minute, but would you like to have dinner?"

Yes! This is what she shouted inside. What she actually said was, "That sounds nice."

"Is six thirty too early?"

"Six thirty would be great." She would ask Gemma to close up and leave the shop early enough to change and get ready.

"Great. I'll see you then." He gave her a last long look, then turned and walked out.

"You may not think there's any 'thing' between you two, but his eyes said different." Gemma stepped out from behind the divider. "I'll close up the shop tonight," she said.

"Thanks." Anna squeezed Gemma's arms and walked back to the worktable, though really, she felt as if she were dancing or floating, carried along by this wonderful anticipation.

At five thirty, Gemma nagged Anna into leaving the shop. They had spent most of the afternoon arranging yarn in the new cubbies, and they weren't done yet. Everything they moved into the new display left a gap elsewhere that had to be filled. What Anna had envisioned as a few hours' work was clearly going to take much longer. "We can work on this more tomorrow," Gemma said. "Go. Make yourself gorgeous."

"I'm not aiming for gorgeous," Anna said. "Just moderately attractive."

"Don't sell yourself short," Gemma said. "You can definitely do gorgeous."

Anna laughed, snapped on Jacquie's lead, and she and the dog headed home.

At the house, she started toward her bedroom to shower

and change, but took a detour to the kitchen, suddenly starving. The half a stale sandwich she had eaten for lunch had vanished long ago. She needed to eat something to tide her over until dinner was served.

She spotted the bakery box on the counter and her mouth watered. There was one cupcake left—perfect. She opened the box and admired the pink-frosted cake then peeled off the wrapper and broke the cake in half. The one she had enjoyed yesterday was a plain chocolate cupcake, but this one was one of Dave's Surprise Cakes. A hollow inside the cake contained a swirl of rich chocolate ganache.

For nonedible surprises, Dave used a plastic capsule—the kind found in gum machines—to contain the charm, ring or other object. "I don't worry about anyone accidentally swallowing that big plastic capsule," he had explained to Anna when they were discussing the cakes for her and Jonas's wedding. "The last thing I need is someone suing me because their girlfriend accidentally ate her engagement ring."

The cupcakes for their wedding had contained silver charms that represented aspects of her and Jonas—a hammer and saw for him, knitting needles in a ball of yarn and a tiny pair of scissors for her. In her jewelry box, she kept a charm bracelet with all the different mementos from those desserts.

Smiling at the memory, she took a bite of the cupcake, letting the chocolate melt on her tongue. The cake was fresh, though she wondered if Sandy had gone a little overboard on the red food coloring in the frosting on top. Anna could taste the bitter chemical tang from the coloring. Still, the chocolate cake did a good job of making up for that. She finished the cake then deposited the bakery box in the trash, ready for the rest of her evening.

She showered and changed, fed Jacquie, then returned to her bathroom to do her makeup and hair. But as she looked in the mirror, a wave of dizziness swept over her. She clutched the edge of the counter, fighting a sudden onslaught of nausea. Then she sank slowly to her knees, too dizzy and sick to move. She pressed her head to the side of the cabinet and closed her eyes. She had had food poisoning once before, years ago. Had it felt like this? Her only real memory of that time was feeling sicker than she ever had before.

Chapter Fourteen

Lucas paused at the bottom of the steps to brush a hand through his hair. The knowledge that Anna hadn't hesitated to accept his invitation encouraged him. He was sure she was attracted to him, but he worried her lingering feelings for her late husband would prevent her from acting on that attraction. He knew only one way to find out. He mounted the steps and rang the doorbell.

Inside, Jacquie barked and he heard the click of her toe-nails on the hardwood floor as she raced to the door. She pressed her nose to the window to the left of the door and barked again. Lucas smiled, anticipating Anna's greeting.

But the door remained shut and no footsteps moved toward it. Jacquie barked again and Lucas pressed the button for the doorbell. The chimes sounded clearly, but even if they hadn't, Anna couldn't have missed Jacquie's increasingly frantic clamor.

He knocked. "Anna! It's Lucas! Is everything okay?"

Maybe she was in the shower. He checked the time. Six thirty-five. He took out his phone and dialed Anna's number. The phone rang and rang then went to voice mail. He ended the call and tried the doorknob. Locked. Could he break it down?

Before he could decide, the door eased open. Anna, gray-faced and bleary-eyed, sagged against the doorframe. Jacquie ceased barking and came to press against her mistress, face full of concern.

"Lucas, I'm so sorry," Anna said, her voice breathy and weak.

"What's happened?" he asked, alarmed. "You don't look well." Probably not the thing to say to a woman you wanted to date, but it was the truth. Anna looked ill.

"I don't know what's come over me." She covered her eyes with one hand. "I'm not feeling well."

She pushed herself away from the door frame and swayed. Lucas caught hold of her and steadied her. "I'm so sorry," she said again, then pulled back and staggered away.

He stepped into the house and followed her. He found her kneeling in front of the toilet in the hallway bathroom, being sick. "Oh, Anna," he said, and knelt behind her to hold back her hair. When she had finished retching, she sat up, one hand to her mouth.

"Lucas, this is terrible," she said.

He patted her shoulder, stood and wet a rag at the sink. He wiped her cheeks then gave it to her, left once more, and returned shortly with a glass of water. "Just sip this," he instructed, and handed it to her. Then he flushed the toilet, closed the lid, and sat on it, facing her. How many times had he done this for Jenny when she was sick from the chemotherapy?

"It must be food poisoning," Anna said. She pressed the washcloth to her cheek. "Gemma told me not to eat that chicken sandwich. I should have listened to her." Her eyes met his, watery with tears. "I'm sorry I won't be able to keep our date."

"That's okay." He looked into her eyes and noted that her pupils were slightly dilated. "Are you sure you're okay?" he asked. "Do you need to go to the hospital?"

"No!" She sat straighter, suddenly more alert. She gathered her legs under her as if to rise, and he stood to help her. "I'm already feeling better. I threw up once before you got here. Whatever it was, I think it's mostly out of my system now." She laid the washcloth on the edge of the sink and leaned forward to study her reflection. "Give me a minute and we'll talk."

He left the bathroom and waited in the hall while water ran. She emerged smelling of mint toothpaste, her hair combed, still pale, but the gray cast was gone. "Let's go in the living room," she said.

She didn't object when he put his arm around her and led her to the sofa. Her skin was warm but dry and she seemed steadier on her feet. He settled her on the sofa, then went into the kitchen and found crackers and flavored seltzer. "These may help," he said, bringing them to her.

"Thanks."

He sat beside her, Jacquie on her other side, while she nibbled crackers and sipped the soda. "Before you got sick, how was your day going?" he asked.

"Good," she said. "We had some new shelves installed in the shop, something I've wanted since I opened the place. The guy who was just leaving when you arrived was the carpenter. He used to work for Jonas."

"The one who wants to buy the Dart."

"That's right." She set aside her glass and the crackers. "Would you like to see it?"

"I would," he said. "But it can wait until you're feeling better."

"I'm much better." She stood. "Let me show you."

He didn't detect any signs of weakness or dizziness as she moved through the kitchen to a door that led to the garage. She flipped on the light then moved to a tarp-covered vehicle on the far side of the space. He helped her fold back the tarp to reveal a red-and-Bondo-gray classic Dodge Dart, the insides gutted. "Jonas found it in a client's barn five years ago and bought it for a few hundred dollars." She smoothed her hand along the hood. "He spent a lot more than that restoring it, but I know he loved every minute of it. It's so sad he didn't get to finish it."

And she had kept the half-finished project in her garage all these months since Jonas's death. Because it reminded her of him? Because it made her feel closer to him? Probably all that and more.

She looked up at him. "I should have sold it a long time ago, but I don't know." She shrugged. "It almost felt like I was betraying him. Silly, I know. Do you have something like that from Jenny that you saved? Or do men not do that?"

His instinct was to look away, to brush off the question. But she deserved his honesty. "I don't have anything like that," he said. "But I didn't love Jenny the way you loved Jonas."

"What do you mean?"

He took her arm. "Let's go back inside and I'll tell you the story." Better they both be sitting down for this.

They settled onto the sofa and she sat back and studied him. "What's the story?" she asked.

He looked up at the ceiling, as if he might find the right words written there. "Once upon a time there was a man named Lucas who dated a woman he liked a lot. He loved her, but not enough to marry her. Not enough to make a commitment to stay with her forever. He thought she understood that, but after they moved in together, he realized she believed there would be more—a ring, a proposal, a ceremony, a happily-ever-after.

"He wanted to make her happy. To give her all the things she deserved, but in the end, he let her down. He couldn't commit to marriage. So she started packing her things and looking for an apartment, and they tried to part as friends. Then she started feeling sick and went to the doctor and found out she had cancer. They stayed together and he looked after her. But she never got the happy ending she wanted."

He rested his elbows on his knees and hunched forward, trying not to read rejection in the silence that stretched between them. Then her hand caressed his back. "Oh, Lucas," she said.

"Her sister hates me," he said. "She thought I should have married Jenny anyway, knowing she was dying."

"That's very unfair," Anna said.

He straightened and found the courage to look at her. Her expression was soft, sympathetic. "I was going to do it, too. I got a ring and proposed and everything. But Jenny was smart and she saw through me. She told me no, that we made better friends than lovers."

"You were a good friend to her," Anna said. "You stayed with her until the end. You loved her in a different way."

"I think she knew that, but I still felt like a terrible person," he said.

"Lucas, you didn't do anything wrong. It would have been dishonest to let her think otherwise."

"Maybe dishonest, but would it have been kinder?"

"Maybe, but you can't know that." She tucked her hair behind one ear and looked down at her lap. "I know in the last months Jonas was alive, the best thing I could do for him was to listen when he wanted to talk and to be a presence in the room when he was too weak to speak. You were those things for Jenny, I think."

"I still feel guilty."

"Welcome to the club." She sighed. "Guilt is a part of death, I think. No matter how much we do for our loved ones, there is always the thought that maybe we could have done more. What if I had insisted Jonas go to the doctor the first time he'd come home complaining of a back ache? But the man worked construction. Aches and pains were part of the job."

"So how do you deal with the guilt?"

"Maybe I hang on to a car he loved, even though I never liked it all that much." Anna's smile surprised her, almost as much as the realization that she could now see the humor in such a sad situation.

"Maybe now you're ready to move on," he said.

She leaned closer to him and slid one hand across his back to rest at his waist. It was an intimate touch; one that made her aware of the heat building within her. A longing for things she had thought out of reach. "How do you know when you're ready to move on, to take the next step?" she asked.

He angled toward her, his eyes locked to hers. "I think you have to simply move and see where your steps take you."

She slid her hand up his back to cup his head and lifted her lips to his. He stilled, his mouth against hers, caught and held. He made a sound in the back of his throat like a groan and nudged against her. His mouth moved, and his hands, gathering her close and pressing her against him.

A flood of sensation—relief, exhilaration and desire—rocketed through her. She caressed the nape of his neck, warm and silky, the ends of his close-cropped hair tickling the backs of her fingers, and slanted her mouth to his, wanting to explore every sensitive millimeter of him.

And she wanted to be closer. She rose up to straddle him. He was hard, his erection pressed against her. The sensation made her feel hot and lit up inside, sparks at every erogenous zone. She kissed him more passionately still, eyes closed on the edge of complete abandon.

Then he pushed her away, just enough that he could look at her. "Are you okay with this?" he asked. "If you're still feeling unwell, we can wait."

"I feel great," she said. "Fully recovered, I promise." She had never shaken off a case of food poisoning this quickly, but maybe sex—or at least arousal—had health benefits she didn't know about. She leaned in to plant a soft kiss on his jaw. "I want this," she said. "I've wanted it for a while now."

"I want it, too." She thought he would kiss her again, but instead he continued to look at her, his hands at her waist, still holding her a little apart from him. "You are so beautiful," he said.

Another side effect of desire, she thought, since her hair was uncombed, her face bare of makeup and probably too pale. But he made her feel beautiful, and that counted for a lot. It helped make her less nervous, and his own honesty with her made her want to return the favor. "I'm a little nervous," she said. "We might need to take it slow." She trailed one hand down his chest, unable to look him in the eye. Doing so would make her forget what she needed to say. "Don't feel bad if I cry a little. I'm a pretty emotional person."

"We'll take it as slow as you need," he said, and started with a long, slow kiss.

Eventually, she led him to the bedroom, where they undressed, also slowly, and the sight of him, naked, made her heart race. Then she registered the adoring way he was looking at her and felt a little dizzy, but in a good way. She sat on the bed and took his hand, intending to pull him down. He hesitated, and pain flickered through his eyes.

"What is it?" she asked.

He shook his head. "It's nothing."

She considered how she might have felt if they had been in his apartment, in his bedroom. "Don't worry," she said. "I redid this room last summer. This is a brand-new bed."

He looked sheepish, but also relieved. "It wouldn't have mattered," he said.

"It matters to me." She hadn't purchased the bed with the idea of making love to another man in it; she had wanted to spend the night not sharing space with all the memories of her and Jonas together. Now she could make new memories with Lucas.

They lay facing each other, studying one another like explorers mapping new territory. He discovered the scar on her shin from a bad fall in rocky terrain while training Jacquie, and she smiled at the almost perfectly heart-shaped birthmark on his hip. And then looking and touching turned to tasting and stroking. "Do you like this?" he asked. "How about this?"

"What if we do this?" she suggested, and so they negotiated their passion.

Her body woke as if from a long sleep and every sensation felt new. She arched against him and cried out with pleasure, and couldn't seem to stop smiling. By the time he rolled on a condom and positioned himself against her, she welcomed him eagerly.

I still remember how to do this, she thought as they began to move together. She closed her eyes and surrendered to the flood of emotions, letting the wonderful tension build, moving toward release.

In the end, she didn't cry, but he did. Silent tears clung to his lashes as he leaned forward to kiss her as they clung together, sated. "I didn't know I could be this happy again," he said.

"I know." She kissed his eyes, tasting the salt. The worst thing in the world had happened to them both but they could still find joy. It was a kind of miracle, one that deserved both his tears and the smile she couldn't erase from her lips.

ANNA WOKE THE next morning to the sound of the shower running. She looked beside her in bed, at the rumpled sheets and the imprint of Lucas's head still on the pillow, and a warm thrill spread through her. She hugged herself, scarcely daring to believe how happy she was.

The bathroom door opened and Lucas emerged, towel around his hips, the muscles of his arms and shoulders bunching as he rubbed a second towel over his hair.

Anna sat up, pulling the sheet around her. "Good morning."

"Good morning." He smiled and moved to the side of the bed to kiss her. "How are you feeling?"

"I'm feeling great." A little tired, a little sore, and not ready to face a huge meal, but considering how sick she had been when he'd first arrived, she felt fantastic. "I think I'm fully recovered."

"That's good," he said. "I didn't want to wake you, but I have to be at work early today."

"That's okay," she said. "I have training at Search and Rescue headquarters this morning." She reached for her robe and slid into it, aware of him watching her.

Before she could cinch it closed, he moved to put his hands around her waist and pull her close. "I really do hate to leave," he said, nuzzling her neck.

"Mmm." She pressed against him then forced herself to pull away. "You're very tempting, but we'd both better get dressed."

He sighed. "You're right." He picked up the clothes he had worn last night from the chair by the bed and began to dress. She indulged herself in openly admiring him. This was a picture that would carry her through even the most boring training class.

Only when he was buckling his belt did she move into the bathroom to get ready herself.

When she emerged ten minutes later, he was waiting with a cup of coffee. "I can't stay to eat," he said. "I need to get home and change into my uniform."

"Maybe I'll see you after your shift," she said.

"Maybe. What are you training for today?"

"Wilderness first-aid triage. There's a lecture, then some practical exercises." She took Jacquie's leash from a hook by the back door and the dog danced over to her. "I need to walk her before I head to the class. She's not going to be happy about being left behind. When I put on my Search and Rescue jacket, she thinks she's going to work."

"Poor abandoned baby," he said, and rubbed the dog's ears. Jacquie leaned against his leg, momentarily forgetting about her walk.

They said goodbye and Anna walked Jacquie along their usual route to the town park, around the track twice, then back home. She fed the dog, made sure she had plenty of water, and slipped out the door while Jacquie was still eating.

All of the rookies and most of the veteran Search and Rescue volunteers gathered at SAR headquarters, a large concrete-floored building with roll-up metal doors that housed all the search and rescue equipment and provided meeting space for the group. Anna sat with fellow rookies Grace Wilcox, Nancy Phillips and Caleb Edmond.

Chris Mercer soon joined them. The blue-haired artist wasn't a rookie, but she had been away from SAR for a year while she'd served as artist-in-residence at Rocky Mountain National Park. "I've taken this class before," she said as she settled onto the folding chair next to Anna. "But it's been a few years. I figured it would be a good idea to refresh my memory."

Nurse Danny Irwin, a veteran volunteer, was teaching the class, assisted by Hannah Richards, an Eagle Mountain paramedic and current medical officer for the group. Anna forced herself to focus on the slide presentation that began the class, outlining the most common injuries they might encounter during backcountry rescues.

But when the course shifted to a lecture on identifying, assessing and treating a lengthy list of possible injuries, her mind kept drifting to last night and her wonderful encounter with Lucas. The evening had been so much better than her fantasies. She had thought she would be nervous, but they had been so into each other, she really hadn't had an opportunity to overthink what was happening.

"Let's take a break and, when we come back, we'll go through some mock exercises," Danny finally announced.

Anna and Nancy headed to the ladies' room then joined the others at a table set with coffee and tea, doughnuts and fruit. Anna was pouring hot water over a tea bag when phones began going off all over the room, including her own.

"Somebody is lucky today," Ryan Welch said as he looked at his phone. "We've got a callout and everyone is already right here."

Sheri was already on the phone with the 9-1-1 dispatcher. "A helitracks chopper spotted someone in a vehicle stuck up on Black Eagle pass," she said.

"That road is still closed, isn't it?" Danny asked. "There's still a ton of snow up there."

"It is," Tony Meisner confirmed. "This person either didn't know that, or thought he could get through."

"It happens every few years," Ryan said. "People look on a map and see the shortest route to their destination is on a road that they don't realize is four-wheel-drive only or open only seasonally."

"Ten years ago a couple froze to death when their mini-van got stuck and they tried to hike out," Sheri said. "This guy is lucky the helicopter pilot spotted him." She surveyed the group. "We'll take the Beast and a couple of four-wheel-drive vehicles, but we'll probably have to stop at some point and snowshoe in. We don't know how long the driver has been up there. The chopper pilot said he only saw one person, but it's always possible there were passengers in the vehicle, so let's be prepared."

Within ten minutes, Anna was in Grace's Jeep alongside Chris and Nancy, following the Beast, a specially equipped

Search and Rescue Jeep, up Dixon Pass, toward the turnoff to the backcountry road over Black Eagle pass.

"We're following a vehicle's tracks," Tony radioed shortly after the SAR caravan turned onto the Jeep road. Ten minutes later, everyone was forced to stop.

Anna piled out of the vehicle with the others and Sheri walked back to them. "There's a little snowslide blocking the road," Sheri said. "We'll have to snowshoe from here."

Everyone donned snowshoes and slipped on packs and began the climb up the road. "The helicopter pilot said he spotted the stranded motorist almost to the summit of the pass," Sheri said.

"How did he make it all the way up there?" Nancy asked.

"After you pass the Homestead Mine, it's too narrow to turn around," Tony said. "He probably just kept going forward until he couldn't move anymore. There's no phone service up here, and no one else was going to come along. If he didn't have snowshoes, hiking down was going to be pretty grueling. The snow's at least four feet deep."

Even snowshoeing was pretty strenuous. Before long, they were all unzipping jackets and stripping off hats. Anna marched along behind Grace, legs already aching, but she wasn't going to complain. This was what rescue work was—lots of hard work on behalf of a stranger.

Another half hour passed and a shout rose up from the head of the line, the message passed back to Anna and the other rookies in the rear of the column. "They've spotted the car," Grace told Anna.

Moments later, they were gathered around a very cold and very grateful young man. Darryl Singh's teeth chattered as he thanked them and accepted blankets and hot packs, and hot chocolate from a thermos. "I was trying to get to Eagle Mountain," he said. "I've never been here before and the map said this was the shortest way." He looked around him, at the snow piled higher than his head on three sides, the nose of his small sedan buried in a wall of snow. "I'm from Florida," he said. "I've never seen so much snow in my life."

"Who were you going to see in Eagle Mountain?" Sheri asked.

He shook his head. "Oh, that doesn't matter."

"If someone is expecting you, they're probably worried," Carrie said. "We can radio and let them know you're all right."

"I was just making a delivery, as a favor for a friend," he said.

"Who was the delivery for?" Sheri pressed.

"A bakery."

"Do you mean Weiss Bakery?" Anna asked.

"Yes, that's it." Singh looked pained. "I don't even know what the package is. I'm just doing it as a favor. And to earn extra money." He looked back at his car, expression mournful. "How much is it going to cost me to get back down from here?"

"We'll take you to town for free," Danny said. "But you'll have to hire a wrecker to come up and get your car. And it won't be cheap."

Singh looked as if he wanted to cry.

"How long have you been up here?" Tony asked.

Singh pushed back the blanket to check his watch. "Five hours. I was wondering how long it would take to freeze to death."

"You're lucky a helicopter pilot spotted you and notified us," Sheri said.

He nodded, expression still sorrowful. "Yes. I am very lucky."

They had brought extra snowshoes, and fitted Singh with a pair and started back down the road with him in the middle of the group. They had traveled halfway back to their vehicles when he let out a wail. "The package!" he cried. "I forgot the package for the bakery!"

"Leave it," Tony said. "You can get it later when they retrieve your car. It's not worth risking hypothermia to get it back."

He looked as if he wanted to protest, but Tony slung an arm around his shoulder. "Come on," he said. "You really do need to get somewhere warmer."

Back at the cars, they settled Singh into the Beast. "We'll take you to the sheriff's office and they'll help you arrange to take care of your vehicle and get you back home," Sheri said. "How are you feeling?"

"Very upset," he said. "But warmer."

"Warm is good," she said.

The caravan started back down the mountain. "I don't think that guy knows how lucky he is," Grace said as she piloted her Jeep through the icy ruts in the Beast's wake. "He didn't have any kind of emergency gear in his car and he wasn't dressed for the weather. He was wearing tennis shoes and didn't even have a winter coat."

"He thought he was making a quick trip to Eagle Mountain," Chris said.

"I wonder what he was delivering to the bakery," Anna said.

"I guess some kind of specialty ingredient or something," Nancy said.

Back at SAR headquarters, everyone pitched in to clean up the materials from the training class. Sheri and Tony drove Darryl Singh to the sheriff's department and everyone else left for home or work or wherever they needed to be.

Anna started home but detoured to the bakery instead. She found Sandy decorating cupcakes, each chocolate-frosted cake topped with a pink or blue rosebud. "These are for a baby shower tomorrow," Sandy said. "As soon as I finish them, I'm closing for the day."

"Do you know Darryl Singh?" Anna asked.

Sandy shook her head. "Never heard of him."

"I just came from a search and rescue call." Anna settled onto a stool beside Sandy's worktable. "He was stuck up on Black Eagle pass. He saw the route on the map and thought it was a shortcut to Eagle Mountain."

Sandy snorted. "I guess he's not from around here?"

"He said he was from Florida."

"He's lucky he didn't freeze to death up there."

"He said he was on his way to Eagle Mountain to deliver something to you."

Sandy stilled. "What was he delivering to me?"

"He didn't say. He just said a friend had paid him to drive the package over to you."

"Where is the package now?"

"He left it back in his car. Do you know what it is?"

Sandy shook her head and went back to adding icing rosebuds to the top of the cupcakes. "No idea. Maybe it was something Dave ordered before he died."

"Do you get deliveries like that very often?" Anna asked.

"We get supplies from all over the place," Sandy said. "Whoever can give us the best price. That's how a small business has to operate to make a profit."

"It just seemed odd to have a guy like that driving something here personally on a Saturday morning."

Sandy laid aside the icing bag and faced Anna. "Why are you so interested? What do you care where we get our supplies?"

"It just struck me as odd," Anna said, determined not to let Sandy cow her.

"It isn't odd. There are lots of specialty suppliers in food services." Sandy picked up the icing bag. "These bags come from a place in Denmark. They gave us the best deal, so that's who we bought from. If somebody in Junction or Denver or Timbuktu has what we need at a good price, we're going to buy from them. Not everything has to come from one big wholesaler, you know."

Anna nodded. "Okay. Well, whatever it is, I hope you don't need it right away. Until Mr. Singh gets his car hauled down, your package is stuck up on Black Eagle pass."

"I'll manage." Sandy picked up the tray of cupcakes, carried it to a glassed-in cooler, and slid it inside.

"Thanks again for the cupcakes you sent home with me," Anna said, hoping to thaw some of the frost that had chilled Sandy's attitude. "They were delicious, as always."

Sandy frowned at her. "So you ate the cupcakes? Both of them?"

"I did. I had the second one yesterday afternoon." She grimaced. "I guess it was kind of wasted, though." She rubbed her stomach. "I made the mistake of eating a sandwich for lunch that had been in the refrigerator at my shop for more than a few days. Not long after I ate that cupcake, I was sick as could be. Food poisoning."

"How are you feeling now?" Sandy asked.

"Much better. I threw up a couple of times and I guess

I got it all out of my system." She shook her head. "I'll be a little pickier about what I eat from now on," she said. "Jonas always teased me about my sensitive stomach. He could eat all kinds of things, but if something is the least off, I can't handle it."

"I need to close up now." Sandy walked to the door and turned the sign to Closed.

"I'll leave you to it," Anna said. "I just wanted to let you know about that package."

"Forget about the package," Sandy said. "I'm sure it's nothing important."

Anna left and drove home.

Sandy had always been a hard person to read, but lately she confused Anna even more. One moment she was asking Anna for help and giving her cupcakes, the next she was ticked off that Anna had stopped by. A lot of people might have written her off, but Anna remembered how grief had played with her own emotions. She had cycled from anger to despair in the blink of an eye, and had probably annoyed more than one person who'd tried to help her. She didn't want to abandon Sandy to go through that storm alone. For now, at least, she would continue to check on her and try to help her, if not for Sandy's sake, then for Dave. He had loved her and he would appreciate that Anna was trying to be there for her.

THAT AFTERNOON, Anna stood on the side of the driveway and watched as Bobby winched the Dart onto his trailer. Bobby's wife, Melody, eight months pregnant, stood beside her. "Bobby is so excited about getting this car," Melody said. "Though I don't know when he's going to have time to work on it, between the business and the new baby." She rubbed the swell of her abdomen and smiled.

"Jonas would be glad to know it's going to someone who will love it as much as he did," Anna said.

Melody's smile faded. "This must be hard for you," she said.

"Not as hard as I thought it would be, really." Anna turned to Melody. "I guess that's a good sign that it's time to let go."

"We would have been happy to pay you for the Dart," Melody said. "I'm sure it's worth a lot of money."

"It's worth more to me knowing it's going to you. I'm sure that's what Jonas would have wanted."

Bobby moved around the trailer to join them. "All set," he said. His grin made him look very young. "Thanks again."

"Thank you for giving it a good home." Anna moved toward him to shake hands, but he wrapped his arms around her and pulled her close in a hug. "Don't be a stranger," he said.

"I won't."

She watched them go, then closed the garage door and went inside the house. She felt lighter. Not happy, exactly, but not as sad, either. She really was letting go.

Moving on. She took out her phone.

I just gave away the Dart to Bobby Fitch.

Lucas's reply came quickly.

How are you feeling?

Good. It was time.

Good.

Want to come over tonight?

I'd like that.

She hesitated, hand hovering over the screen. Bring a toothbrush, she typed. She intended for him to stay with her all night.

HOURS LATER, after dinner and an evening of leisurely love-making, the tinny chimes of his ringtone pulled Lucas from sleep—the kind of sleep where waking feels like surfacing from deep under water. By the time he struggled to open his eyes, Anna was sitting up in bed beside him, the blanket pulled to her shoulders, staring at the phone that vibrated and buzzed on the bedside table. He grabbed the phone and swiped to answer the call. "Hello?"

"Deputy Malone, this is Shaylin Brown. I'm sorry to wake you so early on a Sunday, but I'm worried about George."

Lucas shifted his gaze to the clock on the bedside table. Six fourteen glowed in red numerals. Not the middle of the night, but early for a call from someone who was practically a stranger. "What about George?" he asked.

"He didn't come home last night." Shaylin's voice was ragged, as if she had been shouting, or crying. "I keep calling his cell phone and I don't get an answer. He's not at the office. None of his friends or best clients have heard from him."

"Have you contacted the Junction police?" Lucas asked, becoming more awake by the moment.

"I did. They told me I can file a missing person's report, but they said a grown man failing to come home isn't that unusual. But it is. George is always home by nine. Usually earlier."

"Do you and Mr. Anton live together?" Lucas asked.

"Yes. And he always comes home. He calls if he's going to be late."

Lucas ran a hand through his hair. "When was the last time you saw him or spoke to him?" he asked.

"At the office yesterday afternoon. He said he was driving to Eagle Mountain later that evening to see Sandy Weiss. He said he'd meet me at the house, and not to worry if he was late. But he never came home at all. He doesn't answer his phone. I tried contacting Mrs. Weiss, but she's not answering, either."

Lucas could have told Shaylin that this wasn't really his jurisdiction or his case, but the connection to Sandy Weiss interested him. "Was it usual for George to meet with clients that late in the day, especially on a weekend?" he asked.

"He meets with them when people are available," she said. "He often meets with restaurant owners in the evening, but sometimes with suppliers, too."

"Did George indicate there was anything unusual about this meeting with Mrs. Weiss?" he asked. "Was he fearful of any kind of trouble?"

"He was going to ask her about the things you had told him about her wanting to close the business and stop paying on the loan he had made to Dave. He said he wanted to work something out with her."

"Was George angry about that?" Lucas asked.

"No. That wasn't George. He wants to help people. He wants to make a living while he does so, but he loves putting people together who can help each other. He loves his work. But after what happened with Dave Weiss, I'm scared. What if whoever hurt Dave goes after George?" Her voice broke.

"I want you to be honest with me, Shaylin," he said. "Was George involved in any way with dealing drugs?"

"Absolutely not!" Her voice rose and she talked faster, even more agitated. "George heard there was a group of people selling drugs out of restaurants. He knew some people who got arrested, and the local cops questioned him about it more than once. But he didn't have anything to do with it, and he swore he would turn in anyone he found out was involved. He had a younger sister who died of an overdose when she was twenty-two and he's been absolutely set against drugs since then."

It was a good story, but was it true? Michaela had told him the Junction cops were watching George Anton and hadn't found any evidence against him, but he wouldn't be the first dealer to outsmart the police. "I want you to call the Junction sheriff's department and ask to speak to Del Alvarez," he said. "You tell him your story, and that I sent you. He'll help you."

"I'll do that, but will you at least look for George in Eagle Mountain?"

"I'll drive over to the Weisses' place and ask Sandy if she's heard from George," Lucas said.

"Please call me as soon as you hear anything," she said. "I've been up all night worrying."

"I will." He ended the call and turned to look at Anna, who was still sitting up in bed, watching him. "George Anton is missing," he said. "He was supposed to be on his way to Eagle Mountain to meet with Sandy Weiss yesterday evening and he hasn't been heard from since."

"You need to talk to Sandy," she said.

"Yeah." He glanced at the clock. "And the sooner, the better."

"I'll make coffee." She pushed back the covers and he had a tantalizing glimpse of her, naked, before she pulled on her robe. He would have liked nothing better than to pull her back into bed and spend the day making love to her. But Shailyn's barely suppressed panic over George's whereabouts cooled his desire. He still had little proof that Dave Weiss hadn't committed suicide, but too many things associated with the Weiss Bakery didn't make sense. He and the rest of the sheriff's department were always one step behind everyone involved in this case, from the anonymous note-writer to the person who had shattered the window of the bakery. Maybe this was his chance to get one step ahead for a change.

Chapter Fifteen

Anna set coffee to brew and returned to the bedroom to watch Lucas dress. She wasn't going to get tired of watching him do anything for a long while, she decided. She still tingled with the memory of their lovemaking last night. Why had she waited so long? "Let me call Sandy," she said. "She's more likely to answer a call from me at this hour, I would think."

"That's a good idea." He threaded his belt through the loops of his slacks and fastened the buckle. "Don't say anything about George. Just tell her I need to stop by and talk to her."

"All right." She pulled out her phone and found the number for Sandy and Dave's home. The number was still tagged as "Dave-Home." She hit the button to dial and waited while the phone rang and rang. Then it fell silent, not even going to voice mail. Next, she tried Sandy's cell phone. This time she received the message that said, "You have reached a number that is no longer in service."

"That's so odd," she said. "The number is programmed into my phone, so I know it's right." She punched in the number for the bakery. It rang and rang. "No one's answering at the bakery, either."

"Maybe she's busy with something and can't get to the phone." He finished putting on his shoes and straightened. "I'll try the bakery and, if she's not there, I'll check her house," he said.

Anna relaxed. "Of course. She's probably just swamped with customers." People wanted fresh pastries for breakfast, especially on a weekend morning.

Lucas moved to her and pulled her into his arms. "I'm sorry to have to leave like this."

"I understand." She snuggled closer. "Maybe you can come back tonight."

"I'd like that." He kissed her. A long, deep kiss she was sure was guaranteed to keep them both thinking about it all day. She wanted to cling to him but she didn't. They both had lives to live and work to do.

When he was gone, she dressed and drank a cup of coffee, then slipped a harness on Jacquie. Her usual routine was to walk the dog, then return to the house for breakfast before she settled in to read or garden or catch up on chores. Sunday was the only day Yarn and More wasn't open.

She and Jacquie often headed toward the dog park by the river, or the trail near the school. But this morning, she took a different route; one that would take her past Sandy and Dave's house. She didn't expect Sandy to be there, but it wouldn't hurt to check, would it? She hadn't heard all of the call from Shaylin Brown, but Lucas's side of the conversation had sounded serious. So many strange things had been happening to Sandy since Dave's death. Shaylin had telephoned because she was concerned about George Anton, but Anna wondered if Sandy wasn't the one who was really in danger.

A chill hung heavy in the air as Jacquie and Anna walked

briskly toward the Weisses'. Lights glowed in most of the houses they passed, and she waved to the few people she saw. Jacquie sniffed around the garbage cans awaiting pickup at the curb, and barked at a gray squirrel that raced across the street in front of her. Anna pulled her coat more tightly around her and breathed in deeply the cold, crisp air. If not for her worries about her friend, this would have been an enjoyable walk; a reminder that she should vary her route more often.

Lights glowed in the front rooms of Sandy's home, too, and her Jeep sat in the driveway. Anna climbed the steps to the door and rang the bell while Jacquie sat at her side and stared at the door. After a long moment, the door opened and Sandy peered out. "Anna, what are you doing here?" she asked.

"Jacquie and I were out for a walk and I saw your light," Anna said. "I figured you'd be at the bakery at this hour, so I stopped to see if everything was okay."

"I had to close the bakery for a few days," Sandy said. "Until the window can be replaced."

Anna nodded. How much should she say about Lucas and George Anton? She thrust her hand in the pocket of her coat. "It's cold this morning," she said. "Could I talk you out of a cup of coffee?"

Sandy frowned, and Anna was sure she was going to make some excuse, but she opened the door a little wider. "Sure. You can keep me company while I pack."

Anna and Jacquie followed Sandy through the darkened living room, but even in the dim light, Anna couldn't help notice the room was almost empty. "What happened to your furniture?" she asked.

"I sold it." She headed for the bedroom, and Anna rushed

to keep up. A suitcase lay open on the unmade bed, clothes piled around it. "Where are you going?" Anna asked.

"Since I have to close the bakery anyway, I thought it would be nice to get away for a few days." She picked up a stack of folded shirts and fitted them into the suitcase. "It's been a little tense. I thought maybe a trip would help me relax."

"That's a wonderful idea," Anna said. "Where will you go?"

"Someplace warm, I think." Sandy added a stack of shorts to the suitcase. "I'm tired of cold."

"Do you need me to do anything while you're gone?" Anna asked. "Water the plants or collect the mail?" Sandy didn't have pets that would need care.

"I've got that all taken care of." Sandy fitted a pair of sandals in the side of the case.

"I tried calling you this morning," Anna said. "But I got a message your phone was disconnected."

"Why were you calling me?" Sandy continued to fit items into the suitcase.

"George Anton is missing," Anna said. "I was wondering if you had heard from him lately."

Sandy turned and stared, as if Anna had grown an extra head. "Why would I know anything about George?"

"His assistant said he had a meeting with you yesterday afternoon, here in Eagle Mountain."

Sandy shook her head. "I don't know anything about that."

You're lying, Anna thought. "I always wondered if he was the person who threatened you," she said.

Sandy turned back to the suitcase. "I never did get you

that coffee," she said. "There's some in the kitchen. Why don't you fix us both a cup while I finish up here?"

"Sure." Anna left the room, more certain than ever that Sandy was hiding something. But was it something important, or just Sandy's usual instinct to resist any attempts by Anna to get closer? Jacquie trotted after her, probably hoping for her usual after-walk biscuit. Anna found mugs and filled them from the coffee machine by the sink. Did Sandy take cream or sugar? She couldn't remember. She moved to the doorway. "Sandy, how do you want your coffee?" she called.

"Black is fine," came the answer.

Anna added creamer from a carton in the refrigerator to her own cup and then carried both mugs back toward the bedroom.

She only got as far as the living room. Sandy met her there, a gun in her hand. "You can set the coffee down," she said. "No sense spilling it on the carpet."

Anna stared at the gun, which Sandy held pointed at her. "What are you doing?" she asked.

"The problem with you, Anna, is that you don't know how to take a hint."

THE BAKERY WAS shut tight when Lucas arrived. The large front window was boarded up and a hand-lettered sign on the front door said Closed for Repairs. No cars sat in the lot. Lucas made a wide circle and parked with his SUV facing the road, then got out and walked around the building. Nothing looked disturbed. He took out his phone, looked up the number for the Weiss home and dialed it. It rang and rang, but no one answered, and eventually it fell silent once more.

He stopped at the back of the building, at a pair of metal

double doors that apparently led into a massive freezer. When this had been a meat market, this freezer would have held meat that would be carried through these doors and loaded onto trucks. Ashley Dietrich had said the Weisses stored flour and other ingredients here. He reached up and tried the door, but it was locked by a heavy hasp and padlock.

He turned away, but a thumping noise froze him in his tracks. The noise came again. He stared at the freezer doors then eased one hand to the butt of the pistol in the holster at his side. "Who's there?" he called.

The thumping continued. Not louder, but more rapid. Lucas approached the door. "Who's there?" he shouted.

A noise, almost, but not quite, like a voice. He pressed his ear to the freezer door and listened.

Help, he thought he heard, faint and muffled. *Somebody help.*

Chapter Sixteen

The sheriff arrived at Weiss Bakery shortly after 7:00 a.m., along with two deputies and a locksmith. The locksmith went to work right away, drilling out the lock, while Lucas and the others waited a short distance away. "Who do you think is in there?" the sheriff asked.

"Either Sandy Weiss or George Anton," Lucas said. "They're both missing."

Travis, hands on his hips, looked around them. "This would be a good place to receive or transport drugs or stolen goods," he said. "Lots of space. No neighbors."

"Are you thinking Dave Weiss was involved in something like that?" Lucas asked. "And that's why he was killed?"

"It's something to consider," Travis said.

"Got it," the locksmith called, and swung the hasp away from the door. Lucas and Deputy Dwight Prentice moved forward to tug at the door. Sunlight illuminated the interior of the freezer, where the still figure of George Anton lay on the floor, wrists bound behind his back, rope wrapped around his ankles. His eyes were closed, and frost clung to his skin.

"Call an ambulance," Lucas said, and dropped to his

knees beside the man. He touched one icy cheek. "George!" he said. "George, can you hear me?"

"I TRIED TO do this the easy way," Sandy said, the gun still leveled at Anna. "The drugs I put in that cupcake should have made you go to sleep and never wake up."

"You poisoned the cupcakes you gave me?" Anna didn't quite believe what she was hearing. "That's why I was so sick?"

"Just one of the cupcakes," Sandy said. "I didn't want to take a chance on you eating the poisoned one first and the cops testing the other one. But, apparently, you've got an extra-sensitive stomach and you didn't keep the drugs down long enough for them to do their job."

"Why would you want to kill me?" Anna asked.

Sandy's mouth twisted into a sneer. "Why would anyone want to kill sweet, perfect Anna?" she mocked. "Maybe because you wouldn't stop asking questions. You were the one who spotted the ladder imprints and made the sheriff's department think that maybe Dave hadn't killed himself after all. And you were the one who sent the cops looking for George Anton, too. You kept questioning my story about being in debt, and that made your boyfriend, the cop, question it, too. I don't think you're smart enough to figure things out on your own, but you might stumble on the truth by sheer luck."

Anna's legs felt almost too weak to stand, but she was terrified that if she moved at all, Sandy would shoot her. She had to stay strong. To figure a way out of this. She had to keep Sandy talking. As long as they were talking, the other woman wasn't shooting. She latched onto the most alarming thing Sandy had said so far. "Do you mean Dave didn't commit suicide?"

"He was just like you, always asking questions. I thought he didn't pay any attention to the money side of things. He always said he was happy to leave me in charge of the finances. I would have bet half my savings that he never even looked at the books." Sandy waved the gun in the air, making Anna flinch. "Then one day he asked why we didn't have more money in the bank. And why was the payment to George Anton late? And why was I at the bakery when I had told him I was going out for a run? And who was the man I met there?" Her eyes blazed and her face reddened. "He had *followed* me. Can you believe that? And he had the nerve to accuse me of cheating on him."

"But you weren't cheating on him," Anna said. She glanced from Sandy's face, so angry, to the gun in her hand. Sandy seemed distracted, remembering this interaction with Dave. Could Anna use that distraction to her advantage?

"Of course not. I wouldn't do that. Everything I did was for us! To secure our future, so we wouldn't have to work so hard."

"What were you doing?" Anna asked.

"Why is everyone so nosy?" Sandy waved the gun again. Anna worried it would fire accidentally. She wanted to ask Sandy to stay still, but guessed anything she said at this point was likely to upset her more. So she stayed silent, hoping Sandy would keep talking.

"I told Dave I was being careful. And it was so easy. Just bake a dozen cupcakes, hollow out the centers and put a packet of drugs in each. Mark the cupcakes with a special design on the top and ship them off to restaurants, where the right people would spot the design, remove the packets

of drugs and fill in the gap with chocolate. And who suspects cupcakes?" She laughed, and Anna shivered. There
was nothing cheerful in the sound.

She cleared her throat. "So you were smuggling drugs
in the cupcakes. Where did you get the drugs?" she asked.

"Why would I tell you?" Sandy asked. "Even if you aren't
going to be around to talk."

"Dave found out?" Anna hastened to add. Anything to
get Sandy to focus on something else. "And you had to get
rid of him?"

"He insisted on double-checking the next shipment of
baked goods and found the cupcakes with the extra 'surprise.' He went ballistic. A full-blown screaming fit. The
whole time we were married, he never raised his voice to
me, but he actually *threw* the box of cupcakes at me. He
insisted we go to the sheriff and tell him everything. I told
him that was the fastest way to get us both killed, but he
wouldn't listen."

"What did you do?" Anna asked. She kept her voice quiet,
as if making casual conversation. She wanted Sandy to say
that the drug dealer had murdered Dave. That the dealer was
the one who had threatened Sandy and shot out the window
of the bakery. But part of her already knew that wasn't right.

"I suggested we go for a drive to calm down and talk
things out," she said. "I made coffee to take with us, and a
couple of bear claws to go with the coffee. A little picnic.
But I put a big dose of that dog tranquilizer in his coffee.
He didn't even notice, but it calmed him down enough that
I could deal with him."

"Where did you get dog tranquilizers?" Anna had told
herself she was going to be quiet, but she couldn't keep
back the question.

Sandy looked smug. "I lied to the cops. Dave did have a dog, years ago. Before we married. Bruno had seizures, so Dave had to give him phenobarbital. The dog died while we were still dating, but Dave never threw anything away. I was cleaning out a cabinet after I moved in and found them, but I decided to hang on to them. You never know when something like that will come in handy."

Anna tried to hide her revulsion. "But the medication didn't kill Dave," she said.

"I told you, I wasn't trying to kill him. Not with that. I wanted people to think he'd killed himself, so I had him drive out to Panther Point. I thought about pushing him off a cliff and telling people he had jumped, but decided it would be better if people thought I wasn't anywhere near him when it happened. So I decided to hang him."

Anna swallowed down a wave of nausea. "I saw the scene," she said. "How did you ever get him up in that tree?"

"He was all doped up. I walked him way back there to that cottonwood and we had our little picnic, then I suggested he lie down and take a nap. I went back to the truck and got the ladder and some rope. I set everything up, then coaxed him up the ladder. He was so out of it he didn't protest, but that also meant I had to do most of the heavy lifting." She laughed again. "Good thing I had all that practice carrying dead weight in firefighter training. I got the noose around his neck and the other end of the rope secured around the tree. Then all I had to do was pull the ladder away." She paused and studied Anna. "Don't look so horrified. He didn't suffer. He died within seconds."

Anna swallowed. "What happened to the ladder?" she asked.

"I drove farther into the mountains and dropped it down a

mine shaft," she said. "Then I drove back to the place where
the truck was found and left it there and walked home. I
hid when any cars came by, but there wasn't much traffic,
so I didn't have much trouble. I cleaned up the cupcakes,
baked a new batch for the drugs, and played the part of a
worried wife."

"What about the threatening notes?" Anna asked. "And
the person who shot out the window of the bakery?"

Sandy smiled. "That was all me. I figured it wouldn't hurt
if the sheriff thought I was in danger, too. And it was the
perfect excuse for me to take the money I'd saved up and
disappear. I let my supplier know what was going on and
he agreed that was a good idea. We parted on good terms
and he said he'd be happy to work with me again any time."

"Was it George Anton?" Anna asked.

"Everyone is going to think that, aren't they?" Sandy
asked. "That was another great thing about this whole setup.
George is the perfect suspect. Of course, I can't take credit
for that. My supplier made sure the cops would focus on
George. But good old George was just a patsy. He transported the drugs from me to the various pickup points at
restaurants, and people there distributed the dope on the
streets. George had no idea."

"Surely, he would have figured it out eventually," Anna
said.

"Maybe." Sandy shrugged. "It doesn't matter now anyway." She steadied the gun again. "Now, I just have to take
care of you and I can leave."

Chapter Seventeen

George groaned and his eyelids flickered. Lucas felt for a pulse and located a weak flutter. Even here, in the open doorway, he could feel the frosty chill of the freezer. Had George been in there all night? How had he not died? "Let's move him into the sun, where it's warmer," he said. He took off his coat and draped it over George's still figure. The sheriff and Dwight did the same, then they carried him to a spot on the loading dock in full sun.

The sheriff went into the freezer and emerged shortly, shaking his head. "We'll want to take a closer look, but I don't see anything incriminating in there."

The wail of an ambulance siren grew louder, and Dwight went around front to meet it. Lucas looked down at the still, unconscious man. "Who do you think put him in that freezer?" he asked.

"Whoever it was, what have they done with Sandy?" Travis asked.

The siren quieted and two paramedics raced around the side of the building. "What's the situation?" Hannah Richards asked.

"He was locked in a deep freeze," Travis said. "We don't know how long."

Hannah and EMT Emmet Baxter set to work, checking vital signs and placing warming packs around George's body. Hannah started an IV and began a saline drip. "The saline will help warm him, too," she explained. "There's a little frostbite on his bare fingers, but right now it doesn't look like he'll lose any digits."

George groaned again, more loudly, and turned his head from side to side.

Lucas knelt beside him. "George!" he called.

George opened his eyes and stared up at him. "You're going to be okay," Lucas said. "But we need to know what happened to Sandy."

George shook his head. "No," he said. "No, no, no."

Lucas gripped his shoulder. "You're going to be okay. But where is Sandy? We need to find her."

"Don't...know." George forced out the words. "She... did...this."

The sheriff joined Lucas next to George. "Are you saying Sandy did this to you?" he asked.

George nodded. "Tried...to...kill me."

"Why did Sandy try to kill you?" Lucas asked.

"I...found out...about...the drugs."

"What drugs?" Lucas asked. "What did you find out about the drugs?"

But George's eyes were closed and he didn't make an effort to speak again.

"We need to get him to the hospital," Hannah said.

Lucas and Travis both rose and stepped back. "Do you think he's talking about the drugs that were being distributed by workers at the restaurants in Junction?" Lucas asked.

"Junction law enforcement suspected Anton was the source of the drugs," Travis said. "But maybe that wasn't the case." He looked up at the bakery. "Maybe they were coming from here."

"Those Surprise Cakes," Lucas said.

Travis nodded. "Maybe Weiss was baking more than party favors and chocolate into those cakes."

"Then why was he killed?" Lucas asked.

"Maybe he tried to double-cross his dealer."

"George said Sandy is the one who tried to kill him," Lucas said.

"We'd better find her," Travis said. "Let's check her house. Maybe we can figure out where she's headed."

Lucas pulled out his phone. "I'm going to call Anna," he said. "Just in case Sandy tries to get in touch with her."

"Tell her to stay away," Travis said.

He nodded and listened to the phone ring. And ring. "She's not answering," he said. His stomach tightened. Was she not answering because she was in the shower—or because Sandy had already gotten to her?

As SANDY LEVELED the gun, Anna turned to run. She wasn't going to stand there and be shot point-blank.

Jacquie whined and both women looked at the dog. "Jacquie, go!" Anna shouted.

But "go" wasn't a command in the dog's repertoire. Instead of leaving, she took a step toward Sandy, body tense, growling low. "Jacquie, no!" Anna shouted. Sandy had swiveled the gun at the dog. Anna tried to think of some command the dog would obey. Anything to get her out of harm's way.

"Jacquie, search!" she cried.

Jacquie looked to her, clearly confused. She hadn't been given a scent to focus in on. But she was also trained to do

a more general search, the kind she might do after an avalanche or when searching for a body in a lake. "Search!"
Anna said again, and pointed toward the kitchen.

She almost collapsed with relief when Jacquie turned
and headed for the kitchen. But she had no time to savor the
feeling as she turned to see that Sandy once more had the
gun pointed at her. She forced herself to look in the other
woman's eyes. There was nothing in Sandy's expression
that she recognized as the woman Anna had once wanted
to be friends with. All she saw was a chilling blankness.

"Sandy, don't do this," she pleaded.

"I'm actually going to enjoy this one," Sandy said. She
slipped her finger into the trigger guard. Anna turned to run.

Jacquie barked, and her toenails scrabbled for purchase
on the hardwood floor. The gun went off. Anna screamed
and Sandy roared with rage.

Anna whirled around to see Sandy on the floor, trying to
fight off Jacquie, who had her by the arm and refused to let
go. The gun lay several feet away, half under the sofa. Anna
crawled toward it and picked it up. Carefully. She had no
idea how to shoot, but she knew enough to keep the weapon
away from the woman who wanted to kill her.

"Stop! Police!" The door burst open and Lucas, followed
by the sheriff and two other deputies, burst into the room.
Anna let the gun fall from her hands and sagged against
the sofa. There was more shouting, more barking, but she
was only dimly aware of any of it.

"Are you all right?" Lucas knelt beside her, one arm
around her shoulders.

She nodded and let herself lean against him. "I'm okay,"
she said.

"Could you call off Jacquie?" he asked.

She looked toward the dog, who stood over Sandy, her teeth still clamped around the other woman's wrist.

"Jacquie!" she called. "Jacquie, come!"

Jacquie released her hold on Sandy and trotted over. Anna let go of Lucas so she could hug the dog close.

"Good girl," she said. "Such a good girl."

Sandy swore and fought against the two deputies who put her in handcuffs and led her away. The sheriff came to stand beside Anna.

"What happened?" Travis asked.

"Sandy killed Dave," Anna said. "She was smuggling drugs in cupcakes, from the bakery to restaurants in Junction. Dave found out and wanted to tell you, and Sandy killed him." She shook her head, still dazed by all that had occurred. "I think she might have killed George Anton, too. She said the person who was supplying drugs to her had set up Anton to look like the person behind the whole thing, though he really didn't know anything."

"She tried to kill George, but he's alive," Lucas said. "He's on his way to the hospital, but I think he'll be okay."

"That's good." She covered her mouth with her hand, trying to hold back a sob. "Poor Dave. He really loved her, and she did that to him. She gave him dog tranquilizers then made him climb a ladder and put a noose around his neck. The way she talked about it was so...cold. And she faked those letters and shot the window out of the bakery herself."

Travis nodded. "She took advantage of the bakery's remote location, and she reckoned none of us would want to think a grieving widow could be responsible."

"Do you think you can stand?" Lucas asked.

She nodded and he helped her up.

"We'll need your statement," Travis said. "As soon as possible."

"Of course." She straightened. "I'm okay to talk about it." She turned to Lucas. "I didn't have food poisoning," she said. "Sandy doped one of the cupcakes she gave me. It was supposed to kill me, but I got sick before much of it could absorb into my system."

His expression looked grim. "We'll add that to the charges against her."

"Come on," Travis said. "You can tell us everything at the station. I'll meet you there."

He left and Lucas pulled her closer. "I'm so glad you're okay," he said and kissed her cheek.

She turned in his arms and kissed his mouth, hard and long, and not caring that the room was full of other people who were probably watching. "I'm glad I'm okay, too," she said when they finally broke apart. "I would have hated to die just when we had found each other."

"I can't even think about that." He stroked his thumb down her cheek. "I want to believe we have the rest of our lives to get to know each other."

Her breath caught at that vision. She had promised someone forever before and it hadn't worked out, but the thought of making that promise again didn't frighten her so much anymore. Maybe because this time she knew how fragile their time together could be, and it made her want to try harder not to let a moment slip away unnoticed. "Let's plan on it," she whispered.

GOING OVER EVERYTHING that had happened that afternoon took longer than the events themselves, Lucas realized after

Travis finally switched off the recorder in the interview room and Anna signed her statement.

"Sandy Weiss isn't saying anything," Travis said. "But between your statement and George Anton's, plus the evidence we found at her home and at the bakery, she'll be charged with drug trafficking, murder and two counts of attempted murder."

"Why would she kill Dave?" Anna asked. "They always seemed so happy together. I know she said he was upset about the drugs, but still."

"We'll search for the ladder she talked about," Travis said. "I'm hoping she'll tell us more, but it sounds like, after she gave Dave the phenobarbital, she was able to either persuade or force him to climb the ladder. Dave was a big guy, but she's stronger than most women. She used to compete in power-lifting competitions. Plus, he might have thought if he went along with her, he could talk her out of what she was doing. Until it was too late."

"She might have killed me if it hadn't been for Jacquie." Anna leaned down to pet the dog, who hadn't left her side since the ordeal had ended.

"I'm going to buy her a steak," Lucas said and leaned over to pet the dog, also.

"We're working with Junction law enforcement to track down the dealer who was supplying the drugs," Travis said. "The DA is still hopeful he can make a deal with Sandy to give them a name. It looks like she had a lot of money stashed in an overseas account, and we found a passport with her photograph and a different name, ready if she decided to leave the country. The sous-chef at Red Mesa, who Junction PD arrested, admitted to regularly retrieving drugs in the baked goods from Weiss Bakery. Apparently, every shipment included a box marked 'For Staff' and the drugs were hidden in plastic capsules in hollowed-out places in cakes and other pastries. We're also putting pressure on Darryl Singh to tell us who hired him to deliver that package to the bakery. I sent Gage out with Tony Meisner to retrieve the package from Singh's car. The box they brought back was full of fentanyl pills." He stood. "Thank you for your help, Anna. Lucas can take you home now."

"Are you ready to go?" Lucas asked when they were alone.

She met his gaze, her expression so weary but tender, too. "Can we go to your place?" she asked. "I'd like to see it."

"Of course." He stood and she rose, also, but instead of moving toward the door, she moved into his arms. He tightened his arms around her, wishing he could find the words to ease her distress. She would need more than words; she would need time, and he would give that to her.

"I couldn't believe Dave would kill himself, but I never would have thought Sandy would murder him," she said. "They seemed so much in love."

"Some people aren't capable of loving as much as others," he said. He rested his chin atop her head. "I used to think that about me. All Jenny wanted was for me to love her enough to commit to her for the rest of my life, and I couldn't do it."

"That doesn't make you a bad person," she said. "Not like Sandy. You were loyal to Jenny and did as much as you could for her. But marriage is a big commitment not everyone is ready to make."

"It is. But now I think that even though I couldn't make that promise to Jenny, I might be able to make it one day."

He shifted so that he could look into her eyes. "To the right person."

"I know what you mean," she said. "One day. When the time is right."

"We don't have to rush," he said. "But I want us to be together."

"I want that, too." Her smile was shaky and her eyes glimmered with unshed tears. "I believe in you, Lucas. And that makes me believe in us."

"Yeah." He kissed her lightly, a seal on a promise, one he could make this time and keep. Forever.

* * * * *

WYOMING MOUNTAIN COLD CASE

JUNO RUSHDAN

For Gloria—my aunt, my second mother, my best friend.

Prologue

November. Five years ago.

I'm going to die!

  On this freezing mountain, he's going to kill me.

  No, no, don't give up. Don't let him win. You have to fight!

But how?

Tiffany Cummings tugged at the thick ropes that dug into her wrists, trembling from the fierce sting of icy wind on her bare flesh. She was on the frozen ground, bound with each arm tied to a tree. Her ankles were tied tight together. Unable to even scratch at the rope, she had no idea how she could possibly get free, much less fight.

A gust of wind howled through the snowcapped, forsaken mountain ridges surrounding her. She might have a chance...if only she was alone.

But she wasn't.

The madman who had lured her in and kidnapped her was close. She couldn't see him now, but she felt his dark presence as surely as the bite of the wind.

He was getting ready to take her life.

Why had she been foolish enough to trust him, to accept his help? What had it been about him that caused her to lower her guard?

Had it been his concern for her? His charming smile? His handsome face? His kind words of assurance? Those intelligent green eyes? That it was the holidays, the day after Thanksgiving in her small, peaceful town that had always been safe?

Regardless of the reason, when she'd gotten the flat tires, she'd trusted him and had been deceived. He'd chased her through the mountain. No...hunted her. Like a predator stalking his prey. Knocked her unconscious. And when she came to, opening her eyes, she was trapped in her worst nightmare.

Stripped down to her underwear. Shivering. Bound. Gagged with duct tape over her lips. Barely able to breathe. Waiting for him to kill her while her body grew numb from the cold and the fear.

Snow crunched beneath his feet, footfalls drawing nearer.

Her heart raced. She yanked on the ropes again. Pain cut through her shoulder. Bitter cold from the hard, frozen ground seeped deeper into her bones and she set her jaw against it.

His breath crystallized in the air above her near the trunk of the sturdy pine as he stepped into view. A vicious wolf in sheep's clothing.

He'd even howled like a wolf, baying at the moon when he'd started hunting her.

Now his green eyes found hers, pinning her with his cruel gaze. She kicked out at him, but it was no use. He stayed well out of the range of her feet.

Something glinted in his hand. Metal winked in the moonlight.

A knife. Big and long. Razor-sharp. The kind used for butchering and gutting game.

Her stomach clenched. Hot bile flooded her throat.

Why? She blinked back tears, but the warm drops fell nonetheless, freezing on her cheeks. *Oh God, why me?*

His mouth was covered by a ski mask, but she could tell he was smiling from the way his eyes lit up like it was Christmas. And she was the gift he was about to rip into.

No, no, no!

She couldn't let him get away with this. He had to be stopped. Punished. She'd fought him earlier and scratched his skin. The police would trace his DNA under her fingernails. They'd find him and catch him.

They had to.

But how long before her body was found? Nobody would notice her absence or report her missing. No one might stumble upon her until the next hunting season started.

He lowered to the ground, kneeling beside her.

Panic surged through her blood, making her heart thunder.

"No!" Tiffany tried to scream, but the duct tape muffled her cries. She tried to break free of her restraints, but the ropes were too thick, too tightly fastened. If she were able, she'd beg for her life, offer to do anything if only he'd spare her.

Dear God, help me.

Looming over her, he stared down at her face. Those icy green eyes gleamed in the moonlight. He peeled the tape from her mouth.

A million different things whirled in her mind, but she could only muster one word. "Why?"

"Because I can."

Tiffany whimpered. There was nothing she could say or do to stop him. Nothing at all. "Why me?"

"Someone had to be the first and you made it so easy. So much fun toying with you."

A sob bubbled up her throat, but he pressed the tape back over her lips before her cries left her mouth.

"You won't be alone," he said. "There'll be others." He raised the knife.

Tiffany squeezed her eyes shut, knowing…she was as good as dead.

Chapter One

In the waning light of day, Sheriff Daniel Clark crouched down beside the dead woman. The cool October wind kicked up and the tang of fresh blood hit him, the smell like wet pennies mixed with musty earth.

He'd been in law enforcement for a long time. Eighteen years, most of which had been at the Southeastern Wyoming University's police department. He'd experienced the gamut over nearly two decades, but in this part of the country crime was low and things stayed relatively uneventful the majority of the time. Until he'd taken over as sheriff and the floodgates from hell opened. In the past twenty-four months, there'd been one thing after another: domestic violence, murder, rape, arson, drug cartel activity, a hostage crisis, even domestic terrorists shooting up the town in an attempt to kill a federal agent.

The depths to which humanity could sink no longer shocked him, though it always sickened him. But this was different. He'd never seen anything quite like it.

The woman had been stripped to her undergarments, her arms extended and wrists bound to the base of tree trunks with rope. Ghostly white skin that was turning blue. Her throat had been viciously slashed. Multiple uneven bloody gashes in her chest.

Whoever this woman was, she had once been beautiful. Angular face. Slender body. Her brown eyes were wide and still with that startled expression death tended to leave them in. Long, dark hair was fanned out around her head, as though it had been carefully positioned that way by her killer, like a crown.

The person who took her life had taken the time to make a spectacle of her death.

Daniel looked around past the flash of yellow crime scene tape, ignoring one of his deputies who was embroiled in a dispute over jurisdiction with a police officer. He took in the isolated surroundings of the woods, where the woman had been stumbled upon by two campers.

Why here? In this heavily wooded area with minimal foot traffic if the killer had planned to go through the effort of putting her on display.

He glanced at the neatly folded pile of women's clothing off to the side, and then over his shoulder. "Officer? You didn't touch the clothes, did you?"

"No way, Sheriff," said the LPD patrol officer. "Left the body and clothes in situ," he said.

Good. If they were lucky, they might find a wallet or ID in a pocket. He didn't dare disturb anything until forensics took pictures of the entire scene.

As the heels of his boots sank into the grass, he looked back down at the victim. From the deep ligature marks, it appeared she had struggled while tied up before she died.

Jane Doe was a fighter.

But there weren't any defensive wounds or other bruises on her face or body. Yet, the perpetrator had managed to undress her without any apparent injury to her. Had she been drugged?

Peering closer at her wrist, he noticed a tattoo. A crescent moon next to a sun with an eye at the center. The symbol of the Shining Light cult.

For a few breaths, he stayed crouched, marking the woman's passing. The loss of a daughter, possibly a sister, someone's friend.

"Deputy Russo." Daniel beckoned to her as he stood.

Ashley, a sturdy redhead with long hair that she wore in a single braid, approached him with frustration stamped across her flush face. "LPD is going to make a stink about this. *She* has already been called and is on the way."

Daniel knew precisely who *she* was without his deputy needing to say it.

Chief of police Wilhelmina "Willa" Nelson. As much as he enjoyed the sight of her, as well as her company once upon a time before they'd both held their respective positions, he was not looking forward to their next conversation.

"You measured it?" Daniel asked.

Ashley gave a curt nod. "Just like you requested. Measured it twice to be sure. That tree line there marks the end of Laramie city limits. Fifteen feet from the body. This one is ours."

It was a good thing Ashley was meticulous. He could count on her accuracy, which he was going to need in the next few minutes.

"Okay." He stifled a groan. Willa would fight it. Almost everything between them had become a point of contention. "The victim has a tattoo of the Shining Light." He turned toward the expanse of woods. "Any idea how far their compound is from here?"

"Not exactly. Rough guess would be two, maybe three miles that way." She pointed in the direction he was already facing.

Daniel had limited interaction with the leader of the cult, Marshall McCoy. The man was as charismatic as he was evasive. McCoy had a reputation throughout law enforcement circles for cooperating only when it suited his own interests and a knack for stonewalling when it didn't.

"Forensics is here," Ashley said.

Coming up the hill was their crime scene investigator, Deputy Nina Pruitt. A new hire and transfer from Cheyenne as a result of the increase in budget he'd finally gotten approved. Up until then, they hadn't had a trained forensic scientist in the department. His small team had to collect the evidence themselves and send it to a third party to be processed.

A few feet behind Deputy Pruitt, Willa emerged—a striking brunette in jeans and a white button-down with her badge displayed on her hip.

"Give Nina a hand while I handle this," Daniel said, removing his nitrile gloves as he slipped under the yellow tape cordoning off the area.

"Better you than me." Ashley gave him a wary look. "Good luck." She greeted the other deputy.

Daniel nodded hello to Pruitt. She was young, but seasoned and smart. They were fortunate to have gotten her when she had other opportunities. Some might say bigger and better ones with more room for advancement.

He refocused his attention on the formidable woman making her way to him like a heat-seeking missile. Tall and slender, Willa was all sinewy muscle with the perfect balance of curves. She radiated strength. Not only in her trim build. More so from her sharp mind and her unyielding spirit.

Beneath her cowboy hat, long, dark hair fell to her shoulders in loose waves, framing a compelling face that he took far too much pleasure staring at. Willa aimed a steely glance his way as she slowed her ground-eating stride. "Sheriff Clark."

Daniel gritted his teeth at the cool formality between them that had replaced the warmth of familiarity. "Chief Nelson," he said, tipping his Stetson at her.

He wanted to believe that if they had been alone, which they never were these days, rather than in the presence of subordinates, things might have been closer to their former normal. No posturing. No titles. Only the sweet ease and sultry heat they'd once shared.

"According to my officer," she said, "the body was left in the same manner as my current case."

"From what I read in the paper, it was." He wouldn't have to speculate on the similarities of the crimes if she had loaded the case in ViCAP, the Violent Crime Apprehension Program database that allowed investigators to compare incident details with thousands of other crimes. But that would have assumed Willa had the time to do so. He was aware time was something she was short on with the current constraints of the LPD. "I'm not sure what information you withheld from reporters. There was no mention of any identifying marks on the body. Did yours happen to have a tattoo?"

Willa nodded. "Shining Light symbol. On her shoulder. I take it this one is the same."

"It is. But the tattoo is on her wrist."

She folded her arms. With those razor-edge cheekbones

and rigid stance she looked ready for tug-of-war. "Then I think we can both agree the murders are linked. Since I'm already neck-deep in an open investigation it only makes sense that this case is also mine."

"Not so fast. This body is beyond town limits."

"I'll need to verify that and even if it is, by how much?" she asked, her brown doe eyes narrowing. "One foot, two? We're talking mere inches. No need to muddy the waters on this one."

"Fifteen feet. Which makes this victim unquestionably beyond your authority. Makes it *mine*." He took a deep breath. "We're on the same side and have the same goal. To catch a killer. I don't want to fight with you."

"Then don't." She placed her hands on the snug denim over her hips, the small movement dragging his mind to a moment when they'd both been free from the responsibility of their current positions, skin to skin, the heady taste of her on his tongue.

The memory made his chest ache. He wasn't quite sure why. Their fling, if it could even be called that, had been sudden, intense, scorching, like a flash fire. Not meant to last.

"If only it was that simple," he said.

"It is. Step aside and stay out of my way."

The harder they tried to stay out of each other's orbit, the more circumstances beyond their control yanked them back together. First, his department was located in her town out of all the others in the county. There was no way to avoid one another. Just last month the domestic terrorists gunning for a federal agent had left them no choice but to join forces to save countless lives and protect the town.

Now a serial killer was driving them together once again. Collaboration was inevitable, whether she liked it or not.

DANIEL STRUCK HER as a good guy, not the kind to manipulate her with the power of his position, but she'd been fooled before by the wrong man. It had nearly cost her her life.

Why couldn't he make this easy for both of them and simply agree to let her handle this case?

For some reason, he wasn't going to. It was written all over his handsome face, so handsome it should've been illegal. She saw it in the hard set of his jaw, in the stiff defiance of his six feet two inches of lean muscle. All of which only irritated her more than his obstinance.

"Afraid I can't do that," he said in that smooth, easy tone of his that would brook no argument.

The smell of cinnamon gum and cedar drifted over her, an enticing mix she'd come to associate with Daniel. "Why not?"

"The killer placed the victim here. Outside of your jurisdiction. Nothing I can do to change that. Also, you have to consider the perp might not be finished. Another body could turn up. The next one could be even farther from the town limit."

A distinct possibility that spiked her irritation even higher. It was one she'd rather not entertain, but it was unavoidable. "What do you propose?" she asked, rolling back her shoulders, steeling herself for his response.

If he insisted on taking over the case and cutting her out, which he could do as the highest law enforcement officer of the county, then she'd fight it tooth and nail. Not that she'd have much recourse. Even so, she wasn't going to simply hand him her case. With as many supporters as she had critics, every day she had to prove herself. This might be the twenty-first century, but it was still a male-dominated field, where many still didn't trust her to do the job on the sole basis of her gender.

Everything she had she'd either earned or fought for, and this case was no different.

"Our departments should work together on this," he said.

Surprise had her struggling not to flinch at the idea. She stared in his eyes, cool, brown and unfathomable. "Working with one of your deputies is acceptable. My preference would be Holden Powell."

She knew enough about Powell to believe they wouldn't have a problem getting along. He'd been injured in the shoot-out with the domestic terrorists, but he was on the mend and back in the office.

"Holden returning to work so soon after being shot didn't sit well with my sister. He's on vacation."

"Let me guess, they're dating."

"Actually, they're engaged and living together. It happened rather quickly. Too quickly."

Not even three degrees of separation in this town. "Well, then, assign someone else."

A smile curved his lips. "I was thinking you and me on this one."

Willa scoffed. There were several good reasons for that not to happen. Top among them being distraction. This job required her full focus. The pressure was immense. There wasn't room for diversions. Or complications. "I'd prefer to keep this investigation clean. No muddy waters."

She'd taken great pains to ensure her personal life didn't bleed over into her professional one. Particularly since when it did, it tended to hemorrhage.

Once she started as chief of the LPD around the same time Daniel donned the badge as sheriff, she'd ended things between them. Before their hearts got entangled and it became something serious that was destined to end badly, as things invariably did for her.

An ounce of prevention was worth a pound of cure.

"Look, the LPD is overwhelmed right now," he said. "You've lost most of your detectives and you're running a barebones department. Any assistance, even if it's from me, should be viewed as helpful."

All true, not that he needed to rub her face in the fact. The mayor had hired her not only because she was qualified but also because she was from Wayward Bluffs and not Laramie. There had been suspicion of dirty cops in the LPD. She was brought in to clean it up and she had. Though the fallout was greater than anyone had expected, leaving a serious personnel shortage and her working double duty putting in eighteen-hour days.

Daniel eyed her, probably trying to figure out her reluctance. "If you're worried about which department will get the credit—"

"It's not that." The only thing that mattered was catching a killer. "I don't want lines to blur," Willa said, hoping he'd understand her concerns without the need to say more with others in earshot.

Unfortunately, some people, a few of them cops, had the gall to imply she'd slept her way to the top. The last thing she wanted was for her brief dalliance with Daniel two years ago to become known and end up as fodder for the local gossips.

"Two women have lost their lives," he said. "I think we can keep it professional. Clean slate?" He proffered his hand.

As much as she wanted to, she couldn't dismiss the sincerity in his eyes. "All right." She shook his hand. His palm was incredibly warm, the heat enticing her to relax. She ended the contact before he did, but his touch left her fingers tingling.

Willa looked away at the crime scene. The evidence tech had finished examining the body. She treaded around carefully, photographing the area, circling the grim landscape, documenting every angle and piece of whatever had been left behind.

"Where exactly did you find the last body?" Daniel asked.

"Not far from here." She pointed east, closer to town. "Less than a quarter a mile."

"What did Marshall McCoy have to say about the first victim when you questioned him?"

She frowned. "I spoke with a public relations representative. McCoy was *indisposed*." All acolytes forsook their worldly possessions and took the new surname Starlight, sometimes changing their forenames as well after their vows. Willa didn't get the appeal of the cult. Apparently, many others did. There were more than five hundred people living on the compound. "They claim the victim, Blue Starlight, formerly Beverly Fisher, was no longer a part of their community and was considered to be one of the Fallen."

"The Fallen?"

"That's what they call someone who has left or been kicked out and is no longer welcomed to return."

Daniel quirked a brow. "Did they say why she left?"

"Not really. Only that she decided the commune was no longer for her about four months ago. That's it. Fisher ended up homeless."

"Do you buy it? Why would she give up shelter, safety and hot meals to live on the streets?"

Willa shrugged. "McCoy and his front person for the Shining Light clearly have an agenda. The preservation of their pristine reputation. They won't say anything that'll reflect poorly. Fisher leaving four months ago checked out. No one in town she associated with afterward knew why she'd left. There's definitely more to the story, but the cultists aren't talking."

"With two murdered women from his commune, McCoy will have no choice but to talk."

"Sure, he'll talk. His mouth will open, words will spill out, but he won't say anything pertinent." The man had dodge-and-evade down to a science. "Let's wait until we know more, time of death and hopefully a name of the victim, before we go knocking on his gate." She meant that metaphorically since the last time she was at the compound they'd requested she make an appointment if there were any additional questions. "Ideally, I'd like to talk to someone who knew her outside of the compound first. It'd be nice to have something to go on when we question McCoy."

"All right. That'll give me a chance to look at your case file. I can input the details into ViCAP."

Loading the case in the database would have made coordination with the sheriff's department easier if she'd already done it. "I've barely had time to eat, much less sleep, with none to spare on ViCAP." Nonetheless it was a valuable tool. One she should've made time for sooner. "Sorry about that."

"I wasn't criticizing. You've got your hands full. I never did get a chance to tell you how impressive it was the way you cleaned house, getting rid of all those dirty cops. Couldn't have been easy."

"Took patience and persistence. A lot of sleepless nights devising a way to catch them without any of them seeing it coming." All those police officers had been cunning enough to get away with corruption for years. Nailing them had been the most difficult undertaking of her life. "Bringing in the state attorney general's office was the key. I wouldn't have managed it without one of their undercover agents from DCI," she said referring to the Division of Criminal Investigation.

"You'll accept help from the DCI with no problem, but not me?"

"I don't like to be beholden. Especially not to someone who lives in my backyard."

"Well on this, we'll be helping each other."

"Yeah, sure," she said, her voice clipped, her mouth dry. In the end, she hoped that was how it worked out. "I'll make sure you get the file."

"Sheriff!" Deputy Pruitt called. "There's an ID in her pocket."

Willa and Daniel headed back to the cordoned-off area.

"With Fisher, did you find a wallet or identification in her clothes?" he asked Willa.

"Nope. If only we'd been so lucky," she said. "They had to ID her for us at the compound."

"What do we have?" Daniel asked as they approached the boundary of the yellow tape.

"Her name was Leslie Gooding. Student ID card. SWU."

Convenient that Daniel had been the chief of campus police. "Do you know any school officials willing to come in after hours to access student records?" Willa asked him.

"I stay in contact with a couple of administrators. At least one of them might be able to help out tonight. Worst case, first thing in the morning, but I should give my replacement on campus a heads-up about this."

An unnecessary courtesy since the body wasn't discovered on school property. It spoke volumes about Daniel as a professional and as a person.

"While you're doing that, I'll formulate a statement for the press. Similar to what I put out about Fisher." It was better to feed the reporters her narrative before they caught wind of another murder and painted their own picture.

"I think we should give them more details this time. Mention the tattoo of the Shining Light."

"Are you sure that's a good idea?"

He didn't look certain. "It'll put public pressure on McCoy to cooperate more fully if nothing else."

It could also backfire in a number of ways. "We'll see how it plays out." Willa glanced back at the tech. "Any estimate on the time of death?"

"Based on the body temp and conditions, I'd say it's somewhere between midnight and five a.m. Once I take her in, the medical examiner will be able to give a more precise time. The stab wounds to her chest are deep. Jagged edges to the cuts. You're looking for a serrated knife. Like one used for hunting. Fairly big."

"The same as with Fisher," Willa said. "We didn't find one at the scene." Her cell phone buzzed. She pulled it from her back pocket and glanced at the screen. Wayward Bluffs police department. She groaned at the inkling of why her former department would be calling. "Excuse me. I've got to take this," she said. Turning, she stepped away and answered, "This is Nelson."

"Hello, Chief. This is Cannedy."

"What's up?"

"Bad news." The somber tone of his voice struck her.

"Spit it out, Cannedy. You know I hate suspense."

"Sorry to bother you, but it's about Zeke."

Her heart nearly dropped out of her chest. "Ezekiel?" With suddenly trembling hands, she started down the hill toward her SUV. She checked for any lurking reporters as she hurried but didn't see any. "What happened? Was there a car accident?" Her son had a reckless streak. He always drove faster than he should, taking tricky turns at a high speed. Blood-curdling images flashed in her mind. First, of his body trapped in a mass of twisted metal and then him in a hospital on life support.

What would she do if she lost him?

"No, ma'am, nothing like that. He's okay." Cannedy took a breath, but Willa couldn't shake the fear of a senseless tragedy snuffing out the life of her only child. "He's been arrested."

In an instant, her panic slid to anger. "Arrested?" That boy was going to be the death of her. "What has my son done this time?"

Chapter Two

As Daniel finished inputting the details of the Fisher case into the national database, his thoughts careened back to Willa. She'd taken off from the crime scene in such a hurry. Only an emergency or a herd of wild horses could have dragged her away. He hoped everything was all right.

He'd known her two and a half years, but he didn't *know her* in that way. Only the first six months counted toward the getting better acquainted part until she'd ghosted him. He'd spent some time with her, enough to get a bead on her personality, read her mood. Even then, she'd been too guarded to let him in. He didn't know a thing about her past, or about her life. Other than the fact she was single and had spent almost half her life as a cop in Wayward Bluffs.

That hadn't stopped him from asking her if everything was okay after her phone call tonight. Her tightlipped response, which had told him absolutely nothing, had been expected.

A knock on his door pulled his gaze from the computer up to his injured chief deputy and future brother-in-law.

"What are you doing here?" Daniel asked. "Are you trying to get me into trouble with my sister?" Their relationship was strained enough. Daniel didn't need to do anything to make it worse.

Holden chuckled as though Daniel had been joking. With an arm in a sling, his chief deputy leaned against the doorjamb. "Grace and I are running errands in town. While she's at the hospital discussing changes to her schedule with her supervisor, I thought I'd swing by, see what was going on and invite you to a big family dinner out at the ranch tomorrow night."

Swallowing a sigh, Daniel lowered his head.

"Before you say no, for the third time," Holden said, "not coming won't make the invitations stop. It'll only add fuel to my mother's fire to break bread with you and discuss the wedding."

"Pick a date for the ceremony, tell me what to wear and I'll be there on time. You don't need me for wedding planning."

"I don't. But Grace does. Which means Holly Powell has made it her mission to include you every step of the way. Once my mama gets fixed on something, nothing can stop her. Just ask my dad."

Daniel wasn't buying it that Grace wanted him there. When she'd relocated from California to get away from their overbearing mother, he'd offered her a room at his place—a run-down ranch their father had bequeathed him, where he kept two horses. With his full-time job as sheriff, he'd imagined getting a couple more mares with her help. Showing her what their dad had loved about the Cowboy State, the land, the great outdoors—this place. But his younger sister had turned him down flat, opting to rent an even more ramshackle cabin instead of staying with family and saving money.

Now she was living with Holden. Blissfully fitting in among the Powell clan out on the six thousand gasp-inducing acres of a working ranch, the Shooting Star.

He wanted her to be happy, to find a place where she belonged. What decent brother would begrudge her that?

It was nice she was here, nearby. If only her proximity had brought them closer.

With a twelve-year age gap and their father dying before she was born, they had never had a typical sibling relationship. He'd moved out by the time she was six. During his visits while she was growing up, he'd done his best to fill in the holes of whatever was missing in her life, but he never seemed to get it right.

"Are you sure your mom isn't the one pushing for me to come?" Daniel asked. "For the sake of appearances." He'd play whatever part they wanted for the ceremony, but he didn't want to go where he wasn't truly welcomed. "My sister isn't the one here asking." And invites to dinner didn't start coming until there was chitchat of a wedding.

"She doesn't know I came here to talk about this." Holden crossed the threshold, stepping into the office. "I think she's uncertain where you stand on our relationship. I am, too, to be honest. It's not as if you've given us your blessing."

Daniel leaned back in his chair, the words hitting him like a sucker punch. "I didn't think she needed it." Or cared about it for that matter. "You're two consenting adults and I congratulated you both."

With a half-hearted nod, Holden said, "Sort of. There didn't seem to be any joy behind the words. It was…awkward."

Their relationship, much less their engagement, had been a shock to Daniel. At the time, his deputy had merely been a colleague looking out for Daniel's little sister. Grace was safe and although she was single, she'd never even indicated she liked Holden. "I went out of town for two weeks. Ten days to be precise. And I get back to find out Grace was nearly killed and suddenly living with you." Talk about awkward. "Then you two are engaged after only a couple of months." Six weeks to be exact. "It was all rather fast. Unexpected. I didn't mean to give the impression that I didn't approve." Though he didn't see the reason to rush down to the altar either. "Even if you didn't ask my permission or for her hand in marriage."

He might only be her brother, but he was also the only father figure she'd ever known. Nonetheless, his opinion didn't matter when they started their relationship. It certainly wasn't a factor regarding their engagement. Why was he supposed to think his blessing—or lack thereof—would concern either of them?

"Is that the problem?" Holden asked.

Not wanting to go down that road, Daniel stood. "There is no problem. Honestly, you're great for my sister. I've never seen her so happy and at ease." She even transitioned from working palliative care that had been draining her emotionally to getting her master's degree in nursing administration. "I'm glad you two connected. I only wish it had happened under better circumstances. Okay?"

"Then you'll come to dinner?"

"You just don't give up."

Holden shrugged. "It's a part of my charm. I guess I get it from my mom."

Ready to inform Holden that his charm was a figment of his imagination, another knock on the door saved him.

"Sheriff, am I interrupting?" Pruitt asked.

"No, you're not." *Right on time.* "Come on in." Daniel waved her inside the room when she hesitated.

"The medical examiner will start the autopsy at eight a.m.," Pruitt said.

"There's a second body?" Holden asked.

"Yeah," Daniel said with a slight nod. "This one is ours. She's been identified. One of my contact's at SWU, where the victim was a student, gave me her parents' contact information in Cheyenne. The local PD will notify them tonight. But Chief Nelson and I will be working the case together."

Holden's brows rose in surprise. "Chief Nelson? I'm shocked she agreed."

Not that Daniel had given her much choice.

"Do you want me to take a look at the case?" Holden asked, gesturing to the file Pruitt held in her hand.

"That's all right. Grace will be waiting. I don't want to keep you." Daniel took the file from Pruitt and set it on his desk. "Let her know that with these murders, I'll have some late nights ahead. Dinner will have to wait."

Holden's mouth flattened into a grim line. "She won't like it, but she'll understand. My mama on the other hand is a different story."

The perfect way to handle Holly Powell was with two words. Selene Beauvais. "The person who should really be involved in all this is our mother."

Holden grimaced. "No disrespect, but I think her participation in the planning might stress out Grace. We want to keep things simple."

There was no doubt about it. Selene Beauvais was stress personified. For everyone. But she was still their mother.

"There's no way I can tell my mom I'm included in wedding planning while she isn't." Daniel threw his hands up.

"It might be best for the mothers of the groom and the bride to Skype, FaceTime, something." Let Holly deal with it, sparing both Grace and him. "Before my mother decides to hop on a plane and invite herself to dinner, which is entirely possible if she feels excluded." Then Daniel would have to clean up the mess that would be left in the wake of Hurricane Selene. He stepped around the desk, putting a hand on Holden's shoulder, and steered him to the door. "Tell my sister I can always make time to have a cup of coffee with her."

"Understood." Holden took the hint and left.

"Do you need anything else tonight?" Pruitt asked.

He'd nearly forgotten she was still standing there, silent as a fly on the wall. "No. It's getting late. You should head home." The phone on his desk rang.

"I'll be in early tomorrow," Pruitt said. "Have a good night."

"Night." He picked up the phone. "Albany County Sheriff's Department. Sheriff Clark speaking."

"This is Detective Johnson of Cheyenne PD. We notified Mr. and Mrs. Gooding about the death of their daughter. I'll email you a copy of their statement, but they intend to drive down to Laramie tomorrow morning to speak with you. They also want to see their daughter's body."

Daniel couldn't imagine what those poor people must be going through, the magnitude of grief. "It'll be good to speak with them firsthand. Do they know an autopsy will have to be performed before they can see her?"

"I told them. But they insisted. You should expect them first thing in the morning."

"All right. Thank you, Detective."

Hanging up, he sat at his desk and opened the file. It was a digital world, but he was old-school and it helped him to have everything in black-and-white in his hands. Staring at the photos of Leslie Gooding, his heart sank, but a fire to find her killer ignited in his veins.

Daniel took out his cell and texted Willa.

DOING HER BEST to keep shame from surfacing on her face, Willa followed Cannedy back to the holding cells. Her cell phone in her hand chimed. She read the text.

Tomorrow a.m. Gooding's parents are coming from Cheyenne. My office.

Too distracted to be annoyed the interview would take place at his office rather than hers, Willa sent a quick reply.

Sure. Be there at 9. Let me know if they show sooner.

She doubted that they would. It was a forty-five-minute drive from Cheyenne. The Goodings probably wouldn't get much sleep tonight, but she didn't expect them to knock on the sheriff's door at the crack of dawn. Her phone chimed.

Ok. Autopsy will begin at 8. Hope all is well with you.

Everything was not well. It was a mess, but it could've been worse. At least Zeke was alive. She could still wrap her arms around her son and hold him tight. If he'd let her.

Instead of responding to the text, she slipped her phone in her pocket. Oddly enough, the timing of having assistance on this case was working out in her favor. With Daniel handling things at the moment, she could focus on her son, who needed her full attention.

"I really appreciate the phone call, Sergeant," she said. On the outside, she was unflappable. On the inside, her chest was deflating like a tire with a slow leak.

"The new chief says this is the last favor," Cannedy said, keys jangling in his hands. "Two strikes so far. Next time we have to bring Zeke in and—"

"I understand." Her son would be treated like anybody else. Booked, charged and forced to face the consequences of his actions. "Thanks again for calling me."

"Think nothing of it. Least I could do." At the cell, Cannedy unlocked the door. "You're free to go."

Pushing his long hair back with his fingers, Zeke lifted his head, his gaze meeting hers. "Uh-huh," he said, as his way of greeting, and she stiffened. Hopping up from the bench, her twenty-one-year-old problem child smirked. "Color me surprised."

His ingratitude made her blood boil. "Not another word from you until we're outside."

He snapped his heels together and gave her a mock salute.

Cannedy, his eyebrows two thick slashes of disgust that matched his flattened lips, let go of the opened cell door. "I'll leave you to it, ma'am."

Once the sergeant was out of the holding area, she said, "Come on, and don't do anything to embarrass me further on the way out."

Zeke trudged out of the cell past her, reeking of alcohol.

Thank God he was alive. Unhurt. That was her one consolation.

They walked down the corridor in silence and through the bullpen. Most of the officers in tonight avoided eye contact. Those who didn't stared at her with either pity or disdain. She hated being the subject of either.

Throwing a hand up in farewell to Cannedy, she shoved outside the front door of the police station. Zeke was right on her heels.

"Drunk and disorderly conduct?" she asked in a low voice, pressing the key fob for her SUV. The headlights flashed as the doors unlocked. "That's a class C misdemeanor."

"Better than a felony."

Shaking her head, she opened her door and climbed inside. After her son hopped in, she cranked the engine and pulled out. "How did you manage to get into a fight in a bar when you were supposed to be at work?"

"Had the day off."

"Are you sure you weren't fired?"

He grumbled something under his breath. The only words she caught were curses.

"There you go," he said, "always assuming the worst of me."

Things had never been easy with Ezekiel. But she'd always told herself that it wasn't his fault. Pregnant at sixteen and strong-armed by her parents into marrying the father, another high school kid who she didn't love, she hadn't given Zeke the best start. For three years, she'd tried to make the marriage and the picture of a happy family work until she couldn't pretend any longer. Shuttling her son between the homes of contentious parents hadn't been much better. But when her ex, a police officer, had been killed in the line of duty, Zeke spiraled out of control.

No mother would ever give up on her child, but she didn't know what more she could do, what else she could say to get him on the right path.

If only his father, Zachariah, were still alive. They might

not have been good as a couple, but her ex had been great in a crisis.

"Can you drop me off at Grandma's?" he asked.

She expelled a low breath. "Why not your place?"

His place being a single-wide trailer in the Happy Meadows mobile home park.

"They cut off the heat. It's freezing in there at night. And before you get on me about paying my bills, I did. Mailed the payment on time. It must've gotten lost at the post office," he said, staring out the window into the darkness. "I don't know why they can't do their job properly, but it's not my fault."

That was the narrative she'd been telling him his whole life. Nothing bad that happened was ever his fault. Maybe it was time that she changed the story.

"How about I take you home with me?" she asked, softening her tone. It was little more than a rustic cabin in the mountains, but it was cozy and warm, and she had a spare room for him.

He snickered. "So you can yap my ear off about fiscal responsibility and not fighting. No thanks. At least I'll get some peace and quiet with Nana. She doesn't nag me like you do."

His paternal grandmother believed the sun rose and set with him. In her eyes he could do no wrong.

"You'd get plenty of peace and quiet in a jail cell," Willa said with extreme patience.

"I can see you gearing up for a lecture. Spare me. Okay? I'm not in the mood."

Not in the mood? As if she was after being pulled away from her job because he'd gotten himself into trouble. "Let's talk about you taking some responsibility for your actions.

You chose to go to the bar and drink." When he should've used the money to pay his gas bill. "The fight was as much your fault as it was the other guy's."

"How would you know? You weren't there. I can't believe you're defending a stranger instead of sticking up for me. Maybe I had just cause. Way to go to be supportive, Mom."

"No one is justified when alcohol is involved." Far too many drunks have believed otherwise. "And if I wasn't supportive, I would've told them at the station I didn't need another favor and to charge you. Next time they'll book you, take your fingerprints, a mug shot and you'll be in the system forever. Is that what you want?" She took a breath, chiding herself for letting him lure her into that argument. "A class C misdemeanor could get you up to six months in jail and a fine of seven hundred and fifty dollars. What were you thinking?"

Hesitation. "Guess I wasn't thinking. Just feeling."

One honest thing from him. "Zeke? Please tell me you didn't get into a fight over Sheila Sanders."

"Fine. I won't," he snapped, growing even more defensive.

She could wrangle a suspect twice her size into a restraining hold, cuff him, haul him to the station, handle all sorts of verbal abuse, even from colleagues, put a perp in his place with a few well-chosen words, but when it came to her son, she was a pushover. An illogical, emotional move-heaven-and-earth-for-him softie. Her first job was a mother, doing anything to protect him. In her heart, he was still her top priority.

In her head...she had a higher calling as chief of police.

Willa pulled up to his grandmother's house. "I thought

you and Sheila broke up." The girl was trouble, but Zeke wouldn't listen. At least not to his mother.

"We did."

"Then why did you get into a fight over her?"

He clenched his fingers into fists so tight his knuckles popped.

Her gaze fell to his lap. She stared at the tattoo on the back of his left hand—a moon and sun with an eye in the center.

The only time her son had seemed at peace was as a member of the Shining Light. A blessing as well as a curse.

She put her palm on his forearm, her heart aching in her chest. All she wanted was to keep him safe. For him to be happy, healthy and productive. She'd thought she'd lost him to McCoy's cult and when he came back, at first, she'd been relieved. But Zeke had only been filled with more anger and darkness. Drinking. Fighting. As if he was lost.

"What happened to you on the compound?" she asked in a whisper. "Why did you leave?"

More questions sprang to mind. Had he known Beverly Fisher and Leslie Gooding? Had he seen either of them in the last month?

She didn't dare voice her thoughts. Bringing up anything related to the Shining Light only agitated him. This was already pushing it, begging for a conversation, for a peek into his life.

He jerked his arm away. "Stop asking questions I don't want to answer, Mom. It's not like you ever wanted me to stay on the compound anyway. Just let it go." He got out and slammed the door.

Every time she probed into what happened, he clammed

up. Those who'd known Beverly had claimed she'd done the same whenever the Shining Light was brought up.

Watching Zeke climb the porch steps, she wished she could let it go like he wanted. Simply forget his past association with the religious movement she didn't understand. Pretend as though he'd never gotten that tattoo.

But the coincidence of her son returning shortly before the murders started had her stomach twisting in a knot.

Chapter Three

Mrs. Gooding dissolved into tears as she hunched over in her chair and dropped her face into her shaking hands. Her husband wrapped an arm around her, trying to comfort her, but it only brought tears to his own eyes.

Daniel nodded to Deputy Ashley Russo, who he had waiting in the corridor for this very purpose. She swept inside and helped Mrs. Gooding up and out of the office, shutting the door behind them. The grieving mother's sobs echoed in the hall.

"I'm sorry," Mr. Gooding said. "I thought my wife would be able to make it through this interview."

"You have absolutely nothing to apologize for." Willa moved from her seat beside Daniel around the desk to sit next to the distraught father. "You've suffered a horrible loss."

"We'll do our best to get you out of here as quickly as possible," Daniel said, and Mr. Gooding nodded. "With Leslie being from Cheyenne, how did she first come into contact with the Shining Light?"

"Her grandparents live in Evanston. She's been taking the bus from Cheyenne over there every summer for the last eight years. The bus stops here in Laramie. That's where those kookie people from the cult got to her."

Willa nodded. "It's one of their top recruiting spots. I think it's because so many who are unhoused hang around the area. There are no homeless shelters in Laramie, leaving them vulnerable to predators like the Shining Light. That's also the place where we have the most transients passing through, giving them exposure to people."

Once a month, Daniel had seen them, about fifty or so, wearing Shining Light T-shirts, spreading the word about their religious movement around town, handing out fliers, offering food and shelter to those in need.

"I guess she got curious." Mr. Gooding shrugged. "They filled her head with all sorts of nonsense. Brainwashed her. Instead of going to her grandparents, she ended up on the compound this summer. She joined. Took her *vows*, as if she was marrying the commune," he said with disgust. "Became Lila Starlight, like the name we had given her wasn't good enough anymore."

"Why did she leave the movement?" Willa asked.

Daniel supposed it must have been something compelling to break through the brainwashing.

"She'd been saving up to go to the university," Gooding said. "The time it was taking discouraged her, so we agreed to pay for it. We told her that if she gave college a try, just one year, and didn't like it that we would support her going back to those people. We even took out a second mortgage on our house for the school tuition. The one thing we couldn't get her was a car, but she agreed…on one condition. If, after a year of school, she chose the Shining Light instead, we'd give them a sizable donation."

Daniel exchanged a look with Willa. There hadn't been

any mention of money in the statement they'd given the detective. "How sizable?" he asked.

"Ten thousand dollars. Half of one year's tuition."

Willa gave a low whistle. "That's quite a lot. And the commune agreed that they would let her return, if that was what she wanted?"

"I guess so. Leslie seemed pretty certain that it wouldn't be a problem."

Her brow furrowed, and Daniel made a note to circle back around to find out what troubled Willa about that later once they finished with Mr. Gooding.

"Was Leslie taking school seriously?" she asked.

"I think so. She was doing great on her exams. Studied hard. Socialized and went to parties on campus, like we hoped she would. She even joined the track team." He broke down crying. "She'd readjusted to normal life. We thought we had our little girl back."

Daniel handed him more tissues. "Do you know where she liked to go running?"

"Around campus for a quick jog." Gooding dabbed at his eyes. "For anything longer, she preferred the trails through the foothills of the Elk Horn range."

The foothills were close to where they'd found her body. Daniel leaned forward, resting his forearms on the desk. "Did she ever go running at night?"

"Sometimes. But you said her time of death was after midnight. She wouldn't have gone running that late."

"If she didn't have a vehicle, how did she get around town?" Willa asked.

"The public transportation bus service offered by the university, Secure Ride."

"I'm familiar with it," Daniel said. "It's free and operates until two in the morning and goes anywhere in town. She could've gotten to the Elk Horn trail easily depending on where she was dropped off and whether she was running. Riders can use an app, but we didn't find her phone." He'd check with dispatch to see if she scheduled a ride for the night.

"Did she mention a boyfriend?" Willa asked. "A guy that she spent time together with, or anyone she was having trouble with?"

"No. She wasn't dating anyone to our knowledge. She was a sweet kid who got along with everyone." Mr. Gooding straightened. "Are you saying that someone she knew killed her?"

It was not only possible, but likely. Stranger homicide was extremely rare. "Women are far more likely to be murdered by a man known to them than a stranger." Daniel didn't mention that it was also possible that they were dealing with a serial killer.

What they knew for certain was that both women had been between nineteen and twenty-two, with dark hair, slender builds, and had been former members of the Shining Light.

"Thank you for taking the time to speak with us in person," Willa said. "Where are you staying in town?"

"At the Quenby Bed and Breakfast. We'll be there until we can take our daughter home." Mr. Gooding looked between them with glassy eyes. "When can we see her?"

"Later today." Daniel stood. "I'll have Deputy Russo stop by the B and B. She can take you over to the morgue when it's time."

Somberly, Mr. Gooding rose from his chair. "Please, find who did this and make them pay."

Willa put a hand on his shoulder. "We'll do everything in our power to bring Leslie's murderer to justice."

He nodded and left the office.

The weight on Daniel's shoulders only seemed to get heavier. He could still hear Mrs. Gooding's wailing in his ears and see the devastated look on her face. No one wanted to force a parent to rehash their child's final days, but it came with the job. Such interviews had to be conducted sensitively, with compassion.

Now that they were alone, Willa's placid expression gave way, like a mask slipping. She looked at him, stricken. They were both feeling a bit raw.

For a few heartbeats neither of them said anything, as though they weren't ready to move on from the Goodings misery quite so quickly.

Daniel sat and reviewed his notes. Finally, he broke the silence. "When Mr. Gooding mentioned that his daughter would be allowed to go back to the compound if she decided school wasn't for her, you looked skeptical. Why?"

Willa paced in the office. "After you take your vows, if you decide to leave, they consider you one of the Fallen. They don't welcome you back with open arms according to their PR rep."

"Maybe they do if your parents are writing a check for ten grand."

Stopping, she stood still, her gaze meeting his. "I wonder if they've done that before."

"Let someone come back for a price?"

"Yeah." Willa folded her arms. "What if McCoy realized that Leslie was readjusting and might not return with all that money?"

"You're thinking motive. But what about Fisher? You

weren't able to track down any family and she was living on the streets. No potential loss of cash with her."

"It's possible one of his acolytes, a real zealot who wasn't happy about people leaving, specifically women, took matters into his own hands. It is a patriarchal religious movement."

His cell phone buzzed on his desk, and he grabbed it. "Autopsy results on Leslie Gooding." He turned to his computer. "I'll pull it up here. We can look at it together," he said, motioning for her to take the seat beside him.

For some reason, she hesitated.

WILLA STARED AT the chair Daniel had hauled around the desk next to his earlier—a gesture to communicate to the Goodings that they were equals, partners, on this case, even if they happened to be in his office. She considered sitting there, close enough to catch the scent of cinnamon and cedar. Close enough to feel his body heat.

Whether he was clean-shaven or had a day's worth of stubble covering his masculine jaw, like now, there was no denying he was a handsome hunk. Smooth brown skin. High cheekbones. His eyes always cool and direct. Her gaze dropped to his full, sexy lips, and she remembered his kisses. On her mouth, her cheeks, her neck, diving lower…

She cleared her throat as well as her head. "I'm good. What does it say?" she asked.

A narrow groove appeared between his eyebrows as he studied her. She swiveled on her heel, turning her back to him, and faced the bullpen. On a side table was a copy of the *Laramie Gazette*. The latest murder was on the front page along with an image of the Shining Light symbol.

There were a lot of people who either didn't understand

the religious movement, such as her, or who simply didn't like them, or were afraid of their presence and ever-growing power as their numbers continued to increase. In Willa's experience, it was easy for fear to turn volatile with the right spark.

Two dead women between September and October, only four weeks apart, might just be it.

Clacking on the keyboard filled the air as he pulled up the report. "Know that, know that…" he muttered.

"Time of death?" she wondered.

He read aloud under his breath. "Here we go. Estimated to be between midnight Saturday and two a.m. Sunday."

"Was she raped?"

"No evidence of sexual assault."

The same as Fisher. She stepped closer to the desk, picked up the file, and opened it. "Drugs in her system?" she asked, staring at the photos of Leslie Gooding.

"Preliminary toxicology didn't find a sedative," he said, staring at the screen. "There is strong reason to believe that the victim was impaired at the time of death. Based on the clean wounds, the body was still as she was stabbed. The victim hadn't thrashed or moved about. If something like chloroform was used it would be difficult to detect unless a lethal amount was used."

"That's consistent with the trace amounts of chloroform we found in a tent used by Fisher and explains why there were no defensive wounds or bruising on either. She was probably just waking up when he killed her since her eyes were open." The guy wanted her to know who did this to her. That's why he waited for her to regain some consciousness. "The cut to her throat wasn't the fatal one. It was done postmortem, right?"

"Yes. Immediate cause of death was exsanguination. Four stab wounds to the chest, some deeper than others. Three missed the heart by millimeters. One didn't."

Frustration welled inside her as she set the pictures down. "Any DNA?"

"Nothing significant under the nails or on the body."

"Once again, no blood, no hair, no saliva, no semen, no prints." No DNA. "But he took his time with her and left quite a mess. What does that say to you?" She turned toward him.

"The killer was careful," Daniel said. "Used gloves. Probably wore something to cover his clothing and possibly his hair."

"How long did he watch both of them, planning this?" It was a rhetorical question that neither of them could answer. What if he was stalking his next victim right now?

With a knock, the door to the office opened. Peggy Tuckett walked in, carrying a pot of coffee. "Figured you two could use a refill," she said, sympathetically. The office manager looked to be in her late seventies, with salt-and-pepper hair and hazel eyes.

"Thank you," Willa said, going to the desk and picking up her mug. "I could definitely use some more hot coffee."

Peggy topped up her cup, and then she went around and did the same for Daniel. "Let me know if you need anything else." She started to leave when her gaze shifted to the photos on the desk, and she stopped. Two deep lines appeared between Peggy's brows as she stared at the victim.

"What is it?" Daniel asked.

"This reminds me of a cold case we had a few years back," Peggy said, peering closer at the pictures. "Four dead women. Tied up like that. Stabbed. No suspects. One day, the murders simply stopped."

Willa cupped her mug with both hands. "How long ago was that?"

"I can't say for certain," Peggy said, with a one-shoulder shrug. "Maybe four or five years."

Relief trickled through Willa. If the killer had done this before, then...

Deep down she knew that despite Zeke's rage at the world, her son wasn't capable of this. Not of murdering anyone.

She glanced up and found Daniel studying her. Quickly, she schooled her features.

"Who was on the case?" Daniel asked Peggy with his keen gaze still on Willa.

"The previous sheriff. Jim Ames. He worked it alone. But the more time that passed, the less effort he put into it."

"Nothing came up in ViCAP." There was no mistaking the frustration in his voice.

Peggy sighed. "Ames never used it to my knowledge."

The database was designed specifically to analyze information about homicides that were known or suspected to be part of series, apparently random, motiveless, or sexually oriented. Though it wasn't a requirement where no sexual assault had occurred, Ames should have made more of an effort to input the cases.

Daniel muttered something under his breath, and she caught a curse. "I should've let Holden look at the file like he wanted to last night. He was here back when Ames had the case."

"I wonder why the medical examiner didn't mention the similarities," Willa said, thinking aloud.

"That ME only started three years ago and wouldn't have performed those autopsies, but I can pull up the files for you," Peggy offered.

"I've got it," Daniel said, clacking away on the keyboard, not wasting any time.

"I'll place an order for lunch over at Delgado's Bar and Grill. Sandwiches all right?" Peggy asked.

With a grunt, Daniel nodded. "I'll take a Reuben, please."

"Any kind of soup and a Caesar salad with grilled chicken for me." Willa wished she had an office manager as efficient and thoughtful as Peggy. "Thank you," she said.

"Only doing my job." The older woman headed out of the office, closing the door behind her.

"I found it. The murders happened five years ago spanning from November to January. They referred to him as the Holiday Elk Horn Killer since the first one occurred over Thanksgiving weekend and the last on New Year's Eve. All the bodies were found in and around the Elk Horn Mountains."

Willa stepped closer. "The timeline is shorter. Four murders in three months."

"I'll bring up all the autopsy reports and case files. Want to take a look with me?" Daniel met her gaze. "Promise I won't bite." The corner of his mouth hitched up in a grin that chased away her hesitation.

The quiet, straightforward way about him was one of the things she'd enjoyed most. Over the years, she'd had her fill of pushy Neanderthals that only made her want to push back in return. Her father. Her ex-husband. Daniel didn't fit that mold. He didn't find the need to be a domineering alpha male, even though he was in a position of power.

She slid into the seat next to him. "Might be faster if you

let me use Holden's computer since he's out. We can split up the reports."

"If that'll suit you. Then again, it might be easier to compare and discuss if we're in the same office," he countered, and it was hard to disagree.

He brought up the autopsy report on the first victim, who had been identified as Tiffany Cummings, and they perused the findings.

"Many of the details seem to match our current cases. Except for…" His voice trailed off as she caught what had stopped him.

"She had a scalp hematoma at the base of the skull like she'd been struck. And bite marks on her neck and shoulder."

He turned to her. "Sorry, about what I said a few minutes ago. It was in poor taste."

"Well, you did promise *not* to bite," she said, "and there was no way for you to know what we'd find in the report."

Daniel smiled at her, and her belly tingled in response. He clicked on the case file, bringing it up on the screen and they scrolled through it.

"Look at that," she said. "All the victims were found about a mile from their vehicles."

"And two tires had been shot out with a .223-caliber bullet."

"He used a high-powered rifle to disable the victims' cars," she said. "And then what? How did they end up one mile away?"

"It's possible the victims didn't realize their tires had been shot out and thought they had simply blown. Unless your ear is trained to recognize the difference in the sounds, it's easy for a civilian to confuse."

She had been shooting since she was ten years old and

would know the difference. "Maybe they walked to get help and he got them then." She flicked a glance back toward the bullpen. "One minute." More details that differed from the current case might pop up. She needed to see the cases spread out in front of her. Sometimes if she mapped it, she was able to figure out the why that led to the who.

Willa went to the bullpen and grabbed the standing whiteboard near the wall that she'd spotted. Since it wasn't in use, she commandeered it and rolled it into Daniel's office, then went hunting for markers. Once she had the board set up and had acquired markers from the office supply closet Peggy showed her, she started to make notes about all the victims on the whiteboard.

"Keep going," she said to Daniel. "I'll highlight the differences and then we can fill in everything else we know."

Two hours later they had finished. Stepping back, Willa and Daniel studied what she'd done, including taping up photos of all the victims and one of McCoy centered over the latest ones.

The whiteboard was a good start. "We can add to it as we discover more," she said. For now, the order helped her breathe a little easier.

"It helps me to see everything laid out like this, too. Looking at it, I'm not so sure the killers are the same."

"Copycat?" Willa stared at the board, seeing the possibility. "But some of the specifics that were never released to the public are identical. The way the women were bound. All with nylon rope. Their wrists tied to tree trunks. Stripped down to their undergarments, but not violated. None of that had been in the papers."

"Although all the victims had been dark-haired, the first set had a wider range of ages, twenty to forty. They were also drugged. Medetomidine was found in their systems whereas as chloroform was used with the latest victims."

The report had stated medetomidine was used in veterinary anesthesia. "Maybe he ran out of the stuff or couldn't get access to it anymore."

"The murders that happened five years ago were more brutal—the hematomas and the bite marks. Why hit them if he had drugged them?"

"He used the drug to slow them down and hit them because he enjoyed it. Maybe he was more passionate about it five years ago because he was just getting started. Leaving behind his DNA was sloppy. Perhaps he learned, evolved."

"The first set of victims were killed over the holidays. None on a full moon. Why the five-year break? Why start targeting women from the Shining Light?" Daniel asked. "Why move from the Elk Horn Mountains to their backyard?"

"Let's say it's the same guy. What if he stopped killing because he joined the Shining Light and started up again because they kicked him out? It would explain the break and provide motive for targeting the new victims. Also, the two areas where the bodies were found aren't that far apart." She pulled a map and marked where all the bodies had been discovered. "The location of the last victim from five years ago is only three miles from Leslie Gooding."

"I've got your lunch order." They turned to see Mercy McCoy—Marshall McCoy's daughter, who recently left the movement and had become one of the Fallen—standing at the door to the office, holding up a bag of food from Delgado's where she now worked.

Willa turned the board around to hide their notes.

"They won't talk, but I think we have someone else who will," Daniel said, looking at Mercy.

McCoy's daughter knew the inner workings, understood the Shining Light's beliefs, but was no longer a believer. Her boyfriend had been the federal agent targeted last month by domestic terrorists who had been linked to her father. If there was anyone who might be willing to tell them the truth about the cult, it was her. In fact, she might be their greatest resource of information from the inside.

"Thanks," Daniel said, taking the lunch delivery from her. "Would you happen to have a few minutes you could spare?"

"This is a busy time of day at the bar and grill."

"It's important," Willa said. "We just have a few questions."

"Okay. I guess I could use my break." Mercy gave a polite smile. "Questions about what?"

"Please, take a seat." Daniel motioned to a chair. "We were hoping you could help us out with a case."

Mercy sat, folding her hands in her lap. "The one in the paper about the victims who were former Shining Light members?"

"Yes." Willa nodded. "Did you know Beverly Fisher and Leslie Gooding? They went by Blue and Lila Starlight on the compound."

"I did, but Blue left the commune a while ago. Back in February. And Lila wasn't with us long either. She left in July. Two months before me."

Something struck Willa. "You said that Lila wasn't with the community long *either*. How long were they members?"

"Blue was with us for a year and a half, but she didn't become a member until January. Weeks later she left. Whereas

Lila came to us around March, I think, and took her vows right away. Then was gone soon after, too. The paper said that they were stabbed." Mercy tensed as she wrung her hands. "Did they suffer?"

Willa didn't want to lie, but they didn't need to burden Mercy with the truth. The young woman had an innocent quality about her, probably from her sheltered life on the compound. In the past month that she'd been free, she'd blossomed while retaining her kindness, extraordinary empathy and positive outlook that Willa envied. She didn't want to be the one to taint that.

"No," Daniel said, "they didn't."

"When did they die?" Mercy asked. "The *Gazette* was vague. It simply stated that Blue had been killed last month. And Lila yesterday?"

Willa nodded. "Leslie Gooding was murdered between midnight Saturday and two a.m. Sunday. Beverly Fisher on September 19 between ten p.m. and midnight."

"Oh, my God, that's the same day I left the compound for good." Her gaze fell and roamed like she was thinking.

"What is it?" Willa drew closer. "If something occurred to you, no matter how small you think it, you should tell us."

Mercy chewed on her lower lip. "It's only that the day I left there was a full moon. There was one on Sunday, too."

Daniel took out a notepad. "Is there a significance to that?"

"For the Shining Light, definitely." Mercy nodded. "We, I mean they believe that a full moon is about transformation, where the seeds planted on the new moon are brought to fruition. But last month on the 19th was a supercharged version. A time for one thing to end and something else, something big to begin."

Was Fisher's murder the beginning of a killing spree?

Daniel stopped writing. "Do you know why Blue and Lila decided to no longer be a part of the movement?"

Shaking her head, Mercy pushed her blond hair back behind an ear. "My father didn't want me to be a part of any dealings with the process of the Fallen. Looking back, I wonder if he thought it might encourage me to leave. Feed into my doubts. Do you know why they were killed? Is it because they used to be Starlights?" Concern riddled her face.

Daniel sat on the edge of the desk, facing the young woman. "That's what we're trying to figure out."

"We believe you can provide answers that we desperately need," Willa said. "Your father refused to speak to me. I got the runaround from the PR person, Sophia Starlight."

Mercy laughed bitterly. "PR. What a joke. Sophia is my father's fiancée. Anything she told you came directly from him."

"Are there any circumstances in which your father would let someone go and then agree to take them back?" Willa asked.

"Penumbroyage. It's when a person from sixteen to twenty-four is allowed a year away before taking their vows."

Daniel looked at Willa, the same thought probably going through their heads. "What about after taking their vows?" he asked.

"No. It's forbidden. Someone would be considered the Fallen."

Willa still had her doubts. "Has your father ever accepted money to take back someone who was once Fallen?"

Mercy's gaze fell to her lap, her body tensing.

Willa put a hand on her shoulder. "You can talk to us

without fear of reprisals from your father or anyone else on the compound."

"It's not that. I'm not afraid of my father. But I can't honestly say what line he wouldn't cross when it comes to funding and protecting the commune. Anything is possible."

"Do you know anyone on the compound who might be fanatical enough to kill two women because they left?" Daniel asked.

"The one person who would have been, tried to kill me. But he's dead."

Willa nodded, understanding. The LPD had handled the case. "Is there anyone on the compound who can tell us more about Blue and Lila's time there? Why they left? If they had upset anyone in the commune?"

"*Can* and *will* are two different things. Most of them won't betray my father by answering your questions honestly," Mercy said, and Willa wanted to get McCoy on obstruction so badly it was like an itch under her skin, but it would be hard to prove. "His hold on them is too strong."

"Most, but not all." Willa pinned Mercy with a stare. "Who might talk?"

The young woman's bright blue gaze bounced between them. "Arlo. She's an educator at the compound and an elder on the council. She's the only one to ever question my father when no one else would. They had an argument not long ago about how the Shining Light got their tax-exemption status as a religious organization. She was upset that he was hurting former members somehow to achieve it."

"Hurting them in what way?" Daniel asked.

Mercy shrugged. "Arlo might tell you."

"Might?" Willa studied Mercy. "Is there any way we can persuade her?"

Her gaze fell. "Tell her you spoke to me. That I left because…my father is the true devil. A liar. Evil. His darkness has tainted everything he's built," she said as Daniel took furious notes, "and will one day be destroyed because of his wickedness. One way or another."

Willa could tell it wasn't easy for Mercy to say those things.

"But questioning her in front of others would only endanger her," Mercy added.

"There must be some way to get her alone," Willa wondered.

"She participates in the recruitment of new members in town during the new moon. She'll be wearing yellow, the color for educators. Glasses. Gray bob cut. Arlo stands out."

Daniel got up and went to his computer. "When's the next new moon?"

"In fourteen days," Mercy replied before he had a chance to look it up.

Willa groaned in frustration. "We can't wait that long to talk to her."

Mercy's gaze fell, unease creeping through her expression. As Willa thought she might have to gently nudge her to talk, Mercy finally said, "Arlo also leads smaller weekly excursions to neighboring cities. Every Wednesday they leave shortly after sunrise. They take the same route to get to the interstate. But she won't be alone. If you talk to her, others will report it. There might be a better way to find out what you need to know about Blue and Lila. Empyrean," she said, referring to the name acolytes called Marshall McCoy, "keeps meticulous records. Everyone goes through an unburdening session before they take their vows, where they confess their deepest and darkest secrets to him. He records it and has been known to use it against current members as well as former."

"Use it how?" Daniel asked, raising his brows. "Are you talking extortion? Is that how they got their tax-exempt status?"

"I don't know for certain. If I did, I'd tell you, but I wouldn't put it past him. My father isn't a good person. He needs to be stopped."

"Does he also keep records of why people left?" Willa asked.

Mercy met her gaze. "He does, but only on those who were members. Not on the transients who don't take vows. The files are restricted to him and the council of elders. There's a process to someone leaving. They discuss it and document it. Everyone has to approve, but they generally follow Empyrean's lead. The community says their good-byes and they're driven off the compound."

"Driven?" Daniel stopped writing and looked up from his notepad. "By who?"

"We—they—don't have dedicated drivers. It's always someone from the security team, but they keep a logbook to track it."

"Where are the unburdening records and restricted files kept?" Willa asked.

"In the security building."

Thinking about the prospect that the killer was hiding on the compound, Willa had another question. "Is it possible for someone to stay on the compound without becoming a member indefinitely?"

Mercy considered it. "I suppose, yes, it is. I was there for twenty-four years without taking vows. They don't impose time restrictions on those who come to us as adults. They want people to embrace the Light when they're ready."

"And there's no documentation on a new recruit, someone who hasn't decided?" Daniel asked. "Not even if they were kicked out for doing something wrong?"

Mercy shook her head. "None. They never saw the need for it."

The perfect place and way for a killer to hide, off the grid, no paper trail, no online footprint.

"Thank you," Daniel said. "You've been very helpful."

Mercy bowed her head with a solemn look. "It doesn't feel like it."

"Trust me," Willa said with a nod, "you have." With a witness to attest to the existence of the unburdening tapes, restricted files, and logbook of drivers, they now had enough for a warrant.

Daniel picked up the phone. "I'll get the district attorney to expedite a warrant for us."

Willa nodded in agreement.

DA Allen Jennings had been trying to bring down the Shining Light at least since Willa had taken over as chief of police. She didn't know why he had the group, specifically Marshall McCoy, in his crosshairs, but if anyone could get a judge to sign off on a warrant in less than an hour, day or night, it was him.

"I'll walk you out," Willa said to Mercy.

The young woman rose from her seat, and they left the office, giving Daniel some privacy.

"Thank you again for your assistance. I also want you to know that we don't believe you have any reason to worry about your safety so far, but it's best to increase your situational awareness and not go anywhere alone at night until we catch the killer." Since Mercy had blond hair and blue eyes, a stark difference to the dark-haired, brown-eyed victims, she doubted that the young woman would become a target. She also had an added layer of protection by living with her boyfriend who was a federal agent.

"I will. If you need anything else, don't hesitate to ask."

A chair scraped against the floor, drawing Willa's attention.

Peggy hopped up and hurried toward her. "You're never going to believe this. There's another body."

Mercy gasped as the words sent a cold chill skittering down Willa's spine.

"Who called it in?" Willa asked.

Peggy grimaced. "Hikers out near the foothills of Elk Horn. They saw vultures circling in the sky, went to check it out, expecting to find the carcass of an animal and found a dead woman instead. One of the hikers called his cousin, a cop on the Laramie PD. The officer checked it out since family was involved even though it was well outside of the city limits."

And a violation of protocol, but Willa kept the thought to herself.

"The officer just called it in," Peggy added, "since it's our jurisdiction and he knew you'd be here at our office."

"I bet she was killed last night." Mercy wrapped her arms around herself like she was suddenly cold. "Before midnight. While there was still a full moon."

"There's one more thing," Peggy said. "The officer stated that the victim didn't have a *tattoo* of the Shining Light from what he could see."

The deviation from the new pattern made Willa's stomach churn. More concerning, two women had lost their lives in the span of less than twenty-four hours, and whoever did this was out there free to kill again.

"But…" Peggy's expression was sober as her voice trailed off, "the symbol had been carved onto her stomach."

Mercy gasped.

The murders had already been gruesome enough. But the carving made her wonder. "On second thought, Mercy, there is one more thing you can do. Come with us and see if you can identify the woman."

"If she doesn't have a tattoo, I'm not sure how much use I'll be, but I'll come if you want me to. It's just they're expecting me back at Delgado's."

"I'll call them. Work it out so it doesn't impact your job. Thank you." Her gut told her there might be a connection between the victim and the cult. Then again it could be nothing more than wishful thinking. Either way, Mercy would help them to establish or eliminate a link.

Willa was betting on the former.

Chapter Four

Taking the camera from Pruitt, Daniel headed to the grove of trees, where Willa waited alongside Mercy. From there, they were able to see the yellow crime scene tape draped around trees that cordoned off the perimeter and the officers canvassing the area, but not the body.

Willa said something to the young woman, who nodded in reply, and broke off, meeting him before he made it within earshot of Mercy. "Is it like the last two?" she asked.

"Sort of. The one change was instead of a tattoo there was the carving. Pruitt estimates the time of death to be between seven p.m. and midnight yesterday. She was right," he said, hiking his chin toward Mercy. "The victim was killed during the full moon. Same type of stab wounds as well as a cut across the throat."

"Whoever the killer is," Willa said, "he's familiar with the Shining Light's beliefs. Mercy said the back gate to the compound is less than three miles from here. I asked her if any Starlight can use one of the compound vehicles." Willa shook her head no. "But any of them can take a horse out for a ride."

"We'll have to conduct a wider search for horse tracks."

"Only problem with that is there's a dude ranch two miles due east," she said.

The ranch would offer horseback riding off the property. Any tracks they found might not lead back to the cult's compound.

Tipping her head back, Willa's jaw hardened. "The audacity of this perp to think he can kill two women in one day and get away with it."

"It makes me think of the way he fans their hair out around their head," Daniel said. "Making them a spectacle. As though he's demanding our attention."

"Well, he's got it all right. I don't care how many sleepless nights it takes—we have to catch him before the next full moon."

He nodded in agreement. Next time, the killer might take three lives, escalating the pageantry of these murders. "Let's see if Mercy can ID her," he said.

They started down the slight incline toward her.

"Were you able to get a hold of Rocco?" he asked, referring to the young woman's boyfriend. Willa had thought it best to contact him.

"Yep. I explained the graphic nature of the pictures that she would see," Willa said, keeping her voice low, "and how it might be hard on Mercy to look at them. He's on the way. One of my officers is out in the woods, near the road to lead him up here."

Mercy stood trembling, her arms wrapped around her stomach like she was trying to hold herself together.

Daniel wished there were a better way to investigate a possible connection to the victim and the cult than involving Mercy any further. But their options were slim, and they were running out of time. He pulled up a picture on the viewfinder. He zoomed in on the dead woman's face, so she didn't have to see any of the gruesome wounds. Still, it would be difficult for a civilian to look at with the victim's eyes open, skin gray, hair deliberately positioned, postmortem. Truth be told, although he'd gotten used to the horror, it never failed to repulse him.

"This won't be easy," Daniel said, in an effort to prepare her. "But it's important that you take your time, okay? We need you to be sure. One way or the other." He turned the viewfinder toward her.

Her jaw unhinged. She rocked back on her heels, the blood draining from her face.

"Take a deep breath." Willa clasped Mercy's shoulders. "Do you recognize her?"

For a long moment, Mercy stood silent and trembling, staring at the horrid image.

"Do you recognize her?" Willa repeated gently. "If you're not sure, that's o—"

"Gemma with a *G*." Mercy's voice was barely audible. Her gaze transfixed on the screen. Tears welled in her eyes. "Her name is Gemma Chavez. Oh, my…" She put a hand over her mouth. Tears fell, rolling down her cheeks, and Daniel shut off the camera. "I helped recruit her. I think it was last October before the first snow. It was so cold out. She was shivering and I could see the wind cutting right through her. She was still at the compound when I left."

"Was she planning to take her vows?" Daniel asked. "Become a Starlight?"

"I don't know. I don't think so. She seemed like she was biding her time, not really interested in learning about the Light. Is this my fault for encouraging her to come to the compound? Did I make her a target?"

"This is not your fault," Daniel said.

"You aren't responsible for the sick actions of another person." Willa patted her back. "Don't you dare blame yourself."

"I think I'm going to be sick." Whirling around, Mercy rushed off, not making it far before she leaned against a tree trunk and retched.

Willa took a few steps in her direction, then they noticed Rocco Sharp hurrying through the woods, escorted by an LPD officer and Deputy Livingston. The ATF agent spotted Mercy and ran to her. He slid a comforting around her, bringing her in to a tight hug.

It was a good thing Willa had the foresight to call Rocco. Mercy would need someone close to her for reassurance and support.

Deputy Livingston approached them. "The warrant came in." He held it up.

Daniel took it and perused it with Willa. "The warrant isn't as wide in scope as I would have liked." He slipped it in the back pocket of his jeans. "The victim's name is Gemma Chavez," he said to Livingston. "Get statements from her family and friends. See if they know why she lived on the compound. Get them to confirm dates. See if she had any intention of taking her vows."

Livingston nodded. "I'm on it."

"Let's go knock on McCoy's door," Willa said. "This time it'll go much differently."

Indeed, it would. Even if Marshall McCoy tried to stonewall, now they'd at least get access to some of his records.

They made their way through the woods back to his vehicle. Driving up to the compound, they passed protesters that had gathered near the front gate. The group was small, no more than ten people. But they were loud. They held signs that read STOP KILLING WOMEN WHO REJECT YOU and CULTY MURDERERS. Through bullhorns they chanted, "Shining Light, you are a blight!"

Daniel pulled up beside the guardhouse and rolled down his window.

"Afternoon," said the armed guard. "May the Light shine upon you."

Not sure how to respond to the greeting, Daniel simply nodded. "Sheriff Clark," he said, loud enough for the security guard to hear him and pointing to the star fastened to his shirt, "and chief of police Nelson here to speak with Marshall McCoy."

"*Empyrean* is unavailable unless you have an appointment or a warrant."

Lucky for them they had both. "We have an appointment. Chief Nelson called ahead earlier and notified your PR rep that we'd be stopping by."

The guard nodded. He went back inside the guardhouse and made a call. The guy had to cover his other ear just to hear over the protesters. After a minute, he returned. "You can go on up to Light House. It's the main building at the top of the hill. Security will be waiting for you." He hit a button and the wrought iron gate swung open.

Daniel tipped his hat in thanks, and they proceeded up the long driveway. In the late afternoon light, the large building made of glass and steel gleamed like something straight out of a modern fairy tale.

"They're completely self-sufficient here," Willa said, looking out the window. "Sophia gave me the spiel about how they grow all their own food, make most of their clothing and furniture."

"Wow. Really?"

More guards were scattered across the grounds. All had handguns holstered to their hips or rifles slung over their shoulders. Agent Rocco Sharp had uncovered arsenal on this compound, but it turned out that none of their weapons were illegal, and they had enough to arm a small army.

"They're also vegetarians," Willa added. "Or vegans. I forget which."

"Ashley, Deputy Russo, has been here once before. She told me that they use Light House for everything from celebrations and meetings, to communal meals. But only McCoy lives here. His children used to." He parked where a security guard indicated in front of the building, and they climbed out.

The chanting from the other side of the gate could easily be heard.

"Follow me." The guard led the way up the wide stone steps.

Neighboring the main house was a ten-bay detached garage. A couple of dual-sport motorcycles and one white van with their symbol painted on the side were out front.

The guard opened the door, letting them in. "Please wait here for Empyrean. He'll be with you shortly." Then he closed it, leaving them alone.

"Tight security," Daniel whispered, in case anyone was lurking out of sight, eavesdropping.

"I get having armed security at the guardhouse, but it's odd to have so many guards on the compound when people are supposedly free to leave whenever they want, don't you think?" she asked.

He took off his Stetson while Willa left hers on. "I agree. It is."

Standing in the impressive two-story foyer of Light House, Daniel looked around. He took in the entryway of polished steel and ten-foot-high windows that spanned the walls, the gleaming chandelier and veined marble floor. A lot of money had been poured into this building and the entire compound, a hundred acres surrounded by a brick wall, complete with a guardhouse and fancy wrought iron gate.

"Big bucks paid for all this," Willa whispered, echoing his thoughts, and he gave a subtle nod. "And it's spotless. You could eat off the floor. I wonder how many people it takes to keep this place looking so pristine."

"My apologies for the delay." Marshall McCoy came down the hallway, wearing a white suit that had been impeccably tailored. He was accompanied by a bald middle-aged man, dressed in a yellow tunic and matching pants and a woman in her early twenties who wore a green dress.

Daniel had learned the Shining Light had a color system to represent a person's function in the community. Educators wore yellow. The creative types dressed in orange. Gray was for security. The woman in green was an essential worker.

"I was waiting for our community lawyer, Huck Starlight, to join us," McCoy said indicating the bald man. "And Sheriff Clark, this is our PR rep, Sophia. Chief Nelson, I believe you're already acquainted."

Willa flashed a tight smile. "I am indeed."

"If you wouldn't mind removing your shoes before we proceed to my office." McCoy gestured to their boots.

Daniel noticed the others were barefoot. "We can conduct the interview here. We won't be inside Light House long."

McCoy clasped his hands in front of him. "I understand you have questions about the recent murders of two former members."

"That's correct." Daniel was itching to get through the preliminaries. "Do you know why Beverly Fisher and Leslie Gooding decided to leave the community?"

"I believe, after careful consideration on their part, they decided that the Shining Light wasn't the right fit for them."

"Can you be more specific?" Willa asked.

"I don't recall specifics." McCoy pulled on a placating grin. "I have more than five hundred in my flock. Everyone seeking the Light is welcomed here. At times, we take in twenty or more potential recruits a month. We tend to get quite a few young people who have nowhere else to go." His gaze shifted, locking solely on Willa. "Especially those having difficulty at home with judgmental parents who can't accept them as they are. They receive unconditional love here." His smooth smile spread wider, and Daniel couldn't help feeling as though he was missing something. "Not all decide that our way is for them. After they've received rest and nourishment of body, mind and spirit, some choose to move on. I don't commit to memory all their reasons for leaving. If the message of the Light isn't for them, that's fine. In the end, we might have saved a life. No one is held at the compound against their will. Our mission here is to help people. To make the world a better place."

"That's a nice speech," Daniel said. "But let's focus on the victims. There's a third one. We found her three miles from your back gate. Like Beverly and Leslie, she was murdered during the full moon."

McCoy, Huck and Sophia all exchanged guarded glances.

"Any idea why the killer might choose the full moon to act?" Willa asked. "Is there a special significance to the Shining Light?"

Another practiced smile. "I can't imagine what might be

going through the mind of a killer. As for the moon, all of its cycles have significance for us," McCoy said, then Huck put a hand on his shoulder and whispered in his ear. "I have no idea why the killer would choose the full moon, but as stated in the *Farmers' Almanac*, it's considered a good time to harvest. Perhaps he got the idea from there. I doubt it has anything to do with us."

"Unlike the victims who have a direct tie to your..." Willa drew in a deep breath but did a great job of hiding the frustration she must have felt. "Religious movement," she said, stopping short of calling it a cult to his face.

The cagey responses were certainly testing Daniel's patience, as well. "The latest victim has been identified as Gemma Chavez. A recruit. She came to the compound a year ago, last October."

"According to whom?" Huck asked.

"One of the Fallen who was here during that time period," Daniel replied.

Huck's jaw hardened.

But McCoy didn't even flinch. "Gemma left us last week after deciding not to take her vows."

"Why did she wait a year?" Daniel asked. "Did something happen?"

"Last month the domestic terrorists who were after agent Rocco Sharp also made a threat against us. For the safety of the commune, I instituted a lockdown. If you've never been through one before, it could be scary. At the same time, my daughter chose to turn her back on the Light and embrace darkness. It instilled serious doubts in Gemma. We tried for three weeks to help her overcome them. Ultimately, fear won over faith because she was weak. And the devil found her out there, where the world is cruel."

"The fact that the latest victim also had a previous connection to your organization will be made public," Willa said.

The easy smile slipped from McCoy's face. "News of the murders has spread throughout the community, putting everyone on edge. As if that weren't enough, now we have protesters, with their bullhorns to ensure their voices carry, thanks to the latest article in the *Gazette*. Nice touch calling him the Starlight Killer."

"Seemed fitting," Willa said.

McCoy stepped closer to her. "The only problem with that is Gemma Chavez was not a Starlight."

"She was one of your recruits," Daniel said. "Lived here as a de facto Starlight for more than a year and her killer carved your symbol onto her torso. I'm inclined to agree with Chief Nelson. It's fitting."

McCoy's Adam's apple started bobbing like he was suddenly nervous. "It's unfortunate to hear that."

Willa cocked her head to the side. "Might be even more unfortunate if the number of protesters outside continues to grow. It's in your best interest to cooperate with us unless you have something to hide."

Every cell in Daniel's body told him that McCoy had plenty to hide.

"Here I stand." McCoy outstretched his arms. "Fully cooperating."

"Then you wouldn't mind showing us your logbook of drivers for the dates Fisher, Gooding and Chavez left the compound and were dropped off," Daniel said, and McCoy's expression turned deadpan, but Sophia suddenly looked nervous. "In addition to the unburdening tapes and restricted files detailing why they left."

McCoy opened his mouth to speak, but Huck stepped forward, stopping him.

"Not without a warrant," Huck said.

Daniel pulled the document from his back pocket. "Just so happens we have one."

Glaring, Huck snatched it from his hands and read it. "The logbook of drivers, yes. A list of members who joined within the past five years along with a list of those who became the Fallen this year." For a minute, he was quiet as he read the warrant. "But only the audio recordings of unburdening sessions and files for the two women who were once members."

Daniel had hoped for greater leeway regarding access to other files, but the district attorney had warned that the judge would view it as a violation of the Fourth Amendment and the right to privacy of the other members, past and current, unless they could show sufficient probable cause. Which they didn't have. Yet.

For now, this would have to suffice.

"We also need a list of everyone over the age of eighteen who has been on the compound for the past four to five years, but hasn't taken vows," Willa said.

Huck scowled. "We don't have any documentation on individuals who are not members. We can't give you what we don't have."

"Surely you know who is and isn't a member and how long they've been with you," Willa insisted.

Huck took McCoy off to the side. The two spoke in hushed tones too low to be overhead. After a moment of deliberation, McCoy nodded, and they came back.

"We are happy to comply," McCoy said. "It will take us

some time to get you that list since we have hundreds here. We should have it ready for you in a week."

"You have forty-eight hours, and one more thing." Daniel hooked his thumbs on his duty belt that carried his gun, handcuffs, radio, baton and pepper spray. "Did you agree to let Gooding return to the commune in a year if her parents paid you ten thousand dollars?"

"Now that you mention it, I do recall granting her a form of penumbroyage since she was so young and her faith wavered. One year to fully commit. Though nothing was predicated on money. We do, however, accept all donations with hearts full of joy."

"Isn't that a violation of your rules?" Willa asked. "Since she had already taken her vows."

"I granted her special dispensation. As Empyrean, I have that liberty," he said, clasping his hands, and Daniel found it funny how his memory had suddenly improved after they produced a warrant. "Sophia will take one of you to the security building where we store the recordings and files. Huck will go with the other to the garage. The logbook is in there."

Sophia and Huck slipped on shoes from a mat near the door.

"Sheriff Clark, if you'll come with me," Sophia said.

Daniel glanced at Willa. "Okay by you?" He didn't think it mattered how they divvied up the task, but it was always good to check.

She hesitated a moment. Then she gave her classic tight smile that he'd learned meant she was uneasy or displeased. "Fine with me."

Outside at the bottom of the stairs, they separated. Putting on his hat, Daniel followed Sophia around to the side of the house. He looked over his shoulder and caught Willa glancing back at him. This time he was certain what the look on her face meant. Unease. But he didn't understand what she was worried about.

He lost sight of her and quickened his step to keep up with Sophia, who marched along as though she wanted to get through an unpleasant chore. With light brown hair and eyes, she was attractive, but beneath her artificially sweet exterior was a toughness that made him wonder if she was what his grandmother would have called an old soul. Maybe she was simply a survivor.

Behind the main house, the whole compound opened beyond an expansive meadow. "What are all those buildings?" he asked. One looked like a chapel.

As she explained, she pointed out the barracks for new-comers contemplating becoming members. Beyond that there was the sanctum, which he gathered to be the church, a schoolhouse, a playground filled with kids, then a series of trailers she called the wellness center, as well as communal bathroom facilities.

"Empyrean and I have a private restroom in the main house, where we live together." She put a hand to her belly in that way pregnant women did, though she wasn't showing. "We also have a farm, stables, an apiary, huts that our single members share and small cabins for families on the far side of the compound. These are some of our newest recruits."

They passed a group all dressed in blue, spinning in circles while someone played a drum and another person, wearing yellow, directed them with instructions on breathing and emptying their minds.

"Would it be possible to speak with some of your elders from the council?"

Sophia smiled, but it didn't reach her eyes which narrowed ever so slightly. "Did you have someone particular in mind?"

"No. I just wanted to get the perspective from a council member."

"You spoke with *her*, didn't you? Empyrean's daughter?"

"You mean Mercy?"

Her lips flattened into a grim line as she bowed her head, averting her gaze. "We do not speak the names of the Fallen."

"I'm afraid I'm not at liberty to disclose our confidential sources, but there are a number of Fallen in and around town."

"You're right. There are. But only one with the level of information you used for your warrant." She made a humming sound. "Here we are." She opened the door to a long building with a tin roof. "This is our security hub."

Inside were five guards working at computer stations. As they walked through, he glimpsed a couple of screens. They were monitoring the entire compound. The cameras had been discreetly placed because he hadn't noticed any of them.

A man came out of an office. "Can I help you, Sophia?" he asked while looking at Daniel.

"Sheriff Clark, this is our head of security, Shawn Starlight. Shawn, they have a warrant to take some materials. We're just here to collect them and we'll be out of your way."

"Do you need any assistance?" Shawn asked.

Although he offered assistance, he sounded like he meant protection.

"No, it's okay. Thank you." Sophia led him down a hall

to a room. Above the door handle was a keypad. "If you wouldn't mind." She gestured for him to turn around.

He pivoted on his heels. Beeps resounded behind him and a door clicked open. He turned back. "How many people have access to the records in there?"

"Only Empyrean and the six elders on the council."

"And you, don't you mean."

"I've only been given access recently. I'm still adjusting to my new role as Empyrean's assistant and public relations representative."

"Why the change?" he asked, and her expression soured. "If you don't mind me asking."

"When Empyrean lost his children, everything changed."

The last month must've been difficult for those on the compound with all the upheaval. It was possible the events that led to Mercy leaving, the domestic terrorists attacking a federal agent, and McCoy's son dying could have some-how been the catalyst causing the killer to act.

"Has anyone on the compound acted differently since then?"

"No," she said without even taking a second to think about it. "Here are the records."

There were rows of five-drawer file cabinets for current members, those on penumbroyage, and the Fallen. He hoped more information about the victims and why they left might fill in the missing pieces they needed.

He opened the drawer labeled GHIJ in the penumbroyage section. Sure enough, Leslie Gooding's file was in there. He pulled out the folder. Inside was a thumb drive and a two-page document.

"The audio file of the unburdening session is on the

drive, but there should also be a transcript in the folder," Sophia said.

Daniel went to the cabinets designated for the Fallen. They had been categorized by decade then alphabetized. He opened the drawer under DEF and thumbed through the file folders searching for Fisher.

But another name stopped him.

Ezekiel Nelson.

PORING OVER THE logbook in the garage, Willa noticed that one person in particular had been a driver during every recruiting event—the monthly as well as the weekly ones out of town—and dropped off all the Fallen and those who left the community before taking their vows within the last year.

"Why is Fox the only one to have driven those who were no longer a part of the Shining Light off the compound?" she asked Huck and the security guard in charge of the garage.

"All the guards in training do rounds in every area before being assigned primarily to security," the guard said. He had a kind demeanor unlike the stern, stony-faced Huck. "When he did his time here in the garage, he loved driving and afterward he volunteered so many times I considered him my go-to guy for drop-offs. He still helps me out with maintenance of the vehicles whenever he has a chance."

"What's Fox's real name?" she asked.

Huck's mouth puckered like he was suddenly sucking on a lemon. "That is his *real* name." The offense in his voice was unmistakable.

She wondered what they called her son while he was with them. He'd always hated the name Ezekiel. Surely he'd changed it. Not that it had been Willa's first, second or third choice. His grandparents had picked it from the Old Testament of the Bible and insisted.

"What's his legal name? The one he came to you with?"

The guy looked at Huck, and the lawyer gave his approval with a nod. "Miguel Garcia."

"Where can I find him?"

"Is he in some kind of trouble?" the guard asked. "Fox is a good guy. He wouldn't do anything wrong. Not on purpose. He's always the first to offer help."

"I have some questions for him. No one is in trouble." Not yet, at least.

Another look at Huck. Another nod. "I can radio and ask him to come over."

She saw no good reason to give Fox a heads-up. "That's all right. I prefer you not to radio. We'll go to him. Where is he?"

"At breakfast he mentioned he worked out getting assigned to patrol near the farm today."

"Thank you." She looked at Huck. "Let's go."

"It's a bit of a walk. Ten or fifteen minutes. Do you mind?" Huck asked, as though he was the one who minded. "I don't know if you're in a hurry."

"I can take her over," the guard said, "on one of the motorbikes. If you want to save time, ma'am."

"What's your name?"

"Everyone just calls me Ry."

"I'm ready whenever you are." She looked over at Huck. "We'll need to take the logbook with us but will return it as soon as we can."

Grabbing a set of keys from a hook, Ry headed out of the garage. She trailed behind him. He cranked the engine to one of the motorcycles parked outside.

She swung her leg over and got on the back. Her Buck Budgie—pocketknife—dug into the crease of her pelvis. Compact but sturdy, she never left home without it if she was working. She adjusted it in her front pocket until she was comfortable. Putting one hand on Ry's shoulder, she held her hat down with the other.

With a rev of the engine, they sped off.

There weren't any paved paths for him to drive on, but the bike didn't have any trouble zipping through the grass. The ride provided an impromptu tour of the compound. She'd been so curious for so long. What did McCoy and his acolytes give her son that she didn't?

They receive unconditional love here.

McCoy's words rang in her ears. Even the sound of the motorcycle's engine couldn't drown it out.

But had he been right? Had they not judged Zeke, not criticized? Had they freed him to be his best self?

Zeke never talked about this place after he'd been kicked out. Not the people, the facilities, what he'd learned. Not even the food.

Only that he no longer ate meat.

Part of her wished she'd been the one to retrieve the audio files and documents. The other part of her knew it was better not to be faced with the temptation of stealing her son's. Crossing that line would change her. A slippery slope leading someplace she didn't want to go.

But when it came to Zeke, lines tended to blur.

As they pulled up to an orchard, Ry slowed the bike and stopped. He turned off the bike, leaving the key in the ignition, and put the kickstand in place.

They both climbed off. She looked around and spotted

a man wearing a gray shirt and slacks carrying a basket of apples, at the same time Ry pointed out the same guy.

He was a little older than her son. She guessed twenty-three, maybe twenty-four.

Willa approached him. As she unhooked her badge from her utility belt and held it up, his eyes grew wide, and he went rigid. "Miguel Garcia—*Fox*—I'm Chief Nelson from the LPD. I have a few questions to ask you about Beverly Fisher, Leslie Gooding and Gemma Chavez."

He dropped the basket, spilling apples across the ground, and took off running into the orchard.

Swearing under her breath, Willa almost bolted after him, but then she had a better idea. She ran back to the motorcycle and hopped on. Turning the key in the ignition, she fired up the bike and backed off the center stand.

"Hey!" Ry said. "You can't take that."

Willa took off her hat, shoved it into his chest, and cranked the throttle. She kept one foot on the ground while she pivoted the bike, the backside swinging wildly as she roared off. By the time she could follow, she'd lost sight of him.

Good thing the workers in the orchard gave him away—confused looks, heads swiveling in the direction he'd run.

She sped down the dirt walkway, taking a right through the trees.

There!

He'd gotten farther than she had expected. The guy was fast.

Quick as a fox.

She raced through the orchard after him. He threw a panicked glance over his shoulder, his eyes flaring wide as saucers as he must've realized he couldn't outrun the motorcycle.

Wending around trees, taking sharp turns, she was grateful for the teen years she'd spent off-road racing with her ex, Zach, on the cheap motorbikes he'd fixed up for fun.

Miguel sprinted out of the orchard into a clearing, giving her the opportunity that she needed.

In a wide-open space, there was no contest. She easily caught up to him. "Stop!"

But the kid kept running like his life depended on it.

Slowing the bike, she put her heel down as she swung the rear end, bumping the guy. He stumbled and fell.

She stopped the dual-sport, staying mounted, and drew her weapon before he could bolt again. "Down on your knees. Hands behind your head."

Once he did as he was told, she climbed off the bike and unhooked her handcuffs from her duty belt. "Since you ran, we get to have our little Q and A down at the station."

Chapter Five

"Miguel," Daniel said, "let's talk about your previous association to Beverly Fisher, Leslie Gooding and Gemma Chavez." He set down a picture of each deceased woman on the table inside the sheriff's interrogation room and slid them in front of the suspect.

"I—I—I didn't associate with them," he said. "Not really." Putting his unrestrained hands on the table, Miguel lowered his head and looked at the pictures. "Oh, God. I could never do something like this. I would never hurt anyone."

Huck, seated beside him, shoved the photos away.

"Beverly was on the compound for a year and a half," Willa said. "Gemma for twelve months. Leslie for four. Do you expect us to believe that you didn't interact with them at all the entire time until the day they left?"

"I might have talked to them in the dining hall in passing, but I always sat with the security team. Maybe during one of our celebrations or some other event we might have spoken or something, but that's the extent of it."

Others on the compound had confirmed as much when Daniel had asked around after Willa had put Miguel in the SUV. It's possible they were covering for him, in an effort to protect their image of the Shining Light, but looking at Miguel now, Daniel wasn't quite sure that they were lying. The kid was scared. He didn't strike him as a murderer.

Then again, far too many serial killers came across as normal. Likeable. Twenty-four-year-old Miguel Garcia was both. There was also the fact that he had a record in Idaho. For rape.

"You love being a member of the Shining Light, don't you?" Willa asked, and he nodded. "Why?"

"It's safe for everyone. They don't judge your past. They help you be your best self. We're a community. We look out for each other. Protect one another."

"Even lie to protect a Starlight?" Willa leaned forward. "Maybe even kill to preserve the reputation of the Shining Light?"

Miguel jerked backward, a horrified expression on his face.

"You don't have to answer that," Huck said.

"No, I want to. We walk the path of truth and atone for our transgressions."

"Tell us about the last time you saw each of the victims," Daniel said.

"When someone leaves our community, we usually drop them off at the main bus station in town, after lunch, with their bellies full. With Blue and Gemma, it was different. Blue was the only person I dropped off the entire month of February. People don't leave by choice during the dead of winter. I was told to take her to the church that's across the road from the bus station. And it was right before dinner."

Daniel made a note of it. "Who told you and why?"

Miguel cast a furtive glance at Huck. The older man whispered in his ear.

"Empyrean," Miguel said. "He didn't give me a reason. But I remember that Blue looked sick. She was really pale, sweaty, shaking like she had tremors or something."

Daniel glanced at Willa, but she was entirely focused on Miguel.

Huck put a hand on his shoulder. "You don't have to elaborate," he said in a low voice. "Just answer the question. Keep it simple."

"What about the other two?" she asked. None of the fire had left her tone.

"I don't really remember Gemma, other than she was nice and didn't seem as if she was taking things seriously."

Willa cocked her head to the side. "How would you know if you didn't associate with her?"

"Folks whispered about it. During the winter months we get a lot of people looking for a warm bed and a hot meal. There's a pattern to the drifters. People pick up on it. Most weren't surprised when she said her goodbyes."

"Were you surprised?" Daniel wondered.

"Kind of. The ones like her, who aren't serious, usually leave in spring or summer. Not as it's starting to get cold. She wanted out really bad the day I dropped her off and she didn't want to wait until after lunch."

Which begged the question, why did she hightail it out of there then? Had something or someone scared her enough to make her leave?

"And Leslie?" Willa asked.

"I remember Lila. I was sad because she had just committed to the Shining Light and then she was leaving all of a sudden, but she wasn't unhappy."

Willa propped her elbows on the table and steepled her fingers. "Were you sad? Sure you weren't angry she left?

Angry enough that you'd rather see her dead than living in darkness?"

According to Mercy, that's how they saw the Fallen, as cast out of the Light into the darkness.

Huck's green eyes narrowed to slits. "My client has already stated his feelings."

"I didn't kill anyone," Miguel said. "I thought—we all thought—she was one of us. Then something happened. I don't know what. Next thing I know I was told to drop her off. She talked the entire ride to a couple of other people who decided they didn't want to stay at the commune, telling them she was going to college to make her parents happy. Before she got out of the van, she told me that I'd see her again when she rejoined our family next summer."

Huck put a hand on his shoulder. "Brevity is best."

"What?" Miguel asked the lawyer. "I was just trying to explain that it didn't make any sense to me. I said goodbye and hoped she'd come back to us. I was sad. Not angry."

"Maybe you hit on Beverly, Gemma and Leslie as you drove them," Willa said, "and they didn't appreciate your advances. So you killed them to make them pay for rejecting you."

Since Miguel had a conviction of rape, Willa was playing the right angle with him. Bad cop who thought the suspect had an issue with women.

"It's okay," Daniel said in a softer tone, playing good cop. "You can tell us if things got out of hand and something happened that you didn't intend."

"No way, sir." Miguel shook his head. "I didn't kill those ladies."

Huck took a deep breath. "Chief Nelson, Sheriff Clark, suppositions are not questions. We're done here."

"I only have three more questions." Willa cut her gaze from the lawyer back to Miguel. "Where were you from midnight Saturday to two a.m. Sunday and last night from seven to midnight?"

Daniel wasn't surprised she hadn't asked him about September 19 since the compound had gone into lockdown that night. Anybody with a half a brain, would have claimed that was his alibi whether or not it was true.

"At the compound," Miguel said. "Saturday night I was asleep. I have three roommates who saw me."

Didn't mean he didn't get up while they were also sleeping soundly and sneak out. If the killer was living in the commune, then he was smart enough to have found a way to get out undetected.

"Last night was our full moon celebration," Miguel said. "Dinner was done around seven thirty. We all went to the sanctum and listened to a homily. Afterward, we went around and gave thanks and then we went out to the quad. Danced and sang under the full moon until midnight."

"What was the homily about?" Daniel asked. If he was there, he'd be able to give specifics.

"Empyrean spoke on giving thanks for our ordeals because they're like sandpaper, refining us, making us better. It was inspiring. Uplifting."

"With five hundred members it must be easy for someone to slip away unnoticed," Daniel wondered.

"I suppose." Miguel nodded. "But I danced with Maria most of the night. Empyrean matched us as a couple this summer. She works in the orchard. That's why I requested a work assignment there today. And after the full moon ceremony, I helped the musicians put away their instruments in storage."

"Countless members would have seen him last night," Huck added in a tone implying that Miguel's alibi was solid.

"Then why did you run?" Willa asked.

"Because…" He lowered his head. "I knew this would happen. That you wouldn't listen to me. That you wouldn't believe me. That you wouldn't care about the truth." He glanced up at Daniel with watery brown eyes. "I thought you would be different, but I guess not."

"Why did you think that?"

"You're a Black guy. I'm a brown Hispanic, we don't always get a fair shake."

Daniel had faced his share of struggles. Sometimes people judged him based on the color of his skin before they got to know him as a person, but these two situations were not the same. "That's true. But you ran from an officer of the law after she stated she only wanted to ask questions. Guilty people do that. And you have a record for rape. This doesn't look good for you."

"It was statutory rape," Huck clarified.

"We were both in high school. I was eighteen. My girlfriend was sixteen. And white. Her parents didn't think I was suitable," Miguel said. "They tried to break us up, but Jasmine and I wanted to be together. They went to the cops and had me charged. In Idaho, statutory rape is simply rape. Even though Jasmine made a statement on my behalf and I was an honor roll student, I ending up serving three years. Three. After I was released, I was put on the sexual offender registry. Do you have any idea how hard it was for me to get a job? An apartment? I was like a pariah when people found out. Except at the Shining Light." He looked at Willa. "I'm sorry I ran, really, I am. I freaked, but that doesn't mean I'm guilty. Please, I didn't do this."

Daniel believed him. One thing for certain, they could eliminate him as the killer in the cold case murders five years ago because Miguel was sitting in an Idaho prison. For another, others on the compound would back his alibi.

"What's your final question for my client, Chief Nelson?"

"Foxes are predators. Is that why you chose the name?" she asked.

The guy hunched over, a defeated expression sweeping over his face. "Did you know young foxes are preyed upon by eagles and coyotes? The adult ones are attacked by larger animals, bears, mountain lions. They're fast, but they can't outrun a wolf. The biggest predator to a fox is humans."

Now even Daniel was curious. "Then why Fox?"

"When I was younger, I got obsessed with reruns of the show *X-Files*. I always thought the name Fox Mulder was cool. The Shining Light gave me a chance to forget my past. To reinvent myself. To accept me as the Light would have me be."

Daniel's heart broke a little for the guy if the rest of his story checked out.

Willa leaned over and whispered, "Hallway."

He followed her out of the room and closed the door. "I don't think he did it."

"Neither do I." She put her hands on her hips. "But I want to verify his story about what happened in Idaho."

"Of course." They needed to dot every *i* and cross all their *t*s.

She turned, heading toward the office, and he caught her arm, stopping her.

"Who is Ezekiel Nelson?"

Stiffening, she schooled her features. "I should have mentioned it sooner, as soon as I saw what was granted in the warrant, but I didn't know how to bring it up."

He wished like hell that whatever she was about to say she'd told him two years ago. Not now because she felt boxed in and had no other choice. "Just tell me. Who is he?"

She shifted her gaze before meeting his as though she was considering telling him a lie. But with a shake of her head, she said, "Zeke is my son."

Daniel didn't see that one coming. He'd assumed a brother, uncle, possibly a cousin. "After you verify Miguel's story, we need to talk."

"THANK YOU FOR your time answering my questions," Willa said over the phone to Jasmine Emmer.

"Anything for Miguel. How is he? I mean, is he happy, healthy?"

"Yes. He's doing well."

"That's nice to know after what my parents put him through. At the time, they didn't believe me when I told them that he was the love of my life. But it's still true. I think about him every day. Is he married?"

"I believe he's dating someone." Willa wasn't sure how the matchmaking worked.

"Oh." Disappointment resonated in Jasmine's voice. "Good for him. Well, I was happy to help."

"Have a good day." Willa hung up.

Miguel's story was not only true it was heartbreaking. Years ago, he'd been treated unfairly, robbed of three years of his life, for loving the wrong person. But Willa didn't regret getting tough during questioning. That was the job, to push and poke and see if they got a break. They still had a killer to find before he struck again.

Daniel came back into his office and closed the door. "The dispatch from Secure Ride at the university stated that Leslie requested a ride through the mobile app, pickup point the far side of town at seven p.m. Saturday. I figured that's where she would have most likely been if she was coming back from a run at Elk Horn. But then she was a no-show when the driver arrived."

"Because the killer got to her first. Used the chloroform and waited until the time was right."

"Campus police finally tracked down her roommate. The girl has been sleeping at her boyfriend's, but she crossed paths with Leslie on Saturday evening. She came back to get some clothes and Leslie was heading out for a run."

"If the killer is someone on the compound, the full moon event would have been the perfect distraction to disappear, especially if he's a loner that no one would miss."

Daniel mulled that over. "But Saturday night would've been difficult."

"Difficult, sure." She put her feet up on the edge of his desk and rested back in her chair. "Not impossible. Especially if McCoy sanctioned the murders. What if the Holiday Elk Horn Killer joined the Shining Light, unburdened about his taste for blood, and McCoy asked him to do this with his blessing?"

"That's a big leap."

"The murders didn't start up again until after his heir apparent, Mercy, chose the outside world over the one she had been raised in. Rejected her father and the religious movement he started in front of the entire commune. I'm sure it caused doubt to spread like a disease throughout his flock. Killing a few nonbelievers who had turned their backs on the cult, preaching the devil took them, might be his way to restore faith in the herd."

"A grisly way to restore faith that's bringing them the type of attention they don't want."

"Unless they spin it," Willa said with a look of disgust. "Think about it. Every time something horrible happens in this town, their numbers only grow."

There was no denying that was true. "It could also be someone with a grievance against the Shining Light. You saw those protesters. Half of this town has been aching to get rid of them for years. Don't forget the reason we need to speak with Arlo tomorrow. If it's true Empyrean has been blackmailing former members, people have killed for far less."

"Gemma didn't have a tattoo. How did the killer know Gemma had spent time among them unless he was one of them? The compound, the rules, the lack of a vehicle, the vows to the Light, it's all the perfect cover for a killer. I guarantee you not everyone who joins gives up all their possessions. Easy enough to stash a car not far away. Use an account that he didn't turn over to Empyrean to pay for the gas. It's feasible."

Daniel nodded. "It is." He pulled down the blinds to his window overlooking the bullpen and closed them. He did the same for the ones over the glass door and leaned against it. "Did your son give up everything when he joined?"

Willa's stomach soured. This was coming, she'd been aware, but it didn't make her any more ready to have the conversation. Setting her feet down on the floor, she stood and folded her arms. "He didn't have much to give up. He ran away from home and joined when he was seventeen."

"Why did he leave?"

"Ever since his father, my ex-husband, Zach, was killed in the line of duty, he was never the same." She should've taken him to grief counseling. His grandmother had mocked the idea, putting it into his head that only the weak cried to a therapist. Still, she should've dragged him anyway. Explained that getting help was a sign of strength. "He ended up on the compound. Zeke told McCoy I was a cop. That combined with his age was the only reason I received a phone call, letting me know he was there before I put out an APB on him."

"Why did you let him stay?"

"McCoy talked to me. The man is very good at what he does. Charming. Convincing. It was the end of the school year. Zeke was already failing his classes and had been expelled for fighting. McCoy persuaded me to let him explore the community over the summer. To see if it made a difference in him. I was desperate. All I wanted was for him to get better."

"And he did?"

She nodded. "He was like a different person. Happy. Smiling. Laughing." It had brought her tears of joy to see him that way. "They had even worked with him on his studies. Helped him to get his GED over the summer. He told me he wanted to stay because he'd found the Light. McCoy warned me that if he left, he'd fall back into darkness. He tapped into my greatest fear."

"Of course, you supported him staying."

How could she not? "After he took his vows and became a Starlight, he didn't want to see me or his grandmother. He claimed everything he needed was there on the compound with his new family." The words had been like a hot knife in the heart. "That was my baby. I loved him so much, but I let him go." Every parent had to at some point. She learned to love at a distance, relinquish her expectations and embrace his choices. "Until he came back to me a few years later after he was kicked out."

"For what?"

"I don't know. You have no idea how tempted I was to be the one to get the files."

"What does he say when you ask him?"

"To leave it alone. Then he clams up and storms out or shouts and storms out. Either way, I, the chief of police, can't get a straight answer out of my own son." Saying it aloud only made her even more disgusted and disappointed with herself.

Daniel crossed the room and clasped her shoulders. "You're being too hard on yourself."

Was she? "I'm failing him. I'm so afraid I might lose him if I don't figure out how to fix whatever is wrong. I should be able to do more, but I feel…helpless when it comes to him."

He pulled her into a gentle hug. She wanted to relax into it, but part of her didn't deserve comfort for not doing a good enough job with her kid.

"You're more than a cop. You're a single mother doing the best you can." With one arm around her, he rubbed her back with the other. "I was raised by a single mother. My dad died when I was twelve."

The same age as Zeke. Was it a sign all hope wasn't lost?

"I had some troubled years. My mother threw money at the problem, thinking her wealth was the solution," he said, his voice warm and soothing as a shot of whiskey, and she leaned against him. "Don't get me wrong, when I got kicked out of one private school, she bought my way into another.

But it wasn't until I left home, stopped blaming her for everything that was wrong in my life, claimed my inheritance, my father's ranch out here, that I was able to fix it for myself. Then I became a cop."

"You grew up with a silver spoon in your mouth?"

He chuckled, the smooth sound vibrating through her. "After everything I told you, that's your takeaway?"

She gave him a sad smile. "It distracted me."

"Well, if you need a distraction, I can do better. My mother is Selene Beauvais."

Surprise slid through her. "No way." She'd never been the type to buy fashion magazines or read about runway shows featuring couture, but she would have to live under a rock not to have heard of the legendary supermodel Selene Beauvais.

He hitched up a shoulder. "Way." He stroked her hair, his fingers feathering her ear and her gaze dropped to his mouth.

She missed kissing him, lying in bed, snuggled close. Even if it had only lasted a few months. He'd made an impression that she couldn't forget.

"The point I want you to remember is single mothers are heroes, but superheroes don't exist. Cut yourself some slack. You can't do the work for him."

Everything he said made perfect sense in her head. She just needed her heart to accept the logic. "You're right. Thanks for the support."

"I'd like to support you more. But for some reason you simply cut me off. Can I know why?"

She dropped her arms, ending the embrace, but stayed close to him. Absorbing the smell of him. His warmth. His quiet strength.

"You have no idea how hard it's been for me. Not only as a single mother. But to climb the ranks in the police force and become the first female chief of two different departments."

"Yeah. How would I, the first Black sheriff of Albany County, have any idea what you might be going through professionally. When I first got this job, it wasn't through an election. I was appointed because the last sheriff had made such a mess of things and caused a scandal. It wasn't until I faced an opponent and became elected by the people that my critics started to treat me differently."

Once again, he was right. They had much more in common than she had realized. "We were lovers, but we had also been friends. Sort of." On the verge of becoming such. "I'm sorry I never stopped to consider what you were facing. But it's different for me. As a woman people make assumptions about how I got here. If they knew we had been seeing each other at the time it only would've fed into the narrow-minded notion that I had somehow slept my way to the top even though the mayor appointed me."

He nodded. "But that was then. We've kept our distance, and both proven ourselves for the last two years. Why can't there be an us now?"

A knock at the door had them separating by a good two feet.

Willa was grateful for the interruption. She needed time to think. Her first response would have been that the job was too demanding, requiring all her time and effort. But the truth was the biggest hurdle of cleaning up the department was behind her. Now it was about replenishing her ranks with good police officers and catching a serial killer. Beyond that, Daniel faced the same demands as her and if anyone would understand and accommodate without complaint, it was him.

"Enter," he said, his gaze lingering on her like a soft caress until the door opened.

Deputy Russo came in. "I read the transcripts of the unburdening sessions that McCoy conducted right before they took their vows. The women had been given ayahuasca, a drug they use in their religious ceremonies."

"You're saying they were high when they unburdened," Daniel said.

"Precisely. Nothing noteworthy came up with Gooding. Jealousy of her friends who had cute boyfriends, enough money for college and a sense of purpose. It was the last one that McCoy focused on with her."

Willa put a little more distance between her and Daniel. "And Fisher?"

"She had a history of prostitution and stealing because she was struggling with substance abuse."

"And he dosed her with ayahuasca?" Daniel asked.

Russo nodded. "According to the document that detailed why she left, the ayahuasca triggered cravings that had gone away. It was difficult for her to stay clean again. She broke into the infirmary twice and offered sexual favors to the security team if they would get her something, anything to get high. McCoy couldn't help her. So, when they kicked her out, McCoy had her dropped off at a church that holds NA meetings."

"Unbelievable." Daniel folded his arms. "McCoy got her clean only to mess her up all over again."

"He's playing God on that compound. It's shameful." Willa shook her head. "What was the situation behind Gooding leaving?"

Russo's mouth twisted. "Not quite sure. It stated that she was *allowed* to leave to attend college for a year. It would appease her parents and facilitate a smooth transition if she decided to return. But she would be considered one of the Fallen until the day," she said, pausing as she looked at her notepad, "and I quote, 'The Light spoke to Empyrean guiding him to do otherwise with the sweet child Lila,' end quote."

"He created a loophole," Willa said. "One to allow her to come back and for him to cash her parents' check. No mention of money by any chance?"

"Nope. Sorry." Russo frowned. "The ME won't be able to start on the body for a few hours. Family emergency."

"Okay," Daniel said. "Go to the church—see what they have to say about Fisher. Also question the employees at the bus station. See if they saw or heard anything strange or out of the ordinary."

"I'll head over there now." Russo left the office as Livingston entered.

"Statements from Gemma Chavez's parents and her best friend," the deputy said. "I'm still trying to get in contact with other friends her parents mentioned."

Daniel took the folder. The phone on his desk beeped. He put it on speaker and answered, "What is it, Peggy?"

"District Attorney Jennings and Mayor Schroeder request your and Chief Nelson's presence at the mayor's office over at city hall. Right now."

Daniel groaned. "All right." He hung up. "One guess what the topic of conversation will be," he said, sarcastically.

This case and three dead women. Willa met Daniel's gaze. "Right about now, I'm glad you suggested we work together on this one."

"Why? So we can share the heat?"

She smiled even though they were about to walk into the fire. "Exactly."

"Then I think you owe me one. How about you buy me a drink?"

"Just a drink?" she asked, knowing better.

A deep chuckle rumbled in his chest. "Well…let's play it by ear."

The sound of his laughter and the suggestion of one drink dragged her back to their first meeting at Crazy Eddie's. The bar was a dive outside of Wayward Bluffs before you reached Laramie, in the middle of nowhere. A place for truckers and ranch hands. She'd never worn makeup or a smile and didn't accept drinks someone else had purchased. Her reputation for being the tough woman no one bothered had been hard-earned until Daniel had waltzed in and had the guts to claim the stool beside her.

With a scowl, her brush-off had been, "Cowboy, no offense, but *I* don't want company and if *you* don't want trouble, you'll take a hike."

Still, that hadn't discouraged him. "Depends on the kind of trouble."

She'd pointed to her Wayward Bluffs badge on her hip that had sent most men skittering. "I'm Chief Nelson, so we're talking police trouble. Still interested?"

He had simply flashed his own badge from the SWU campus police. "Nice to meet you. I'm Chief Clark, but I'd prefer it if you called me Daniel."

She had been a goner right there, but something in her wouldn't let her buckle. The more she'd played hard to get over the weeks that had followed, the more interested he'd seemed. One night, she'd taken the time to explain her reasons why a relationship of any kind was out of the question. Though she was single, she had a complicated family— leaving it open to interpretation—and a job that demanded all her energy. A man in her life would have required time and effort she didn't want to give.

"I've picked two duds before, which is proof that dating isn't for me," she had confided, breaking her rules and engaging in conversation with him every time he'd walked into that bar.

"Maybe the third time is the charm."

She'd given him more honesty. "I don't have that kind of luck."

"I do." Another irresistible smile that made her thighs tingle. "I've got enough for both of us."

Unsure what exactly it had been, his infectious confidence, his calm demeanor, his easy way with her or that he'd simply worn her down, she'd suggested that they get a room at the motel down the road. Eventually, the motel had turned into nights at his place.

Then she'd gotten the job in the LPD and had ended it.

"Hey." Daniel waved in front of her face, bringing her back to the here and now. "What do you say?"

"It's never just a drink, cowboy."

He gave her another slow grin that sent a zing of anticipation jolting through her, and she smiled in return. "No, Willa, I guess not." His chuckle was low and knowing. "I suppose when it comes to you, it's always more than just a drink."

Conversation. Lovemaking. Snuggling. Showers together. Sometimes even breakfast, too.

Her body ached for all of it. She'd gone two years without being touched. Not even a hug from her son. But her head told her to slow down. Not to throw caution to the wind without thinking it through first.

"Let's talk after we deal with the mayor and the DA."

Chapter Six

"Good evening, Mayor Schroeder, DA Jennings," Daniel said, taking off his hat.

"What can we do for you?" Willa asked.

Sitting behind his oversized mahogany desk, the mayor glanced at the DA, who stood beside him, red-faced and clearly steaming.

"I'm going to cut right to it," Allen Jennings said. "You two came to me, requesting assistance on a quick turn-around warrant, and I was more than happy to oblige. You went to the compound, questioned a suspect and released him. We have three dead women. Three! Why wasn't he charged?"

Word spread fast, which meant Daniel had someone in his office leaking information to the DA's office. But that was an issue for another time. More pressing was that if Daniel knew anything about Willa, it was that she would not abide anyone talking to her that way.

While he on the other hand had perfected the art of not letting it get to him. Well, not letting it show anyway.

Before he could get a word out, she opened her mouth first.

"He had an alibi and we had no evidence." Willa put her

hands on her hips. "Simple as that. It's called adhering to the law."

Narrowing his eyes, Jennings marched around the desk. "Don't presume to dictate to me about the law."

"We're all on the same side, working toward a common goal." Daniel stepped in between them. "I think we need to bring the temperature down a couple of degrees and let cooler heads prevail."

"McCoy is behind this." For a small wiry man with a thick shock of white hair and a penchant for bow ties, Jennings had a big presence that filled a room and a voice that belonged to a man twice his size. "What is it going to take for you two to do your job and bring me something I can convict him on?"

"I'm inclined to agree with Chief Nelson," Daniel said. "Evidence."

"Then find some, damn it. Every day that menace of a man plays the pied piper, stealing more children, brainwashing wives, corrupting husbands and sucking up souls like the devil on earth with a spiritual vacuum cleaner is a day that you," Jennings said, pointing at Willa, "and you—" his finger swung to Daniel "—have failed to do your jobs and handicapped me from doing mine!"

Whoa. To Daniel this almost felt personal. Jennings's comment about stealing children must've struck a nerve with Willa because she didn't respond. Daniel looked to the mayor to gauge where he stood on this.

Schroeder's face was solemn, but he remained quiet, which told Daniel that Jennings had gone running to the mayor and made a fuss.

"We're doing everything we can to stop a killer," Daniel clarified. "That may or may not give you McCoy." He doubted that it would.

"I was so close. This close," Jennings said, holding up to two fingers separated by a mere inch, "to getting the Shining Light and that sanctimonious Marshall McCoy on tax fraud charges, then my witness got scared and went quiet on me before handing over evidence. The next thing I know his cult somehow managed to get tax-exemption status like pulling a bunny out of a hat."

"Who is your witness?" Willa asked.

Jennings finally shut up, his gaze bouncing between them.

Daniel sighed. "You can't drag us in here, berate us and not trust us enough to put your cards on the table and tell us the truth. We need to share information."

"He's right," the mayor said. "Tell them."

Jennings scrubbed a hand over his face as he considered it. "Arlo Starlight. She won't talk to me anymore. I think she's worried that the evidence will be traced back to her."

Willa looked at him, the question gleamed clear in her eyes. He gave a curt, subtle nod. After all, he was the one advocating disclosure in the spirit of cooperation.

"Mercy McCoy told us that her father uses the unburdening tapes," Willa said, "where members share compromising information, against them."

Jennings jumped on that. "Against them how?"

Daniel shook his head. "We don't know. But we plan to find out."

"When?" the mayor and Jennings asked in unison.

"Tomorrow," Daniel said. "If we learn anything, we'll let you know." The last thing he wanted was to be a hypocrite by withholding information, but Mercy had trusted them to approach Arlo about this in a sensitive manner. Honestly, Daniel had serious doubts regarding Jennings's ability to be sensitive.

"Listen, I'm going to give it to you straight," Mayor Schroeder said, "we have protesters outside the Shining Light's compound. Once the news breaks about the third body, the numbers are going to triple. I don't want this city turning into a tinderbox. Your top priority should be to find this killer and put him behind bars. Secondary is solving the problem of the cult. We all suspect illegal activity is happening on the compound. Thus far, we've been unable to get anything on Marshall McCoy. And that's after I brought in a joint task force to focus on them." He put an elbow on his desk and rubbed his brow. "Willa, you did an outstanding job clearing the debris out of the department. But I need more from you. I'm planning on running for governor and on that same ticket will be Allen for attorney general. We need this Starlight Killer caught. And McCoy. Or I'll have to appoint someone else who can do it."

She rocked back on her heels. "Are you threatening my job?"

Schroeder shook his head. "I don't threaten. I inform. I incentivize. Your son is no longer a member of the Shining Light, but it's my understanding that he's having difficulty reacclimating," he said, and Willa suddenly looked worried as if surprised he had that information. "Allen's daughter is a Starlight, spinning in circles and dancing under the moon. You both have skin in the game. You just need a little extra motivation." His gaze shifted. "Daniel, where do you stand regarding the Shining Light?"

"I stand on the side of the law. If McCoy is guilty of something and we can nail him, we will. But my job doesn't solely cover their compound. I'm responsible for all of Albany County and my duty is to the citizens who elected me. Regarding the serial killer, we may be dealing with a copycat. Someone murdering women in the same manner as the Holiday Elk Horn Killer."

"Your office mishandled that case," Jennings said full of vitriol, as though Daniel had been the sheriff five years ago. "It would behoove you to ensure your department doesn't let a cold-blooded murderer get away a second time, especially if he's a member of the Shining Light."

The DA was practically foaming at the mouth with hatred for McCoy. Now knowing that Jennings had skin in the game—a daughter who had become a Starlight—he couldn't help but wonder how far the district attorney, a father, would go to tear down the Shining Light.

"If this tinderbox ignites," Mayor Schroeder said, "it will be the problem of everyone in this room. Do not let that happen. Not on my watch."

A riot in town, or worse, an attack against the compound, wouldn't look good on the mayor's résumé in his bid for governor. But Daniel had hoped the man's primary concern would have been the protection of the citizens, not safeguarding his political future.

"I can assure you we will do everything in our power to keep that from happening," Daniel said.

Schroeder leaned back in his chair. "See that you do. Both of you." He fixed his gaze on Willa. "Because if this turns into an unmitigated disaster, the fallout won't land on this office," the mayor said, reaffirming his intent to place the blame on the chief of police.

In the corridor, on their way down the hall, Daniel said,

"If this doesn't shake out the way we'd like, don't worry, I won't let the mayor railroad you out of your job."

"And how precisely would you stop him?"

"I'd hold a press conference. Tell everyone that I took over the case from you and accept full responsibility for any failure. Then I would sing your praises about how your office did everything possible to assist. If he tried to fire you after that, it would come across loud and clear to the public for what it was. A politician trying to cover his own behind."

She put a hand on his shoulder, stopping him. A look he couldn't quite decipher came over her face. "Why would you do that for me?"

He cared about her, and she did not deserve to get fired to advance the political career of a selfish coward. "You're an excellent chief. You accomplished something in your department that your predecessors couldn't. And I don't like bullies. We work damn hard, risking our lives for this job. We shouldn't be treated as pawns." Schroeder rubbed him the wrong way, and now Daniel would do what he could to protect Willa.

She stared at him for several heartbeats, and he wished he could read her thoughts. "We didn't get a chance to eat lunch earlier and now it's time for dinner. How about we leave the delivery order in the fridge for tomorrow and you come back to my house?"

He grinned, happy for the invitation. The possibilities of where the night might lead ignited a fire in his bloodstream. He remembered every inch of her body, long and trim, athletic and strong. Full breasts. Sinewy legs. Every time they'd slept together, he had reveled in the feel and taste of her, drawing out every sensual moment, savoring the bittersweet sensation, like that experience might be his

last with her. But their first night, after weeks of flirting—
and it had been a while for him—he'd needed her so much
he'd been a wild man. Looking at her now still triggered
that gut-aching desire.

Not love, but more than like, his affection for her combined with his sexual impulses created one heck of a reaction in his body.

"I mean for work," she clarified, dampening his excitement. "We can make a quick bite to eat, review the Chavez
statements, cross-reference the lists of members against
those of the recent Fallen and wait for the autopsy report,"
she said, listing the mountain of work they had to do.

During their fling, they had not gone back to her place
a single time. At first, he'd simply been thrilled about the
upgrade from the impersonal motel to his house. Then he'd
figured that she had needed the convenience and ease of
leaving when she wanted, avoiding the awkwardness and
hassle of asking him to go. But after she had cut off all com-
munication without explanation and stopped showing up at
Crazy Eddie's, he'd realized she had never wanted him to
know her phone number, much less where she lived.

It wasn't as if he would have gone looking for her at her
job, which struck him as borderline stalkerish. His mother
had raised him to be a gentleman and he had the common
sense to take a hint.

"A working dinner sounds good to me." Since they weren't
eating in the office, he wanted to take this as a sign that she
was willing to trust him even if it didn't mean more than that.

"I have to warn you, my place is small," she said. "Actually, it's a tiny cabin in a remote area. But if Wayward
Bluffs is too far for you to drive, then we could do dinner
at your place."

There was no way on earth he was turning her down. If he did, he might not get a second chance. "Your place is perfect."

DANIEL STOOD IN Willa's cramped kitchen, chopping vegetables like a proper sous chef. "This was a great idea," he said, and she spotted a flicker of desire in his eyes.

"Yeah." Willa hoped she didn't come to regret it. She'd never brought him here before in an effort to keep their dalliance from blossoming into something more. She hadn't worried he would have shown up unannounced. Pointing a loaded shotgun at a person had a way of dissuading a guy from returning without an invitation. It was just that once she opened her life to someone, invited them in, it was hard to close that door.

Maybe Daniel was right. They'd both proven themselves. He'd won his election. She'd been praised by the mayor and the media for cleaning up a dirty department—an accomplishment no one could take away from her. If they could stop this serial killer and nail McCoy, she'd have no qualms about exploring the possibility of a relationship.

Daniel got her. Her need for space and discretion. The hardship of being a single mother. And no one else would understand better than he did the commitment and sacrifices this job demanded.

Not only did she respect him, but she felt safe with him, trusted him and desired him in a way that she had never experienced before. She'd been attracted to him from his opening lines in Crazy Eddie's, and she knew she'd never tire of appreciating him physically ever since watching him build a fire at his place one night when his shirt had lifted, exposing bare skin. But she stayed careful. Cautious.

Less so now that she was aware what he was willing to risk for her. He treated her as more of a partner on this case than the man she'd foolishly and reluctantly married. She was amazed that he was willing to jeopardize his position as sheriff to save her job.

No one had ever been on her side in that way.

"Add the veggies to the sauce," she said.

He dumped the chopped zucchini, spinach, kale and mushrooms in. Leaning close, he watched her stir the pot of quick homemade marinara. She flicked a glance at his handsome face, letting her gaze slide to his broad chest, the ripples of muscle straining against his shirt. A little thrill whipped through her. A memory came rushing back, of how it felt to run her fingers over his bare skin, the masculine sound of pleasure he made when she pressed her lips to his—

Nope. Going there would only mean trouble.

The timer beeped, refocusing her. "Mind draining the rotini?" She already had a colander in the sink.

"Sure." He slid around behind her, his body grazing hers in the narrow galley kitchen, and grabbed the pot.

"Save a little of the water to add to the sauce along with the pasta."

"That's a trick I use myself. My mother's chef taught me."

She still found it hard to believe that his mother was rich and famous and one of the most beautiful women in the world. Now she knew where he got his good looks from— and he was hot. "Must have been nice growing up with all that wealth."

He poured a quarter cup of water into the sauce and then added the pasta, and she went back to stirring, giving the rotini a chance to absorb the flavors.

"Not really. She wasn't around too much when I was younger, always jet-setting off for work or fun. The privileged lifestyle catered to her—not to kids. But when you grow up with a silver spoon in your mouth as you say, you can't complain."

"Sure, you had safety, shelter, private schools, a chef, probably tutors," she said, and he nodded, "and never wanted for any material thing, but that doesn't replace a mother's presence. Trust me, I know. My son reminds me every chance he gets that all his life I've put my career first, with the long hours and overtime. Then as a cop you have to separate the horror and awful stuff that desensitizes you over time from your home life and there are moments when you're so drained, you're a shell of person, going through the motions. Giving as much as you can, but it's never enough."

She took a deep breath, not knowing where all of that had come from. But it felt good to say it, to get it out. That was the effect he had on her. Got her to lower her guard and talk.

With a sympathetic look, he put a hand to her back and rubbed. "Even though I've never been married and don't have kids, I get it. A few months before we met, my girlfriend of three years dumped me." He met her gaze and must've seen the questions in her eyes. "For all the reasons you mentioned. I didn't want to bring the darkness home, didn't want to talk about it and she felt shut out. The hours and the emergencies were too much for her. On campus we were understaffed, and you wouldn't believe the number of incidents that occurred. She eventually accepted a job in Omaha. Not long after I started as sheriff, she asked me to visit to be sure our breakup wasn't a mistake."

She started plating the food. "I guess it wasn't."

"After being with you I knew it wasn't because I had

stopped missing her. Then when I got there, she wanted me to change career fields and move to Nebraska. Become a real estate agent of all things. Can you imagine?"

They both laughed.

She handed him a plate and grabbed a bottle of wine. "One glass with dinner?"

"You do owe me a drink."

They went to the table and sat. She put a small dish of grated Parmesan cheese down. He sprinkled a healthy amount over his pasta as she poured the wine.

"Sonia didn't understand that this job is a calling." He dug into the food and gave a satisfied moan. "This is excellent."

In high school, she'd known a Sonia—a selfish, mean girl. "Being a cop gets in your blood. Becomes a part of you that you can't shut off." She took a mouthful as well, pleased she done a good job with limited ingredients and in a hurry.

"Exactly," he said with a nod. "What made you want to become a police officer?"

"My dad was a cop. My ex, too. Zach joined the force a year before we separated. After the divorce, I had been working two jobs to make ends meet on my own, in an effort to show my father that I would never be anything like him because he was an alcoholic, verbally abusive, distant tyrant who wanted me to be a cop. Anyway, I had started entertaining the idea of accepting my boss's invitation to go out on a date. He promoted me to assistant manager at the grocery store. One night, we were the only ones there and he thought I should be nicer to him."

"As in sleep with him nicer?"

"You've got it. A conversation turned heated, there was grabbing and then hitting and the next thing I knew I was fighting for my life. I hit him with something hard and knocked him out cold. Called the police. And I had never been so happy to see a couple of uniforms show up. He came to and when they put him in cuffs and shoved him into the back of a cruiser, I wished that had been me. Cuffing him and taking him to the precinct. I applied the next day."

"You're a fighter. A survivor. You didn't let him steal your peace of mind or your power."

She took a sip of wine. "You?"

"I worked on a ranch when I moved out here. The owner turned out to have been an old friend of my father's. During those long, hard days I learned what it meant to be a cowboy, from understanding the grass cycles to timing the calving season to maximize those cycles, bull genetics and diseases. It wasn't easy."

"If it was easy, everyone would be a cowboy."

A hint of a smile tugged at his mouth. "Anyway cattle kept going missing. The owner would file reports with the local brand inspector, the Livestock Board, the sheriff. Nothing. I investigated on my own. Found the culprit. In the process of bringing him to justice, I took two to the chest."

She'd seen the gunshot wounds and had asked. All he had said was it had been the price for getting justice for a friend.

"Anyway, I ended up becoming a criminal investigator for the Livestock Board. I loved wearing the badge and solving cases, but there was no room to grow. An opening with the campus police popped up right when I was looking for a change. I took it and worked up the ranks fast."

"Nearly dying didn't scare you off. Because you're a fighter, too."

"Guess we're two peas in a pod." He slid her a sexy look that sent a flutter through her belly.

The room shrank around them, becoming more cozy, more intimate.

"I guess so." Averting her gaze, she struggled and failed to shake off the sensation.

She shoved more food in her mouth before she said something provocative. Around him she felt sexy and seen and she didn't intimidate him. He took her in stride. Her suggestive comments seemed to stoke a fire in him and when they came together they both burned.

Less talking. More eating. And get to work.

She glanced up and found his gaze on her. "Why are you staring? Do I have something on my face?" She touched the corner of her mouth.

"A bit of sauce." He reached over, wiped the opposite side, and sucked it from his finger.

She squeezed her thighs together at the way he made the simplest action sexy.

"But you are awfully hard not to notice," he said with a devilish grin.

Her face heated, and she cleared her throat. "Which folder do you want? Chavez statements or cross-referencing the cult's lists?" she asked, pointing to the folders she'd left on the counter.

"The lady gets to choose." There was a flirtatious twinkle in his eyes.

"I never said I was a lady." She was treading into dangerous territory, but the words had left her mouth without thinking.

One of his brows quirked. "You're certainly not in the bedroom. Part cougar I think from the way you pounce and the marks you leave on my back." He let out a low chuckle as his gaze skated down her body.

She tingled all over. "Flip you for it."

"Are we talking a coin, or do you want to wrestle again?"

The wrestling match in the motel room had been a result of too much whiskey and her trying to prove she could take him. She had too, pinning him quickly. Until he'd shoved his pelvis up, flipped her over, and became the one on top with her happy to be trapped beneath him. Then they had stripped each other in a mad rush, kissing and tasting. Lips running over bare skin. Arms tangling. His hips urging her legs to part.

"On second thought, I'll just take the lists."

She stood.

So did he, sidestepping to block her. She could have easily walked around him if she'd wanted, but she didn't move. She barely breathed.

Standing in front of each other, toe to toe, he gripped her chin between two fingers and tilted her face up a fraction, meeting her gaze. "The one thing we've both learned is that life is short. We have to make the most of the time we have."

Not suppressing the primal urge, she did.

She wrapped her arms around his neck, pulling his mouth to hers, and kissed him with all the pent-up emotion begging for release. He kissed her back, hot and hungry. She wanted him. Body and soul. And she didn't care about tomorrow or the consequences. She wasn't going to let this moment slip away from her.

He groaned as his arms tightened around her, one warm hand pressed to her spine and the other cupped her backside, pulling her closer. There was an urgency in his touch, in his kisses.

Her lower belly heated, desire spreading through her, rushing in her veins, pounding in her ears. It had been so long since she'd been held, touched like this, and never had she been so impatient, her body rousing with each sensation he made flare.

A car door slammed closed outside.

Her eyes flew open, gaze going to the window. Footsteps stomped up the porch. Keys jangled.

Sighing at the awful timing, she let Daniel go and hurriedly fixed her appearance, smoothing her hair, hoping the flush was gone from her cheeks.

The knob turned. The door opened.

Zeke stepped inside, slamming the door closed and stopped short. "Who in the hell is this?"

"Hello to you, too," she said, straining for calm and patience. "This is Sheriff Daniel Clark."

Her son grimaced, his gaze taking in the room. "I can't believe you're dating a cop. You'd think you'd have the common sense to find somebody with a profession *less* dangerous and *less* stressful than yours."

"We're not dating." Her cheeks heated. "We're working a case together."

Zeke rolled his eyes. "Yeah, okay. I'm going to grab some food, go to my room and you two can get back to wining and dining. I mean 'working,'" he said using air quotes.

Embarrassment was like a red-hot poker in her gut. "For your information this is a working dinner."

"Whatever." He stormed past her into the kitchen and peered into the pot. "Is this vegetarian?"

"Yes." She'd gotten into the habit of making meatless meals in an effort to help him with his transition. "What are you doing here? I thought you were staying at your grandmother's," she said, flicking a glance at Daniel.

He sat down and went back to eating.

"She got upset with me, so I bounced. I'm going to crash here for a bit. They changed me to the graveyard shift over at the gas station. I've got to be there at two a.m. Can you believe they told me at the last minute and expect me to show up?"

"Yes, it's a called a job. You had yesterday off." Willa went up to him in the kitchen and put a hand on his shoulder. "Why is your grandmother upset?"

He must've seriously messed up if the older woman wasn't happy with the boy-who-did-no-wrong.

Zeke jerked away from her touch. "It's my business with Grandma." He ladled a mound of pasta into a deep bowl. "You don't want me up in your business, right? Or would you rather I eat at the table and get an up-close look at you in action. *Working.* Don't you usually go over cases in an office?"

Shutting her eyes for a moment, she drew in a deep breath. How had it gotten this bad? Had it happened slowly or in a great horrendous slide like an avalanche, burying her.

"You won't speak to me that way." She fixed him with a stare. "Not in my house."

Zeke put his hand up to his mouth, motioning like he was inserting a key and turning a lock. Spinning on his heel, he strode to the table, put Parmesan on his food, gave Daniel a two-finger salute and stormed off to his room, slamming the door closed. A second later the television came on.

Willa was mortified. She could melt into the floor. "I'm so sorry—"

"Why are you sorry?" Another sympathetic look. "He's the one who should be apologizing."

"But I'm the one who lets him get away with it." If she scolded him, putting her foot down, she'd only drive him away.

At least she knew he was safe, warm and well-fed while under her roof.

Daniel got up, came over to her, and clutched her shoulders. His steel grip steadied her from the outside in. "It's complicated. You two have been through a lot together. Add in the Machiavellian factor of the cult and who is to judge? Certainly not me. Cut yourself some…"

"Slack?" Easier said than done.

He grabbed the folders from the counter and handed her one. "Let's show him what *work* looks like. Besides, we have to be up at the crack of dawn in order to catch Arlo in the morning."

He turned to go to the table, and she caught his hand.

"Thank you."

"For what?"

Being so incredible. "Understanding. Not judging." And if he was, he kept it to himself, thankfully. "Making me feel better." A miracle in itself.

"That's what partners do. Good ones anyway."

She'd been saddled with lousy ones for sure, but she wondered if he was only talking about work and them on this case.

Sitting down and opening the folder, she decided it didn't matter. For as long as he was her partner, whether it was a day, a week, or longer, she wouldn't take it for granted.

Chapter Seven

Picking up his coffee from the cup holder in the SUV, Daniel took a sip. At the early hour, with the sun barely up, his body needed the caffeine, but his restless mind kept churning over the case. According to Gemma's best friend, she'd left home because her stepdad had been handsy. After bouncing between jobs, with no stable place to live, sleeping on her best friend's couch, she'd picked up a flyer for the Shining Light. Her friend had gotten a boyfriend. Gemma hadn't wanted to overstay her welcome. The compound was a good alternative until they had a lockdown after receiving a threat that terrorists might attack the commune. That combined with Mercy leaving the community was a sign that she should go, too.

"I can't stop thinking about the Chavez statements," Daniel said to Willa.

"You doubt the veracity?" she asked from the passenger seat.

"No. I buy the reasons for her turning to the cult. I even believe what McCoy told us, that the lockdown and his heir apparent, Mercy, choosing to become one of the Fallen was enough to send her running for the hills. Miguel dropped her off a week ago. Surveillance footage at the bus station shows it. Then she doesn't visit her parents or her best friend and simply disappears until we found her dead body yesterday?"

"Do you think the mother, or the girlfriend is lying? The stepdad took her, killed her? But what about the other two?"

"I'm not saying they're lying. I'm saying that it's strange for her to disappear." He took another sip of the strong, hot brew. "What if the killer grabbed her and held her for a week waiting for the full moon?"

"No defensive wounds," she said, referring to the autopsy report that had come in late last night. "Pretty hard to hold a woman against her will without her getting some. I suppose he could've drugged her, but nothing was found in her system. It would've been tedious to use chloroform for that long."

"He could've dosed her with something for several days. Then used chloroform short-term, giving the other drug time to leave her system and we wouldn't pick it up."

"Either way, it supports your theory that the killer is someone on the outside." She took a gulp of her coffee. "I was really hoping that cross-referencing the two lists would have given us something. I thought for sure a member who had joined four to five years ago, right after the Holiday Elk Horn Murders stopped, would have been on the list of the Fallen, who had been cast out or had decided to break their vows this year."

"We do have something. A list of potential suspects to question." Once Livingston got into the office, he would start working on tracking them all down. Four individuals, one being Ezekiel Nelson. They had to question him, surely Willa was aware of that, but Daniel had yet to discuss it with her.

The white van with the Shining Light symbol on the side

came around the corner, headed down the road in their direction, where they weren't easily visible behind a sign.

Mercy had told them which route to take. On this particular stretch of road, it was easy to exceed the speed limit unless the driver was a stickler for watching the gauge.

They were hoping to get lucky.

Willa held up the velocity speed gun, aimed and pulled the trigger. The van passed. A smile spread across her face, and she turned to display the screen to him.

There was nothing complicated about how Wyoming's absolute speed limits worked. If you drove faster than the posted speed, you'd violated the law. In this case, the driver was going thirty-six in a thirty-mph zone.

Daniel hit his lights, not bothering with the siren.

It took the driver less than a minute to respond, stopping on the side of the road.

Daniel pulled up behind them and they both got out, approaching the driver's side.

Miguel was behind the wheel and rolled down the window. He looked crestfallen to see them. "Hi, Sheriff, Chief Nelson. Is there a problem?"

"You were speeding," Willa said with a stern face. "Six miles over the limit."

"Oh, I'm so sorry. I didn't realize it."

"Who's in charge of this outing?" Daniel looked over the passengers, his gaze settling on the woman with glasses and a gray bob.

"I am."

"Ma'am, can you step out of the vehicle." Daniel walked around to the passenger side as Willa resumed going through the motions with Miguel.

The sliding door whooshed open, and Arlo climbed out.

"My apologies for exceeding the speed limit. Fox is usually such a careful driver."

"Please close the door and follow me."

Her face twisted in confusion. She slid the door shut and trailed behind to the SUV.

He stopped in front of his vehicle, keeping his back to it where he could keep an eye on the rear of the van and track how Willa was doing.

"What's going on, Sheriff?"

"State your name for me," he said, double-checking he had the right person.

"Arlo Starlight. We have all the proper documentation. Fox's license is current."

"Mercy thought you might help us," he said, with no time to ease into it.

Her eyes fluttered with surprise "Help with what?" She was about to look over her shoulder.

"Don't turn around. Stay focused on me," he said, and she did. "We know you were working with DA Jennings to get him evidence of tax evasion."

"I can't help with that." She shook her head, her expression grim. "If I provide documentation, it will trace back to me."

"Has McCoy used information from unburdening sessions to blackmail or extort present or former members?"

She stood still and silent, her gaze not wavering as she deliberated how to respond.

Daniel frowned, watching Willa review the documentation that Miguel handed her. "We don't have much time."

Finally, she nodded.

"How did he use it against them? Was it to get the tax-exemption status as a religious organization?"

More deliberation.

Willa glanced at him, checking in.

He shook his head, indicating he needed more time. "Please," he said to Arlo.

"The entire commune will suffer if the tax-exemption status is revoked," she said. "With the amount of back taxes, we might lose the land. We'd all be homeless with nowhere to go."

Miguel got out of the van and Willa started giving him a field sobriety test.

Daniel took out his notepad. "Mercy said to tell you that she left because her father is the devil. A liar. *Evil.* His darkness has tainted everything he's built and will one day be destroyed because of his wickedness."

Arlo hunched over, clutching her chest like the words had sent her into cardiac arrest.

"You must have your doubts about him, too," Daniel said.

Another nod.

"Give me names of the people he blackmailed."

She sucked in a strained breath. He could only imagine how her faith must have been rocked to the core.

"Not about the taxes," she said, her voice shaky. "The rest of us have too much to lose. We do such good work. Save so many lives. Marshall is corrupt. We must cut him out as a doctor would a cancerous tumor. I have believed this for a long time. But I won't endanger the commune."

"I don't want five hundred people to suffer because of the wrongdoings of one man. You must know something that I can give to the DA so he can go after him. Just him."

A tear leaked from the corner of her eye, and she whisked it away. "Roger Hines," she said, and he started writing. "Elmer Clayborne and Felicia Pietsch."

"Councilwoman Pietsch?"

A slow, grave nod. "Marshall extorted them for money."

"Are you sure?"

"I was there when he approached the councilwoman at her home back in June. He alluded to her husband's unburdening session. She played dumb. He asked me to leave the room. We left with a check for seventy-five thousand dollars. Marshall and I fought over it. He dismissed my opinion and commanded me to silence. Two more checks came in following his visits to the others. A quarter million in total. He used it to buy us time with the taxes until he could finagle our status as a religious organization."

The sum was shocking. "Do you know what he had on them?"

"Not all of them. After the incident at Pietsch's house, I listened to her husband's audio file."

"And? How damaging is it?"

She leaned in close and whispered what it was.

Pietsch would want to bury that. If it ever leaked, it could ruin her politically, and she had already announced her intent to run for senator. "Is her husband still one of your members?"

"He left after going through the unburdening session but before taking his vows. The councilwoman came and dragged him home, irate over how his joining would affect her politically. It was my understanding that he moved into the apartment above the garage and they are staying together for appearances."

"Thank you," he said with a sincere nod, understanding that she was putting herself at risk by talking. "You can be on your way."

"May the Light be upon you, Sheriff."

He gave Willa the signal, and she waved Miguel back to the vehicle.

After the Shining Light van pulled off, they climbed in the SUV.

"I felt bad for putting Fox through that after how hard I questioned him yesterday," she said. "I apologized for the inconvenience. Did Arlo give us anything?"

"Three names. All we need is for at least one of them to corroborate that McCoy blackmailed them for money, then we've got him."

"Do you want to hand this off to one of your deputies?" she asked.

"They've got their hands full following up on things related to the murder case." Besides, he wasn't sure if they would apply enough pressure to get the three to talk. They were wealthy and powerful and did not want their dirty laundry being aired. "Not much we can do until Livingston gets us contact information for the list of the Fallen. Our efforts this morning might be better served on this. If we have a chance to get McCoy, even a slim one, we have to take it." He put the SUV in Drive. "What do you say if I drop you off at your car and we can divide and conquer, each taking a name? We can join forces to tag team the last person later. I think it will take both of us."

"Who are we talking about?" she asked, curiosity gleaming in her eyes.

"Councilwoman Felicia Pietsch. Catching her off guard at her office might compel her to cooperate to keep any of her subordinates from overhearing."

"Interesting." Willa thought for a moment. "I think we should pay her a visit right now. Before she's coiffed and caffeinated. Without the armor of her makeup and a suit, it might be easier to get her to talk."

He trusted her judgment and was open to any ideas that would get them a cooperative witness. "Let's get an address for her."

WITH DANIEL STANDING beside her, Willa rang the doorbell of the Pietsch residence and braced herself for what was to come. She had to be convincing, more persuasive than ever before in her life. The pressure was immense to collar McCoy. She just hadn't realized she was on the clock with her career, her future, at stake because the mayor had lofty ambitions to be governor.

"We're closer now?" he said, the words sounding like a mix between a question and a statement, as he shifted his body so that she could see his full face.

For a heartbeat, she lost herself in his gaze. "To getting McCoy?" she asked, her voice a tad rough with her wondering if he was not discussing the case any longer, but in fact, their relationship. "Yes." She nodded, also answering the unspoken question in his eyes.

A crisp breeze sent a chill through her, making her shiver despite her zipped-up jacket.

Daniel gave her a half grin. "We can do this. Together."

"I hope you're right."

This was a gamble. Pietsch could throw them out of her house, slam the door in their faces and lawyer up.

Footsteps padded on the other side of the door before it swung open. A freckle-faced teenage girl stood facing them. Her light brown gaze fell to the star pinned to Daniel's shirt and swung to the badge on Willa's hip. "Mom!

The cops are here!" She stood, holding the door until her mother hurried down the stairs.

Wearing fuzzy slippers and a robe that was open, revealing pink satin pajamas, a flustered Pietsch came to the door. "Go get dressed, honey," she said to her daughter, who scampered off. Yawning, she wiped the sleep from her eyes, her dark, messy hair looked as though she had just rolled out of bed. "What brings the sheriff and the chief of police to my door at such an early hour? I hope no one is hurt. Or dead."

"Ma'am," Daniel said. "May we come in?"

She appeared uncertain for a moment, then shook her head as if clearing a daze and stepped aside, opening the door wider. "Of course."

They both stepped into the foyer and removed their hats but kept their jackets on.

"Can I get you two some coffee? The machine is on a timer, and it hasn't perked yet, but I can switch it on and it'll be ready in a jiff."

They were going to pass on the coffee and not give her a reason to get up and leave the room once the conversation had started. "Ma'am, is there someplace where we can speak privately? Without your daughter overhearing?"

Her eyes grew wide with concern. "Yes, certainly. Follow me." She shuffled down the hall in her slippers, leading them to an office, and shut the door behind them. "What is this about?" she asked, fully awake now, and tied her robe closed.

Daniel gave her a look of pity. "Please, have a seat."

She stumbled to sit on a loveseat at the back of the room. Willa and Daniel grabbed chairs that faced the desk, turned them around, and sat.

"You're starting to worry me," Pietsch said. "Why are you here?"

"Did Marshall McCoy come to your home in June and blackmail you?" Willa asked. "Extort you for money?"

Bewilderment swept over her face. "I have no idea what you're talking about."

Willa narrowed her eyes, taking in every nuance of the woman's body language. "Are you saying he didn't come here?"

She crossed her legs at the ankles and folded her hands in her lap. "No, he paid me a visit. We had iced tea and a lovely chat."

"About what?" Daniel asked.

Uncrossing her legs, she licked her lips. "He asked me for a donation to help his organization."

"In exchange for keeping quiet about what your husband shared during his unburdening session," Willa said, a statement, not a question.

Her face paled and she swallowed, making an audible sound. "He did no such thing. Marshall is an upstanding citizen. A pillar of the community who has dedicated his life to helping the less fortunate."

"Ma'am, we're sensitive to your position." Daniel scooted to the edge of his chair and leaned in. "You're probably sweating bullets right now, fretting over how much we know, how it'll effect your reputation, your chances of winning a seat in the senate when it comes out that your husband defrauded investors of more than two million dollars and used some of that money to finance your campaign. The press will have a field day with it."

Pietsch pressed her lips tight and stiffened. Her eyes swam with guilt.

"You're not alone," Willa said, needing to hit her with an ice-cold dose of logic to make her see reason. "McCoy did this to others. This story is going to break. We're not here for your husband. Or for you. We want Marshall McCoy for extortion. Blackmail. Since there are others who are also guilty of something, the first one to speak might be able to cut a deal with the DA for immunity. If you're that person, then your husband would go to jail. Not you, if you got a deal."

Jennings loved to cut deals for immunity to get a witness to talk. This would give him the boon he needed for his political aspirations, but she seriously doubted that more than one person would get an offer.

"This will destroy any hope of a political future." Pietsch lowered her head and clutched her hands. "If you're here, then it means the DA doesn't have everything he needs. Not yet. Maybe not ever."

"Are you willing to take that chance?" Willa asked, drawing Pietsch's gaze back to her. "We know what your husband did. It's only a matter of time, days, possibly hours, before it's leaked. Once the press gets wind of this, you will be tried in the court of public opinion and the DA won't stop until there are convictions in a court of law." Not only for McCoy, but for whatever crimes the others had committed.

"If you can get immunity, you can get in front of this with the press," Daniel added. "Control the narrative rather than letting it control you."

"This doesn't have to be the end of your political career. People might see you as a victim if you were the one to turn your husband in and helped bring down McCoy." Anything was possible.

Daniel nodded. "He extorted a quarter of a million dollars."

"Someone is going to talk first. That person will fare the

best. The others…" Willa shook her head. "This is survival of the fittest." She truly meant sleaziest. "Be smart. Be the first one to sit down with the DA. Tell us what happened."

Pietsch took a sobering breath and straightened, holding her head high. "Marshall did come to see me. *Me*, not Richard. He talked around what he was after. But honestly, I had no idea what Richard had told him while doped up on that drug they use. I had imagined an affair. Proof of multiple affairs. Then he asked Arlo to leave us alone. Things took a turn and got serious. Direct. He flat out told me that my husband had embezzled over two million dollars from his company and had used it to pay for the maintenance of his mistress, her condo, clothes, manicures, trips. To buy expensive toys, his watches, the suits. None of it would've played well in the press for me, but those things I could have survived. I mean if a president's wife can overcome her husband's affair to run for president herself one day, surely, I could rise above this. I refused to give him one cent."

Willa agreed. "How did McCoy take your refusal?"

"Not well. That's when I saw a different side to Marshall. He became vicious. Apparently, Richard had also funneled half of the illegal money into my campaign fund. Because he felt guilty about what a lousy husband he had been to me. But all he did was inadvertently tie me to his crime. I was so shocked and appalled to discover it that I didn't know what else to do besides write the check that Marshall wanted. Or he was going to leak the tape. I *am* the victim here."

Her story sounded good. Almost plausible. But Willa found it hard to swallow that she didn't know her husband had defrauded investors and given her one million dollars to help her win a senate seat. More believable was that they had worked out an arrangement that benefited them both.

Daniel shifted in his seat. "Did you ever tell your husband about McCoy's visit and the payment?"

"Of course. I was furious. The money came out of Paige's college fund."

The teen didn't deserve to suffer for her parent's mistakes, but millions took out student loans every year to pay for college. Willa had. "How did he respond?"

"He was horrified. Then he broke down in tears. After that I made him move his things to the apartment over the garage and end his affair."

"Richard didn't get angry about losing his mistress?" Daniel asked. "Or about shelling out seventy-five thousand dollars to a man he had once trusted?"

"If he was angry, he didn't show it. Probably because I was mad enough to spit nails. He was apologetic. Dejected."

"Do you know where your husband was between ten and midnight on Sunday?" The autopsy report had narrowed the window for the time of death.

"Why?" Pietsch tensed.

"Do you know his whereabouts?" Willa pressed.

"He was here."

Daniel sighed. "How can you be sure if he was supposedly in the apartment above the garage?"

"Because he was in the living room camped out in front of the big-screen TV watching Sunday night football and drinking himself into oblivion. The last game started at eight p.m., I think. I was here, in the office, working until ten thirty, listening to him boo and clap. Sometime after eleven I told him to turn it down so I could sleep. Monday morning, I found him snoring on the sofa."

Willa glanced over to Daniel to see if he had any other

questions. From the look he gave her, they were both satisfied. "Thank you, councilwoman," Willa said.

"I'm going to call my attorney, get dressed and sit down with Allen Jennings this morning. I'll be damned if I let Richard's shenanigans torpedo my life."

Pressure ebbed from Willa's chest as she was one step closer to securing her job. "You're doing the right thing."

Chapter Eight

To Daniel's surprise, DA Jennings was not only willing to cut an immunity deal with Felicia Pietsch for turning in her husband for fraud and agreeing to testify against Marshall McCoy for blackmail, but the other two as well, provided they weren't guilty of murder or any crime involving a child.

Jennings was furious with McCoy for stealing his daughter. So much so that he wanted to get him on three counts of extortion and put him away for life more than he wanted to see the others behind bars.

By late afternoon, Roger Hines had also worked out a deal, but Elmer Clayborne had lawyered up and stuck to his story that his check for ninety-five thousand dollars—the largest of the three sums—had been a willing donation.

Neither were feasible suspects for the murders. Hines had stage four emphysema and couldn't get through a ten-minute conversation without requiring oxygen. While Clayborne was tough as nails, he was almost eighty-one and had a private nurse who tucked him into bed every night at 9:00 p.m.

They were certain they were looking for a big guy, athletic, under sixty, strong enough to carry an unconscious woman up to one mile, based on where bodies were found in relation to roads and the fact sedatives had been used.

One smart enough to lure them into traps. A sharpshooter, if both killers were the same, with excellent accuracy.

"It'll be a relief once McCoy is behind bars," Willa said as they walked through the courthouse, heading toward the sheriff's department.

The hallway had a faint lemony smell that spoke of cleaning compounds. A scent he found oddly comforting. "A relief we'll have to wait for."

McCoy wasn't going to be arrested today. The DA had to get a few more pieces together first, but it would be soon. Maybe even tomorrow.

The question on Daniel's mind: Was Elmer Clayborne's sole concern getting through this unscathed, or would he give the cult leader a heads-up about the impending charges?

"Thanks to Arlo, and Mercy," Willa said, "that is one less thing to worry about. Now we can fully focus on finding our killer."

They reached the end of the hallway and turned left. Two doors down another corridor they came to the open set of double doors, with SHERIFF'S DEPARTMENT stenciled on the front.

Sweet home away from home.

Livingston was hard at work on the phone, talking and taking notes. After grabbing a bite to eat, Daniel wanted to start questioning the list of the Fallen.

Russo spun out of her chair and was on her feet, making a beeline toward them. "I've got good news and bad news."

Better a mix than purely the latter. "Bad news first."

"We widened the search radius for horse tracks at the crime scene for Gooding and Chavez. Both were a no-go, which leads me to believe the killer used a car and carried the victims to the site."

"Good news?"

"In widening the radius, we found two items. A necklace that must've fallen off the victim had DNA from Chavez on it. The other was a ring. Totally clean. No DNA and no prints on it. Based on where we found them, we can tell from which direction the killer approached the site, which leads to an auxiliary dirt road. No cameras."

Daniel swore under his breath. He was from Los Angeles, the most populous city in the United States with thirty-five thousand CCTV cameras. About nine for every thousand residents. There was a tiny fraction of that here, which didn't even cover every major intersection. When he didn't have a killer on the loose, he was grateful for the small-town feel, the slower pace, the tight community and the light traffic that didn't necessitate thousands of closed-circuit cameras.

But today, he had to tamp down his frustration.

"The two items are on your desk." Russo followed them into his office. "Father O'Neill at the church confirmed Fisher had been dropped off right before the start of an NA meeting. Some attendees helped get her inside. She was experiencing severe withdrawal symptoms at the time. They took her to the emergency room. The priest checked on her after she was discharged and got her to a shelter in Cheyenne. Sometime in late summer, he couldn't be sure exactly when, he spotted her back in town. Strung out and picking up johns at the truck parking lot across from the weigh station not far from the church. He encouraged her to come to the NA meetings, to get a hot meal that's offered once a day at their soup kitchen—they're open four days a week. He heard she was living in a tent near Cottonwood Park."

"That's where we found her tent," Willa said.

"None of the employees at the bus station recall seeing

any of the women," Russo said, "and nothing strange or out of the ordinary on the days they were dropped off there or in the vicinity. I'm heading over to try the truck park next. See if I can find any of Fisher's regulars. It's a two-minute walk from the bus stop. There might a connection between a trucker and all the victims."

Daniel picked up the sealed evidence bag that contained the necklace and looked it over. "It's worth a shot," he said as Willa grabbed the second bag. "Good work."

Livingston knocked on the door and waltzed in. "Got a minute?"

"Sure." Daniel glanced at Willa. Her forehead creased with unease as she stared at the ring in the bag, her skin turning pale.

"I've contacted all four individuals listed as the Fallen and departing the compound this year," Livingston said. "One guy, Roy Albertson is up in Montana. He left because his father passed away and one of the conditions of receiving his inheritance was that he had to manage the family ranch personally for five years and get married. Roy sounded happier than a pig in slop. After his dad disinherited him, he joined the Shining Light. His father's dying wish was to bring him back home."

"I guess it worked." Daniel put a hand on Willa's arm. "Everything okay?"

She nodded, but she looked the opposite. Not meeting his eyes, she set the bag down and faced Livingston.

"Alice Valdez and Louis Brooks chose to leave at the same time and are currently living together at her mother's house."

"What's their story?" Daniel cast a furtive look at Willa. She folded her arms and appeared to be lost in thought.

"The two met and became a couple on the compound. But according to the cult's rules, unions are arranged based on the 'Light' speaking to Empyrean. Marshall McCoy had intended to separate them and match them to different partners. They weren't on board, so they left."

"Miguel Garcia mentioned that he was matched with someone, as well. How are Alice and Louis doing? Happy like Roy Albertson?"

"Not quite." Livingston frowned. "Alice told me they fight all the time now and she regrets leaving the Shining Light. She wonders if Empyrean had been right about them not being a good match. Something to do with a karmic debt of their two souls and needing to heal spiritually with other partners. I didn't really understand what she was talking about. But she claims they were together with friends last weekend playing *Dungeons & Dragons* until the wee hours both Saturday and Sunday night."

"Maybe their relationship woes are a self-fulfilling prophecy. Someone told them that they were doomed to have trouble and now they read that into everything, trying to find it."

"I suppose." Livingston hiked up a shoulder. "Only one person on the list refused to talk to me." His gaze swung from Daniel to Willa. "Ezekiel Nelson. He's also the only person who joined the Shining Light four years ago *and* left this year," he said, and Willa remained stoic. "So I had a deputy bring him in. Nelson is sitting in the interrogation room, complaining that he has to fill in for a coworker tonight."

Awkward tension swelled in the room. "You made the right call." Daniel gave a little nod. "Can you give us a minute?"

"Sure thing." Livingston hurried out of the office, closing the door behind him.

"Talk to me," Daniel said and waited, but when she didn't respond, he closed the blinds to the window and turned back to her. "Why didn't you tell me that he joined four years ago?"

"I didn't think it mattered." Her voice was low.

"Of course it matters."

She looked up at him. "You think a seventeen-year-old kid was capable of being the Holiday Elk Horn Killer, responsible for viciously stabbing four women to death? Do you think my kid is capable of that?"

"What I think is that I should've heard it from you and not Livingston. You know as well as I it all comes down to the details. It's all important." But he felt like a fool for not reviewing the lists himself and simply trusting her.

"You're right." Turning, Willa gripped the edge of the desk and stared down at the evidence. "The ring...it's Zeke's."

Shock jolted through him. "What? Are you certain?"

"It was his father's class ring. Sterling silver with a dark black tone. Garnet center stone. Personalized side emblems and engravings. I gave it to him for his sixteenth birthday in the hopes it would encourage him to do better in school and graduate, to make his father proud. Yes, I'm sure." She shook her head, staring at it. "But I haven't seen him wearing it since he came home from the compound. There is a reasonable explanation for this. I know it. There has to be. My son is not a killer."

Daniel eased closer. "Do you know where he was the night of the murders?" he asked, wondering if he could even take her at her word.

"Sunday night I dropped him off at his grandmother's house, but the truth is, I don't know about the other evenings."

Her honesty was a relief. "Would you be willing to call the grandmother to see if he was there all night? On speaker?"

Willa's gaze lifted to his and she nodded without hesitation.

He put a hand on her shoulder and rubbed her arm. "Let's get to the bottom of this."

She picked up the receiver on his desk, dialed the number, and hit the speaker button. The line rang.

"Hello," the older woman answered.

"Irene, hi, it's me, Willa."

"Oh, I almost didn't pick up. I didn't recognize the number."

"I'm over at the sheriff's department working on a case. Hey, I had a quick question. After I dropped Zeke off on Sunday, did he stay there with you all night?"

The grandmother made a sound of exasperation. "Funny you should ask. Your son took my car after I told him *no* because I could smell the alcohol on his breath, and I was worried about him getting into an accident."

Willa grimaced. "What time did he come back?"

"Not until three in the morning. I am too old for this. He's going to give me a heart attack or a stroke from worrying about him. Later that morning I took him to pick up his own vehicle, which was parked outside a bar. I told him that if he wants to stay with me while the heat is out at his trailer and it's freezing over there, then he's going to have to start going to church with me. No ifs, ands or buts about it. And what does your son do? He goes running back to you because you'll tolerate his outrageous behavior. Spare the rod and spoil the child. You should have listened to me—"

"I've got to go." Willa squeezed her eyes shut. "Bye, Irene." She slammed the receiver down.

"I need to question Zeke. Now," Daniel said, heading toward the door.

"I'm coming with you."

"No, you're not. I'm bringing Livingston in with me."

She rocked back on her heels and stared at him in disbelief. "Why? That's my son we're talking about."

"Precisely. Someone in my office is feeding Jennings and/or the mayor information. There's no other way he found out about us questioning and releasing Miguel Garcia so fast. What do you think is going to happen the second he finds out that your son is a suspect? You can be in the observation room or stay in here until it's over. End of discussion."

Chapter Nine

Arms folded across her chest, Willa stood with her feet firmly planted, watching Daniel and Deputy Livingston interview her son through the one-way glass in the observation room that overlooked the interrogation room.

It was all surreal. Like a nightmare she couldn't wake up from. Zeke was troubled. Disrespectful. In pain. But he did not, could not murder one woman much less seven.

As the chief of police, related to the suspect, she didn't belong in the interrogation room. As a mother, willing to do anything for her child, there was no other place for her, but this was as close as she could get.

"Do you know Beverly Fisher?" Daniel asked as Livingston set a picture of the deceased down on the table.

Zeke reeled back in horror. "Oh, my God. No."

Willa licked her bone-dry lips, wishing she had brought in a bottle of water. Her throat was parched, and a headache was starting to throb behind her eyes.

"Where were you the night of September 19th between ten p.m. and midnight?"

Her son shrugged. "I don't know. Can I see a calendar?"

Daniel looked at Livingston and nodded. The deputy

pulled out his phone, tapped some buttons and showed Zeke the screen.

"I was off that day. I went to the Frontier Sports Bar," he said, and Livingston made a note. "I stayed until about one maybe."

"Can anyone verify that you were there?" Daniel asked.

"The bartender. A couple of waitresses. Patty for sure because she said I was a horrible tipper and needed to work on it."

Daniel nodded. "Do you know Leslie Gooding or Gemma Chavez?"

Zeke cringed at the next two photos the deputy put on the table. He looked away from them. "No. Is this why I'm here? You guys think I did this?"

Willa's chest ached at the resurgence of the pressure ballooning behind her sternum. If she could spare her son from looking at those photos—the horrendous images that would stick with him for the rest of his life—then she would. But showing suspects crime scene photos was a beneficial tactic that allowed the interviewers to gauge their initial response, which could be telling.

"We're not accusing you of anything," Daniel said. "We just need to get through these questions. What about this past Saturday? Where were you between ten and midnight?"

"I, uh, I was home. Alone."

Straightening, Daniel put his forearms on the table. "Home? In your trailer, where it's freezing cold because the heat has been shut off?"

Zeke looked up, past Daniel, to the one-way mirror. Her son's green eyes flared wide, anger giving color to his cheeks, and in that moment, he looked exactly like his father. "Did you tell your boyfriend that?" he said, and Livingston stared at Daniel. "Huh? What kind of mother betrays her son?"

Misery flooded her. This might be the breaking point in their relationship where he no longer wanted to have anything to do with her, even though she hadn't uttered a word about the lack of heat in his trailer. It didn't matter. Because he wouldn't believe her no matter what she told him.

"Hey." Daniel slapped the steel table. "Your mother has nothing to do with this interview."

"Interrogation! Call it what it really is."

Daniel took a breath. "Tell us about Sunday night. We know you weren't at Grandma's so don't bother lying."

Zeke scowled and lowered his head with a shake.

"Talk to me," Daniel urged. "Staying silent will not help you and it doesn't look good."

"Yeah, well, telling you where I was won't look good either."

"It's got to be better than looking like a murderer." Daniel leaned forward. "All I want is the truth."

"I was at Sheila Sanders's place."

What? That didn't make any sense. Willa prayed he wasn't lying. But if he wasn't, why would he be reluctant to give them an alibi?

"If I call Sheila Sanders, she's going to tell me that you were there with her?" Daniel asked.

Zeke shook his head. "I wasn't inside her place. I was at her place. Out front. In my car. Watching her through the window with Frankie Young."

Willa's skin crawled. Her son was a stalker? Hadn't she raised him better than that?

"Why were you there?" Daniel's tone was far gentler than hers would have been.

"We were on and off again in high school. After the Shining Light, we hooked back up. But it was different. I don't know. Things had changed, but I told her I loved her and she said the words back. Then we had a fight."

Livingston stopped writing. "A physical altercation?"

"No. Mostly yelling. She shoved my chest once, but I didn't shove her back. Anyway, we decided to take a breather from each other. You know, give each other some space to clear our heads. I'm at the bar and Thomas told me she started seeing Frankie. But I didn't believe it because she made me swear that we wouldn't see other people during the break."

"Thomas got a last name?" Daniel asked.

"Mills," Zeke said, and Livingston made a note. "So I drove over there to see if it was true. Sure enough, they were snuggled up on the sofa watching horror movies. That's Sheila's classic MO to get a guy to make a move on her. She was encouraging him. Then I met up with Thomas for an early dinner before his shift on Sunday—"

"Where?" Livingston asked. "Time?"

"Pinky's Pizzeria. Around five. I was telling him all about it and in walks Frankie with his buddies. And I don't know what happened next. I like blacked out and when I came to Thomas was pulling me off him and Frankie's friends were helping him up. I warned him to stay away from Sheila. Then Wayward Bluffs police officers showed up and hauled me in for drunk and disorderly conduct. Later that night, I went back to see if he listened. The dude was there. Again. Watching another movie."

"Which ones did they watch?" Livingston asked, and Zeke rattled off two from some chainsaw or jigsaw series.

Zeke might be a stalker, but at least he had an alibi.

Daniel put the evidence bag with the ring on the table. "Do you know what that is?"

Her son picked up the bag and peered close. Surprise washed over his face. "Yeah, it's my dad's class ring. My mom gave it to me, but it was lost."

It was lost? Not he lost it?

Daniel scratched at the stubble on his jaw. "Lost when?"

With a shake of his head, Zeke shrugged. "I have no idea. When you decide to take your vows to the Shining Light and become a member of the community, you hand over all your possessions. I gave them my wallet, my clothes, my ring. It was liberating. But when I was forced to leave, they gave everything back. Except for the ring. They verified in the logbook that I had given it to them, but they couldn't tell me what happened to it. The ring was just gone."

The paper trail would corroborate what he said. It had to.

"Why were you kicked out?" Daniel asked.

"It's against the rules for one Starlight to strike another."

Fighting. Yet again.

How was it possible for her son to have so much anger when she had given him so much love? And why did he think he could solve his problems with his fists?

Even as a child he was quick-tempered and always got into scuffles on the playground.

"Who did you hit?" Livingston held his pen at the ready to jot down the name. "And why?"

"Fox from security," he said, and Willa groaned at the bad luck. "I was into this girl, Maria, and I thought she was into me, too. One day, Empyrean announced he was matching her and Fox together. I pulled her to the side and told her we shouldn't accept it. If we left, we could be together. She didn't want to. She thought Empyrean knew best. I didn't want to leave either. I loved it there, but every time I saw them together, smiling, holding hands, I just couldn't stop thinking, *Why is Fox getting what I should have?* I never should've hit him. I really hurt him, and he did nothing wrong. I apologized, but Empyrean said that my lack of acceptance would only fester and that I would be a problem for the community. So he made me leave. And every day since I've been back, I've hated Empyrean. Hated him for making me love that place and believe that new family would always be mine. Hated him for taking it all away without giving me a second chance. And I can't wait for him to get what he deserves someday and hurts the way he made me hurt."

Willa rubbed the back of her neck, wishing she could massage the ache from her chest. More than that, she longed for him to have love and happiness and inner peace. But he was never going to have any of it until she got him the help that he needed, and he started taking responsibility for his actions.

The door to the observation room swung open. Melanie Merritt, the deputy district attorney, walked in. "We have the warrant for Marshall McCoy's arrest."

"That was faster than expected. We didn't think your office would request one until tomorrow."

"We were working on charging him not only under the state law but also the federal blackmail statute. If we get the conviction on both counts, for Pietsch and Hines, he could receive up to twenty years in prison. Allen called in every favor to make this happen as soon as possible. He doesn't want the great Empyrean to spend one more night in his plush bed. He wants to dethrone him tonight."

Arresting McCoy would ruffle plenty of feathers on the

compound. No one would want to cooperate with her, letting her simply look at their inventory register for the belongings of new recruits after they slapped handcuffs on their Empyrean.

It wasn't enough that Zeke had an alibi. She needed to prove that the ring wasn't in his possession at the time of the murders. The only way to do that without waiting for a warrant of her own was to go ahead of Daniel to the compound.

"You should know that us getting McCoy is like having a weight off the shoulders of my office," Melanie said. "We can all breathe again. Thanks to you and Sheriff Clark."

"We didn't do it alone. Mercy McCoy and Arlo Starlight helped."

"Arlo? I'd assumed she'd gone dark forever."

"She was afraid of hurting everyone on the commune if they lost the tax-exempt status. The sheriff got her to see that there's more than one way to skin a cat. Excuse me, I have to take care of something. Would you let the sheriff know that I'll meet him at the compound?"

"No problem."

Willa hurried out the door and down the hall.

THE CROWD OF protesters at the front gate of the compound had tripled in size as the mayor had predicted. The chants through the bullhorns boomed around her as she pulled up to the guardhouse.

After rolling down her window, she and the guard yelled back and forth, keeping it short, and she was waved through the gate.

Her cell buzzed. It was Daniel.

She put the call through the Bluetooth. "This is Nelson."

"Spare me the formality," he snapped, sounding annoyed. "What are you doing?"

"Getting the evidence my son needs to clear his name."

"We can get a warrant for it tomorrow."

Not good enough. She was going to ensure that her son didn't have to spend the night in jail without worrying about backlash from the mayor or the DA on how they had released yet another suspect. "Why wait when I can get it tonight? You should be praising my efficiency. By the time you arrive, I'll have it."

"We're supposed to be a team. Doing this together."

"I've got to go." She disconnected.

Despite the intrusion to their dinner, Sophia was waiting at the bottom of the stone steps in front of Light House along with Huck.

"What can I do for you, Chief Nelson?" she asked as Willa vacated the SUV, raising her voice to speak over the chants of the protesters.

"When my son, Ezekiel, left this August, he said that he was supposed to be given back all his possessions, but a ring he had was missing. Can we see if any notes were made in the inventory list?"

Sophia looked to Huck, but they nodded in unison. "I see no reason why we can't accommodate that request. Right this way." Sophia started walking and Huck ascended the steps, going into Light House. She keyed the radio. "Shawn, could you meet me at the shed with the key?"

"I'm coming now," the head of security said.

"At what point, is someone required to hand over their belongings?" Willa asked.

"Nothing is required here. Everything is a choice. We encourage everyone to go through the process of exuviation—the casting off their former selves in preparation to become something and someone new—as soon as they feel ready to do so. Some shed their belongings as soon as they arrive, even if they don't become members. But every recruit who has decided to fully embrace the Light and take their vows has already done this well in advance."

Willa dug deep not to roll her eyes. "Do you ever sell any of the member's possessions?"

"Definitely not. If for some reason a member must leave us, then we wish to restore them as they came to us."

"Does that include money?"

A coy smile. "We don't give back donations."

They went around to the back side of the garage and stopped at a building that was roughly half the size of the ten-bay garage. Although the overall shape resembled that of a shed, the name was misleading.

Shawn ran over, meeting them at the door. He input the code on the keypad and with a beep, the red locked light flashed green.

"Who has access to the shed?" Willa asked.

"Most members of the security team, ma'am. It gives us the flexibility to open it without delay whenever a member departs." He opened the door for them, and they stepped inside.

Sophia hit the light switch, illuminating rows and shelves filled with boxes of tagged items.

"How does the process work when a member leaves?"

Sophia turned to a shelf with books lined up in chronological order by the year printed on the spine and grabbed one. "We find out what year they arrived," she said, opening it and flipping through the pages, "find their name." She stopped on Ezekiel's. "Everything is listed and the member initials it. We tag everything and store it. When they are ready to go, we use the serial number on the tag to locate the items, turn them over, and the member departs."

The initials *EN* were beside each meager personal thing he'd described in detail.

"Here's the note," Sophia said, pointing it out. "His ring couldn't be located. Someone from security searched for twenty minutes. It's odd and quite rare for something to go missing."

"I'll need a copy of that page in the ledger," Willa said, and Sophia looked prepared to protest. "But if that's going to be a problem, I'll simply be back tomorrow with a warrant."

"Shawn." Sophia handed him the book. "Please make a copy for Chief Nelson."

With a curt nod, he took the ledger and hustled off.

"It'll only be a moment."

Willa looked around. It would be easy enough for someone who was waiting to receive their belongings to slip their hand in a box and swipe an item from the shelf, especially something as small as a ring, if the security guard's back were turned for only a few seconds.

"I'm sorry I intruded on your dinner," Willa said.

"You didn't. We're always finished by seventy thirty."

"How is it coming with that list of individuals who have been here awhile without taking vows?"

"It's coming. The sheriff did give us forty-eight hours."

That he did. "Are you truly happy here?"

Sophia flashed a genuine smile that reached her eyes. "It's the closest to paradise on earth. On our compound, there's no violence, no rape, no murder. Everyone is treated with dignity and respect. We seek to enlighten and as we improve ourselves, make the world a better place."

Sounded good in theory. For those who had lived and thrived on the compound for decades that might have been true, but Willa was struggling with how broken her son had been after being cast out of this paradise. The animosity he had toward Marshall McCoy concerned her, but if her son felt that way, there must have been others. It made her wonder, what if the killer wasn't one of the Fallen, or a guy on the compound, but someone else? They were missing something.

Shawn returned with the copy and locked up while Sophia walked her back to her vehicle. By the time they reached her SUV, the genuine smile on the young woman's face dissolved as two sheriff's vehicles came up the drive with flashing lights that indicated this would be a different kind of visit.

The front door of Light House flew open, and Huck hurried down the steps. Marshall McCoy, his last day clad in an all-white suit, appeared in the doorway and moseyed down as though they couldn't possibly be there for him. In his mind, he must have thought himself untouchable.

Daniel slid her an irritated glance and she held up the copy of the document. Shaking his head at her, he handed Huck the warrant and strode past him up to the mighty Empyrean. "Marshall McCoy, you're under arrest for blackmail," Daniel said, handcuffing him as he read him his Miranda rights.

Pale as death, obviously in shock, McCoy looked to Huck to get him out of this.

All the lawyer said was, "I'll meet you at the station."

There would be no wiggling out of this one. Jennings had made certain before getting the warrant.

Russo and Livingston took McCoy by the arms and got

him into the back of the SUV. Their presence was starting to draw a crowd of onlookers.

Sophia stood, gaping and trembling in disbelief as Starlights gathered around her, watching as their Empyrean was hauled off in cuffs.

Daniel strode up to her, his expression stern, but she wasn't going to apologize.

"Did you release Zeke?"

"Yeah, I did. We'll verify everything he told us, but he's not going anywhere. In fact, he was on his way to work to relieve a coworker who needed to leave early. Livingston called the gas station and confirmed it."

"Here you go." She gave him the copy. "Jennings is happy with us for now, but neither of us needs the mayor making a stink out of this."

He sighed. "I don't want to argue with you."

"Then don't." She grinned at him, and his mouth lifted in a slight, reluctant smile. "We've both been up since five this morning. I'm famished and can hear your stomach growling. How about we have another working dinner, but with less work." Far less since Zeke wouldn't intrude tonight. "I've got a theory I want to run by you."

"I'm in. But I need to be at the station when we process McCoy and see if he'll make a statement."

"He won't. Huck won't let him say a word."

"My thoughts exactly."

"Want to do dinner at your place or mine?"

"Yours. You've got the tasty leftovers. I'll even build a fire," he said, and she shivered, not from the cold, but pure anticipation. "Provided McCoy stays silent, I won't be far behind you."

"I need to swing by Zeke's job and check in on him. See how he's doing."

"Take care of your kid. That's got to come first."

He really was the best. Almost too good to be true. *Almost.* "See you soon."

Chapter Ten

After Marshall McCoy had been booked and shown into the interrogation room, Daniel sat in front of him and his lawyer, Huck.

"I exercise my right to remain silent," McCoy replied to the fifth question.

"Is it true that you used the money you received from Pietsch, Hines and Clayborne to pay off the back taxes on the compound?"

"I exercise my right to remain silent," he repeated, staring down at the table, looking bored.

This was a golden opportunity, having McCoy down at the station. Daniel decided not to waste it. "Did you ask or authorize someone on the compound to kill Beverly Fisher, Leslie Gooding and Gemma Chavez?"

McCoy's gaze flicked up to his. "No."

Daniel had just been fishing to see if the man would bite. "Did the murders of those women keep your flock from running after Mercy rejected you and your movement?"

Huck turned to him with worry stamped on his face, a muscle working in his jaw.

"No," McCoy said plainly, and the lawyer whispered to

him, whatever he was saying was accompanied by enthusiastic hand gestures.

"Do you know who killed Fisher, Gooding and Chavez?"

Lowering his gaze, McCoy returned to playing the silence game.

"Do you have suspicions as to who it could be?" Daniel asked.

They were back to more of the same, and this was why Daniel hated having lawyers present during interviews. Invariably, it made his job harder.

Daniel was willing to bet that he could've gotten more out of McCoy. The killer was tied to the Shining Light somehow, which meant Marshall either knew who he was or could help lead them to him. "The court might show you some leniency if you identified the serial killer. More innocent lives could be lost. Lives you can save by giving me a name." Daniel stared at him, waiting, hoping. "You make yourself out to be a savior but you're nothing more than a hypocrite." He shoved to his feet. "You'll spend the night here in a holding cell. Tomorrow you will be remanded to the county jail until your bail hearing."

"I'd like my one phone call," Marshall said.

"Your lawyer is already here."

"Clearly."

Huck could pass along any message he wanted back on the compound. "Who do you want to call?"

"My daughter."

Huck stared at him with as much surprise as Daniel felt. "I'll see that you get your phone call."

"And her number. I'll need that as well," McCoy said.

With a curt nod, Daniel left the room and headed to his office. For a minute, he'd gotten the man talking. How? Was it because Daniel had been asking the right questions? Or the wrong ones?

"The mayor is on line one for you," Livingston said.

Groaning, Daniel scrubbed a hand over his face. "Did anybody get me what I needed?" he asked to the other deputies in the bullpen.

Mitch Cody, the prior army helicopter pilot Daniel had persuaded to join the department, hopped up, rushed over and handed him a piece of paper. "Thomas Mills confirmed Zeke's statement. Sheila Sanders did watch the movies named with Frankie Young. The waitress Patty Weber couldn't remember if he was there on the 19th, but she said he never pays in cash, always credit card, making it easy for us to verify, and he is a horrible tipper."

Armed with that and the documentation Willa had procured, showing that the ring in question had been lost or stolen on the compound and not returned to the kid, should be enough ammunition.

"YOU WERE THERE behind the one-way mirror, watching me being grilled weren't you, Mom?"

Denying it wouldn't help either of them. She didn't want a relationship built on lies. "I was."

Zeke glared at her from behind the counter at the gas station in Wayward Bluffs. "And you did nothing to help me. In fact, you violated my trust and told them my heat was shut off."

"I said nothing about your trailer or the status of your bills." Taking a breath, measuring her words, she put her hands on her hips. She was grateful to be free of the weight of her duty belt she'd left in her vehicle. "Listen to me. I know you're not a murderer. I believe in you. Always have and always will. You mean the world to me. I also have faith in the system and this is how it works. Questioning is a part of it."

"You could've advised me to keep my mouth shut and gotten me a lawyer."

He was right. She could have. "Then you would still be under suspicion, and I would have been forced to recuse myself from this case. You answered the sheriff's questions and—"

"Don't you mean your boyfriend?"

Ignoring that, she continued. "And I got the proof from the compound that your ring was never returned to you. Once they verify everything else you've told them, you'll be officially cleared. Which is a much faster, cheaper and more efficient way than hiring an overpriced lawyer." That took some of the steam out of him. "The mayor is scrutinizing this case closely. Schroeder will not like it that you were released. I know you don't care if I lose my job over it, but there's a lot at stake." She pulled her wallet from her pocket, fished out three twenty-dollar bills and slapped them down on the counter. "Pay your gas bill, apologize to your grandmother for taking her car without permission and don't you ever drink and drive again. Not only can you end up wrapped around a tree, but you could also kill someone else. You're smarter than that. Start acting like it." She turned to leave, then hesitated. "What do you have to say for yourself?"

"Thanks. Not just for this," he said, picking up the cash. "And I do care if you lose your job. I just don't want what happened to Dad to happen to you."

He still carried the grief of losing Zach, but she didn't want him to fear that the same would happen to her.

"I love you," she said, turning for the door, not expecting him to say anything in return.

"Ditto," he grumbled behind her.

Smiling, she climbed into her SUV and headed home. Normally after a tough day and working a case she needed to crack, she'd go to the gym. Get in thirty minutes of vigorous cardio and weightlifting to keep her muscles toned and her body strong. Once she got into a zone, her mind would empty and any issues she had resolving a case would start to unravel.

Tonight, she wanted company—Daniel's—and conversation instead cardio, though she was open to getting sweaty with him. It was nice to have someone in her corner, who she could rely on. A hot cowboy and a cop all rolled into one.

Not much farther now. This last road would take her home. She wondered if she'd have time to shower before Daniel arrived.

Willa took the corner way too fast, and her SUV's tires slid a bit, but she corrected. She'd been on this hilly road hundreds of times in all sorts of weather, even blizzards, but she was exhausted and starving, driving a tad too aggressively. She took another bend in the road and began to slide, lucky to finagle her way out of it before the SUV hit the shoulder and careened over the side into the gorge that was Devil's Canyon.

She shifted down, slowing. The tires slid again as though the road was slick with black ice close to the top of the hill. *Not that cold yet.* Only a little farther to go and she'd be headed down the hill, toward home. She'd be there in minutes.

Hopefully, Zeke was all right.

Once more the vehicle slipped, the wheels losing their

grip. It had been a while since she had replaced them. Low tread could reduce tire traction. Maybe that was the prob—

Crack!

The canyon echoed the blast of a high-powered rifle shot—the sound unmistakable to her.

Gut instinct made Willa duck. Her SUV shuddered. Someone was shooting at her vehicle.

Keeping one hand on the steering wheel, she fumbled for her firearm that was in the passenger seat on her duty belt. Then it occurred to her what was actually happening.

Those weren't just shots at her.

It's the Holiday Elk Horn Killer. This is how he first isolates his victims. Shooting out their tires.

Oh, God!

Fear speared her heart.

She had to make it down the hill, beyond the canyon. Almost, almost. She was almost there, but the tires hit another slick patch.

It wasn't cold enough for ice. Was it oil?

The SUV spun, tires skidding. Her seat belt gripped tight, digging across her chest, and there wasn't anything she could do behind the wheel.

Faster and faster her vehicle whirled. She had to do something before it was too late. Frantically, she snatched her cell from the magnetic mount on the dash and dialed Daniel, but the phone slipped from her hand as the SUV slammed into the guardrail.

Metal shrieked and groaned, giving way, and the SUV slid over the edge. All she could do was hang on and pray she didn't die. The drop into the forest—*thank God not the canyon*—was only a few feet, but her vehicle tipped, landing on its side and rolled.

With the crunch of steel and shattering glass, she pitched forward at the same time the airbag deployed. It slammed her back against the seat, pressing hard against her face and chest. Pain ripped up her neck and shoulder. The scream of twisting metal filled her ears. Sharp rocks and debris tore through the broken windows. The front panels crumpled. A tire popped during the roll down the slope.

She couldn't focus on the warm blood that oozed from the side of her head. The vehicle flipped over, landing upside down. The roof crunched on impact, jarring Willa to her bones.

Fire whipped through her shoulder. The airbag squeezed her tight, the grit from its deployment making her eyes burn.

Agony fogged her brain. Her lungs were tight, so tight it was though the air was being squeezed from her lungs. Cool night air whipped through the car. She could barely think, barely breathe, but she fought to stay conscious.

The killer was out there, the hunter. Watching. Making his way to her. To stalk his prey.

Awareness slid over her. She still held her sidearm. That was something.

If he dared approach her while she was trapped in the SUV, she'd shoot to kill. No questions asked.

This was bad. Dire.

Get out. Now! Get out and run!

She pressed on the release button of her seat belt and tried to push the airbag from her face. Neither would budge. Pain rippled up her shoulder and she let out a wounded yelp. Something was wrong with the airbag—a defect in the construction or a mechanical error.

Despair welled inside her.

Come on. Think. You're running out of time.

He was out there. Somewhere in the darkness. Moving closer. She sensed his presence like an ominous shadow slithering overhead. His intention was clear and deadly.

All she could think about were the first victims on Elk Horn. Images of them flashed through her mind. Stripped and tied, their wrists bound so tightly to tree trunks that their skin was bruised and broken. Their chests stabbed. Throats slashed. Bitten. Dead. Skin gray. Brunette hair fanned out like a crown.

Nausea punched through her stomach as she realized she fit the profile of the first victims. Aged twenty to forty. Slim. White. Dark hair. Single. Driving alone when he struck.

No, no, no! She couldn't let that happen to her. *Move! Get the hell out!*

Groaning against the pain, she shoved her fingers down and pushed hard on the seat belt release button. Nothing.

She jabbed down on it harder, again and again. But it was no use. It was jammed.

Ice-cold panic flooded her veins. At any moment that sick murderer would pop up, a nightmare made flesh and blood, and stuck in this position, trapped by the air bag, she was a sitting duck. It would be the end of her.

She listened for approaching footsteps, snapped twigs, any noise that would give him away. But he was hunting a cop. Not just any officer but the chief of police. He had the audacity and the smarts to set the perfect trap. He'd expect her to be armed and she expected him to be prepared.

Teeth chattering from the pain and the fear, she struggled to wrangle her thoughts.

Don't give up! Keep fighting!

If she could move the air bag enough to breathe or reach her phone or…

The knife in her pocket.

Grimacing through the throbbing ache, she struggled to slip her hand into her pocket and reach her Buck Budgie. Swallowing back her panic, she shoved her fingers deeper. The tips grazed steel. *Almost. Come on.* Frantically—adrenaline driving her to hurry—she gritted her teeth and eased her hand farther.

Any second she expected him to appear.

Her heart pounded furiously, beating hard as a drum. Desperation and anger swept through her as she clenched the knife. *Yes! Thank God.*

Sharp and sturdy, the blade would set her free. She pulled the knife to her chest slowly, so it didn't fall through her fingers. Hands shaking, she slipped open the blade with her left hand clenched around her gun. Furiously, she stabbed the air bag.

After a *pop*, it hissed and slowly deflated. The strong chemical smell it left behind tainted the air, making her cough. She shoved the collapsed bag out of the way and started on the seat belt. If not for her injured shoulder, she would have made quick work of slicing through it. As it was, the sawing motion took effort, adding pressure to her rotator cuff, and irritating her bruised flesh.

Sawing through the seat belt, she sensed rather than saw she wasn't alone. She turned her head to look around and grimaced. Hurting all over, she was one hell of a mess. But alive.

She had to get out if she intended to stay that way.

Listening again, she didn't hear anything besides the howling wind and her wild heartbeat. In the darkness, she only saw trees, the ground, and shadows playing tricks on her mind.

But she knew he was out there. Watching and waiting.

She aimed the gun out the window, hoping to get a glimpse of him. *Show yourself.*

Seconds ticked by in her head matching the rhythm of her pounding heart.

Nothing.

She turned back to the seat belt. Her only thought now was to hurry and get out. Moving faster—the pain making her vision blur—she continued sawing until the belt broke free and she dropped to the roof.

Agony exploded through her shoulder, her spine, her neck. Tears burned behind her eyes. Her shoulder was dislocated. The gut-wrenching sensation was familiar. She had an old injury that flared up if her shoulder was hit with enough force at the wrong angle. Hands trembling badly, she managed to close the knife and stuff it in her pocket. Shifting her Glock to her right hand, she braced herself to crawl over the broken glass and out of the vehicle. But once she did, she'd be exposed with no more cover.

He might be waiting for her to make that very move.

A sharp prick stung the back of her leg.

What in the hell?

Had she cut herself? She touched her hamstring and felt something small and metallic lodged in her muscle.

She yanked it out and stared down at a dart with a tiny needle. Her heart turned to a block of ice.

Oh, no. He shot her with something worse than a bullet. There was no telling what kind of drug was inside the tiny silver cartridge. If she stayed there, giving it time to work through her system, it was all over.

Panic-stricken, she searched for her phone to call for help.

But she didn't see it anywhere. Had it been thrown from the car? She swore under her breath. Where was her duty belt?

She shoved a branch that was in the car aside and found it. Grabbing her radio, she keyed the transmit button. "This is Chief Nelson."

"Go ahead, Chief," the duty officer replied.

"I'm in imminent danger. I rolled over off Route 4 less than two miles from my home," she said, and it struck her like a bolt of lightning that this sick monster knew where she lived. How long had he been following her? Stalking her? Planning this? Since she was first in the news making a statement about Fisher? But why now? Were they close to finding him? "I believe the Holiday Elk Horn Killer is after me. He blew out my tires, causing my vehicle to go off the road, and shot me with some kind of tranquilizer dart." Medetomidine. That's what he used. "Contact Sheriff Daniel Clark. He may be the closest to me to respond immediately. Send backup. Proceed with caution. He slicked the road with something and he is armed and dangerous."

A crack shot for sure, to disable her car and send it careening off the road. An ace marksman. A hunter.

"Yes, ma'am," the duty officer said and switched over to a different line for a moment and then returned. "Can you see him, Chief?"

"No. But he's out there." Closing in. Hunting her. Time was running out. She had no idea how long it would take before she was incapacitated. If she didn't move now, she was going to die here. "I'm moving from the wreckage of my vehicle." He'd expect her to continue downhill, where the ground plateaued. It made the most sense. So she was not going to do what he expected. "I'm injured, but I'm going to try heading back uphill toward the road," she said.

Willa pictured him waiting for her in the darkness. Patiently. Quietly. Finger on the trigger, ready to put a bullet in her chest. But then he wouldn't have bothered to drug her.

She forced herself to crawl out of the car through the busted window. Shards of glass bit into her left palm that she used to pull herself forward.

Blinking hard through the pain, she stood and brought up her pistol. She turned three-sixty, scanning the woods for him. Numbness seeped through her. Holding the weapon up was getting harder. Already her fingers and limbs were having trouble responding as a tingle spread through her.

The sedative was working fast. Too fast.

A howl broke the quiet. It sounded like a wolf, but it had been made by a man. Of that she was certain.

That predator was coming for her.

But she wasn't going to make it easy. Holding tight to her gun, heart drumming, Willa ran.

Chapter Eleven

Punching the accelerator, his SUV fishtailing, Daniel straightened out the wheels with some effort. He took the winding road, which had been made even more treacherous with a slippery substance, as hard and fast as he dared. The point was to find her, not to get into a wreck himself. He kept hoping for a glimpse of Willa's car, any sign of her or an accident.

He glanced at the GPS. Three miles from her house. In the middle of nowhere. Why did she live in such a remote, isolated area in Wayward Bluffs?

Space, privacy and few neighbors but they're all nice, she'd told him.

He cursed every single one of her reasons now, even though he couldn't throw a rock from his place and hit any of his neighbors' houses.

Where are you, Willa?

His SUV slid, sending his pulse skyrocketing, and he tapped the breaks, careful not to go into a spin. He'd finally reached the slickness she had mentioned. As much as he ached to slam on the gas and get to her as soon as possible, he had to slow it down. Just enough to avoid getting into a wreck himself.

Two and half miles from where he expected to spot her or her vehicle.

There had been no mention of any slick substance found on the road near the victims' cars in the cold case files. But the killer wouldn't have needed it with civilians. Taking on Willa, on the other hand, a trained professional, the guy was probably stacking the deck in his favor. Handicapping her as much as possible to ensure he got his prey.

Daniel slapped the steering wheel. If they'd gone together, had left at the same time, then this wouldn't be happening.

But there would have been another moment, sooner or later, when she would be vulnerable and unsuspecting and alone. Then this predator still would have pounced. To-night—*thank God*—Daniel had planned to come out here and was already on the way, and Zeke was out of harm's way, safe at work. If nothing else, Daniel estimated that he wasn't too far behind Willa based on the time the call came through about her accident.

Rounding another bend, his headlights swept over a busted portion of the guardrail—gnarled steel split wide.

That's where she must have gone off the road and over the side. His gut clenched. How far was the drop? Noting the mile marker, he slowed to a stop and threw the vehicle into Park.

Hopping out and treading carefully around the vehicle, he got on the radio. "This is Sheriff Clark. I've found where Chief Nelson was forced off the road. Route 4, mile marker 7." He popped the trunk and grabbed his emergency road-side kit.

"Copy, Sheriff. Notifying inbound units, the ambulance and your helicopter pilot."

The wind shrieked in the surrounding canyons, sounding too much like a wounded animal. His mind was playing tricks on him. He was just keyed up and needed to focus on the only thing that mattered right now. Finding Willa.

He unzipped the bag and grabbed a road flare. After locating the rough striking surface on the cap on one end of it, he tore off the plastic lid. He held the flare away from his face and lit it much the same way he would strike a match.

The flare sprayed ignited, molten material that would burn for an hour. He tossed it a hundred feet behind his SUV, where approaching vehicles would easily spot it. He hurried forward, past the SUV, toward the mangled opening in the guardrail.

His thoughts took a dark turn as he considered his father, James Clark, and his final minutes. On a road not too different from this one. Also, here in Wyoming. Near Laramie in the Snowy Range Mountains. A brutal storm. Poor visibility. A tragic accident where his car had gone over the side of an embankment. Died on impact before Grace had even been born.

But that was twenty-six years ago. The past would not repeat itself. There was no storm, no mischance at work here.

This was the cunning machination of a vicious serial killer. Willa was alive, fighting for every breath, and she needed him.

Clutching his kit, he rushed to the opening and peered over the side. Trees and darkness spread as far as the eye could see. The bloated moon was bright and the sky clear, but the woods were so dense the moonlight didn't hit the forest floor.

Where the hell is she? He didn't even see her damaged vehicle. Not because the drop had been too far, but because it had rolled. The savage bulldozed path the wreckage had cut made him wonder how bad the accident was and how serious her injuries might be.

Worry gnawed at his insides, reminding him that every time he found a sliver of happiness it had slipped right through his fingers, like grains of sand he couldn't hold on to.

Not this time. Not today.

After two long, long years, fate had brought Willa back into his life, and she was the best thing to have happened to him since he'd moved out here at the age of eighteen and learned what it meant to be a cowboy. From the second she'd flashed her badge in Crazy Eddie's he'd been drawn to her like a dying man in the desert to a lush oasis.

"Hell," Daniel grunted. He had it bad. It was a wonder how she'd managed to have gotten under his skin so quickly. *You let her, you fool. Now look at you.* She'd slipped in a while ago when their no-promises, no-strings-attached fling had evolved into a full-blown affair. Only he hadn't realized it until she had cut him off completely before they'd started to border on a relationship.

And that's what he wanted with her. A relationship. Cooking together. Cuddled up in front of the fire. Supporting one another. Building each other up. He wanted to be a haven for her.

But there was a killer on the loose who had put her in his sights.

Dread caused stomach acid to bubble up his throat. Scanning the terrain below, he searched for any sign of her. Still, nothing. Desperation sent him shuffling down the side of the hill without any gear to prevent him from falling if he took a nasty stumble.

Another blast of wind shrieked through the canyon. Listening closely, it sounded like a wolf howling. Urgency pounded through him as he scurried along the rocky terrain. His mind was racing, his heart throbbing with a mix of fear and fury.

DARKNESS DANCED AROUND the edge of her vision. She blinked, fighting it, and an image of Daniel floated in front of her. Relationships ended badly for her. Once nearly tragically. Perhaps this was the universe's way of telling her that Daniel would be good to her and good for her—body, mind and soul—but to balance the scale, this was how she would meet her end. At the hands of a sadistic madman.

Daniel's face vanished, but he was coming for her. Help was on the way. She simply had to hang on, keep moving, keep fighting. She scrambled up the slope, her body slow, her footing unsteady. Her shoulder was in agony, but she clung to the pain, grateful it was the only thing preventing her from succumbing completely to the drug coursing through her veins. But not for much longer. The adrenaline, the stark fear, wasn't enough anymore. It was getting harder and harder to clamber up the hill. To hold…on to…her gun. She shook her head, desperate to clear the fogginess.

She stumbled and swayed before she dropped to her knees. Unable to make herself stand back up, her brain refusing her commands, she tipped backward, hitting the ground.

Blinking hard, she was starting to fade. Numbness crept through her limbs, her mind clouding.

Her head lolled to the side, as she tried to look for the devil. Her fingers loosening around the gun until her grip was no more and her firearm slipped free.

The sky began to spin—the world, the moon dimming.

"Chief Nelson," he said, turning her heart to stone. His tone was congenial and warm like he knew her.

He was close. Only a few feet away.

"No," she said, her voice shallow, her tongue thick, her throat dry.

This was her son's greatest fear, losing her to the darkness of the job. She couldn't die like this. For Zeke's sake. She had to survive to repair the dysfunction between them, to give him a chance at the future he deserved. She had to truly start living herself, letting in love, giving herself permission to be happy. Not only preach the way, but show him, leading by example.

She struggled to find her weapon. But failed.

It was there. On the ground beside her. Somewhere… somewhere. She was starting to slip beneath the surface of consciousness.

"Looks like you're having car trouble. Do you need help?" he asked, taunting her.

This was what he had probably said to his victims, getting them to lower their guard, letting him get close. But he was just toying with her. For sport.

And then he came into view, his features covered by a ski mask, night vision goggles shielding his eyes. A figure in black painter's coveralls.

"Want me to give you a hand?" he asked, extending his toward her. Metal glinted in his other hand. A large, hunting knife.

Chilling, bone-deep terror sliced through her.

Mustering the last of her waning strength, she growled at him as she extended her fingers, feeling around for her pistol. "Drop dead."

"Not before you," he said in a singsongy voice that gave

her chills. "But first, we're going to have some fun. At least, I am."

"Go to hell." Battling the sluggishness overtaking her more and more every second, she groped for her Glock. This time her fingers hit cold steel. She heaved it up into the air. If only she could aim. She fired.

Pop, pop, pop.

But all the shots had missed, flinging up dirt and breaking off bits of bark from a nearby tree. No, no, no.

"Aww, that's too bad, Chief. Nice try, though. I'll give you an A for effort."

"Cheater." The word lacked the force she had longed to hurl at him.

The only way he could win against her was by slicking the road, shooting out her tires, drugging her from a distance.

Coward.

She raised the gun to squeeze off another round, but her fingers didn't respond. Unconsciousness clawed at her, threatening to suck her under. "Can't win…a fair…fight."

He kicked her sidearm from her hand and stepped on her forearm, dragging a scream from her. As he eased off the pressure, the darkness swooped in, determined to swallow her, and the fear evaporated, leaving only sharp-edged doggedness to end this man's life, if by some miracle, she ever got the chance.

A SERIES OF gunshots echoed through the canyon. Slowing his descent, Daniel pinpointed the direction of origin.

There. Her car. Crushed metal caught the light of the moon. He swept his gaze slowly, steadily up the hillside from there.

Willa! Oh, God. Was someone beside her?

His heart squeezed as he realized that the killer was right on top of her. Willa's agonizing scream carried on the wind, echoing in the woods, ripping through him. Every muscle in his body tensed as a rush of adrenaline flooded through his veins. His need to reach her before it was too late was single-focused and overwhelming. Racing like a madman down sloped terrain, he scrambled faster to get to her, his chest tight, feeling like his lungs might burst.

Daniel wended through the thicket of drooping ever-greens, heading down the razed path her car had made. Pulse pounding, muscles burning, he hurried, needing to do something. *God.* If he didn't reach her in time…

Frantic, his breath punching from his mouth, Daniel slid several feet, narrowly catching hold of a tree trunk to stop his rapid-fire descent. He was close enough now that he could more clearly make out the twisted metal of her wrecked car and details of her assailant. Tall. Medium build. Cloaked in black. And wearing night vision googles.

Cold fear tightened in his gut. He dug into the emergency kit and pulled out another flare. Quickly, he used the striking surface on the cap to light it and threw it. The flare, spitting molten sparks, landed near Willa and in her attacker's eye line because the monster reeled back like the bogeyman from the light.

Daniel drew his sidearm. At the same time, the helicopter swooped in overhead, piloted by his deputy Mitch Cody. The aircraft's bright spotlight shone on the killer. Daniel took aim and fired. Once. Twice. Three times. The third shot jerked him forward, like he'd been hit or grazed on the left arm. Then the predator disappeared in the forest, evading the helicopter's searchlight in the trees.

Daniel rushed the rest of the way down, panting and filled with dread, his gaze locked on Willa's unmoving body. He tripped. Righted himself. And dashed over to her. Dropping to his knees, he pulled her into his lap and felt for a pulse.

She was alive! Her breathing shallow from the drug the killer had used on her, but she was going to be okay.

Chapter Twelve

"You shouldn't have called him," Willa said to Daniel, lying in the bed in the emergency room, holding Zeke's hand.

Daniel gave her one of those sympathetic looks that was starting to grow on her. The inkling of a beard was developing after two days of not shaving and she liked the facial hair on him. Liked it a lot.

"I had to," Daniel said, relief on his sharp features. "He deserved to know what you've just been through."

The last thing she wanted was for her son to know that she had almost been murdered by a serial killer. Unable to ever squash his fears, he'd have nightmares for the rest of his life, always worried whenever she was on duty.

Even though, technically, she hadn't been on duty when that madman attacked her.

"I'm glad he told me, Mom." Zeke stood at her bedside in an oversized sweatshirt and jeans. His dark hair carefully and deliberately mussed.

Taking in both of them at once, with no one fighting or fussing, except for her, they'd never looked so good to Willa.

Tears pricked the corners of her eyes, but she blinked them back, not wanting Zeke or Daniel to see her break down or give them any indication she was unnerved and scared. She had been stalked, attacked and almost murdered. The very idea of the killer knowing where she lived made her blood run cold, and her assailant was still out there, on the loose, most likely planning to terrorize her again.

Luckily, her injuries were minor. Grade 1 whiplash that didn't necessitate a cervical collar. A cut on the side of her head that had required four stitches. A dislocated shoulder, which the doctor had fixed by popping the ball portion back into the socket. It ached right now and would be sore for the next couple of days, but it wasn't anything ice and pain relievers couldn't take care of.

"It's my job to worry about you, not the other way around. Got it?" she said.

But it was too late for that. Her son's skin was paler than usual and the shadows under his eyes were deep. Zeke had been concerned. Scared.

Which made two of them. She glanced at Daniel, her gaze lingering on the lines creasing his brow. Make that three of them.

"Come on, Mom." Zeke rolled his expressive Zach-like eyes. "You and Grandma are the only real family I have. We are supposed to worry about each other."

More tears threatened to well. "Does that mean you're going to be an angel from now on and cause me less stress?" Willa asked, needing to lighten the mood for all their sakes.

Success. She managed to pry a smile out of him. Not a toothy, make your cheeks ache smile, but a real grin.

"Let's not push it by asking for two miracles in one day," Zeke said.

Willa tried and failed not to chuckle, but Daniel laughing, too, reminded her that she needed to do more of that.

Not less. "Until you get your heat turned on, I want you to stay with your grandma."

"Why? Do I have to?" Zeke looked as if he had been ordered to seminary school instead of being expected to accompany his grandmother to church once a week. "You're going to be discharged tonight."

She slid her gaze to Daniel in a quiet plea for help. This was a truth her son didn't need to know.

"You're right, Zeke. I am your mom's boyfriend," Daniel said, and Willa's eyes flared wide as her son's jaw dropped a little. "After this incident, I'm going to be around more and she's going to need a lot of extra rest over the next few days."

Zeke nodded. "Yeah, sure."

When her son wasn't looking at her, she mouthed to Daniel, *What are you doing?*

He shrugged.

"Once I'm a hundred percent and I've wrapped up this case, things will go back to normal. Okay?" When he didn't respond, she repeated, "Okay?"

"I got it." He stared at her with eyes that reminded her so much of his father. "But I'm going down to the gas company tomorrow, so it's not a big deal. I just don't want you lying to me if you're in danger or something. I'm grown. I can handle it. You don't have to keep treating me like a child."

Willa's throat closed. "It isn't safe for you to be at my house. Not right now."

"Then it isn't safe for you to be there either."

"I agree," Daniel chimed in.

She did not sign up for them to gang up on her. "I haven't thought through the logistics yet."

"You can stay with me," Daniel offered.

Zeke eyed him. "Or with Grandma. If I had a spare bed in the trailer, you'd be welcome to it."

There was no way she would ever stay with Irene. Under any circumstances. "It isn't safe for me to be with family. I'd only endanger you." That monster could find her simply by watching the police station and the sheriff's department and follow her from there anytime he pleased. And her nightmare wouldn't cease until they had him in custody or he was dead.

Zeke tightened his grip on her hand, and she didn't miss the shadow that crossed Daniel's eyes. "Are you going straight back to work?" her son asked.

"Yeah. There's a bad guy out there and he needs to be stopped before he kills anyone else."

Daniel raised an eyebrow. "There is a sheriff on the case."

"Are you saying you don't need me?"

"No." He shook his head. "I'm not saying that at all," he said, and it was clear to her that he was talking about more than the case. "I am saying that it's fine to rest and recover. You went through...an ordeal."

"You should listen to him, Mom."

This had to stop. Reaching over, she pushed the call button for a nurse, with her IV connection pulling at her wrist. It was time to get out of there. Morning would come before she knew it and she wanted to be ready. "Sitting around, watching TV and twiddling my thumbs isn't going to help me. And it isn't going to help this case get solved any faster either. Physically, I'm fine. Even the doctor said I don't need down time."

Daniel's expression turned somber as he caught what she didn't say. She wasn't fine on other levels that she was not going to touch with a ten-foot pole until they caught the creep who had made the mistake of going after her tonight.

The door opened and a heavyset nurse with rosy cheeks swept in. "Can I get you something?" she asked and hit a button, switching off the call light.

"Yes. I'd like to be released. As soon as possible," Willa said. "The doctor mentioned I wouldn't have to spend the night and I'd rather be on my way."

"I'm not sure if the doctor is ready to discharge you." The nurse frowned. "But I'll go check, Chief."

"Thanks. Appreciate it."

The nurse backed out of the door, and Zeke's lips twitched. "Mom, why do you do this job? I know we need cops to keep people safe and for law and order. But why do *you* do it, knowing the risks, how dangerous it is?"

"You come from a long line of cops. When I was a bit younger than you, I swore I would never become a police officer. I fought it for as long as I could. I was called to do this job. It fits. It's a part of me. It makes me happy."

He looked her over, from head to toe lying in the hospital bed. "You don't look very happy. And I don't mean just now."

Of course, he'd noticed her living half a life. "I'm planning to make changes. I'm going to stop denying myself the things that fill me with joy and have nothing to do with my job." She glanced at Daniel, and she saw the recognition in his eyes. "I know you were happy on the compound," she said to her son. "But I want you to work on being happy out here, too."

Sighing, Zeke lowered his head. "Yeah, I know. It's just been…hard."

She understood better than he realized. "Change is hard.

But possible. And it doesn't hurt to have help along the way," she said, giving his hand a long squeeze.

Her son tightened his fingers around hers and squeezed back.

Progress. If nearly dying was the crucial element needed to break the storm between them, she'd do it all over again.

She looked at Daniel. A smile slid from one side of his mouth to the other, and a tingle trickled through her. She couldn't help but wonder if this was the start of something real and wonderful that might actually last.

Then she thought better about tempting fate.

THE NEXT DAY, Daniel tried to act like nothing had changed. But in fact, everything was different.

He had finally acknowledged to himself how deep his feelings ran for Willa. The woman whose beauty and backbone had first caught him off guard. She was smart as a whip, athletic and had a sassy sense of humor that never failed to surprise him.

Willa appeared open to exploring her emotions for him. Not only because she had agreed to stay with him for the time being, but in all her truth sharing with her son, she hadn't disputed that they were dating. Zeke's hostility level had dropped from DEFCON 2, next step to nuclear war, to DEFCON 4, strengthened security measures.

Thought most significant and troubling was that Willa, the chief of police, had gone from being the hunter to being the hunted.

He wasn't going to lie to himself, it had kept him awake last night while he ensured Willa slept safely at his ranch.

"Let's hear your theory you wanted to run by me last night," he said to her in his office.

Willa looked good, strong and healthy, for a woman who had come close to dying last night. Her shoulder ached and she had taken pain relievers this morning. All in all, her spirits were high. He only hoped she wasn't putting on a brave face because she thought he needed her to. He didn't.

"I was thinking about Zeke's anger during your interview," Willa said, "when he talked about McCoy and how he wanted Marshall to hurt."

"I think there are plenty of folks in town who feel the same way he does. We passed a couple of them on the street celebrating as they read the headlines about his arrest."

"I'm not talking about schadenfreude," she said, referring to pleasure derived by someone from another person's misfortune. "Is there an English equivalent of that?"

"Epicaricacy."

"You just happen to know that?" she asked, and he nodded. "Your mother bought you an excellent education. Money well spent. Anyway, that's not what I'm referring to. McCoy caused pain on a deep level for Zeke when he took away *paradise*. I felt his pain as he talked about it. I believe the killer might be someone who feels like that."

"If it was a copycat, I could see that," Daniel said. "But how do you explain the Holiday Elk Horn Killer stopping five years ago?"

"I think he found the Shining Light. Perhaps to hide out at first. But after a while he started believing. McCoy worked wonders with Zeke. I think it's possible that he might have done the same for the Holiday Killer. Then something happened a couple of months ago and he got kicked out. Now he's angry, bloodthirsty kind of angry, and wants to hurt McCoy and the cult in the process with these new murders.

That's why this time he's targeting women with some previous affiliation to the cult."

Taking a sip of his coffee, Daniel leaned forward. "But we've already looked at the Fallen who were sent away this year before Beverly Fisher was murdered."

Nodding, she flashed him a knowing smile. "What if there is another category of people who were robbed of paradise, but aren't the Fallen?"

"It sounds like you're asking me a riddle," he said.

"Exactly. Haven't you felt like if we could crack the code and ask the right question that we would get all our answers from someone in the Shining Light?" she asked.

"Déjà vu. I felt that way yesterday when I was interviewing Marshall. When I started asking him certain questions about the murder case, he actually gave me answers." Yes and no responses. Still, it counted. "Until Huck got him to stop talking."

"We need our very own Shining Light Decoder," she said. "I'd call Mercy, but I don't know if she would be up for it."

Daniel looked out at the bullpen. *Talk about timing.* "Only one way to find out. Why don't you ask her?" he said, pointing to Mercy as she strolled from the front around to his office.

Mercy smiled. "Sheriff Clark. Chief Nelson." She wore blue jeans and a purple sweater.

Even though she was going on over a month of freedom from the compound and their rules, and no longer had to only wear white, to this day it was strange seeing her dressed in other colors.

"What are you doing here?" Willa asked. "I was just talking about you."

"I'm here to see my father. He called me last night and asked me to come visit him. Why were you talking about me?"

"It was nothing bad," Daniel clarified, picking up on the uncertainty in her voice.

"I was saying that we need a Shining Light Decoder because we're not asking the right questions."

Mercy stepped into the office. "I have time to be of assistance this morning. Is there anything I can do to help?"

"Maybe. Are there ever any people who are denied *paradise*, aren't allowed to stay on the compound, but aren't considered the Fallen? Not the transients, who don't care and are only looking for three hot meals and a safe bed. Believers who aren't Starlights."

Mercy sat in the chair beside Willa, facing the desk. "Sure," she said. "It happens, but it's rare."

"What do you mean?" Daniel asked.

"Recruits are usually allowed to stay for as long as they like as adults, no pressure to take vows. While with us, they learn our ways, learn about the Light, are given a function on the compound and trained accordingly."

Daniel took out his pad and reviewed his notes. "Do they still where blue, the color of novices?"

"Not once they've been with us for a year or more," she said, as if the question was silly. "By then, they've become embedded in the community. A part of the commune. The only functions they can't serve in are as leaders and council members. When a person has decided that they're ready to take their vows, they go through their unburdening session with Empy—" she said, stopping herself, "my father and sometimes, and it is rare, he sees too much darkness in a person's heart to allow them to join us. Once that happens, they are cast out, but they aren't labeled, branded like the Fallen."

It had been a riddle, but would solving it uncover a killer?

Daniel exchanged a glance with Willa, her warm brown eyes bright and animated, he could almost feel the buzz of excitement sizzle through her veins as it did his.

Nodding, Willa grabbed the logbook she'd gotten from the garage. "This shows not only who the drivers were, but also the passengers who were dropped off. We've been dismissing the transients, not realizing that some of them, a small, rare group, aren't drifters at all, but people who had built a life on the compound and were ready to commit until Marshall deemed them unworthy and cast them out with nothing. No purpose. No home. No family. Alone and angry. I'm betting one of them is our serial killer." She turned the book toward Mercy. "Do you recognize any names that fit the parameters of who we're looking for?"

"How far back do you want me to go?" she asked.

They'd been looking at the last year, but it didn't hurt to go back a little farther. "Look at everyone over the past two years," Daniel said, handing her a notepad and pen to jot down names.

"Can we get you anything?" Willa asked. "Coffee, tea, soda?"

"A bottle of water?"

Willa was about to get up when Daniel motioned for her to stay seated. Instead of being in the office, she should be home resting. He wasn't going to argue. Not with everything else that was happening. If she was in the office, he could be sure she was safe.

He grabbed Mercy a bottle of water and handed it to her. Sitting back down, he became exceedingly aware of the clock ticking off the seconds, of Willa's nervous energy as she paced, the tension evident on Mercy's features as she flipped the pages and scanned the names.

Daniel caught up on some paperwork while Mercy reviewed the logbook. He thought he'd have more time to complete a full task and mark it off his to-do list, but he wasn't complaining when Mercy closed the book.

She took a long swallow of water and held out the notepad.

Willa practically snatched it from her grasp and looked down at the list. "Are you sure? Only one name?"

One?

Another long drink of water. "I'm sure," she said, looking confident. "My father has listened to hundreds and hundreds of people unburden themselves. Not all who come to us are good. But we, they, *my father*, knew that the Light was capable of making most individuals worthy through powerful miracles, changing hearts, saving souls of all kinds. Like I said it's a rare occurrence for him to refuse to let someone take vows and join the community."

Willa sat beside Mercy. "How long was he at the compound?"

The young blonde thought about it. "I remember after my father had announced it was my twenty-first birthday, that man approached me and told me that it was too bad I wouldn't get the chance to celebrate it properly in a bar. I found the comment inappropriate and off-putting."

"He was there at least four years," Willa said, and Mercy nodded. "Fits our timeline for the Holiday Killer, as well. What section did he work in?"

"Security," Mercy said.

"He had the code to the shed where everyone keeps their

belongings from the outside world and could've stolen Zeke's ring," Willa said. "Planted it to throw suspicion away from him."

"What's his name?" Daniel asked. He was going to get every available deputy on the task of tracking down where he lived and worked. Then they were going to bring him in today and put an end to this.

Willa turned the pad to face him.

Simon Yates.

Chapter Thirteen

Willa sat in the passenger seat of the lead vehicle with Daniel behind the wheel. There were two more sheriff's SUVs behind them. None of them had on sirens, but all the vehicles had switched on their flashing lights.

"I can't believe Simon Yates has been under our noses the entire time," she said. "This just goes to show that sometimes the simplest answer is sitting right in front of us."

She wasn't sure if it was a cop thing or just a human thing to complicate things. Like the harder it was to get something gave it more value.

"What I find unbelievable is that he's working as a janitor at the church right across from the bus station. He could sit and watch every single Starlight or drifter being dropped off by the Shining Light van," he said. "From that vantage point, he could also scope out the surveillance cameras of the bus station, to know precisely where to stand so as never to be caught on the security feed."

Yates had failed to take into consideration the surveillance of the convenience store next to the bus station. Cameras covered the store's parking lot and gave a view of the soup kitchen and the church, which showed Yates not only interacting with all three victims, but also him taking

Gemma Chavez into the church. She never left through the front or side doors. No surveillance footage was available showing the rear of the house of worship.

Daniel slapped the steering wheel, and she gave him a what-is-it look. "To think, after Simon Yates was kicked out, his first victim was Beverly Fisher, the drug-addicted young woman who had been dropped off at the church."

"Simon had only been out of the compound for a month and working at the church for three weeks. His emotions still must have been raw, like Zeke's now. He probably started thinking about the idea after he saw Beverly. Then for seven months, he lined up his victims, stalked them, learned their routines and habits before killing them. Can you imagine the degree of patience and level of planning that required?" After last night, she could imagine a multitude of horrible things Yates was capable of.

"Gemma Chavez is the exception to how he operated with the others," Daniel said. "Even then, he was able to act quickly, impulsively, decisively without being seen."

Willa shook her head. "He was seen all the time as a janitor. The problem is no one bothered to notice him. That's why he wasn't caught."

"Father O'Neill has no idea he has allowed a murderer to live rent-free in the basement of the church. With a key, he can come and go as he pleased."

They pulled up to the church located across the road from the main bus station that served as a hub for the university's Secure Ride, as well as Greyhound and Amtrak. Daniel parked in front of the church while the remaining deputies covered the other two exits to ensure Simon Yates did not get away and slip through their fingers if he decided to run.

Suspects tended to run for a number of reasons—survival instinct, fear, panic. The worse the crime, the higher the odds.

"Are you good to go on this?" Daniel asked. The worry in his eyes was touching. "There's no shame being part of the backup."

No shame for him. For her, most certainly there was. "Don't try to sideline me or put me on the B team." Willa could handle a dash and chase. The ache in her shoulder wouldn't stop her from running, though tackling a suspect would prove tricky. Not impossible. She'd have to watch her sore shoulder, but the doctor had cleared her for duty.

Daniel had taken steps to mitigate fight or flight of the suspect from occurring with six of them, three teams of two going in through the only entrances: front, rear and east side.

The time of day was ideal. The church was open, and neither mass nor confession was on the schedule now. The soup kitchen next-door would not get started for another two hours.

Once the other two teams radioed in that they were in position, Daniel said, "We're a go."

Weapons drawn, Daniel and Willa entered through the front. They had a visual on Russo and Livingston. Cody and another deputy weren't visible from the far end of the church.

Father O'Neill was sitting in a pew reading scripture. He jumped to his feet, his head on a swivel as he processed the sight of them. "What is the meaning of this?"

"Simon Yates, Father," Daniel said. "Where is he?"

Wild-eyed, O'Neill hesitated. "Are you sure you're looking for the right man? Simon is hardworking and kind. Has he done something wrong? Perhaps it's a misunderstanding."

Shaking her head, Willa wanted to pull Father O'Neill aside and set him straight, but they'd have to explain later.

"Where?" Daniel repeated the single word.

The priest pointed a trembling finger to a door. "In the basement. That's where he stays. Try not to hurt him."

Tell that to the seven women he's savagely killed.

Daniel took point, reaching the door first, and signaled to her with his eyes. Willa put a hand on the knob. Slowly, she checked it, turning the knob ever so slightly. Unlocked. She slid a glance to Daniel.

One curt nod was the signal. She opened the door, revealing a staircase. He cleared it and headed down. Willa was right behind him, and Livingston followed. The other three remained upstairs near the entrances, on the slim chance that Yates got past them, he was not getting out of that church.

In the basement, they entered a wide corridor. Daniel directed Livingston to the left. The deputies opened the two doors at the end of the hall, looked inside the rooms and closed them. Deputy Livingston made a sharp back and forth motion across his throat, letting them know it was a dead end, and mouthed, *Supplies.*

A toilet flushed up ahead to the right. The three of them swiveled, focusing on the precise point of the sound.

Bathroom down the hall.

The door swung open, and Yates stepped into the corridor, carrying a magazine, wearing a sweater, jeans and boots. He was a big guy in his thirties. Tall. Sturdy build.

With weapons trained on him, Daniel said, "Simon Ya—"

The guy dropped the magazine and darted across the hall, disappearing into another room.

They always run.

And it was their job to pursue them no matter what.

The three of them took off after him. At the threshold, she and Daniel each took a position on either side. She peeked around the doorjamb and checked the room. Storage: stacked tables and chairs. A quick glance to the floor.

Clear. Willa swept into the room first. Then Daniel was at her back and Livingston was bringing up the rear.

They hustled through to find another corridor and came to a cozy a space that looked as if he was using it as a makeshift bedroom. There was a cot, sleeping bag, magazines and toiletries.

The hallway up ahead was dark.

She hated dark rooms since there could always be a nasty surprise waiting—like a suspect hiding in a corner with a loaded gun.

Livingston took point. Moving forward with caution, he ran a hand along the wall. He must've found a switch, and the lights flickered on.

No sign of Yates.

They hustled to the next room. The door was closed. She yanked it open, and it was also pitch-black inside. There was a faint humming noise of machinery, and the temperature was several degrees warmer. She guessed it was a boiler room.

Reaching her hand inside against the wall, she groped for a light switch. Found it and flipped it on. Once again, no Yates, but this was the last room. He was probably hiding inside somewhere.

The three of them exchanged glances. With a nod from her, Daniel crept inside first, and they swept into the room behind him, searching the corners and behind the equipment.

Then she saw it. An opening in the wall behind the boiler.

A steel plate the size of a door had been removed. She signaled the others. Grabbing her flashlight from her duty belt, she clicked it on and shone the light inside.

It was a tunnel.

"What the hell?" she muttered.

Daniel peeked inside and keyed his radio. "Suspect is getting away on foot through what looks like an old bootlegger tunnel that was used during prohibition. Russo find out where this one leads. Cody put out an APB. White. Six-one. Two hundred pounds. Rust-colored hair. Blue eyes. We're in pursuit." He slipped inside.

She and Livingston were right behind him.

Footsteps pounded up ahead in the dark. Yates was making a break for it.

Flashlights up and sidearms at the ready, the three of them bolted down the tunnel. Her adrenaline level was off the chart, determination fueling her, she no longer felt any aches.

DANIEL RAN FULL speed after Yates. Willa was right on his heels, but from the sound of it Livingston lagged a bit behind.

They came to a fork in the tunnel and had to choose. Right or left? Closing his eyes, he listened, trying to hear over the pounding of his heart.

"Right," Willa said, darting past him in that direction.

Just in case she was wrong, he directed Livingston to take the other tunnel because there was no way in hell that he was leaving Willa alone or letting Livingston go with her.

They rushed down the tunnel after Yates. He was navigating in the dark, but he was fast—already familiar with the underground system. He probably had used this network of tunnels to help him orchestrate his crimes.

A sliver of light winked up ahead. Drawing closer, Daniel saw a door as he came to the end of this tunnel. He eased open the door, bracing himself for a sneak attack, or a pot-shot.

But nothing happened, which meant that Yates was getting away.

They entered another maintenance room. At first, he had no idea where they were. Hurrying through into the next room, they came to a hall. They were in another basement. Based on the signs, they were in the library. On the university campus.

Daniel quickly led Willa up to the main floor and down a corridor that opened to the foyer.

Simon Yates dashed through the front doors outside.

If they didn't hurry, they could lose sight of him and then he might disappear forever. They weaved around the folks in the foyer, making their way to the doors. Outside, they each turned in different directions, scanning the area for him.

"Hey!" a young woman cried as Yates pushed her to the ground.

The tall guy shoved through a gaggle of students, knocking another down as he ran toward the Watson Hall building—a twelve-story residence hall. There were too many students around to take a clean shot. The guy crossed the lawn in great, long strides and stormed into the building.

In hot pursuit, Daniel and Willa were right behind him. He keyed his radio. "SWU campus," he said in between hard, ragged breaths. "Watson Hall."

They shoved through the door, scanning the lobby. Where was he?

Daniel recalled there was an underground tunnel from this building to the dining center to accommodate students in the winter. But then he caught sight of Yates.

In the opposite direction, running past the bank of elevators, the man pushed through the door to the stairwell. They sprinted after him, made it through the door in time to see him racing up the steps past the second floor, shoving kids out of his way, slamming them into the wall. Once again, too many students in the stairwell to risk firing his weapon.

Why couldn't more of them be lazy and take the elevator?

"Out of the way!" Daniel yelled to the kids who stood frozen.

They chased after Yates, ascending floor after floor; the higher they went the more the students thinned out in the stairwell.

His thighs were on fire, muscles burning by the eighth level. If Willa felt the strain of the rapid climb, she didn't show it. The top levels were empty except for the suspect and them. "Police! Stop!" Daniel squeezed off three shots, but the guy kept going. He got back on the radio. "Headed to the roof. Watson Hall."

Up three more flights for Daniel and Willa, almost to the top of the tallest building in town, but the man threw open the door to the roof and slammed it shut behind him. Once they reached it, Daniel eased open the roof door. They were met with a deep silence, nothing but the wind.

There were too many places to hide up there. Housings for the air-conditioning units served as dividers down the length of the roof, and Yates could be behind any of them.

"Let's get him," Willa whispered fiercely.

Nodding, Daniel wanted nothing more than to collar this guy. Holding himself perfectly still, he listened for any sound, any noise to give Yates away. There. Panting came from fifteen feet away. He indicated where to Willa and she signaled that she was going around the other way. Daniel edged forward, treading light on the rooftop gravel. Ten feet, eight, five, and the man jumped up like a grouse flushed from the brush.

The guy bobbed and weaved, trying not to get pinned down or shot.

Daniel charged and pounced on him, taking him down to the gravel top. They wrestled, twisting, throwing knees and punches, each trying to gain the advantage. Daniel went for the arm he'd injured on the guy last night, but nothing brought him pain. He slammed the guy's head into the metal housing of the air conditioner.

At the same time, Yates threw a fist to his kidney. The pain was shocking, and Daniel lost his grip on him.

They both scrambled up to standing. Stumbled and staggered.

Willa trained her gun on the suspect. "Don't move."

Raising his palms, Yates was close to the edge and moved closer still.

"Not another step!" Willa warned.

"Or what?" Yates asked and spit blood from his mouth.

"Or I will send you straight to hell where you belong," she said, the gun not wavering in her steady grip.

The creep smiled, his teeth bloody. "I'm already in hell. Ever since Marshall cast me out. Want to join me?"

"You tried that last night," Willa said. "Never again."

Confusion contorted his features. "Tried what?"

Regaining his breath and his strength, Daniel snatched his handcuffs from his duty belt. "You can pretend all you want. We know you're the one who attacked her last night, you monster. You've already murdered seven women and you're going to rot in jail for it." He stepped forward to cuff him.

Yates moved back onto the ledge.

What was he doing? Daniel stood still while Willa kept her gun pointed at him.

"You think I killed seven?" A sinister smile spread across Yates's face. "Then I did good and he'd be proud. But I can only claim three," he said.

No, no. Damn it.

There were *two* killers after all.

"He? He who?" Willa asked.

"The hunter," Yates said. "I woke him up. Or maybe you did." He stared at Willa, his gaze raking over her. "Either way, if he came for you last night, he won't stop until he's tasted your blood and stabbed your pretty little heart."

Not if I can help it, Daniel thought with a sudden burst of renewed fury.

This was the Starlight Killer. A copycat of the cold case murderer. Which meant the man—*the hunter*—who came for Willa was hiding, plotting, waiting for another chance to strike.

This wasn't over. Not even close. And it never would be until they found the first killer and stopped him. One way or another for good.

"We can work out some kind of deal," Daniel said, desperate to get Simon to cooperate and give up a name, "with the district attorney for a lighter sentence, if you tell us the name of the hunter. You don't have to face a sentence of life imprisonment." More like three consecutive life sentences. "Just tell us who he is."

Yates eased back, shifting his heels off the ledge, over the side. "Don't worry about finding him. He'll find her.

And you're right. I don't have to spend the rest of my life in prison." Extending his arms wide, Simon Yates tipped backward, and fell, disappearing over the edge.

"No!" Willa screamed, reaching for him, but Daniel grabbed her by the shoulders, hauling her back and away from the side. She turned, facing him. "We needed that creep alive! We needed him to tell us so we can end this."

"Yes, if Yates hadn't just killed himself and had told us the truth about the hunter's identity, it would've made this easier. But easy or not, we aren't going to give up. Do you hear me? *I* won't stop until we find that sick bastard," he vowed, meaning every single word.

Chapter Fourteen

In the sheriff's office, Willa didn't know how to rid herself of the anxious energy bubbling inside her. She was still on edge.

On the roof of Watson Hall when Yates had talked about the hunter coming for her, to taste her blood and stab her pretty little heart it had been as if a cold, dark wind had blown straight through her soul, chilling her to the bone.

How dare that guy say such awful things and then take the coward's way out? Did he think she was going to crawl up into a pathetic ball, hide away in her house and wait for a serial killer to come for her?

I woke him up. Or maybe you did, Simon had said.

A chill slithered through her body, but she refused to dwell on it.

She didn't operate that way. Letting her mind wander down a dark, twisted path that suggested monsters prevailed or that she had provoked one wasn't going to happen. It was a slippery slope.

Daniel came back into the office along with Mercy who handed her a piping-hot mug.

Willa took a sip and gagged. It wasn't coffee. "What is this?"

"Tea," Mercy said. "Chamomile with honey."

"It's awful," she said, making a face.

"It will calm you down," Mercy said.

Willa set the mug on the desk. "I don't want to calm down," she snapped. "I want to find the man who ran me off the road and stalked me like I was his prey."

"Lowering both your blood pressure and anxiety is always better," Daniel said, and she opened her mouth to protest. "And before you fight me on this just try it. Drink one cup while we run an idea by you."

Frowning, Willa picked up the mug and took another sip. Second time around it was still awful, but it was only one cup. "What's the idea?"

"On our way back here after Simon Yates committed suicide," he said, "I replayed all our theories about who the killer could be and I believe you and I are both right."

She grimaced through another sip. "But we had different suppositions."

He nodded. "I thought it was someone on the outside who was angry and wanted to retaliate. Our Starlight Killer turned out to be Simon Yates. You believed the killer is someone at the compound, who's been hiding out for years, living off the grid. I think that's exactly what the hunter is doing. It's like you said, it's the perfect cover."

Willa leaned forward with interest. "Today is the deadline for them to provide us with a list of individuals who have been there for years and haven't taken their vows."

"There'll be multiple names," Mercy said. "Ten or more."

The number sounded so big, and depressing, compared to Mercy's earlier list of one.

"Ultimately, where will it get us?" Daniel asked, his words generating new anger in her. "We'll question them and the guilty party will lie and evade. We won't be able to prove anything, and you will still be in danger."

None of this was making her feel any better. Not the tea. Not his prelude to an idea, which she had yet to hear.

"What if I told you there's a way to not only identify the killer," he said, "but to have him in custody today and to get the evidence we need to lock him away for the rest of his life, within less than forty-eight hours?"

Willa didn't even try to hide her skepticism. "I'd ask what's the catch. How could that be possible?"

"Through her," Daniel said, pointing to Mercy.

"Yesterday, the sheriff asked if he could give my father my phone number because he wanted to speak with me," Mercy said. "I've worked hard to move on, and I wasn't sure how I felt about it, so I said no. This morning, he had a legal document sent to me. It would essentially make the compound mine and free to do with it as I please."

"But how?" Willa asked. "You're one of the Fallen, the Starlights aren't allowed to speak with you."

"I don't know what his plan is. That's why he wants to talk to me. Anyway, I kept stalling. But it wasn't until you all came back, and I learned Simon is dead and you're still in danger that I understood why."

Willa crossed her arms. "Not to sound ungrateful, but I'm not getting how these two things are related."

"My father wants something from me. It's important to him. That puts me in a position of power where I can ask for something in return. The identity of the killer who is hiding on the compound. If anyone knows, it's him, and I can get him to talk."

There was no doubt in Willa's mind Marshall was aware of all the secrets that his people were hiding. "We could possibly find out who," she said with a nod. "But how do we get the evidence that will convict him?"

Daniel smiled. "I've worked it out with Mercy."

"This all sounds," Willa said, with a shake of her head, "a little too good to be true."

"Sometimes the simplest answer is sitting right in front of us," he replied. "You told me that earlier in the car. Then it occurred to me what the cleanest solution might be."

"Perhaps so. I'm just not used to simple." Willa sipped her tea. "Mercy, in order for you to ask your father for something, don't you have to agree to whatever he wants?"

"I'm sure I can come up with some conditions of my own," Mercy said, leaning forward and putting a hand on Willa's wrist. "We're talking about a serial killer who has set his sights on you. This is your life."

"This is your life, too." The young woman only recently broke free. Willa didn't want to be the one to take away all her new possibilities in the outside world, not even to bring a killer to justice.

"After talking with the sheriff, I think this plan will work. You can have peace of mind. Tonight," Mercy said. "You deserve that. Everyone does." She patted the back of her hand. "Let's go. He's waiting for me in one of the interview rooms."

Willa was stunned they had been working behind her back, albeit to ensure her safety, and their plan was ready to be executed. Right. Now. Her gaze bounced from Daniel to Mercy. "I don't want you to regret this."

"I won't agree to anything that gives me qualms," Mercy said, gently. "All right?"

Willa nodded "Thank you." But it still felt like they were asking too much from her.

"Putting the Holiday Killer behind bars isn't just for you," Mercy said. "It will make the compound safer. It'll show the town that we value the law more than loyalty, and the families of the cold case victims need closure. It's been far too long."

For someone so young, she was wise beyond her years.

They walked Mercy down to the interrogation room and let her in. Then Willa and Daniel went to the observation room.

"Do you really think she can get him to talk," Willa asked, "when he must expect that we're listening?"

"If anyone can do this, it's Mercy," Daniel said. "The good news is Huck isn't here."

Willa hoped he was right. With Yates gone, they needed another way to find out who had tried to kill her a mere two miles from her home. And fast. Before he had a chance to go after her again.

Mercy sat down across from her father and placed the legal document on the table between them, setting a pen on top.

"Thank you for coming," Marshall said to his daughter.

Nodding, Mercy folded her hands. "I was shocked to hear from you since you consider me to be one of the Fallen and to be honest, I don't understand why you've sent me this document."

He looked past her at the one-way mirror, almost as though he could see Willa and Daniel standing there. "I'm taking the charges against me very seriously. I'm preparing myself for the possibility of a conviction, and I want to ensure my legacy lives on through you."

Willa turned to Daniel. "It's like he said that for our benefit," she said.

"Maybe," Daniel said, lifting a shoulder. "But Marshall doesn't strike me as someone to accept defeat."

"At some point he has to acknowledge the reality that there are two witnesses willing to testify against him," Willa said, "in addition to the fact that he's actually guilty."

Marshall turned his focus to his daughter. "The compound, the commune of five hundred," he said to Mercy, "the belief in the Light, the core values, can all be maintained with you at the helm, overseeing things in conjunction with the council of elders."

She scoffed. "You branded me one of the Fallen. No one in the commune will look at me or speak to me. They believe I must be shunned."

The same fate, or rather plight, as Zeke. Willa had never considered how much harder the circumstances must be for Mercy since she grew up on the compound.

Marshall reached across the table and covered his daughter's hands with his. "Forgive me. I was angry and hasty and misguided. You did not reject the Light or the commune. You rejected me. Your father. That's the message I've already communicated to Huck and asked him to spread it to everyone in the hopes you agreed to this. You were always meant to lead. I was just too tainted to see it."

Mercy expelled a heavy breath. "I have a new life now."

Nodding, he leaned back in his chair. "I'm aware. How is Rocco?" her father asked.

"He's good. We're happy together and with the way things are. The council of elders doesn't need me to run things. They can do it by themselves."

Willa glanced at Daniel. "Is she trying to talk him out of this?"

"I don't think so. Sounds like she's asking him to define her value and what she brings to the table," Daniel said.

A sad smile tugged at Marshall's mouth. "Your vision is unique. You can help the Shining Light evolve beyond what it is now. I only ask that you don't let my name be forgotten. I see you capable of building a bridge between the community of this town and the one on the compound, where there won't be protesters at our gate."

"I'm glad you mention it," Mercy said. "With the protesters, their numbers and their anger continue to grow. For me to consider your proposal, I'll need something significant from you."

Marshall hesitated, his brow creasing. "I don't have much to offer from behind bars, but whatever is within my power to give you, I will."

"I hope you mean that. Simon Yates is dead," she said, straightening. "Before he took his own life, he admitted that he isn't responsible for trying to kill Chief Nelson last night." Mercy paused, letting that sink in. "He said—the hunter—will go after her again. The same hunter who murdered four women five years ago."

"My dear," Marshall said, lifting a hand to caress her cheek, "if you take over as leader of the compound, you will have access to all the recorded unburdening sessions and will be able to find him yourself."

She moved away from his touch. "Stop. Lying. I don't believe *the hunter* is a Starlight and I don't believe he has an unburdening tape for me to find." Shoving her chair back with a scrape against the floor, Mercy stood. "If you want to play games, then this discussion is over."

Willa was impressed. Mercy was a tougher negotiator than she had expected.

"Wait. Please, sit." Marshall gestured for her to take her seat, and she did. "You're right," her father admitted. "He isn't a Starlight. He and Simon arrived around the same time. Simon was lost, troubled, looking for a place to belong, but the other one seemed like he was running or trying to hide, but many come to us looking to escape something. They became close friends quickly. They bonded over their difficult relationships with their mothers. Based on the things Simon eventually confessed during his unburdening, looking back on it, I believe his friend, who he referred to as the *hunter*, shared details with Simon about the murders he had committed before coming to the Shining Light. The violent things Simon learned from the *hunter* made him fantasize about doing the same thing. Made him hunger to experience the sick thrill. Simon admitted that he looked up to him, admired him, wanted to become the *hunter*. He had even imagined killing some of our members. That's why, after I made him leave, he emulated the hunter's killings, except with Starlights."

"When did you suspect there was such darkness in them?" Mercy asked.

"What makes you think I did before Simon's unburdening?"

Mercy leaned back, disgust twisting her features. "Because I know you, Father. The way you read people, see inside them is remarkable. Please. I need you to be honest with me, or instead of leading the Shining Light, I'll destroy it."

With a sigh, Marshall lowered his head. "I had suspected for quite some time," he said. "I monitored them closely. Neither of them ever laid a finger on anyone in our community," Marshall said, as though that somehow made who and what those men were okay. "I found out for certain when

Simon chose to unburden in order to ascend and become a member. There was simply too much darkness. The way he fantasized about killing people in our community, I could not make him a permanent member. So I cast him out."

Mercy grimaced. "What about the other murderer?"

"After I made Simon leave, the *hunter* will never unburden out of fear he will be cast out as well."

"How can you let him stay?" she asked, and Willa wondered the same.

There were women and children of all ages on the compound. Surely, Marshall viewed the man as a threat to his community.

"I would never kick someone out based on a suspicion," Marshall said. "A confession is a different matter."

"If you've known all this time who is responsible," Mercy said, "why didn't you tell Chief Nelson and Sheriff Clark?"

Willa could take a guess as to why Empyrean would stay quiet.

"It would reflect poorly on us," he said.

What he really meant was that it would reflect poorly on him.

"The commune would have questioned the sanctity of the unburdening sessions if I had revealed information from one to the police," Marshall said, and Willa was sickened by how he had violated it anyway by blackmailing former members. "And I could visualize the headlines in the *Gazette*: Marshall McCoy unleashes one murderer while harboring another. The Shining Light would not have survived such scrutiny."

"More like Marshall McCoy wouldn't have survived the scrutiny," Daniel said.

It was just as Willa had thought. McCoy was protecting

his image above all else, even at the expense of more lives lost. "If he had only told me the truth after Beverly Fisher, I might have been able to save Leslie and Gemma."

"He's despicable," Daniel said. "It makes me wonder what other monsters are hiding on the compound."

Willa nodded. "That's probably another concern he had. The entire town will wonder the same thing."

"Who is he?" Mercy demanded. "Who is the *hunter*?"

Marshall shoved the contract toward her. "Will you help lead?"

"You should know I'll make sweeping changes," Mercy said. "For starters, I won't live in Light House or on the compound and won't require anyone else to either. Rocco and I are happy on his ranch. Also, I think it's time to do away with the color system. We should wear what we want. And I'll welcome back any Fallen member who desires to be a part of our community once more."

Willa wasn't going to jump for joy about that last part. She had just gotten her son back and wasn't ready to lose him again, but Zeke had to make choices for himself.

"I don't fully agree." Marshall shook his head vehemently. "I believe the chaos it'll breed could overwhelm you. But my opinion won't matter. You run it as you like."

Mercy picked up the pen and turned to the last page. "Give me a name. And I'll ensure the Shining Light survives."

"Orion Vansant."

"Ry?" Mercy asked. "From the security team who works in the garage?"

Oh, my God. Willa's gut twisted.

"Isn't he the guard who assisted you in getting Miguel for questioning?" Daniel asked.

"Yes," Willa said, "he was." Admitting it aloud made her skin crawl.

She had spoken with Ry, touched him, ridden on the back of his motorbike. Had she done something to encourage his homicidal attention? She wondered when the hunter had decided to target her. After her first press release or visit to the compound? Or had it been their personal interaction? Putting him up close with a woman who fit the profile of his victims?

Don't go there.

Ultimately, it didn't matter. There was nothing she could've done differently to prevent him from hunting her because every action she had taken had been to do her job.

"Are you all right?" Daniel asked her.

No, no, she wasn't. Not yet.

"I will be," she said. Once she saw the look on Orion's face when they slapped the cuffs on him, and she read him his rights that would go a long way to making her feel much better.

While they waited for the arrest warrant to come in, Mercy contacted Huck at the compound and arranged to have extra security guards posted in and around the garage where Orion was working, oblivious this would be his last day. No one wanted a repeat of what happened with Yates slipping away.

On their approach to the compound, they had foregone the flashing lights and sirens, not wanting to give Ry the slightest heads-up that he was finally going to pay for his crimes.

Willa needed the sense of agency that came with driving. She sat behind the wheel as they took two sheriff's SUVs to the compound.

Marshall McCoy's message about Mercy had spread like wildfire. Once the guard at the gate had seen her, he had waved them right through. At least a hundred people had gathered on the front lawn of Light House, waiting for her. Not only was she embraced when they arrived, no longer shunned, she was treated like royalty. A large group surrounded her while others waited to talk to her and touch her, their affection for her so genuine.

Willa got of the vehicle with a sense of purpose. Holding the logbook, she headed to the garage with Daniel on one side of her and Livingston on the other.

"Hey, there," Orion said with a bright smile, having the audacity to meet her eyes as they entered the garage. "If it isn't the lovely Chief Nelson, the industrious Sheriff Clark and his trusted deputy. What can I do for you?"

Shawn and two other security guards were tinkering around in the building. From the corner of her eye, she saw them monitoring the situation.

Pulling on her I'm-going-to-enjoy-this smile, Willa said, "Today is about what I have for you." She handed him the logbook.

"All done with it?" Orion asked. "Did you get what you needed from it?"

"Yeah, I think so." Her stomach soured as she considered how he must've thought he had her and the rest of them fooled. *Lovely Chief Nelson. Industrious Sheriff Clark.* Not only was her compliment sexist for focusing on her appearance and the sherifff's work ethic, but he was cocky enough to say it to her face after hunting her like an animal just last night. "Hey, Ry, I've got one more thing for you." As she pulled the warrant from her pocket and handed it to him, the guards closed in around him from the rear.

"What is this?" he asked with a frown, opening it and glancing at the paperwork.

The security guards stopped what they were doing and came closer, taking their cues from Shawn.

"Orion Vansant, you're under arrest," Willa said, drawing the sweetest satisfaction from saying the words.

In nanoseconds, Ry changed, like a switch had been flipped, and he lunged at her, going for her throat, his green eyes bulging with fury. Daniel and another deputy snatched his arms, holding him back, before he had a chance to touch her.

"As I was saying. You are charged with the murders of Tiffany Cummings, Rose Rossini, Jessica McIntosh, Carla Larsen and with the attempted murder of a police officer, leaving the scene of a crime and obstruction of justice. You have the right to remain silent."

She finished reading him his rights while Daniel handcuffed him. Holding Orion's wrists with one hand, Daniel grabbed his left arm with the other. She watched him apply pressure to the area where Daniel had shot and wounded him last night, and the man winced.

"I don't know what's going on." Ry's face flushed red. "This is a load of crap. Some mistake. You've got this all wrong. I haven't done anything wrong."

Once they reached the sheriff's SUV, Daniel put Orion in the back seat and slammed the door shut. "How do you feel now?" he asked.

"Never better," she said with a wink at him.

Huck cut through the crowd surrounding Mercy and greeted them. "Sheriff. Chief." He held up a disposable bag with a cup. "Inside is Orion's cup from our last meal. That should be all the evidence you need for a conviction."

They already had his DNA from the bite marks on the bodies. Once it matched the DNA from the cup that would be all District Attorney Jennings would need.

Willa glanced over her shoulder at Orion, the hunter, in the back seat. She breathed a sigh of relief that the monster was going to spend the rest of his life behind bars where he belonged.

"What's on your mind?" Daniel asked her.

"How good it will be that the four families from the cold cases will finally get the closure and justice they deserve."

"Thanks to you," he said with a grin.

She returned his smile. "Thanks to us."

"You have to admit we make a pretty good team, don't we?"

Professionally and personally. She cupped his face—right there in public, for anybody to see—her heart lighter than it had been in weeks. Maybe ever. "Yeah, the best."

Epilogue

In less than forty-eight hours, they'd gotten a DNA match for Orion Vansant and the district attorney had charged him with four counts of first-degree murder among other things. On the Shining Light compound, Mercy and the security team found a hole that had been dug under the fence and hidden with bushes. They believed that was how Orion Vansant was able to get out of the compound without being seen. Daniel's deputies located a car Vansant had been storing at a nearby dude ranch. Under the church in the tunnels Simon Yates had used, they found evidence that he had kept Gemma Chavez down there before killing her. Marshall McCoy pled not guilty to blackmail and was planning to fight the charges.

In the days that followed, Mercy had started implementing her sweeping changes on the compound. One of the most significant was starting family day, where members were encouraged to invite friends and family from the outside to spend the day on the compound together.

Rather than leaping at the chance to rejoin the Shining Light, Zeke had decided to give it a year on the outside. He and Thomas were now roommates, and he no longer had a problem paying his bills.

One month later, standing outside by their vehicles, Daniel held Willa in his arms and looked down into her lovely face. "You've got nothing to worry about."

"Easy for you to say. You're not the one hauling a resistant son into family therapy," she said.

Daniel smiled, holding back a chuckle. "Zeke agreed to go, albeit reluctantly."

"After months of prodding him," she said, sounding exasperated.

"I still call that progress. Also, I've heard that Dr. Delgado is fantastic at what she does. She even helped the FBI with that hostage crisis situation earlier this year."

"Then she's just what we need, considering Zeke is acting like I'm holding him hostage by taking him." Willa frowned, looking overwhelmed.

She only needed to take it in baby steps, one session at a time.

"Trust in the process. Trust in her reputation." He rubbed her lower back, wanting to caress her curves, but drew on his self-restraint. "Most importantly, trust in the bond you and Zeke have. You'll get through this."

The corner of her mouth hitched in a grin as she held him tighter. "How do you always know what I need to hear to feel better?"

He shrugged. "Call it intuition." The truth of the matter was they fit together. A perfect match. He loved her fiery spirit and she loved his grounding calm. It also helped that they understood the pressures, the long hours, the danger they both faced professionally.

"Thanks for not giving up on me. On the possibility of an us."

"You can thank me later." He lowered his head, brushing his lips over hers before taking her mouth in a kiss that showed her precisely how much he wanted her.

"Ugh," Zeke said, coming out of the cabin. "Save it for the bedroom." He got into Willa's car and slammed the door.

Laughing, they pulled apart.

Willa looked at her watch. "You better hurry up. You don't want to be late picking up your mom from the airport."

No, he did not. Selene Beauvais could be late and leave others waiting, but never the other way around. "I should be good. I checked the traffic. The roads to Denver are clear."

Willa climbed into her SUV, started it and rolled down the window. "I can't wait to meet her."

That's what she said now.

"It'll be nice," Willa continued, "having the focus on Grace and Holden and not us. No pressure."

"That's true. No pressure is always my preference." He leaned down, putting his arm on the door. "Thanks for agreeing to come to the family dinner with me."

"Thanks for inviting Zeke." She glanced over at her son, who nodded while on his phone. "He's always been curious what it's like on the Shooting Star Ranch."

"Which reminds me. I mentioned to Holden that Zeke wasn't happy working as a gas station attendant and was hoping to get a position as a ranch hand. He said they're always looking for hard workers who don't mind starting at the bottom. I hope I didn't overstep by throwing your name out there."

"Are you kidding?" His eyes lit up with excitement. "You didn't overstep. That's great. I guess it's not so bad you're my mom's boyfriend."

Daniel laughed. "I guess not."

Willa swatted her son's arm playfully. "Stop it, Zeke."

She looked over at Daniel. "Thank you. That was nice of you. You didn't have to do that. We appreciate it."

"Play your cards right, young man," Daniel said, "and you'll even get a tour tonight."

Zeke fist pumped the air. "Yeah."

Wearing a beautiful, bright smile, Willa shook her head. "See, it's going to be fine. All you have to do is trust me."

"If that's all, then no problem. Because I do trust you. And love you."

"I love you, too." He never got tired of hearing her say the L-word. Leaning closer, he brushed his lips across hers and kissed her slow and soft.

"Ugh," Zeke said. "Save it for later."

"Sure. We'll save it."

"Hey, I've been meaning to throw this out there," she said. "What do you think about us living together?"

Zeke looked up from his phone. "I think it's a brilliant idea. Where would you live? Wayward Bluffs or Laramie?"

Willa smiled. "I was thinking on Daniel's ranch closer to Laramie. Shorter commute."

"Is there a spare room for me when I visit if I wanted to stay the night?" Zeke asked.

"I've got two," Daniel said, and her son made a sound of approval. He did love her and would do everything he could to make things easier, better, for her and Zeke. "We should do it before Thanksgiving."

"Sounds perfect," she said with a nod, and it warmed his heart to see the confidence gleaming in her eyes. "We're going to be fine." She pressed a hand to his cheek and caressed his face. "The three of us."

He was counting on it. "Better than fine."

* * * * *

COMING SOON!

We really hope you enjoyed reading this book. If you're looking for more romance be sure to head to the shops when new books are available on

Thursday 12th October

LET'S TALK

Romance

For exclusive extracts, competitions
and special offers, find us online:

f MillsandBoon

𝕏 @MillsandBoon

◎ @MillsandBoonUK

♪ @MillsandBoonUK

Get in touch on 01413 063 232